Trained medic and crisis counsellor, C.J. has assisted with many difficult cases involving abuse, rape and homicide. Winner of the Golden Gateway, Readers' Choice, and Daphne du Maurier awards, her short story 'Scutwork' was selected to appear in *First Thrills*, an anthology edited by Lee Child, featuring today's bestsellers alongside the future stars of tomorrow. Her first novel, *Blind Faith*, was a self-published ebook phenomenon in the US, debuting at Number 2 on the *New York Times* print and ebook bestseller list and garnering her legions of fans. *Blind Faith* was shortlisted for the International Thriller Writers Awards 2013 for best original ebook novel.

www.cjlyons.net

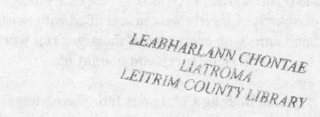

Readers **love** C.J. Lyons

ALSO BY C.J. LYONS

Blind Faith

BLACK SHEEP

C.J. LYONS

WITHDRAWN

sphere

SPHERE

First published in the United States by St. Martin's Press in 2013
First published in Great Britain as an ebook in 2013
This paperback published in 2013 by Sphere

A CIP catalogue record for this book
is available from the British Library.

ISBN 978-0-7515-5235-5

Printed and bound in Great Britain by
Clays Ltd, St Ives plc

Papers used by Sphere are from well-managed forests
and other responsible sources.

MIX
Paper from
responsible sources
FSC® C104740

Sphere
An imprint of
Little, Brown Book Group
100 Victoria Embankment
London EC4Y 0DY

An Hachette UK Company
www.hachette.co.uk

www.littlebrown.co.uk

Dear Reader,

Every book published is born from a community. *Black Sheep* is special because in addition to our normal team, involving the wonderful folks at St. Martin's and my agent, Barbara Poelle, two people volunteered their real-life names for characters in Caitlyn's world as part of charity fundraising efforts. I'd like to thank Mike LaSovage and Mary Agnes Garman for their generosity.

Caitlyn's journey takes her to places both real and fictional. While Cherokee, North Carolina, is real, Evergreen, Balsam County, and the VistaView Casino are entirely fictional. The Cherokee Nation's court case involving the freedmen is quite real and is still in the news today. Butner Federal Correctional Institution is also real, and I'd like to thank Lee Lofland for his virtual tour of their facilities. All embellishments are mine.

One of the best parts of my job is doing the hands-on research. For *Black Sheep* that included participating in hostage situations and building searches while I visited Quantico and the FBI Academy. If you are interested in the FBI's hierarchy or their investigation techniques, you can download a pdf from my website: http://cjlyons .net/wp-content/uploads/FBI-Terms-and-Resources.pdf.

It includes a glossary of law enforcement terms and acronyms as well as a variety of resources I used while creating *Black Sheep*.

As always, thanks for reading!
CJ

CHAPTER ONE

"Drop the gun!" Caitlyn Tierney shouted to the FBI agent.

The agent hesitated, chin bobbing as she tried to decide the correct move to make. Tough choice since Caitlyn held the agent's male partner against her chest as a shield. She'd grabbed his weapon and now used his greater height as an advantage. The only portion of Caitlyn's five-six frame visible to the female agent was Caitlyn's hand holding the male agent's own weapon to his head.

The female agent held her weapon steady, aiming at her partner and Caitlyn behind him. Fat lot of good that was going to do her, but it was standard procedure.

Caitlyn braced herself against the larger agent. He smelled minty fresh, as if he'd chewed gum or used mouthwash before following his partner into this squalid dump of an apartment. Sweat trickled down from his hairline, beading at the back of his collar. His hair had been freshly trimmed; his skin still held tiny nicks from the razor.

She glanced around. He was her only cover. The rest of the apartment was bare of furniture except for a sagging tweed couch shoved against the far wall and a coffee table made of cheap two-by-fours. Back to the wall, Caitlyn's only exit was the door to the right of the female agent across from her.

"Let's talk about this." The female agent's voice quavered, but her aim didn't falter. "Let him go and we'll talk."

"Shut up or I shoot him!" Caitlyn responded, effectively removing the agent's best weapon: her command authority. Hard to negotiate or intimidate when you can't speak. "Drop your gun. Now!"

Make a choice, make a choice, Caitlyn thought. The overhead ceiling fan swooshed, barely stirring the air with its listless movements. The place stank of mold and sweat, of windows that didn't open, shag carpet decades out of date, and too many years of too many people making too many bad decisions. The FBI agent was just one more, standing in the weak light of a naked sixty-watt bulb, her mind stuttering through a minefield of options.

Don't make me do it. Choose. Just choose.

The agent didn't choose. Her aim faltered, dropped down, then raised halfway up in indecision.

Caitlyn shot her in the forehead, followed by a double tap to the chest.

Then Caitlyn touched the muzzle of her weapon to the male agent's temple. "Bang. You're dead."

"Tierney!" The scenario leader yelled her name from his observation post. "What the hell you doing?"

Trying to teach them how to stay alive in the real world, Caitlyn thought. She'd been where these New Agents in Training were: forced to choose between following procedure and taking a chance on her instincts.

Six months ago when she'd had a gun to her head and another pointed at her partner, Caitlyn surrendered her weapon. If she hadn't, she'd be dead—and so would five hundred innocent civilians. But she'd done it consciously, knowing her Glock wasn't her only weapon. That it wasn't even her best weapon.

These NATs needed to learn to think like that. It might save their lives someday.

The scenario leader, Mike LaSovage, one of the FBI Hostage Rescue Team members, clomped over to her, aiming his clipboard as if it were a weapon. "Supervisory Special Agent Tierney, a word, please."

Caitlyn removed her helmet and rubbed her right temple, lifting her short red hair, matted by the training gear, away from the itchy scar. She glanced at the female NAT she'd shot. The woman trembled. Her hand touched her face shield, coming away with neon green paint on her fingers—the color of Caitlyn's Simunition.

"She needed to make a decision," Caitlyn muttered, wiping her own sweaty palms against her black cargo pants. Simulation or not, the scenario hit close to home, awakening memories as well as a surge of adrenaline.

"The purpose of this exercise is to allow agents in training a chance to follow proper arrest procedure, not to throw them into a hostage negotiation." LaSovage turned so his back was to the NATs. Didn't want them to see Mommy and Daddy fighting. The Bureau was above that. Follow the bible—a four-inch binder crammed full of rules, regulations, and standard operating procedures—and you'd go home at night, was the catechism the kids were meant to learn from these exercises.

Despite the fact that a few were close to Caitlyn's age, they *were* just kids. No idea what the real world held for them. Decisions made in a heartbeat, bullets fired that could never be unfired, good people lost because of your actions—or inaction.

"You saw the way they entered," Caitlyn argued, feeling older than her thirty-five years as she spied the crushed expressions on the NATs' faces. Nine years carrying a loaded weapon, almost dying twice, killing a man in close-quarters combat, watching a good man sacrifice his life to save hers: Permanent scars crisscrossed her body and her soul. She couldn't remember ever being as young as these new agents. "He was more concerned about following her lead than the threat I posed. Totally opened his weapon side to me. How could I resist? No real suspect would have."

LaSovage looked over his shoulder to where the two dead agents huddled together commiserating and, hopefully, dissecting their mistakes. "It was a sloppy entrance. But this is their first exercise outside of FATS video training. First real-life scenario. You didn't need to push it that far."

"I'll bet they don't make the same mistakes next time."

He grimaced in agreement. "Maybe. But let's play the rest of these by the book, okay?"

Caitlyn had never done "by the book" well. Used to be she could fake her way through it, pretend her actions were guided by rules and regulations, but after returning from an extended medical leave for emergency brain surgery that saved her life, she'd given up the pretense. Which was why the powers-that-be had left her in limbo, on temporary assignment here at Quantico.

"You doing okay?" LaSovage asked, trying not to stare at her hair, still not fully grown back after her operation. "Can't be easy after—"

"I'm fine." How many times a day did she have to tell people that? Or pretend she didn't notice their stares as she walked through the halls at the academy.

Six months ago she'd have embraced the idea of continuing on as a permanent instructor—she enjoyed teaching and loved challenging her students. But to be stranded here as temporary duty, merely so she could remain under the scrutiny of the bosses without becoming a PR risk? Suddenly her office in Jefferson Hall felt as cramped as a prison cell.

Her last case had earned her an unofficial reprimand from the Office of Professional Responsibility and an official, but grudgingly given, commendation for uncovering corruption in the FBI's higher ranks, the U.S. Marshal Service, and even the sacrosanct FBI National Laboratory.

The brass would have preferred if she'd taken their offer of a medical pension and left the Bureau quietly, but no way was she going to let them bully her into quitting. Given that she knew of several embarrassing skeletons hidden in the FBI's closet, they couldn't fire her, not without risking another blot on the Bureau's public image.

Which left Caitlyn and her career in limbo.

"You sure?" LaSovage persisted. "We could grab a beer or something after we're done here. If you want to talk."

His glance dropped to the top part of the scar that ran vertically up her chest, visible above her tactical vest. The rest of the scar formed a letter *K* with the crossbars slashing above and below her left breast. If it weren't for her fair skin the scars would have been less noticeable, but after six months they were still reddish and she'd given up trying to hide beneath turtlenecks. Just like her attitude, they were now part of her, take it or leave it.

His concern seemed more genuine than the morbid curiosity most of her colleagues had exhibited. Interesting since, although LaSovage was a four-year veteran of the Hostage Rescue Team, the FBI's vaunted equivalent to an elite SWAT unit, he'd never actually had to kill anyone.

During the course of their careers it was rare for FBI agents to draw their weapons outside the range. Which made Caitlyn, so young, yet already almost dying a violent death twice and killing a man up close and personal, a distinct anomaly. She heard the whispers: *Was she reckless? Stupid? Or just plain unlucky?*

She wished she had an answer. "Thanks, but I need to be somewhere tonight," she told LaSovage. "Maybe next time."

He nodded, gave her an uncertain smile as if wondering if she was trying to protect him or herself, then turned to usher the next group into position.

They finished out the remaining training for the day, and she returned to her office in Jefferson Hall to grab her laptop and car keys. She was surprised when the female agent in training from the earlier scenario appeared at her doorway, now wearing clean regulation khakis and a blue polo shirt.

"What would you have done?" the NAT blurted out, ignoring the strict protocol that usually guided NATs' interactions with their instructors. Belatedly she added, "Ma'am."

"What's your name?" Caitlyn took the seat behind her desk, but left the NAT standing at attention. This group was new, hadn't taken any of her classes yet, so she didn't know them personally; she'd merely been playing a bad guy in today's scenarios to help with evaluations.

"Garman, ma'am. Mary Agnes Garman."

Mary Agnes? Sounded like a nun's name. She was only a year or two younger than Caitlyn, in good shape but not as fit as the recruits coming from the military or law enforcement, with an hourglass figure that did not fit her name. Although who knew what nuns looked like under those habits?

Caitlyn filled her mind with an image of a mother superior holding a compass—a mnemonic technique she'd cultivated after her brain trauma made remembering things like names a struggle. Not that she'd ever share that secret with anyone.

"What did you see as your options, Garman?"

Mary Agnes hesitated, not in indecision as she had earlier, but in thought. "You didn't give me any."

"Exactly. What's wrong with that statement?"

Her rigid posture sagged. Caitlyn nodded to the chair across from her, and Mary Agnes slumped into it. "I gave you the power. But—" She scowled in thought, her gaze drifting past Caitlyn to the window, already dark with the early-January sunset. "But I still had no options."

"Tunnel vision. The adrenaline makes you focus on what's in front of you, the direct threat. It does that to your mind as well. But there are always possibilities. Don't ever forget that."

"I could have lowered my weapon, but regulations—"

"Do the bad guys play by the rules?"

"No, but—"

"In here"—Caitlyn gestured to the cement-block walls surrounding them—"you have to know the rules, live by them. And that's not a bad thing. Nine times out of ten they'll save your butt."

"And the tenth time?"

"Look for options. You never considered any other

options today. Instead you hesitated, couldn't commit to a course."

"I froze. I got my partner killed." The remorse and fear in Mary Agnes's voice was real. Good. Better she learn the hard lessons now before the gun pointed at her shot something more lethal than a paintball.

"You did. Next time you won't."

"What would you have done?"

"You still controlled the exit."

"It was too far away."

Caitlyn shook her head. "No. It was only three steps to your right. Adrenaline. It distorts everything. Good thing is, the bad guys are affected as well, have the same limitations."

"I could never abandon my partner." Her voice made it sound like sacrilege, reinforcing the mother superior image in Caitlyn's mind. As if what Caitlyn suggested was as bad as betraying a family member. Which, in a sense, it was. Unless you imagined past the knee-jerk blind obedience to ethics and codes of conduct.

"Yes. You could. Three steps and you would have been behind cover, able to observe, negotiate, call for backup, or shoot if the hostage taker took further action."

"Further action. You mean kill my partner."

Caitlyn stood. Stretched her arms wide. "Look at me, Garman. I'm all of five-six, can bench one thirty, maybe one fifty on a good day. What good would a six-foot, two-hundred-pound deadweight do me?"

"You wouldn't have shot him?"

"Not unless he was no longer useful. And that would only happen if—" She arched an eyebrow, waiting for Mary Agnes to put the pieces together.

It took a moment, but the frown faded as the answers

fell into place for the agent in training. "I blocked your escape. If I was out of the picture, dead, you could make a run for it. By standing there, I gave you *more* reason to kill us both."

"Exactly. You were thinking about what you wanted, but you should have been focused on what the hostage taker wanted. Embrace the possibilities, decide how you can control the outcome."

Mary Agnes took a deep breath, chin bobbing in agreement. She stood with renewed energy. "Thank you, Supervisory Special Agent Tierney. You gave me a lot to think about."

Caitlyn smiled, remembered why she enjoyed teaching so much. "No problem, Garman. Have a good night."

Mary Agnes headed back to the dormitory while Caitlyn took the steps down to the lobby, waved to the guard there, and jogged through the cold, her coat flapping open, to her Subaru Impreza WRX parked in front of Jefferson Hall. A thin coating of frost crackled across the Subaru's windshield, but she didn't waste time scraping it clear. She still had thirty-six miles to drive to Paul's place in DC.

She took back roads, avoiding 95 and the constant snarl of traffic on the interstate. Usually she enjoyed the hour-long drive. It provided needed breathing space.

As extroverted as she was introverted, Paul often joked that if it weren't for him, she'd be living the life of a hermit. She never let him know how close to the truth that was. She'd yet to invite him to her place in Manassas for a night, was more than willing to let him think it was because as a neuroradiologist he had to stay close to GW.

In reality, she simply didn't do entertaining. Or strangers in her space. So much easier to make the drive, enjoy Paul's company, and leave when she wanted. She liked the freedom, needed the control—another thing Paul teased her about.

Only lately he wasn't teasing. He was hinting. Emptying a dresser drawer and shelf in the bathroom for her. Talking about how much her drive took away from the time they had together.

He was ready to settle down. With her. For the long term. And it scared the shit out of her. Caitlyn didn't do relationships, never had. She did longer-than-average flings that ended in shouting matches, bruised egos, guys storming away, and her sighing in relief at another bullet dodged.

Paul didn't shout. He wasn't an alpha male, not like her usual guys, and his ego didn't bruise. He cuddled. Comforted. And actually enjoyed it.

Worse, so did she. Being taken care of was a foreign experience to Caitlyn. Paul wrapping his arms around her, sharing his strength, putting her first—it was sweet and sexy and so very addictive. Another thing that scared her. Ever since she was nine and lost her dad, Caitlyn had lived her life and guarded her heart with one rule: Trust no one.

Paul had snuck past that barbed-wire rule and now she was at a loss how to handle things. Part of her wanted to embrace the life he offered: a normal, stable, caring, trusting relationship.

The child in her screamed to run, run, run before she exposed herself too much.

She'd loved every moment of their six months together. Paul had reminded her that there was more to life than just her work. After almost dying, she'd needed that, needed a little of what everyone else seemed to have: someone to come home to, a connection with the world outside the FBI.

Despite the fact that Paul had given her more than any other man she'd ever been with, she knew she didn't have the feelings for him that she should have. It worried her. What was wrong with her that a normal relationship with a terrific guy terrified her more than facing an armed felon? Paul had saved her life six months ago when he diagnosed her brain aneurysm. If she couldn't bring herself to trust him, would she ever be able to trust anyone?

Caitlyn hesitated before pulling into the underground garage at his building. She could call, make an excuse about the training going late, drive back to Manassas and the peaceful solitude of her apartment. He'd never know she was lying—she was pretty good at it. Her chest tightened. Mouth went dry. She didn't want to lie. Not to Paul.

But she was afraid of what she might be facing when she went inside. Afraid of what she'd do when he forced her to make the choice. She didn't want to lose him, wasn't ready to return to her solitary ways.

Not a ring, please not a ring, she thought as she left the Impreza and waited for the elevator. Her cell rang and she grabbed it like a drowning woman lunging for a lifeline.

"Tierney."

"Excuse me, Supervisory Special Agent, this is the operator at the Washington Field Office. I have an urgent call for you from the prison chaplain at Butner Federal Correctional Institution. Will you accept the call?"

The elevator came and she entered, hit the button for Paul's floor. Who the hell did she have behind bars at Butner? Maybe one of the convictions from her time in Boston had turned and they moved him to the facility in North Carolina? After all, Bernie Madoff and Jonathan Pollard were doing time there, as well as a smattering of mobsters turned witnesses for the prosecution.

As always, her curiosity got the better of her. Not to mention an excuse to delay seeing Paul—the thought felt strange, as if she were betraying Paul, but it also gave her a weird sense of relief. Why did relationships have to be so damn confusing? Give her a felon to take down any day of the week. "Sure, put him through."

"Caitlyn Tierney?" The man's voice was unfamiliar. "I'm Pastor Vince Whitford, one of the chaplains at Butner."

She left the elevator and stopped outside Paul's door. No sense knocking if this was something that was going to take her back to work. "Yes. Why are you calling, Pastor?"

He cleared his throat, obviously uncomfortable. "I've been counseling a prisoner here at Butner Medium who tried to kill himself a few days ago. Eli Hale."

Hale, she'd never arrested anyone—oh, hell. She did know that name. Hadn't heard it in twenty-six years. The image of a man, taller and broader than her father, as black as Sean Tierney was pale, his voice low and husky and shaking with laughter as he chased after his daughter and Caitlyn, playing the scary monster to their damsels in distress, a game that always ended with Caitlyn and Vonnie gathered under Eli's massive arms, giggling as he twirled them around until they were dizzy with delight.

"Eli Hale?" It was her turn to clear her throat as childhood memories flooded through her. Vonnie, her best friend in the whole world—until they'd been yanked apart after Caitlyn's dad was forced to arrest his own best friend, Eli Hale. For murder. "Is he okay?"

"He is now. The doctors are releasing him from the medical unit tomorrow, but I convinced him to agree to meet with you. I think you're the only person who can help him."

Anger and confusion twisted through her, tossing her childhood memories aside. Except the one that never left her: the image of her father lying dead, killed with his own gun, by his own hand. Unable to stand the guilt of seeing his best friend convicted of murder.

She swallowed bile. "I think you have the wrong person. There's no reason on earth why I'd want to talk to Eli Hale. Or him to me."

"Please, Agent Tierney. Don't hang up. A girl's life is at stake."

Caitlyn's fingers closed around the cell phone, almost but not quite touching the end-call icon. She wanted to hang up, to end this painful trip down memory lane. But . . . "What girl?"

"Eli's youngest, Lena."

CHAPTER TWO

Lena. She'd barely begun to walk the last Caitlyn had seen her almost twenty-six years ago. Vonnie adored her baby sister, loved playing and taking care of her. She and Caitlyn had dressed Baby Lena up in swaddling clothing her first Christmas, and took turns playing the Virgin Mary and the angel bringing glad tidings, to the thunderous applause of their beaming parents, their performances rewarded with large helpings of Mrs. Hale's pecan pie.

Caitlyn was an only child, so knowing little Lena was like having a baby sister of her own without having to sacrifice any of her parents' attention. Not that Caitlyn's mom had time for another child. Jessalyn Tierney had worked two jobs: three days a week keeping the accounts for her brother's development company and another three as a receptionist at a Realtor's office in Bryson City while studying for her license. She wanted their family to have a better life than living in a drafty old farmhouse in a drafty old nowhere village in the western Carolina mountains.

That was Jessalyn—even now, decades later, she was

constantly striving for something better for herself; constantly disappointed in the life Caitlyn, her only child, had chosen. One more disappointment in a long line of disappointments. Sometimes Caitlyn got the feeling that her mom didn't always think the sacrifices she'd made for her daughter had been worth it.

Not that she and her mother could ever actually talk about it.

Caitlyn's dad had worked six days a week as well. Four twelve-hour shifts for the sheriff—which usually turned into fourteen- or sixteen-hour shifts—and then two days helping Mr. Hale build houses. Sometimes Vonnie and Caitlyn would tag along to job sites, fetch and carry and even hammer a few nails under their dads' watchful gazes. When the work was done for the day, their dads would take them fishing down on the Oconaluftee, or they'd climb up the mountain and visit the trout farm or just go sit on the Hales' porch, the men in rockers talking sports while drinking beer, the girls dangling their feet over the edge, Mrs. Hale serving them pie or cookies or red velvet cake before curling up on her husband's lap.

Caitlyn's mom never did that. Said it'd wrinkle her dress or slacks or blouse. She didn't bake, either. No time. Instead all she did was work and save money so they could move to a nicer house. Which had made no sense to Caitlyn. Why'd they need more money? They had plenty, it seemed to her. And she loved her house, old and creaky, just the way it was.

Made no sense to Dad, either, and he was the one who'd left his family in Pennsylvania to come live in Mom's North Carolina hometown after he fell in love with her. Before he met Jessalyn McSwain, he'd planned to stay in the marines, go to college, then work for the FBI. Had it all mapped out. But, he always smiled, teeth flashing as he finished the story, love had other plans for him.

"Lena," Caitlyn murmured into the phone, her voice muffled by memory. Little Baby Lena. Except not a baby anymore. "What's happened?"

"She's gone missing."

The FBI agent in her closed the door on childhood sentimentality. "You don't need me. File a missing persons report. Why aren't you talking to her mother and sister? They can coordinate efforts better than I can. It's not federal jurisdiction."

He cleared his throat again. Stalling for time. "I'm sorry. Her mother and sister are both dead. Killed almost four years ago now, hit by a drunk driver."

She sagged against the wall opposite Paul's door, focusing on the polished brass apartment number reflecting the light from the tasteful art deco wall sconces lining the corridor. A small part of her wished she was inside, his arms wrapped around her, protecting her from the sudden slap of grief. She hadn't seen Vonnie or her mom in twenty-six years, there was no reason why anyone would have told her about their deaths, but those cold facts couldn't stop the tears.

She blinked them away before they could make it farther than her eyes. "Lena would be, what, twenty-seven?"

"Not until next month." Right, a Valentine's baby. Caitlyn remembered the blizzard that almost trapped Mrs. Hale at home when she started into labor. She and Vonnie had boiled water and collected towels until Caitlyn's dad made it through the snow in his sheriff's department SUV and got her to the hospital just in time. Whitford continued, "She's graduating law school this summer—"

"Lena's going to be a lawyer?"

"Thought it was the best way to exonerate her father. She never doubted his innocence—neither did her older sister or their mother. Despite his refusing to deny his guilt. But while they seemed resigned to his fate, Lena was, well, stubborn. She was determined to see her father set free."

A twinge of anger cut through Caitlyn. Eli Hale was guilty. Everyone knew it. How could he let his daughter waste her life like that?

"*Was?* Past tense?" Had Lena discovered more evidence against her father? "Maybe she couldn't take the truth of her father's guilt and ran away."

"When her father told her to stop working on his case they had a bit of a falling-out. She was supposed to visit, call, but never did. But I'm sure she didn't run away. And, honestly, I'm not certain Eli deserves to be in prison for the rest of his life." The last came out with a touch of defiance.

"Hale confessed. There is no federal parole. Life is life." The words escaped from her flat, stripped of the emotions that churned through her gut. Emotions she'd spent the last quarter of a century denying. Her father was dead because of what Eli Hale had done, because Hale had betrayed their friendship. Hale himself didn't deny it. Hale had confessed in open court to killing a man and using his relationship with a sheriff's deputy to try to cover it up, further sullying her father's reputation. "He deserves to be behind bars."

She was about to hang up—again—when Whitford made that irritating throat-clearing noise. "After he tried to kill himself, while he was still woozy from the drugs, Eli said something. Something he denies saying now, but I heard it plain as day." His words were rushed as if he realized this was his last chance. "He said, 'Sean was right. Death is the only silence they'll accept.' Sean, that's your father?"

"My father's dead." Vertigo pressed her back to the wall, fighting the urge to slump to the floor and surrender to the flood of memories and emotions. Dad didn't know she was there that day. She'd skipped school because he had a rare day off and Mom was at work and it was a gorgeous spring afternoon, too beautiful to waste inside a smelly old school, and the trout were just waiting for them to grab their rods and head down the mountain to the river. That was the only comfort she had. That he didn't know, hadn't planned for her to be the one to find him.

The door to Paul's apartment opened. The lights were on behind him, silhouetting him. A tall black man, like Eli Hale. For a moment it seemed as if the past had collided with her present. He stepped forward, shattering the illusion: Paul was thinner than Eli, had a lean, runner's body. His brown eyes creased in concern; one hand clenched a kitchen towel, the other reached out to her. "I thought I heard voices. Everything all right?"

She nodded, changed hands gripping the phone as if that would help her suddenly sweaty palms, held it even closer to her ear so Paul couldn't hear, her body twisted away from him. She needed to end this conversation. Lay old ghosts to rest once and for all.

"I know your father kil—is dead. I understand how painful this must be for you," Whitford said. "Yet every time I see Eli he talks about your dad, won't let him go, as if he's doing penance."

"Good," she snapped. "This has nothing to do with me. If he's really worried about his daughter, hang up and call the cops."

"He won't let me. Said if the police got involved, they'd kill her."

Paranoid ramblings of a man who'd spent most of his adult life incarcerated.

Paul stood watching, his concern morphing into irritation when she didn't join him inside the apartment. She wasn't sure why, but she needed to keep this part of her life away from him. Avoid contaminating what she had now with what she'd lost so long ago.

"Who's 'they'?" She immediately wished she hadn't asked. Her curiosity couldn't resist.

"He wouldn't say. But the way he talked—" He paused. "I've been a prison chaplain for thirteen years, Agent Tierney. I don't spook easily, and I know a scam when I hear one. What I felt from Eli was pure fear. Lena's life is in danger if we don't do something to help her. The warden has approved a meeting between you and Eli for tomorrow, eleven o'clock. Please come. Just talk to him. I think you're her only hope. Eli's only hope."

The last words convinced her of his delusion. Whatever was going on with Lena—and plenty of twenty-somethings took off without telling their fathers where they were going, even when their fathers weren't locked up in a federal penitentiary—the minister's agenda was more personal: salvation for a self-confessed killer.

Next thing, he'd be asking her to forgive Hale.

Paul crossed the hall, took her free hand, and she let him lead her the six steps into his apartment. His hand felt so solid, so real compared with the memories buzzing through her mind. Soft jazz rumbled from the stereo; the table was set, wine poured, candles lit, a warm man waiting.

"It's out of my control. I can't help you." She did what

she should have done ten minutes ago. She hung up the phone and focused on the man before her, giving him a bright smile. "Sorry about that, Paul. Work."

"Something important?"

She hauled in a breath, used it to fortify her smile. "No. An old case that's not my jurisdiction. Nothing to do with me."

He bought the lie, took her bag from her, and gathered her into his arms for a proper greeting. Caitlyn held him tighter than she'd intended, but she couldn't help herself. She inhaled his scent: sandalwood and cooking spices blended in a rich, tantalizing medley. This was so good, the best thing that had ever happened to her.

The thought made her wonder about Lena. The irony that Eli Hale's daughter had spent her life trying to prove a self-confessed murderer innocent. While Caitlyn had spent her life putting killers like Eli Hale behind bars trying to win the approval of her own dead father. Both facing impossible tasks. Both leading impossible lives.

Maybe Caitlyn's mom was right: She'd never find happiness until she was willing to put the past behind her. Maybe that's why Paul scared her so much. He offered her a future she wasn't sure she deserved.

CHAPTER THREE

The room was all walls, no windows. Maybe a pantry or walk-in closet with the shelves and hanger rods removed. The floor was carpet old enough and cheap enough that the edges curled up. It smelled of sweaty feet and rancid bacon grease. Overhead, beyond her reach, a bare incandescent lightbulb, its filament whining like mosquitoes on a warm summer's night, a string dangling down to control it. She only turned it on when the darkness became too overwhelming, didn't dare risk it burning out, leaving her with nothing.

No electrical outlets to turn into a Bat-Signal with chewing gum and a bobby pin. If she had chewing gum or a bobby pin. No baseboards to yank off and use as a weapon. Beneath the carpet was plywood, nailed down with headless nails from a nail gun, so she couldn't even pry one out. Not that she didn't try when she got bored enough.

There was no furniture unless you counted the small chemical toilet in the far corner. Only enough room for her to lie down if she positioned the sleeping bag diagonally across the floor. But they'd left a case of water and some Ensure, saltines, and peanut butter—enough for a week if she was careful—and the room, wherever it was, whatever it was before it became her prison, was warm enough as long as she kept her coat on.

She hadn't seen their faces. Not really. That gave her hope.

She had no idea how long she'd been here. Other than searching her while she was unconscious and removing anything that could be used as a weapon, including her watch, which she missed dearly as time passed in fits and starts, they hadn't touched her.

They'd taken her shoes. For some reason she couldn't stop thinking about that. They weren't expensive, just Walmart knockoff dress boots she'd worn under her slacks—wanted to look professional when she spoke to Dr. Bearmeat at the archives office. Without them, only cheap white socks on her feet clashing with her navy slacks, it made this all too real. Terrifying.

Until one of them, the skinny one—all she'd noticed was his eyes, strange, blue with flecks of silver—he'd snuck back alone and returned her chain with its tiny gold cross. Seemed to realize how important it was to her. She squeezed her hand around it now, small comfort in the darkness.

They hadn't even asked her anything—a relief since there was very little she could tell them. She had a lot of ideas, ideas grown into full-blown conspiracy theories after they took her, but no proof, nothing to bargain with.

Why had they kept her alive? No matter how much she prayed, tried to put her faith in God's plan, that question kept nagging at her. Wouldn't it be safer for them to kill her, shut her up for good?

Unless she was the bargaining chip. Being used as

leverage against someone else. And that could only be one person: her father.

"It's no good," she yelled. "He doesn't give a damn about me."

There was no sign anyone heard her. No sounds at all beyond her ragged breathing. The silence encouraged her ranting. Trapped alone in the dark, talking to herself, was better than listening for the sounds she didn't want to hear: footsteps, a pistol being cocked, the nervous laughter of men who'd decided to have some fun before disposing of her corpse.

"What do you want from me?" She curled up in the corner, hugging her knees to her chest, praying. She stopped, listened hard. A floorboard creaked with a man's weight. Or was it just her imagination? She held her breath. *Please, no. Dear God, please help me.*

The creak came again. She was a woman of faith; it was all she had left. But for the first time in her twenty-six years, Lena Hale wondered if maybe God wasn't listening after all. Maybe He was a self-centered bastard, with no regard for His children, just like Eli.

Maybe, just like Eli, He would abandon her, leave her here alone to die.

CHAPTER FOUR

Dinner consisted of eggplant, tomatoes, and braised beef, served with candlelight, a nice Merlot, and strained small talk.

She and Paul had an understanding: He didn't talk about his patients and she didn't talk about her cases. But this was different. She could tell he wanted to ask, was waiting, expecting her to explain what kind of "work" had her so upset.

What could she say? That it wasn't a case but something to do with her father, dead for twenty-six years? Dead because of the man she'd loved as a second father, when she was young and stupid and hadn't yet mastered the art of guarding her heart?

Or the girl. Baby Lena. Missing. Or maybe just not interested in talking with her own father. Who knew? If what Whitford thought was true, Lena was in danger—of course he had no facts, only fears.

After she cleaned the kitchen, Caitlyn used her cell to track down two numbers for Lena, a cell and a residence in Durham. No answer at either. Didn't mean anything.

Law students were allowed to take a night off, not answer their phones. Besides, it was out of Caitlyn's jurisdiction; she couldn't drop everything to start asking questions. Real-life law enforcement didn't work that way.

Another reason not to explain Whitford's call to Paul. He'd never understand. Just like Whitford hadn't. They heard "FBI" and thought she had the keys to some magic kingdom where super computers could spot a face in the crowd at the Super Bowl or trace a smudged fingerprint to anyone in the country in the ten seconds before a commercial break. Damn *CSI*.

"What's wrong?" he asked as they lay together in bed later that night. Distracted dinner conversation had led to distracted sex. Totally Caitlyn's fault. When she was anxious she tended to turn to sex as a diversion. Tonight it hadn't worked.

"Work." Another lie. Well, to be fair, the same lie repeated.

"I thought you were glad they hadn't given you a new assignment." He wrapped his arms around her, pulled her closer, his fingers brushing against the K-shaped scar on her chest. Souvenir from six months ago when she'd tangled with a psychopath. It tingled beneath his touch. She shifted her weight until his hand came to rest over her breast instead. So much better. As she was relaxing into his embrace, thinking maybe it was time for more diversionary sexual fun and games, he broke the mood by saying, "Who knows where they might send you."

His voice held a plaintive tone. She tried to lighten things. "Bismarck, North Dakota."

He sat up straight. "Seriously?"

She managed a smile, although he couldn't see it in the dark. Bismarck was where the academy instructors threatened to send agents in training who screwed up. "No. Just an old FBI joke."

"I don't think it's funny." He lay back, silent, as his thumb traced circles along the curve of her shoulder. Usually his touch was enough to relax her, but tonight it was more of a distraction. One more thing to worry about: leaving him when she was finally reassigned. Hurting him. Being hurt herself.

This—them—was never supposed to last this long. Way past her usual relationship boundaries, she was lost without a map.

When Caitlyn finally drifted to sleep, her dreams were filled with fragments of images, colliding as she tried to piece them together into a coherent whole. Lena, laughing, toddling away from Vonnie, who chased after her with a clean diaper . . . Dad and Eli Hale siting on the porch but instead of relaxing, rocking their chairs as they sipped their beers, their heads leaned together in earnest conversation. It was always funny to see them together like that: pale, carrot-topped Sean Tierney, thin and wiry, head-to-head with a man almost twice his size, dark chestnut skin, shaved head.

"You girls go play," her dad had snapped when she and Vonnie bounded up the steps. "Go on now, leave us be."

Eli said nothing, just gave Vonnie a sharp look that made her eyes go wide as she tugged at Caitlyn's arm, pulling her back down the porch steps. It was a bad time—Eli was in some kind of trouble and Sean Tierney was the only person who could help him.

That's what her dad did, he helped folks. Best job in the world, he said.

Caitlyn wanted to be just like him. She led Vonnie

around to the side of the porch where they slid through a gap in the latticework and crouched immediately below their dads. How could they help if they didn't know what was going on?

"It's the truth," Sean Tierney was saying, his voice raised rather than the calm, even tone that Caitlyn usually found so comforting. "Why should I stop saying it?"

"Stop being so mule-headed. Everything they have says I did it. I killed that man. Best thing for all is if I say it, too." Eli sounded sad, like someone had died or something.

"That's crazy! You can't do that—"

"You let me decide what I can and can't do," Eli answered in a grim voice. "I'll do whatever it takes to keep my family safe."

A man's boots thudded so hard above them dirt rained down on where Vonnie and Caitlyn crouched. "I'm not going to lie. Especially not if it means sending an innocent man to prison."

"Then don't say anything. You need to shut up and just mind your own business about it. Hear me?"

"Eli, I can't—"

"Not asking if you can or can't, Sean. I'm telling you. This is the way it's gotta be." His voice dropped. "Don't make me beg, man. I will. But don't make me do it."

A woman's scream drowned out Sean Tierney's reply. Caitlyn sat up in bed, still half asleep. Was it a dream?

A thud shook the wall behind her. Paul moaned and rolled over, reaching for her. She moved his arm away and slipped out of bed, grabbing her service weapon.

"Don't!" the woman screamed again. The sound of a slap cut her off.

"Caitlyn, where are you going?" Paul whispered as he climbed out of bed and came to her.

"I need to see what's happening, help her."

He grabbed her arm. "Stop. There's no one to save. They go through this every few weeks. Get drunk, bust up the place, then make up again."

"Get the phone, call nine-one-one."

"I'm telling you there's no need. Seriously." He pivoted her to face him. "She's fine. First few times I went over myself just to make sure. They'll break a lot of glass—" Another thud against the wall punctuated his words. "Scream at each other, but believe me, there's nothing you need to involve yourself with. Besides, she gives as good as she gets."

She stared at him. Who was he to make that judgment? Did he have any idea how many women were killed inside their own homes by the men they loved?

"I know why you do it, why you rush in," he continued. Paul always needed to analyze everything, just like he did with his X-rays and MRIs.

"I'm not rushing into anything. I'm a trained federal law enforcement officer. This is my job."

"It's survivor's guilt."

That got her attention. Divided it between what was going on next door and her plan of approach. Never good to have your attention torn when dealing with a domestic, but he couldn't know that. "What?"

"You feel guilty about that guy dying and you living." He was talking about her last case, right before they met. She'd never told him the details, although it had been in the news. Not all of the facts, but enough for him to fill in the blanks. "It wasn't your fault, Caitlyn. You think you owe him something, like somehow you can pay him back if you go out and save the world. But you don't owe anyone anything."

She froze. Caught between Paul and the exit. No cover. Just like her agent in training earlier today. The sounds from the apartment next door vanished. The pistol in her hand felt heavy, holding her in place like an anchor.

Paul stepped forward, placed his hands on her shoulders. For once his touch didn't bring comfort with it. She shrugged his hands away. "Caitlyn." His voice was colored by the slightest hint of irritation—which only pushed her farther from him. "Come back to bed."

Suddenly, shivering in the dark, straining to hear if a woman on the other side of the wall was still alive, clarity lanced through her as sharp as a blade and she knew what Paul really wanted. "You want me to quit."

He didn't even flinch. "You've paid your dues, almost got killed yourself. Twice. I don't know what I'd do if anything happened to you." He reached for her once more, wrapping his arms around her from behind, his lips brushing the top of her head. His scent was intoxicating and she almost relented, almost surrendered.

Sounds of a bed squeaking and a woman's laughter came from the apartment next door. Not dead. Just loud foreplay. Paul was right. About one thing.

Caitlyn stepped away from his embrace and re-holstered her weapon before turning to face him. "You're serious. About me quitting."

He looked surprised. "You're so smart, Caitlyn. You could do anything you want. Why stay in a dead-end job with no chance of advancement when your bosses don't want you there anyway?"

At that moment he sounded exactly like her mother, constantly disappointed that Caitlyn hadn't done more with her life, that she'd chosen to follow in her father's footsteps. Exactly like the voice in her head every time her boss called to tell her that OPR had a few more questions or that her fit rep was delayed again or that the Bureau was searching for the "right" position for her and it might take a while before she received another active-duty assignment.

The brass at the FBI didn't want her there, so why stay? Why wait for them to find a reason to fire her? Why not just leave?

She wished she had an answer.

Wished even more that she could ignore the resentment smoldering in her, lit by Paul's suggestion that she quit. He'd said "we" as if it was his decision as much as hers. As if it was his life.

Well, hell. At least she was back on familiar territory as far as relationships went. She knew where this was headed.

He smiled and reached for her when she sat on the bed. She leaned forward, avoiding his hand, and grabbed her jeans from where she'd hung them on the footboard.

"What are you doing?" Wounded pride undercut his smooth baritone.

"I have to go."

"At this time of night? Where?"

"North Carolina." She didn't bother with her bra, slid her fleece V-neck over her tank top. Her hair came out flyaway static, red strands shimmering in the dim light from the window.

"I thought we weren't going to Charlotte until next month."

Right. The dreaded trip to see her mom, then on to his folks in Atlanta. "Not Charlotte. A federal penitentiary outside Raleigh. I have to meet a prisoner."

Five minutes later she was on the other side of his front door trying to deny the wave of relief that swamped her. He was a good man, didn't deserve this shit. Her shit.

She missed him already.

CHAPTER FIVE

He was most worried about the leopard.

The others had taken to their new homes just fine, like it was meant to be. Well, except the chimps. They'd outsmarted him that first night. Bernie had locked the cabin doors but they'd busted out through a window instead. Hadn't left, though—they seemed to enjoy playing hide-and-seek, leaping down on him when he was feeding or changing the straw he'd put down for the others, chattering away at him from rooftops and trees, scampering from cabin to cabin, exploring. Right at home. Just like the others.

Sure, the three-toed sloth kept gouging at the walls of the cabin it shared with the lemurs, but as soon as he moved a stack of firewood and some downed tree branches in there, it was as happy as a trout gulping mayflies. Even the lion, old and weary and moth-eaten as it was, had settled into its new quarters just fine. Gave a rumble and a toothless smile every time Bernie opened the cabin door to deliver it fresh ground venison.

Bernie was beginning to think that maybe, if he could

figure out a way to keep the Reapers from finding out that he was the one who had stolen the animals, maybe he could actually keep them here with him. Probably not. But it turned out it wasn't as easy as he'd imagined, giving stolen wild animals away to a good home. The zoos he'd called all wanted documents, health records, stuff like that.

Heck, he couldn't even get the leopard to eat. Bernie had taken extra care with its home, placing it in the sturdy log cabin main lodge instead of the more flimsy guest cabins scattered around the grounds. After Bernie boarded up the windows and it couldn't claw its way through the lodge's walls, it tore through the plaster ceiling and holed up in the rafters. Every time Bernie came near the lodge it made a noise like it was sick to its stomach, a soft keening that made Bernie's own stomach clench, his every instinct warning him to flee.

He couldn't abandon the poor thing. Not after everything it'd been through, first with that asshole with the exotic petting "zoo" over in Pigeon Forge, and then after the Reapers had taken the animals when their keeper defaulted on his loan. The motorcycle club figured they'd make money with the exotic beasts, so lost and far from the homes they'd been snatched from. Planned to sell hunters a chance of a lifetime.

So what'd they do once they had the things in cages on the back of a flatbed? Started shooting. Training them for the chase, Poppy said, using an empty Jack Daniel's bottle on the ground below the truck as a target, laughing when the glass flew into the chimps' cage, sending them screeching and flying up the chain link to the farthest corner.

Bernie loved Poppy, loved all the guys in the motorcycle

club. The MC was his family. But just like his real family, sometimes they could be total assholes.

Maybe the leopard was still in shock. Maybe that was why it wouldn't eat or come down from its perch, just lay up there making those noises that rattled his fillings and made his hair stand upright.

He parked his truck in front of the large two-story log cabin. The Teddy Roosevelt Lodge had seen better days. Built back in the 1930s in the hope that the new Smoky Mountains National Park the CCC and WPA were carving out of the mountains would attract families, it sported fourteen separate cabins spread out along the perimeter backing the woods as well as the central two-story main building. The land was rugged, the lodge so high it spent most of the day shrouded in either fog or shadow. It was situated adjacent to the far northeastern corner of the Cherokee Reservation's Qualla Boundary, sandwiched between it and the national park with no room for further development.

The original owner was optimistic the privacy and spectacular view would make building halfway up the side of a mountain a gamble that would pay off despite the only access being a treacherous road that would challenge most vehicles.

He'd been wrong. And so the property had languished, turned over a dozen times to equally enthusiastic developers, until finally Bernie's dad took it on while making a bigger deal, and gave it to Bernie, saying, "Even you can't screw it up any more than it already is."

Best thing Dad ever did for his son. Bernie loved the lodge. There were no neighbors or visitors; no one wanted to drive up the narrow, twisted single-lane road going nowhere. When life with the Reapers got too rowdy and overwhelming, he could come here and think and dream.

He imagined the lodge turned into a real home, he and a girl settling down, raising a bunch of kids who'd grow up with the animals, learning to live together in harmony with nature. Most of his dream came from movies and TV shows he'd watched as a kid, old ones from back when his folks were young themselves, like *Gilligan's Island, Tarzan, Swiss Family Robinson, Doctor Dolittle* . . .

Now he had a chance to live his dreams. First, God had sent him the animals to rescue and care for.

Then, last night, He'd sent the girl. She was perfect: smart and pretty and a woman of faith. A few times he'd leaned against the door and just stood there, listening to her praying, tears slipping down his face. He couldn't say why he wept; guess he finally knew what folks meant when they said the Spirit moved them. She moved him like no one else ever had.

Dad would never approve.

The law would lock him up for good.

If the Reapers ever found out they'd kill him.

CHAPTER SIX

Caitlyn drove past the yellow-and-neon glow of slumbering bedroom communities that dotted Route 28, not worrying about speed limits or flashing amber stoplights. Her phone rang. Paul. She put it on speaker, although usually she hated to talk while driving.

"Baby," he drawled in his best Barry White impression, "I miss you. Come on home before your side of the bed gets cold."

She laughed. Paul was the first man she'd ever been with who could always make her laugh. She was crazy, even thinking of leaving him. But she also couldn't envision a life with him—at least not on his terms. Doubt left her feeling unbalanced. She resorted to a weak attempt at humor. "I told you what I'd do to you if you ever called me 'baby' again."

"Oh yeah, baby, come show me what a bad boy I am." He gave up the impression, too hard to maintain when he was cracking up himself. "Seriously, Caitlyn, come back home so we can talk about it."

Talking with Paul about the future of their relationship. Or chatting up the man responsible for her father's death. Easy choice. "I really do have to be in Raleigh first thing in the morning. I'll call you as soon as I'm back."

"You'll be back for the weekend?"

He sounded anxious. God, he wasn't planning anything stupid involving a ring, was he? It would be just like him to orchestrate an elaborate surprise. Part of her wanted to be that girl, the one who had a man eager to delight and surprise her. Most of her was simply too scared to even think about it. "I'm not sure."

His sigh filled the distance between them. "Okay. Drive carefully. Call me."

"I will." She hung up, her attention focused on the lonely highway ahead of her.

When she made it home, she parked the Impreza in front of the restored Victorian and climbed the creaky outside stairs leading to her apartment on the second floor as quietly as possible. Like Caitlyn, her landlady was a chronic insomniac and prone to stop by for a chat if she heard Caitlyn up and about.

Leaving her apartment would be the second-hardest thing when she eventually was given a new assignment. She loved this place, with its big drafty windows and high ceilings. It was the first time she'd actually turned what started out as temporary quarters into something that felt like a sanctuary.

It wasn't fancy. The sofa shared the living room with her treadmill. She ate standing at the kitchen counter because she'd never found time to buy a proper table or chairs. But every time she walked through the door she felt a weight lift, she could let her guard down. Really relax. Whether it was curling up and reading a good book or working out while watching reruns of *Dr. Who*. Or just sitting on the couch and cleaning her guns.

The focal piece of the room stood in the corner: a small, upright gun safe lovingly crafted from cherry, with an old-fashioned dial lock embedded into the door. It was about the size of a footlocker only half as deep, heavy enough to stand on its own, but small enough to easily fit into the trunk of a car. It was the one piece of furniture she'd taken with her every time she'd moved. The only thing she had left of her dad.

She took a quick shower and changed into working clothes: navy slacks, off-white blouse. Then she crouched down before the gun safe and twirled the knob to unlock it. She loved the way the tumblers clicked as the knob spun—it felt like opening a bank vault. As a kid, she'd press her ear to the door, pretend she was Willie Sutton cracking a safe. Of course she never succeeded. But it was fun trying.

The smell of gun bluing greeted her as she opened the door, a scent she associated with her dad more than any cologne or aftershave. She slid her fingers over the safe's satiny finish, remembered helping him sand its door and walls, sawdust tickling her nose, his smile as they moved together, with the grain, always with the grain.

She selected the backup piece she wanted from the shelves lining the back of the door, a Glock 27. Forty-caliber yet small enough to fit into an ankle holster or wear at the small of her back. The main space was designed to hold long guns: Dad's old deer rifle and her Remington 870 shotgun stood side by side, waiting like old friends.

Not today. Probably didn't need the Baby Glock, much less the ASP extension baton or the Gerber folding knife she carried, but Caitlyn liked to be prepared when she hit the road. Never knew what might be out there.

After grabbing enough clothing for a few days—just in case, she told herself—and leaving a message on LaSovage's voicemail that she was taking a leave day—not that anyone would miss her playing a spare bad guy in training simulations—Caitlyn took off again. She was far enough south of DC and it was early enough in the day that the interstate wasn't crowded, leaving her the left-hand lane mostly to herself. Past Richmond, I-85 through southern Virginia was a monotonous stretch of highway but she didn't worry about falling asleep at the wheel. Too many ghosts to keep her awake.

Her father's face, blood matting his red hair—hair the same red as hers, setting them apart from the rest of the family. The dull film that made his eyes, always before sparking with intelligence and kindness and a hint of laughter, appear fogged, like the mists that clung to the river on cloudy mornings. His skin was still warm when she reached a hand to touch his cheek, unable to believe what her eyes told her. But not warm enough. She knelt there, on the floor of their living room, the room she'd sit and watch cartoons in after school, listening for his boots clacking against the porch steps, waiting for him to open the door and scoop her into his arms, reminding her that the world might be a big, dangerous place but he was there to keep her safe.

A truck driver honked as Caitlyn drifted across the centerline. She yanked the wheel back, blamed it on a lack of coffee even as she wiped her tears with a knuckled fist.

She never blamed her father. Twenty-six years and she'd never blamed him.

Her mom had. The rest of the family. The people at

church, in town, at school. Evergreen, North Carolina, was a small town on the edge of the Cherokee Reservation. The kind of town where everyone knew everyone's business and wasn't afraid to pass judgment.

Weak, they pronounced Sean Tierney. Coward.

She'd gotten into so many fistfights, cursed and shouted down so many adults—including their minister—that her mom confined Caitlyn to her room. Of course, Jessalyn didn't realize Caitlyn could hear everything said in the kitchen and living room through the ventilation duct. That's when she heard the truth: Her dad killed himself because of what Eli Hale had done. He'd been about to lose his job because he was still defending Eli, trying to prove his innocence, saying Eli was with him at the time of the murder, even after Eli confessed to hitting a Cherokee tribal elder with a hammer then burning down the man's house to cover it up.

No, she didn't blame her father for abandoning her all those years ago. For taking a coward's way out. For ripping her world apart.

She didn't blame her father. She blamed Eli Hale.

By the time she drove onto the Butner campus her anger had coalesced into a perfectly foul mood, more suited for a rain-soaked day than the sun-filled, crisp January morning the world presented to her. FCI Butner One, one of several medium-security facilities on the campus, was gorgeous. If you ignored the double ring of twelve-foot fences topped with razor wire, you'd think you were driving up to the corporate headquarters of an environmentally conscious manufacturer.

Trees and ornamental bushes surrounded the courtyard behind the administration building, each bush trimmed into a neat green ball. Large green spaces separated the housing units, named after Atlantic Coast Conference universities. The rec yard boasted a bocce court, running track, baseball diamond, and a sweat lodge for the large Native American population housed here. The only thing separating it from an elite athletic resort was the overhead wire preventing helicopters being used to break out prisoners.

She parked in front of the admin building and wondered if the Native Americans ever gave Eli Hale a hard time. After all, he was a black man who'd killed an Eastern Band Cherokee tribal elder in a particularly brutal manner, bludgeoning the man to death and burning his house down. Maybe life here wasn't the country-club existence the pretty shrubbery and gently curving pathways suggested. Part of her—the nine-year-old part of her—hoped so.

The other part wondered how anyone stayed sane locked up for life, no matter how nice the surroundings. Even after twenty-five years, Hale would only be in his late fifties, still plenty of time left. Time to think about what he'd lost. About how he'd betrayed his best friend. About what he'd taken from Caitlyn and her mom.

Jessalyn had never recovered from her husband's death. Never dated again—at least not as far as Caitlyn knew. Had given up her childhood home to take Caitlyn far away from the bad memories. Had given up everything to offer Caitlyn a new life.

All because of Eli Hale. Caitlyn took a deep breath, trying to choke off the bitterness surging into her veins like a shot of cheap tequila. Another breath followed as she reminded herself she was a federal law enforcement officer here to interview a prisoner. Nothing more, nothing less.

She placed her credentials into her blazer pocket, her gun in a holster on her waist, and secured everything else in the trunk where she had a lockbox bolted to the car frame. Not as nice as her dad's gun safe, but it added a layer of theft deterrence. No cell phones were allowed inside, so that stayed in the car along with her wallet, leather car coat, backup weapons, and overnight bag.

It was still early, just past ten, but she knew it would take time to process her. Since actual visiting hours didn't begin until later in the day, they'd need to pull guards to escort Hale to her, which would take more time. Probably why the warden scheduled the visit to coincide with Hale's transfer from the medical center back to his unit. Efficient use of manpower.

The guard manning the reception desk didn't seem to think so. He grunted without making eye contact after Caitlyn filled out the requisite forms and showed her ID. His entire world seemed to consist of the computer screen and keyboard in front of him.

"We're at almost double our capacity and short-staffed." He answered her unasked question with a defensive tone as if she should just beg forgiveness and leave him the hell alone. "You'll have to wait."

"For how long?" Caitlyn asked. The reception hall was already filling with families queuing for visitation.

"Look, lady, you either wait here or sit in an interview room."

"I'll take the interview room." Better than standing here being scrutinized by resentful women and risk being contaminated by snotty-nosed kids. Another strike against Paul—he wanted a family, would make the perfect father, while she'd be Mommy Dearest at best.

Growing up, her friends all loved her mother because

Jessalyn Tierney treated them like adults, the same way she treated her daughter. No coddling, although plenty of hugs and kisses, but mostly a determination that her daughter would be strong. *Stronger than her father* was the unspoken refrain that colored every moment of their life together.

Watching her mom stand so strong against her grief, while also being treated like an adult, expected to fend for herself since the age of nine, hadn't cultivated any maternal instincts in Caitlyn. Just the opposite: To her kids were miniature aliens from a strange planet invading her world.

"Suit yourself." He waved to another guard, who made her fill out more forms as he took her weapon and locked it into a drawer, then ushered her through the metal detector.

The second guard, Smith was his name, seemed in a better mood than the first. They walked to the visitation area, passing through several layers of doors. Once they were inside he led her down a hallway, nodding to two inmates mopping the floor and a guard juggling a cup of coffee while turning a key in a door leading to the monitoring room.

"So this is why I'm starting my shift early," the second guard said to Smith, eyeing Caitlyn. "Guess it's worth it."

The two inmates looked sideways at her and she stared right back. One, a black man with short dreadlocks, smiled a hopeful smile. Caitlyn arched an eyebrow at him in incredulity. His partner laughed and elbowed him back to work.

Smith led her past the three of them to an entrance to a corridor. Inside there were interview rooms along one side, ringing the main visitation area. The interview room was empty except for two vinyl chairs, too light to be used as weapons, and a table bolted to the floor. Two walls were solid, white cinder block, while the two with doors were made of reinforced glass, floor-to-ceiling, thick enough that as soon as the door closed behind her, all noises of the prison block died.

Smart design, Caitlyn thought. Privacy but without the need for additional staff to monitor them. The single man operating the video feeds and watching out the observation window above them could handle it all.

"Not sure how long it will be," Smith told her. "He'll be coming through the inmate entrance." He pointed out the window to the secured glass doorway on the other side of the large general visitation room. "If you need anything, here's the intercom."

His radio buzzed. He raised it to his lips, gave her a wave, and left, the door shutting with a thud behind him.

Caitlyn took a seat and faced away from the door she'd come in through, out the glass wall opposite. The second door and window led to the general visitation hall, a large cafeteria-like room with chairs swiveling out from round tables. There was a play corner for kids; the far wall was lined with vending machines. If not for the guard sitting inside a glassed-in monitoring room one level above or the signs reminding visitors and inmates of the rules, it could have been a low-priced family-style fast-food joint.

The inmate entrance was below the monitoring room. Hale would be processed through a metal detector just as she'd been and screened by a guard. Then he'd be allowed access to the visitation area and through it the private interview room she waited in.

A lot of fuss to talk to a man she never wanted to see again. But she couldn't stop thinking about little Lena— she might be twenty-six, but in Caitlyn's mind she was still toddling around with a droopy diaper hanging from her hips. What kind of trouble could she have gotten herself into?

The chaplain's words had stuck with her as well. He'd said Hale told him her father was right, that death was the only silence they'd accept. Who the hell were "they"?

The answers were the only reason she was here. Waiting for the man who'd destroyed her family. And if there was one thing Caitlyn hated, it was waiting.

She spent the time counting ceiling tiles: fifty-four; eyeing the video camera in the corner; practicing imitations of movie lawmen from Gary Cooper's tight-lipped expressionless anger to John Wayne's eye-wrinkling scowl—a game she'd played with her dad as a kid; and watching the guard at the monitor station above. From where she sat only the top of his head was visible, but he sure seemed to bounce around a lot for someone whose job was to sit and watch a bunch of video screens. Finally he settled down into his chair and vanished from her sight.

Just in time for her attention to focus on the inmate entrance. The doors slid open and Eli Hale entered.

It was as if twenty-six years had never happened. He didn't shuffle or hunch like many men she'd seen in prison. No, still the same head-high stride, gaze moving from left to right and back again like a king surveying his domain. He saw her and a smile began to crinkle his eyes, just for a heartbeat, before fading into a sorrow-filled nod of appreciation.

He understood how hard this was for her. She dropped her professional facade, caught between the nine-year-old girl's desire to run to the man who'd been a second father to her and the thirty-five-year-old weighed down by decades of pain. Standing at the glass door, waiting, she watched him walk across the empty room, threading his way through the maze of tables.

The doors behind him opened once more. He blocked her view of what was happening, but a quick glance at the clock on the wall told her it wasn't yet time for official visitation. Maybe a guard?

She couldn't hear anything beyond the glass, but something alerted Hale. He stopped, not ten feet away from the door leading into the interview room, turned his head to look back, his body still facing her.

That's when they jumped him.

CHAPTER SEVEN

Two inmates, both Hispanic with shaved heads and Sureno gang tatts. What the hell were West Coast gang-bangers doing waltzing into the visitation area? Caitlyn hit the panic button as one Sureno tackled Hale from behind, grabbing him in a bear hug so tight Hale was lifted off his feet. The other danced forward, his fist grasping a small object.

Caitlyn lunged for the door, but of course it was still locked. Trapping her on the wrong side to watch helplessly.

"We need help in the visitation area," she called into the intercom.

No one answered. She shouted, waved at the video camera, but there was no sign of the guard in the monitoring station overhead. He was probably also the one on the other end of the intercom and panic button. Shit.

No gun, no way to intervene, no one to call for help. All she could do was watch as the Surenos stabbed Eli over and over, smiling and laughing at the overhead cameras, wiping Eli's blood across their faces like it was war paint.

Caitlyn's fury reared up so hard and fast it brought tears to her eyes. She slammed her hand into the thick glass, the pain barely registering as she stood witness to an execution.

The two Surenos finished their work. One blew her a kiss, the other grabbed his crotch and gave her the finger, and they ran out the way they came in. Hale slumped against the table next to the door, blood blossoming into tiny rosebuds across his shirt. Not so much blood, but that wasn't necessarily a good thing, Caitlyn knew. The real damage would be internal.

She pounded on the door, more out of frustration and anger than an attempt to break it down. Her eyes locked on Hale's. He struggled across the length of the table to get closer to her. His mouth opened and closed, but she could hear nothing through the glass.

His body shuddered as he hauled in a breath and pointed at her. Then he slowly mouthed words impossible to deny: *Lena. Save Lena.*

"No," she called to the dying man, willing him to hang on. Childhood memories, her and Vonnie, Eli and her dad, all of them laughing, so happy . . . she'd locked the good times away along with the bad. Now to have to watch this . . . she choked down a sob. It was like her own father dying all over again. "Eli. Hang on. Please."

Her voice cracked and faded. Eli couldn't hear her.

With a final gasp Eli Hale slumped facedown across the table, one arm snagged over the back of a chair, the only thing keeping him from falling to the floor. Caitlyn cursed as the alarm finally sounded and three guards wearing helmets and carrying shields and riot batons ran into the visitation room.

She waved them to Hale. Although it was obvious to

anyone that there was no longer any threat, they still circled the room, ensuring it was empty. Then two of them stood guard while a third checked for life signs. He shook his head.

Eli Hale was gone. Taking his answers with him.

Bernie loved being a prospect for the Reapers. Life would be even better once he was patched in and became a full-fledged member of the motorcycle club. But until then, it was his job to put up with their crap and do all the shit work no one else wanted.

Like coming in early on a Friday to clean up at the clubhouse and the trailer behind it, making sure there was enough booze and beer and snacks to last the weekend of partying. Pushing a broom. Pretty much what his dad had him doing before he left McSwain Enterprises to join the Reapers. Jimmy McSwain had no regrets seeing his son leave to become a biker full-time—in fact, when Bernie had told him about the Reapers' invitation, his dad had taken him out for a drink to celebrate. First time he'd ever done that. Most of the time, he just pretended like Bernie didn't exist.

Bernie loved everything about being a Reaper—until two days ago, when he overheard their leaders planning to kidnap and kill a girl. Now it was as if his entire world had been turned inside out. He couldn't trust his brother Reapers—his only friends—but he couldn't leave them, either, they'd find him and then . . . He shuddered so hard he almost dropped the broom.

What choice did he have but to stay? Try his best to figure a way out of this without hurting the Reapers or Lena.

The Reapers' clubhouse was in an old two-story

A-frame log cabin that used to be a bar called the Pit Stop. Now that the Reapers owned it, it served twice as much booze, but since these were MC private parties, they didn't have to worry about liquor licenses or zoning laws. They held Church upstairs in a private room. On the main floor was a commercial kitchen, offices behind the bar, as well as a dance floor, darts, and two pool tables.

Bernie pried two steel-shafted darts out from the wide-planked pine floor. They were nowhere near the dartboards, instead seemed to have been aimed at the sign near the front door that read: NO SQUIDS ALLOWED! He stashed them behind the bar and went back to his sweeping.

The menial labor kept his hands busy and his mind free to roam. While he swept, he'd see stories unfold inside his head like a movie, only starring him, Bernard McSwain, as the hero. Used to be all sorts of foxy chicks starred opposite him, all with big boobs and adoring glances. But lately the only woman he thought about was the girl.

Lena. Eli Hale's little girl. Which made her off limits for so many reasons. Including the fact that Poppy wanted her dead.

What Poppy wanted, the MC always made happen. Not only was he their leader, their president, he was what held the club together, kept the money flowing and the bikes rolling. Without Poppy and the shadowy figures he and Weasel, the club VP, worked with behind the scenes, the Reapers would be nothing more than another bunch of losers who couldn't cut it in the real world.

Instead, they ran this town. Practically the whole county, for that matter. A fact that used to make Bernie walk proud and tall—unlike when he was being shuffled around from job to job at his dad's company. Only place off limits to a

Reaper was the VistaView, the Indian casino on the other side of the reservation.

Bernie's dad ran the VistaView but Bernie hated it. The casino was built in 1990 when Bernie was just a kid. Even back then it felt old and as out of date as the furniture his mother kept in the living room that was off limits to him and his friends. He couldn't understand why the casino was so popular. Who cared about a bunch of grayhairs hunched over slots or sweating at the live tables, fool enough to lose their money even though everyone knew the house always won?

The MC was more of a family to Bernie than his dad or big sister or even his mom had ever been. And he'd betrayed them.

Acid burned his throat and he popped another Tums and wiped the sweat from his forehead and neck before taking his broom back up. He hated lying to his brother Reapers, hated being caught in the middle like this. It made him feel sick, feverish with guilt. But no way would he give them Lena. God had sent her to him, just like He'd sent the animals. She was Bernie's. He would take care of her, figure out a way to save her . . . save them both.

But how?

"Watch where you're going."

Bernie jumped at the gruff voice. Sweat poured from him—last time he'd tripped someone up while mopping it'd been Weasel. He still had the welts across his back from where the VP had broken the mop handle and beat him with it. As a prospect, Bernie had no choice but to take it. Another reason why he couldn't wait to be patched in as a full member. Real Reapers didn't take shit from nobody.

Thank God the size-twelve engineer boots in front of him now didn't belong to Weasel. "Sorry, Goose."

The man snorted, shifted his feet from the floor up to a chair, and tipped the chair he sat in back onto two legs. The posture looked so damn cool. No wonder all the ladies adored Goose, although his blond hair down to his collar and scruffy beard and all those muscles helped. Every time Bernie tried to lift weights and get muscles like those he just got a sore back. And he'd tried balancing on a chair's rear legs and about knocked himself out when he fell.

He sighed. No way he'd ever be like Goose. That was why, even though they'd both started as prospects at the same time, Goose already not only was a full patch but had just been elected to the coveted post of club enforcer.

Which sucked. Because unlike the other guys who treated Bernie like their own personal slave or, worse, their own personal punching bag, Goose talked to him, treated him like Bernie counted for something.

But it was Goose's job to protect the club from outside threats. Like Lena.

So he was the last person Bernie could ever ask for advice.

"What's wrong, kid?" Goose cracked one whiskey-wearied eye open to focus on Bernie. The MC had had a pre-pre-weekend party last night that had gone on until four in the morning.

Bernie shuffled away so Goose couldn't see his face. He sucked at lying and knew it. "Nothing."

"Don't sound like nothing." Goose tilted the chair back onto all fours, sat up, and grabbed the not-quite-empty bottle of Jim Beam from the table. He took a swig, shook all over from head to toe like a shaggy dog coming in from the rain, and banged the bottle back onto the table with a satisfied grunt. "Have one on me. Sit down, drink up, tell me what's going on in the world of Bernard McSwain."

Bernie swallowed hard before turning to face Goose. Worst thing was, Goose acted like he really was interested by Bernie's pathetic life. Like he cared.

But Goose always did what was best for the club. Poppy would have asked him, as club enforcer, to find Lena and kill her.

Bernie didn't understand exactly why Lena was a threat to the club, but he was not about to let anything happen to her.

Goose kicked a chair out. Bernie sagged his skinny butt into it, still holding the broom by the handle, fighting a wave of nausea.

"What is it, kid? Girl troubles?"

That was close enough to the truth that Bernie didn't have to worry about lying. "Yes, sir."

"I keep telling you. Cut the 'sir.'" Goose was thirty-six, making him only a few years older than Bernie, but as a full-fledged member of the MC, he'd earned the "sir." Of course, Goose called Bernie "kid" or "prospect," everyone in the MC did—and would until Bernie earned his patch. Hell, maybe even after. At thirty-three he was still getting carded. He was skinny like a kid, still had pimples—but only occasionally, thank God—and he barely ever needed to shave. The club made its prospects keep their hair cut real short in a buzz cut or shaved to display the Reaper tatt across their scalp, but even that didn't help Bernie any when it came to earning respect.

"Girl trouble. Gotcha covered—I have an ex-wife and more ex-girlfriends than I can count. You name it, I've been there. She pregnant?"

"No, sir." Bernie shifted in the hard wooden chair.

Last thing he wanted was a discussion of his sex life—a topic the club members were always way too interested in for his taste, setting him up on blind "dates" with hookers and biker groupies, usually the ugly ones. Getting him laid was a constant joke among the Reapers.

"She cheating on you?"

"No. Nothing like that." She didn't even know Bernie existed. Much less that he was risking his life to save hers. But he couldn't explain any of that to Goose, not with the enforcer sitting there, tatts rippling down his bare arms, those dark blue eyes of his reading Bernie like a billboard.

"Can't be that bad of trouble then," Goose said, taking another swallow of bourbon, staring at Bernie appraisingly as he raised the bottle.

Bernie wilted under the other biker's glance, slid free from the chair and the inquisition, and stood. "You're right. I'll figure it out. Thanks."

He shuffled away, pushing the broom before him with random strokes, and escaped to the stockroom. Leaning back against the closed door, sweat poured from him so fast his shirt felt gritty. He took off his leather vest, tugged his shirt over his head, used it to mop his chest dry again, and stood there shivering under the naked lightbulb. A foul, metallic taste filled his mouth and he gulped two more Tums.

How much longer could he keep this up before he screwed up and got him and Lena killed?

CHAPTER EIGHT

The glass walls made privacy impossible, giving Caitlyn no choice but to shove her emotions aside until her work here was finished.

One thing about the Butner staff, they were damn efficient. Twenty minutes later Hale's body had been taken away. Then two men in suits and several high-ranking officers in crisp white Bureau of Prisons shirts toured the crime scene, leaving one man in a suit behind. Now, a mere eighty minutes after a man had been brutally murdered, the lockdown was lifted and two inmates wearing protective gear were finishing cleaning up the blood and decontaminating the area. Just in time for visitation.

Maybe these BOP guys should be running things in DC, Caitlyn thought as she paced the circumference of the interview room for the two hundred and eleventh time. She hated being caged up like this, hated her every move being watched, no contact with anyone except an anonymous guard who'd spoken to her earlier, making sure she was okay and letting her know she'd have to wait for a Special

Investigations Services investigator to interview her before she'd be released.

Like she was a damn prisoner. While the real ones were going on with their day as if nothing had happened.

Beyond the glass the inmates finished cleaning and left. A few minutes later the first of the family members arrived, children scattering across the large room, racing to the play area, women nodding at one another, chatting as they arranged themselves around the tables to wait for their men. They seemed to all know one another, at least the ones with children did, even though they spanned different ethnicities and, from their attire, crossed the socioeconomic spectrum. A handful of the women were alone and dressed more provocatively, pushing the boundaries of the prison-mandated dress code. These gathered at tables on the far side of the room, away from the play area, the targets of scornful glares from the wives and mothers.

Caitlyn felt like she was looking at a scene trapped inside a snow globe. Better yet, a fish tank where adversarial species had been mixed. She couldn't hear anything, but the women's body language said enough. On one side of the silent war were devoted family and loved ones soldiering through. The other, cheap entertainment who'd never stick for the long haul.

And then there was Caitlyn. Obviously establishment, obviously law enforcement. A common enemy.

Observing the women and children helped to calm Caitlyn's adrenaline rush. The initial shock and frustration at being unable to save Eli faded to irritation. And curiosity. She still had questions—more questions than ever.

The door behind her finally opened, bringing with it the smell of coffee brewed too long and a man's citrusy

aftershave. She didn't turn, wanting to keep the SIS investigator off balance and gaining her the chance to observe him via his reflection. Finally, the glass walls were
good for something.

He was the same man who'd documented the crime
scene an hour ago. Not quite six feet, broad shoulders that
strained the seams of his navy suit, late forties, brown
hair with a shimmer of gray, wedding band plain, sensi-
ble. When he turned to sit she spotted a tear along the side
seam of his jacket. Same kind of tear she was constantly
mending in her own blazers—suit coats weren't designed
to accommodate service weapons. But prison officers
didn't routinely carry weapons.

"Anytime you're ready, Special Agent Tierney." Slight
accent. Not New York, more Midwest. "I'm Investigator
Boone. I'll be taking your statement about this morning's
events."

Events? She buried her disdain at the euphemism for
murder. "You were a detective in Chicago before joining
the Bureau of Prisons?"

"Milwaukee. Put in my twenty, retired, but the city went
broke along with my pension, so decided to move south
and go to work for the BOP."

"Your wife must like that you're off the streets, working regular hours."

He reached for his coffee cup, turning away from her.
"She died. Breast cancer. Three years ago."

Three years ago. About the same time he'd retired,
judging from his age. She pictured that: a lifetime together, dreaming about what you'd do once retirement
freed you, only to have the day come with no one left to
share those dreams with. She'd bet the wife's passing had
more to do with his new position than money worries.

Hard for cops to give it up. Especially when there was no one to give it up for.

Maybe Paul was right. Better to get out now, before it was too late.

She brushed the thought aside as she turned to face Boone. He slid the second coffee cup in her direction, gestured to the empty seat across from him. Let the games begin.

Caitlyn sat down and quickly led Boone through everything she'd seen. She finished with a question of her own. "What happened to the guard in the monitor room?"

Boone shifted in his seat before conceding the lead to her. Trying to gain her confidence, no doubt. "Sudden attack of gastric distress. He's in the hospital getting an IV now."

She remembered the two inmates joking with the guard in the hallway. The cup of coffee in his hand. "Poisoned."

"Probably. I'm not a believer in coincidences."

"And the guard at the visitation station?"

He blew out his breath in a short exhalation, quickly cut off. "Him I'm looking into. Says he was sucker-punched, knocked out."

"Helluva long time to be incapacitated by a punch."

"Outside of movies or TV, yeah. Docs are checking him out as well."

"And the two doers?"

"Both lifers, nothing to lose, everything to prove. Funny thing is"—he leaned forward—"Hale had no beef with any cars. Everyone liked him, even the Indians and Neo-Nazis."

"Cars" being a group of prisoners who hung out together, she translated. Usually joined by commonality from life before incarceration, like gang members or former mobsters, sometimes by the length of their sentence or the crimes they committed.

"And," he continued, "those two Surenos were just transferred in from California. They didn't even know Hale."

She thought about that as the women in the visitation hall gathered their children and stood at attention. The doors to the inmate side of the hall opened and inmates began to filter in, pausing to scan the room for their loved ones.

"You all sure took care of things fast." She gestured to the family reunions beyond the window.

"Warden's idea. Figured we got the two killers, on video no less, no reason to keep everyone on lockdown, risk getting folks agitated." He looked down his nose at his coffee. "Warden's a pro-gressive." His derisive tone split the word in two.

"And you're not."

"I want to know why the hell a guy with twenty-five years in without a scratch ends up being targeted for a hit two minutes before he's due to have a sit-down with a fed."

So he agreed. It was a hit. By who? And why? If Hale knew something, he'd been silent for twenty-five years; why kill him now? It had to have something to do with Lena's disappearance. Was it a warning to her? Or those who held her, if she had been taken? Or just tying up loose ends?

"I wish I knew," she told Boone. "You find out, let me know."

He scrutinized her, not buying her dumb act. Too bad it wasn't an act. "You know he tried to kill himself a few days ago. Overdosed on OxyContin. Any ideas about why?"

She shrugged. Remained silent.

"I think he was trying to send a message to someone. Someone afraid of what he knew. Tell them, *Hey, I'll die before I squeal*. Something like that."

"Could be."

"Could be. But then why the change of heart? Why ask to talk to you—I checked, he asked for you specifically. Hale had nothing to do with any federal cases you'd be working on. Unless he heard something here. Maybe he was ratting out another con?"

She stuck with the truth. "I have no idea what information he wanted to pass on. Did you ask his cellmate? Or the others on the block?"

"Of course we asked. No one's saying nothing. And now you're telling me this is all a fluke, some kind of crazy coincidence he got shived on his way to talking to you?" His stare was piercing, trying to break past her facade of nonchalance. A facade easy to maintain because she really did know nothing helpful.

"I don't know." She stood. "Sorry I can't be of more help."

He sat, finished his coffee, in no hurry. Finally got up and led the way to the door, pushed the call button. A rush of relief greeted her as it buzzed open and she crossed the threshold, free of confinement. She'd make a piss-poor prisoner.

"I don't suppose there's any way I could take a look at his personal belongings?" she asked casually.

"Funny thing," he replied, matching her tone. Two cops bullshitting each other and both knowing it. "Before he left the infirmary he wrote a will. Naming you sole beneficiary of his personal documents. We already got them boxed up—confiscated and inspected everything in his cell after he tried to OD a few days ago. Almost like he knew he was gonna die. Got an explanation for that, Agent Tierney?"

"I wish I did, Investigator Boone."

Lena had no idea if it was day or night. The drugs they'd given her had finally worn off, leaving her feeling heavy-headed and bleary, as if her mind was seeing the world through a haze of Vaseline. She was afraid to sleep, afraid she'd miss a chance to escape, afraid of being alone in the dark, vulnerable.

Not that she could sleep even if she wanted to. The thumping she'd heard earlier had returned, coming from different directions. First beyond the door, then overhead, then the side wall. Sometimes it sounded like footsteps, sometimes like fists.

One thing the noise had done: It had oriented her. She'd thought the rear wall was the outside wall but the way the sound changed when it hit the side wall, that had to be an exterior wall. And it didn't sound very thick, either.

Which meant, God willing, there was a way out of this hell.

She sent up a quick prayer of gratitude and went to work. The water bottles were too flimsy; the Ensure ones were made of sturdier plastic. She scraped the mouth of one bottle against the plywood subflooring, trying to sharpen it as much as possible. Then she positioned it against the base of the wall, lay down on the floor, braced her back against the opposite wall, and drove the bottle in with her foot. The bottle stuck, impaled to the drywall.

She scrambled back onto her hands and knees, lever-aging the bottle against the wall. A fist-sized chunk fell. It wasn't drywall, she saw. Beneath a dozen coats of paint was some kind of plaster threaded with long, dark filaments. Horsehair. Which meant it was really old. Supporting it from behind was wire like you'd use for a chicken coop stretched between thin pieces of wood lathing.

Repositioning the mouth of the bottle against the side of the hole, she gouged out more of the plaster. Behind the chicken wire and lathing was yellowed newspaper serving as insulation. She stretched two fingers between a wire loop and snagged a sheet, pulled it free. When she smoothed it open across the floor, she saw the date on it was 1932.

It was slow going removing the paper but she didn't have the strength or leverage to yank the wire out, so the best she could do was to stretch a few loops as wide as possible. Once she had the paper out she could see the outside wall: wood siding, unpainted on this side.

She waved her hand over the hole and was delighted to see skinny rays of sunlight making their way in from the outside. A sense of hope surged through her. As she strained to pry the wire apart she began to sing one of her mom's favorite hymns: "Praise to Thee, Thou Great Creator."

Her fingers were raw, stinging with tiny cuts from the wire, but finally she was able to make a gap large enough to put her entire hand through. She wanted to take a look while the hole inside her prison cell was still small enough to hide. Once she enlarged it, she was committed to escaping as quickly as possible, before the men returned, and that meant waiting until dark.

Please, God, let this work, she prayed as she inserted one of the plastic bottles into the hole she'd so painfully created and wedged it between a gap in the overlapping siding. It was just long enough that the bottom of the bottle extended through the hole. She braced herself once more and kicked it as hard as she could.

A hollow thud echoed through her body as the bottle smacked against the wood siding. Lena held her breath. Could anyone hear?

No sounds came. She pulled the bottle free and checked the siding. The slit between the top edge of one piece and the bottom of another had widened slightly. Should she try again? Or work on making the interior hole large enough for her entire body and kick out a large chunk of siding all at once, knowing that would make a huge clatter?

But who could resist a glimpse of sunlight? She told herself it was to survey the terrain in the daylight, to plan her escape route.

Really, she was simply desperate for any contact with the outside world. She replaced the bottle, this time angling it over the corner of the bottom edge of siding. The gap was large enough that the bottle stuck there on its own. That was hopeful.

She leaned back and kicked again. This time the thud was accompanied by a splintering noise.

Quickly she slid the case of water over the fist-sized hole in the plaster. But no one came to investigate.

Emboldened, she exposed the hole once more and pulled the bottle free. Its mouth was hopelessly cracked, the plastic folded in on itself. That was okay, she had plenty more where it came from. Prone on the floor, she shimmied as close as she could to the hole, pressing her face against the plaster wall.

The bottom corner of siding had splintered. She reached in with her fingers, fought for purchase, ignoring the wire scraping her knuckles as she wiggled the corner free.

Suddenly it came loose in her hand and a stream of sunlight hit her in the eye. She blinked, crying with pain and joy.

Thank you, Lord! Thank you! She tilted her face one way and then another, trying to see more than the tiny patch of dirt the hole in the siding exposed. She put her fingers through it, trying to wiggle more of the siding free, but it stubbornly resisted.

Pulling her hand back inside, she peered through the hole once more, inhaling the crisp air, smelling freedom.

Then the sunlight vanished. Replaced by a large almond-shaped brown eye with no white showing at all and surrounded by heavy ridges of brown-gray skin.

She gasped. The eye blinked. Then pulled back and was replaced by a snout with flattened nostrils flaring above short gray whiskers. Accompanied by the undeniable sound of a chimpanzee.

Lena rolled away from the hole, so overwhelmed with terror that all she could do was press her back against the far wall and curl her body into a small ball. Goose bumps shivered across her flesh, and she hugged herself harder. Where was she? Locked up in some kind of zoo?

"What do you want from me?" she cried out, tears garbling her words. Anger lanced through her. Anger at God, at the men who'd brought her here, at her father—if it weren't for his deceit, she wouldn't even be here. She screamed in fury and frustration and fear.

Her only answer was the sound of fists drumming against the outside wall and more chimps chattering.

CHAPTER NINE

Boone led Caitlyn to a small office in the administration building. SPIRITUAL AFFAIRS, utilitarian lettering on the door labeled it. Inside was a scuffed wooden desk layered with folders, an office chair behind it and two wooden visitors' chairs in front. Its most prominent feature was a box of generic facial tissues, economy-sized.

The man behind the desk stood as Caitlyn and Boone entered. He was a short, balding white man in his fifties wearing a long-sleeved brown shirt with a clerical collar. "Agent Tierney? I'm Pastor Whitford. We spoke on the phone last night."

She shook his hand; his grip was firm but not antagonistic. Neutral, as was his expression when they sat down. Boone stood beside the door, watching. Waiting for some slip of information that would make sense of Hale's murder. Caitlyn had the feeling he might be waiting a long time.

Technically the investigator's case was closed—he had the two men who killed Hale. Hell, the murder was caught on camera. But like any good detective, he wasn't satisfied with just closing a case; he wanted to understand why Hale had been targeted and if there were any further threats to Butner's precarious tranquility.

Whitford reached below his desk and brought up a carton of notebooks and loose papers. "Eli could have been an architect," he said, unrolling a large detailed drawing across the jumble of folders. It was a rendering of the Sistine Chapel drawn on brown butcher's paper, complete with architectural details. Somehow the beauty of the building increased with its skeleton exposed, enhanced by intricate breakout sketches of its most intimate details. "Gorgeous, isn't it? He's helped a bunch of the guards plan additions and renovations, even submitted a design for the new Butner Three facility. Not that they'd ever use an inmate's design."

Boone chuckled. "Be like giving the other team your playbook before the Super Bowl."

"I honestly don't think Eli ever imagined escape," Whitford said thoughtfully. "I met him almost ten years ago, and from the very beginning he seemed, well, content. Working the grounds crew got him outside more days than not, visiting with his family every week, even teaching me to play chess. Compared with the other inmates I've counseled, he's always been rather detached from it all. Like this was the life he was meant to have."

"So why'd he try to kill himself?" Boone asked the question foremost in Caitlyn's mind. She wished he'd sit down. It was irritating having him behind her. She edged her chair sideways so she could keep both him and Whitford in view. "You don't do that if you're all content and Buddha-like."

"I wish I understood the answer to that, Investigator, I

really do. But I'm not sure anyone here really understood Eli Hale."

Boone answered with a *hrumph* noise that said he was as tired of the holier-than-thou mumbo-jumbo as Caitlyn was. Whatever Eli Hale was, he was no saint.

"So all this is mine?" she asked, gesturing to the box.

Whitford rolled the drawings of the Sistine Chapel back into a neat cylinder. He tilted his head to meet her gaze. "Yes. It's all yours."

She took the box. No larger than the milk crates she'd hauled all her earthly possessions in during college. "Okay, then. Guess I'll head back home."

Boone scowled at her as she turned to the door. Not liking the unanswered questions. She didn't blame him. After a beat, he opened the door for her.

"You both have my numbers," she said in parting—more for the chaplain's sake than Boone's. She had the feeling Whitford wanted to say more, but not in front of the SIS investigator.

Boone walked her to the lockbox station out front, where she retrieved her service weapon. "Stay in touch, Agent Tierney," he said as he escorted her to her car. "If there's something more brewing here I need to know about it."

"I don't think you have anything to worry about." The danger wasn't inside Butner; it was outside and aimed at Lena Hale.

"Oh really? That's funny coming from someone who says she doesn't even know why the hell she was called down here to talk with Hale." His glare said it was anything but funny; Boone's professional pride had been wounded. "Real goddamn funny."

He turned his heel and left. Caitlyn placed the box of drawings and notebooks on the Subaru's passenger seat and retrieved her phone from the trunk. She wasn't surprised when it rang as soon as she sat down in the driver's seat. Whitford.

"I couldn't talk with Boone here," he said in a rushed voice. "But before Eli left the infirmary this morning we spoke. He feared something might happen to him—guess he was right."

"Why was he afraid?"

"I didn't tell you the entire truth last night. You see, Lena's spent the past three years going through court transcripts, police reports, trying to prove her dad's innocence. Eli kept asking her to quit. A few weeks ago they had a big blowup over it and she said she was through with him."

"I told you. Hale's guilty. So maybe she did run away." Except that didn't explain why Hale was killed.

"That's just it. She did run away. Or at least stopped answering Eli's calls. But she came back a week later. Told her dad she wasn't going to keep working on his case, she was giving up. Said she was going to clear her family name, try to make up for all the harm Eli'd done."

"How the hell was she going to do that?"

"I don't know and I don't think Eli did, either. But he was real worried. Kept talking about you and your dad. Said Lena must've stumbled into something and gotten the wrong people worried that he might have talked."

"Talked about what?" If the man thought he might be killed, why not give some specifics to help her? Or was this all some paranoid delusion spun out of control?

"He wouldn't say. I think it was something to do with the crime that got him here in the first place because he said something about her digging up the past."

"So why'd he try to kill himself? He couldn't help Lena if he was dead."

"Eli told me that he didn't try to kill himself. Said he'd sent a message that Lena knew nothing, that if they left her alone he'd stay quiet." Again with the mysterious "they." Frustrating. "The next night someone spiked his drink and he woke up in the infirmary half dead."

Shit. "We need to tell Boone the truth."

"No. I promised him. He said they'd kill her."

"With him dead, what's to stop them from killing her anyway? If they haven't already." Hell, now she was beginning to sound just like Hale. Paranoid. Delusional.

"You. He said you could save her. Said you were the only one."

Great. A self-confessed killer her number one fan. "I don't even know where to start looking for her. Surely he gave you some specifics?"

"He said she'd gone home to Evergreen. It's a small town in the mountains, near Cherokee."

Evergreen. Caitlyn's mom's had left her entire family behind when she'd moved Caitlyn away from Evergreen, trying to distance Caitlyn from the memory of her dad. It hadn't worked, but Caitlyn still felt a chill at the mention of the town. She'd been nine years old when she'd last seen Evergreen.

"Yeah, I know the place," she told Whitford.

"Eli said everything you need is in that box."

A bunch of old drawings and notebooks that it'd take her a week to go through—and that Boone and his men had already examined. What did Hale think this was, the freaking *Da Vinci Code*? Twenty-five years being locked up had driven the man insane. Sending her on a wild goose chase after a girl they didn't even know for certain was missing and a mysterious conspiracy that probably existed only in a convicted killer's mind.

Then she remembered the look of anguish in Hale's eyes as he lay dying, using his final breath to call out his daughter's name. He'd trusted her, believed she could save Lena.

But Caitlyn was no miracle worker. She was already breaking every rule in the book just by being here. She might have even gotten Hale killed by coming to see him. The expression on Hale's face as he lay there dying . . . the face of her father, blood everywhere. Too many memories, too much pain.

All leading back to Evergreen. Didn't mean she had to play the game, follow the bread crumbs. Caitlyn yanked the gearshift to put the Impreza in reverse. "If you think of anything else, call me. Anytime, day or night."

"What are you going to do about Lena?"

"I can make some calls. I still have family in Evergreen. It's a small enough place that if she's there, someone will know."

"That's it? Some calls?"

"There's not a whole lot I can do without an official case. And it's out of my jurisdiction, anyway."

His exasperation broke through the airwaves. "So where are you going?"

"Home. Back to Quantico. Where I belong." She hung up, just as frustrated as the chaplain was but for different reasons. She'd done everything she could—more than she should. Hell, what more did he want from her?

She'd been right there when her father died and couldn't save him. Ten feet away from Eli Hale and couldn't save him. How could anyone expect her to be able to save Lena?

CHAPTER TEN

Hunger and a need for caffeine fueled Caitlyn's exasperation as she drove east on Gate 2 Road back to I-85. There was a large truck stop at the interstate, and she pulled in there.

Talk about a day not going as planned. Images of Hale's killing replayed through her mind, over and over at different speeds; each time her frustration at being forced to watch, unable to help the man, etched the images deeper into her psyche. By the time she dragged Hale's box into an empty booth and ordered a large serving of chicken and dumplings, coffee and a glass of milk, her frustration had morphed into anger.

True, the killers were caught and already behind bars, but someone had been pulling the strings. If what Whitford said was true about Hale's overdose being an initial attempt on his life, then there were others inside Butner responsible. While she waited for her food she sipped at her coffee, sorted through the papers lying loose in Hale's box, and called Boone.

"SIS, Boone speaking," he answered in a clipped tone.

"It's Tierney. I was wondering. Could Hale's overdose have been non-accidental?"

"Of course it was non-accidental—he tried to kill himself. Oh, you mean someone else slipped him the drugs?" He paused. "He told the docs he took them himself, said he was"—there came the sound of papers being rustled—"despondent over not seeing his daughter because of an argument they'd had."

So Hale hadn't told the doctors about Lena being missing. But someone had been worried that whatever Lena was doing would give Hale a reason to start talking . . . and as far as she knew the only thing Hale had to talk about was the murder he was convicted of twenty-five years ago.

"Tierney, you there?" Boone's voice interrupted her thoughts. "Doc's note doesn't say anything about the OD not being self-inflicted, but that doesn't mean jack."

"You'll look into it?"

"Best I can. One thing for sure, it wasn't those Surenos. They were locked up in the SHU when Hale OD'd."

She thought. "Did Hale make any phone calls before his OD?"

"We're still checking the records—nine hundred inmates, it'll take another day or so."

"You guys record outgoing calls, right? When you find it, I'd like a copy." She had no official standing to make the request and Boone knew it.

"There's something you're not telling me." His tone was more resigned than accusatory.

"Not really. Definitely nothing concrete."

"Uh-huh. Guess that's why they call you guys 'special' agents."

Like she hadn't heard that one before. "Seriously, if I find anything you need to know, I'll call."

"I'll be waiting by the phone, breathless with anticipation." He hung up before she could come up with an equally snarky reply.

Her order of comfort food arrived on a platter brimming with gravy, accompanied by a glass of milk so cold it gave her a brain rush with the first gulp. She ate one-handed, trying to find some semblance of order in Hale's papers. There were sketches of various well-known architectural wonders—even an inside-out view of an Egyptian pyramid.

The notebooks were filled with similar sketches along with detailed materials lists and step-by-step construction instructions. One notebook had every page crammed with drawings of a house Caitlyn recognized: Hale's home in Evergreen, North Carolina, back up on McSwain Mountain. The only house higher on the mountain was her own childhood home. Above them both was the trout farm, the McSwain family's first major commercial enterprise back in early days of the last century.

Her mom and uncle were so proud of the McSwain name. Uncle Jimmy had bought back almost every parcel of land the family had lost over time; gave Caitlyn's mom and dad the two-century-old farmhouse that was the original family homestead as a wedding present.

Caitlyn loved the old place, built so solid it didn't even tremble in the worst blizzards or spring storms. Dad was always trying to improve it in his little free time. Tearing down wallpaper, refinishing the floors, she and Dad together scraping decades of paint from the original oak cabinets. It'd about broke her heart to leave that house, but after Dad . . .

Jessalyn had been upset about leaving Evergreen for different reasons: She was leaving her family and everyone she knew behind to start over, a newly widowed mother, a thousand miles away from the only home she'd ever known. Her mother's sacrifice had become a sword's edge that divided her and Caitlyn. After trying and failing for years to make her mother happy, she finally simply gave up. No one could make Jessalyn happy, not after Dad was gone.

Thankfully, Uncle Jimmy said he'd keep the old house safe for Caitlyn. If she could ever bear to return home, walking in the shadow of Dad's memory, over floorboards that had been soaked in his blood.

Maybe Uncle Jimmy could help now. The year after she and Mom left Evergreen, he'd gone on to become the developer in charge of the tribe's casino, bringing the VistaView Resort to life from the blank canvas that had been an empty parcel of land along the reservation's outer edge. As director of the casino, he knew everything that happened around Evergreen—all of Balsam County— and most of neighboring Cherokee, as well.

Caitlyn was about to call Uncle Jimmy when she came to the bottom of Hale's box and found a pocket-sized address book. Leafing through it, she found Lena's address and phone number in Durham and, bingo, the name and cell number for Lena's roommate.

She finished her meal, ordered cherry pie for dessert, then dialed the roommate. "Melissa Andersen? This is Caitlyn Tierney. I'm a friend of Lena's family. I need to reach Lena as soon as possible."

"Is it her father?" Melissa sounded like she was in her midtwenties and had a definite South Carolina accent. "A chaplain called a few days ago, said he was real sick."

Caitlyn hesitated. Death notifications should go to the next of kin first, but since that was Lena . . . "I really need to speak with Lena. Do you know where she is?"

"She left for a little town in the mountains, near Cherokee. Evergreen. It's where her family's from. Hey, wait, did you say Caitlyn Tierney?"

"Yes."

"Oh my God. I know who you are. Lena has a photo of you and her sister sitting right there on her dresser. You two were so cute as kids. Covered head-to-toe in mud, only your eyes showing—and your red hair, standing up all over."

Caitlyn knew the picture well. It was one of her father's favorites. She hadn't seen it in decades, not since after his death when her mom packed everything away and moved them to Pennsylvania. "That's me. So Lena left when?"

"Monday night."

She'd been missing even longer than Hale suspected. "Did you hear from her? Do you know where she was planning to stay in Evergreen?"

"No. Sorry. She said she'd only be gone a day or two, but sometimes she loses all track of time. One time when she was volunteering for the Innocence Project she—"

"Is that what she's doing now? Working on her dad's old case?" Maybe Caitlyn could track her down by going through the people involved in Hale's trial.

"Oh no, she's finished with that. Took her years but she finally realized there was nowhere left to turn. I think she was real angry with her dad—can't blame her, all those years she and her mom and sister believed in him, only to realize he really did kill that man." Her shudder reverberated through her voice. "Poor thing. She and her dad had a big fight about it. I think maybe this is her way to get some distance, you know?"

"So you have no idea what she was looking for in Evergreen?"

"No, sorry. Her family still owns a house there, maybe she went there?"

"Was she in contact with someone in Evergreen?"

"Sorry, I don't know. But when you find her, tell her I've got her mail here."

Mail. "Anything in there that might help me find her?"

"Just bills—oh and a letter from a law firm. Must be one of the ones she applied for a job at. Feels thick, like it might be a contract, so she might want to hurry back and open it."

If Lena was accepting a new job, why would she take off? More important, why wouldn't she stay in contact with her roommate?

"Hope that helps," the roommate said. "Tell Lena I'm sorry about her dad being sick."

"I will, thanks." Caitlyn hung up, more puzzled than she was before she called. Looked like she'd have to rely on Uncle Jimmy for info after all.

Only one problem. Other than the occasional Christmas card and a bouquet of flowers when she was in the hospital last year, she wasn't exactly close with Uncle Jimmy or her cousin Bernie. Which meant calling Mom first.

Caitlyn downed the cherry pie, told herself she needed the extra calories for fortitude. Before she could make the call, her cell rang: Paul.

She hated that she hesitated before answering, almost but not quite long enough for it to go to voicemail. "Hi there," she answered in a chipper voice.

"Hey, sorry to bug you at work, but I needed to know if you'd be coming home tonight."

He meant *his* home. Which lately had somehow begun being translated as *their* home.

"I'm still in North Carolina," she hedged. Not that there was any reason why she wouldn't be headed back to DC by evening, but she wanted to know why he needed to know.

"Well." He sighed the word. "I wanted to surprise you, but guess I need to tell you. With the holiday Monday and the long weekend, I planned a special getaway at the beach."

Her first thought was, didn't he have to work Monday? Then she realized he must have pulled a favor to ask for it off—not like doctors had federal holidays off the way Quantico instructors did.

Her second was, anywhere but the beach. All her life she'd avoided visiting the beach. Before he died, her father had promised a family vacation to the Outer Banks, a town called Duck where his family went when he was a kid. It would have been her first time seeing the ocean, and he put her to bed every night telling her stories about the beach and finding seashells and the way the water smelled like magic when the sun sparkled over it at dawn.

Even now, twenty-six years later, it pained her to think of finding that magic without him at her side.

But Paul couldn't know that.

"You still there?" he asked.

"I am. I'm just—wow—I'm shocked. Paul, that was so sweet of you." It was, it really was. How the hell was she going to say no? Why should he have to suffer because of her crazy messed-up father complex?

"I thought we could leave tonight, right after work," he

said. "Wake up to sunrise on the beach. I got us an ocean-front cottage. Only one bedroom but plenty of privacy."

"Sounds fantastic."

An awkward silence hung between them, stretching from North Carolina to DC and back again.

"You're not coming, are you?" he finally asked, hurt coloring his voice.

She hesitated, her gaze caught on a picture of Lena sitting on top of the pile of papers in Hale's box. The photo was taken at Lena's college graduation, her cap sitting at a jaunty angle, the tassel swinging past eyes crinkled with joy. She'd just lost her mom and sister, had made it through school alone and on her own, and despite everything still faced her future with undaunted hope and a blinding smile.

"I can't," Caitlyn told him, the cherry pie suddenly tasting bitter.

"Work?"

She couldn't lie, not about this. "No. A family emergency." Well, almost-family. Kinda. If not for the part where Eli Hale was responsible for her father's death. But she couldn't let Lena suffer for his mistakes. And Lena didn't have anyone else. "I have to go home to Evergreen."

Another silence, this one more sad than awkward.

"I'm sorry," she said, and it was the truth. She should never have let him start planning a life together, should have found a way to leave before it got this far. But he was so damn easy to be with, and after everything she'd been through last year, she desperately needed easy and comfortable.

More than comfortable: Paul was safe.

"I understand. Next time we'll pick a date together so

nothing will get in the way. Drive careful. Call me when you get there."

What could she say to that? Nothing except "I will."

"Love you." He hung up before she had a chance to lie to him again.

Caitlyn stared at the phone in her hand. No more lies. Next time she saw Paul, she'd tell him the truth. She didn't love him. She wasn't sure it was in her to ever love someone, not the way he deserved. There was just too much of her heart that she always had to hold back, protect.

There wasn't enough of her left to give to someone else. No one's fault, just the way she was hardwired. Better to end things now before he was hurt.

Who was she kidding? There was no way in hell she was going to be able to end it without Paul being hurt.

The pie thudded like a millstone in her gut, decadence laced with a heavy syrup of guilt.

Might as well call Mom and make the day's quota of pain and suffering complete.

Lena smiled at her from the photo, adding to her guilt. What if she couldn't find her? Poor thing, she didn't even know her dad was dead.

Christ, she should have gone with Paul to the beach. There was nothing worse than family death notifications; Caitlyn had learned that when she worked a short stint with the National Center for Missing and Exploited Children.

Her phone rang again. Mom. How the hell did she do that? Somehow she always managed to call Caitlyn before Caitlyn had a chance to reach out first and earn filial Brownie points.

"Caitlyn, what's wrong?" Jessalyn Tierney asked, her

tone distraught—not unusual since she seemed to always call when something was wrong in Caitlyn's life. Almost dying—twice—killing a man, emergency brain surgery. Her mom's psychic radar was a fine-tuned instrument.

"Nothing's wrong. Why?"

"Paul just called. Wanted to know if there was anything he could do to help. Said you canceled this weekend because of a family emergency."

Oh shit. "Paul called you?"

"Of course. Who do you think helped him find the rental at such a great location on a holiday weekend?" Her mom had inherited the family's entrepreneurial love of real estate, just like Uncle Jimmy. After Caitlyn left for college, Jessalyn had moved back to North Carolina and partnered with Jimmy to open a real estate investment firm in Charlotte. Not even the housing bubble had slowed their profits.

"You knew about this weekend and you didn't warn me?"

"He wanted it to be a surprise. I think he's been shopping for a ring. I already gave him my blessing, of course. Past time for you to settle down, raise a family of your own."

"Mom, I'm only—" No. She wasn't falling into that trap. Arguing with her mom was like racing along a Mobius strip: Once you got started there was no good end. Ever. "Wait. Paul talked to you about it?"

"We talk all the time," Jessalyn replied flippantly. "Well, maybe not all the time. Three times since Christmas. Which is three times more than you've called me."

Ouch. Jessalyn kept score over everything. "I called you on Christmas."

"No. I called you. After you couldn't be bothered to

make the trip down to see your mother for the holidays. Not like you had to work—you said you were basically a substitute teacher until your bosses decided to fire you or not."

Caitlyn's jaws ground together. "I'm not getting fired. And I told you, Paul was on call."

There was more judgment in her mother's silence than in a judge's gavel banging down. Caitlyn knew better than to try to plead her case—it would just give Jessalyn more ammunition to use during later skirmishes.

Finally Jessalyn asked, "What's the emergency? Paul said something about you going back to Evergreen. Why on earth would you do that? There's nothing for you there except bad memories."

She was wrong. Evergreen would always be home to Caitlyn's happiest memories. But she couldn't say that to her mom; it would hurt her feelings. Jessalyn had done the best she could, a single mom, raising a child under traumatic circumstances, dealing with her own grief. But nothing could take the place of Caitlyn's dad or heal the gaping wound his death had torn in her heart.

"It's Vonnie's little sister, Lena. She's gone missing."

"The Hale girl? What's that to you?" Acid dripped from Jessalyn's words. Caitlyn wasn't the only one who blamed Eli Hale for Sean Tierney's death.

"I promised I'd look for her. She's in trouble."

"Promised who?" Jessalyn pressed. She was merciless that way.

Caitlyn knew better than to resist. "Her dad. Right before he was killed."

"Eli Hale is dead?" Her exhalation rattled through the airwaves, and Caitlyn could almost see Jessalyn's hand pressed against her throat. "What happened?"

Caitlyn told her about Eli's murder.

"You saw it? It happened right in front of you? You never should have gone there. How many times have I told you to leave well enough alone? You're so darn stubborn. My God. A prison riot. And you in the middle—"

"It's my job." A little white lie. Occasionally necessary when dealing with Jessalyn. The FBI may have fine-honed Caitlyn's skills, but it was living with her mother that had prepared her for undercover work with decades of practical experience in lying and hiding her emotions.

Sometimes it felt like Jessalyn had more than enough emotions for the both of them. Anxiety as she fought to protect her daughter from anything bad in the world. Depression and withdrawal as she struggled to create a new life for them both alone in a strange town. Forced happiness celebrating even the most minor of milestones as she tried her best to provide the love of two parents.

"I'm fine, Mom. Calm down."

"Calm down? I'll do no such thing. And you, young lady, aren't going to Evergreen. The Hales have caused enough pain and suffering in this family, thank you very much. You call Paul back right this instant and tell him you're going to the beach."

"I can't." The phone grew hot in Caitlyn's palm—channeling Jessalyn's overwrought emotions, no doubt. "I have to go now." She'd wanted to ask for Uncle Jimmy's number, but hell with it, she could Google it. "Bye, Mom, love you."

She hung up just as Jessalyn was gulping in air for another ultimatum. Turned the phone on mute before it could ring again.

The remnants of her pie had congealed into a scarlet mess the shade of freshly shed blood. Still, she couldn't resist swiping a finger through the sticky goo and licking it clean. Just like she and Dad used to do behind Mom's back.

Her sigh was a strange combination of anxiety, anticipation, and apprehension. Looked like for the first time in twenty-six years she was going home.

CHAPTER ELEVEN

Caitlyn called the roommate back—she'd already forgotten her name—and got directions to Lena's apartment in Durham. If she was going to do this, might as well do it right. Which meant learning as much about Lena as possible.

The apartment was typical grad student housing: tiny galley kitchen, living room–dining room combo with a single window facing into the next building, two bedrooms with a bath between them in the back. Maximum spatial efficiency, minimum fuss. But it was clean, the acrid smell of a fresh vacuuming still filling the air.

The decor mirrored Caitlyn's own place in Manassas: a combination of Ikea and Goodwill. The box-like lines of the sofa were softened by a collection of mismatched pillows and a colorful pashmina thrown over its back.

"So you really think something happened to her?" the roommate asked as she waved Caitlyn to the couch. "Should I call the police? Report her missing?"

Eli Hale had warned against it, but if someone in Evergreen had Lena then there was no way Caitlyn could avoid them knowing she was looking for the girl, so she didn't see a downside to alerting the authorities. Plus, an official report would let her use the NCIC database if any law enforcement officer reported a sighting of Lena or her vehicle.

"That's probably a good idea. You said she's been gone five days now without word?" Caitlyn sat on the sofa—it was more comfortable than it looked—but the roommate kept pacing.

"Yes. Is that long enough? It's more than forty-eight hours, right? Gosh, I can't believe anything could have happened to her."

"Actually that's only in the movies. You can report someone missing at any time if you have reason to fear for their well-being. They'll need a recent photo and information about her car: license plate, color, make, and model."

"That's easy, I can do that." She finally slumped into one of the dining room chairs gathered around a glass tabletop on a chrome pedestal. "What if she comes back? Will I get in trouble for reporting her? Will she get in trouble? We're both applying for jobs right now—"

"Don't worry, neither of you will get in trouble." If a law student had second thoughts about talking to the police when her friend might be in trouble, what did that say about the average person?

Caitlyn shook the thoughts aside; local law enforcement PR was not her problem. She stood. "How about if I look at her room while you collect that information?"

The roommate led her to the second bedroom door then hesitated. "Okay, but don't move anything. She has a system." She opened the door. "You know, she's fine, I'm sure. Probably just found some interesting research—Lena is nuts about research, especially historical stuff. The rarer, the better."

Caitlyn didn't burst the roommate's bubble of denial. She stepped inside the bedroom. Obviously Lena wasn't the neat freak of the two. The room was strewn with books and papers and photos and maps and notebooks, as if a tornado had torn through a library and deposited the debris here. Whiteboards with scribbled notes in a rainbow of colors perched on the windowsills and dresser. The only clear space was the twin-sized bed. It had a sage-green duvet trimmed with lace and a lace accent pillow. No personal mementos other than a Bible with a worn leather cover sitting on the nightstand and a few photos in cheap frames lined up on the dresser.

Caitlyn sucked in her breath as she saw the first photo: the one of her and Vonnie as kids, bundled in snowsuits, covered in mud, laughing. Another of Lena in diapers, Eli Hale bouncing her in the air as Vonnie looked up, clapping in delight. One of Lena's mom curled up on the porch swing of their house in Evergreen, smiling as she shucked peas.

All ancient history. Taken before Lena could possibly remember. There were two newer photos: Lena, Vonnie, and their mom at Lena's high school graduation, and one of Vonnie and Lena taken at a restaurant, the girls giddy, arms wrapped around each other's shoulders, leaning toward the camera.

The entire history of one family gathered on a dresser top. And now Lena was the only one left. Caitlyn's smile at seeing Vonnie's happiness faded, her lips tightening at the thought of telling Lena how her father died.

Sighing, Catilyn turned to the papers. The maps were of the Qualla Boundary, home to the Eastern Band of Cherokee. One was dated 2010; the other was a reproduction of a map from 1883. There was a stack of bound books: copies of the *Duke Law Review,* along with Cherokee Supreme Court, Oklahoma U.S. District Court, and North Carolina State rulings. Beside the books were printed copies of individual federal and state cases. From the abstracts, it looked like they all dealt with the Cherokees' assimilation of the blacks who'd once been their slaves but then became freedmen.

She snapped photos with her phone. Article title pages as well as the whiteboards and the calendar scribbled with names and incomprehensible notes. Homework for tonight.

"She was researching an article for the law review," the roommate explained when she returned and handed Caitlyn a piece of paper with a photo of Lena and all her pertinent info printed at the bottom. "That's one she posted on Facebook a few weeks ago. And a copy of her student ID, driver's license, and car registration."

"She's not carrying them with her?"

"No, she is. But when she gets into a project, she gets a bit obsessed." The roommate gestured to the research materials covering every surface of the room. "More than once she's lost her purse, so she keeps copies of everything here. Easier to get new ones that way."

"I don't suppose you have her credit card info as well?"

"Sure. She only has her debit card, her mom didn't believe in them." She blew out her breath, straightening the photos Caitlyn had moved out of place on the dresser. "I hope she's okay."

Caitlyn found a pile of papers that were stacked alone in the far corner as if they were an offshoot of the main research. They were copies from the State Archives in Raleigh, all dealing with Qualla Boundary land grants and census information.

"Do you know what all this is about?" She raised the first photocopy, a title page with old-fashioned print labeled DEED BOOK R, 1880–1882: RECORDS OF EASTERN BAND OF CHEROKEES, and showed it to the roommate.

"That's what I was telling you about on the phone. After she realized she couldn't prove her dad innocent"— she stumbled while putting the sentence together, too polite to flat-out proclaim Eli Hale guilty—"Lena began working on her law review paper. It's really about the Cherokee Nation in Oklahoma, but she wanted to see if there were any precedents set with the Eastern Band Cherokee who remained in North Carolina. I guess since her family lived there, right on the edge of the reservation, she was interested. I'm not sure what she found, but her family was mentioned in some old record, and she got obsessed with 'vindicating the family name.' Whatever that means." She finished with a shrug.

"So she went to Evergreen to research her family roots?" Caitlyn looked at the dates on the archives. "Like back to the eighteen hundreds?"

"Yeah. She wanted to look at as many original documents as possible. And they weren't all at the archives in Raleigh. She thought some of them might be in Cherokee in the tribal records."

Even if they were, it wouldn't take a crackerjack researcher like Lena five days to find them—not to mention five days of not contacting her roommate. The roommate must have thought the same thing because her hand went to her mouth.

"Oh my God. Something really did happen to her, didn't it?"

Caitlyn wished she had an answer.

* * *

Goose tilted his chair back and ducked his chin into his favorite thinking position. Something was going on with Bernie. The kid was never what you'd call normal—too lost in his own fantasies, half here and half inside his head all the time—but last few days he'd been acting downright weird.

Skipping out early from club parties, coming late to Church, disappearing in the middle of the day and coming back smelling of dead meat and urine.

If it was anyone but Bernie, Goose would think he'd gone all serial-killer psycho. Funny, if he had to bet on any of the Reapers pulling a Manson or Dahmer he'd have tagged Poppy. Even though the dude was in his early sixties, he had eyes dead as steel that could look daggers through you. Thought nothing of beating the crap out of anyone, Reaper or not, who got in his way—or better yet, watching as he ordered one of the other MC members to do his dirty work.

As the new club enforcer, now it was Goose's turn. It was an honorary title more than anything. At least Goose hoped so. Poppy's first order was for him to find the animals the MC had taken from that schmuck over in Pigeon Forge. Not exactly Tony Soprano work. Of course, Poppy had added: And find the bastard who stole them from us so I can kill him. Slowly.

Hard to tell if Poppy was kidding or not. But in his almost year and a half with the Reapers, Goose had never seen them come close to actually killing anyone. Beating the crap out of them, sure—just like they spent most weekends beating the crap out of each other. Pent-up frustrations of being a one-percenter, living on the outer fringes of society's bell-shaped curve, outside the law, beyond conforming, true free spirits.

At least that's how the MC liked to think of themselves. Really they were a bunch of guys—mostly out of work like Goose, who used to be a software engineer in Asheville—who liked to ride, drink, and screw around without anyone telling them what to do.

The ultimate Peter Pan fantasy. Especially when you added in the women who practically threw themselves at the Reapers and the excitement of low-level illegal activities like the deal that had gotten them those damn animals in the first place.

Goose had his suspicions about who stole them. Especially as that was right around the time Bernie started acting all hinky.

The trick was getting the animals back, making Poppy happy, without Poppy knowing the kid was behind it—not easy given that every time Bernie tried to lie his ears turned red—and then convincing Poppy there was no need to keep looking for the thief.

Given Poppy's psychopathic tendencies, a real balancing act.

"Hey, Goose!" Poppy's roar thundered through the empty bar from his office in the back. "I got a job for you. Bring that computer of yours. And your gun."

Gun? Goose scrambled to his feet. He liked the Reapers, the way they'd accepted him without question, always generous with a drink or a loan or a place to crash after he lost his job. But sometimes he worried they carried this idea of living on the fringes of society to extremes.

He grabbed his laptop and headed behind the bar. Weasel, the MC's vice president, was already in Poppy's office. Goose paused outside the door, listening, wondering what the hell Poppy was going to ask him to do this time.

Hoping it was better than hunting for a bunch of stupid animals that were probably dead from the cold by now anyway.

"No more half-assed fuckups," Poppy was telling Weasel. "This time we do things right. I don't want to take any chances."

"Not my fault." Weasel was a small man, barely five-eight, but he made up for it by being the nastiest son-of-a-bitch Goose had ever met. The guy was in his forties, had a shaved head displaying his Reaper tatts, and a line of ex-wives and -girlfriends a mile long, each skankier than the last.

"Did I ask whose fucking fault it was? Goose," Poppy bellowed. "I said, get your ass in here."

Goose popped through the door as if he'd just arrived. "Sorry, had to grab my laptop. Whatcha need?"

"There's a fed coming to town. Nosing around. Thinks we have something to do with some law student that's gone missing."

"You want me to find the student? See if I can track him online?" Goose asked. Computer searches were much more his forte than hunting lions and leopards through the mountains.

"No," Weasel said, yanking on the lapels of his leather vest as if shaking off an insult. "I'll take care of her."

"Wait." Poppy leaned back so far his desk chair creaked. "You can do that?" he asked Goose.

"Sure. Give me her name, Social if you've got it, and I can dig up her latest credit card charges, maybe even phone records, GPS if her car has it, you name it. Plus, if she uploads a photo to Facebook or anywhere, I can tell you when and where that picture was taken."

Poppy inclined his head, obviously impressed. "Guess having a geek around can come in handy. Weasel, catch him up with the info he needs."

Weasel frowned as he dug in his pocket for a paper. "Want me to take care of the fed while brainiac here sits on his ass surfing porn?"

"No. I want you to keep looking for the girl. She gets found, the feds get off our backs. We don't need no extra attention with the poker run this weekend. And you"—he aimed a finger at Goose like he was pulling a trigger— "take your fancy toy with you and work on finding where this girl has been and where she might go while you tail this fed and bug her room, her phone, her car, anything you can get your hands on. She'll be staying at the VistaView so you need to get cleaned up before you head over there. No colors."

The VistaView? The tribal casino was the one place usually off limits to the Reapers—a way of keeping peace with the locals without scaring off the tourist trade. Most of the Reapers didn't have the cash to lose gambling, anyway.

"Sure thing, Poppy." Goose turned to leave, then turned back. "Why do the feds think we have anything to do with this law student going missing?"

Poppy played it cool, not a flicker of emotion in his expression. But Weasel tensed.

"We don't have anything to do with her going missing," Poppy said. "But apparently she stopped here on her way out of town, I dunno, asking directions or something. We got to be proactive, get ahead of things. Last thing we need is trouble with the feds. That good enough for you?"

"Yeah, sure. Knowing she was here helps me start track her movements. Did anyone see what kind of car she was driving? That'd help, too, if it's new enough to have GPS on it."

Weasel answered. "Honda Accord, about ten, twelve years old at least. I think it was dark red, hard to tell, it was night and she was only here a few minutes."

"You talked to her?"

"Yeah." Weasel turned and glared like Goose was asking for a three-way with his old lady or something. "I talked to her. Told her how to get to the interstate. She drove off and that was all."

Poppy handed Goose the slip of paper Weasel had given him. "Here's all the info you should need."

"Okay, I'll get right on it." Goose left the office but didn't shut the door the whole way. He glanced at the paper. Lena Hale. Age twenty-six. Black. Five-nine, one forty, brown hair, brown eyes. Social Security number, car registration info, address, phone number. How the hell did they get all that from a thirty-second encounter? And why was the club interested in some law student from Durham?

"As soon as he finds her, you take care of business. No fuss, no muss, you understand?" Poppy said to Weasel. Goose leaned forward, straining to hear more details. It was his job as enforcer to take care of club business, not Weasel's.

Unless they were talking about killing the law student. God, he hoped not.

"And the fed?" Weasel asked.

"We need to know how much she knows and who else she's talked to first. Then we'll decide."

Decide? As in possibly killing a federal agent? The muscles in Goose's neck bunched. No way in hell would he let that happen.

"It's a plan." A chair scraped back. Goose took his cue and hustled back out to the bar. He was working on the laptop when Weasel emerged.

"Haven't found her yet, hotshot?"

Goose shook his head. "Just setting up search parameters so it can run while I head over to the VistaView and start working on the fed. Oh yeah, they got a name?"

"Tierney. Caitlyn Tierney."

CHAPTER TWELVE

Emotions churned through Caitlyn as she drove west toward the Smoky Mountains, but she boxed them up to be dealt with later. She had a case to work.

The Butner chaplain couldn't have known it when he reached out to her last night, but Caitlyn had a good deal of experience with missing persons cases—which was actually, despite Hollywood, fairly unusual for a FBI agent, especially now when ninety percent of the Bureau's resources were devoted to counterterrorism and financial crimes.

Caitlyn's first assignment after the academy was working with a multi-agency FAST team: Fugitive Apprehension Strike Team. After that assignment she'd been transferred to Boston, where she worked the Violent Crimes Task Force before being loaned out to the National Center for Missing and Exploited Children after Katrina to locate kids taken by predators who'd used the storm to cover their actions.

But she never thought she'd be searching the mountains where her dad had taught her to hunt. It was eerie, as if things were always supposed to be this way. Her dad teaching her how to track and shoot and most of all to think like whatever animal they were after. The FBI fine-honing those skills, even though they'd intended to forge her into an entirely different kind of hunter. And now Eli Hale, the man who'd shaped her life, who'd started her on this path, sending her back home to search for his daughter.

A shiver shook her but it had more to do with the sun slipping behind the mountains and the spitting snow than anything else. She cranked up the heat, turned on the defroster, and pressed down on the accelerator.

She'd left a message for Uncle Jimmy at the casino and he called her back just as she headed down Route 19 through Maggie Valley. She pulled off into the empty parking lot of Ghost Town in the Sky to talk to him.

"So you're coming for a visit? What a great surprise. Can I ask what prompted this? I figured we'd never see you back around these parts ever again." He and Aunt Lacey had brought her cousin Bernie for a visit a few times when Caitlyn lived in Pennsylvania, but she and her mom had never returned to Evergreen. Not while she was growing up, at least. Jessalyn had gone back for Lacey's funeral ten years ago. Caitlyn wasn't sure if she ever made the trip from Charlotte to Evergreen any other time. If so, Jessalyn had never mentioned it.

"I'm trying to trace a missing girl. Lena Hale."

"Lena—you mean Eli Hale's youngest?" Disapproval sharpened his tone. "Why would she come here?"

"I don't know, but her roommate said she was heading to Evergreen and she's gone missing. Would you check your records and see if she stayed at the resort?"

"I guess I could. But there are plenty of other hotels

around here now that the VistaView has become such an attraction."

Hard to imagine Evergreen needing more than one hotel, but a lot could change in twenty-six years.

"Thanks, I appreciate it."

"No problem. There'll be a room ready and waiting for you when you get here. Just tell the girls at the front desk to call me soon as you arrive."

"There's no need to make a fuss—"

"Nonsense. You're family. And I haven't seen you since you graduated college. Can't wait to see what a real-life hotshot FBI agent looks like in person." He hung up before she could protest.

She pulled onto the highway, mountains north, south, and west of her, their shadows darkening the road. No turning back now.

Lena huddled in the far corner of her prison. For the first time since they'd taken her, she allowed herself to break down. Not just cry. Hit bottom. Hard. She sobbed and screamed and begged for mercy, hugging her knees to her chest, rocking back and forth so hard her head banged against the wall.

How had her father withstood twenty-five years of being locked away?

She was still angry at him—and furious at herself for believing in him. After all, he'd never lied about what he'd done. It was her blind faith, passed on by her mother and Vonnie, that had led her to believe in his innocence.

He'd been so angry with her when she'd visited him a few weeks ago, wanting to take his case to the Innocence Project. She'd never seen him like that, not in her entire life. He'd stood up from the table, drawing the attention of everyone in the visitation room, and yelled at her. "Once and for all, just leave it be," he'd said, his face flushing to the point where she worried he might have a stroke. "I killed the man, Lena. I'm right where I should be. I'm guilty, goddamn it!"

He'd stalked away, leaving her speechless and alone.

Alone. She'd spent most of her life feeling that way— never fitting into her mom or sister's well-rehearsed dance. Vonnie and her mom always returning from a visit to Dad, talking about their last visit, planning their next. Like he was somehow still a part of their family.

For years Lena had played along. After all, he was the only dad she knew, and having him in her life was a lot more than many of the kids she grew up with in the Hayti district of Durham. Most of her schoolmates never saw their fathers or even knew who they were. At least Eli tried to play the role, always interested in her life, giving her advice, asking for details, staying involved.

Until Mom and Vonnie were killed. While going to see him. Leaving Lena alone. Truly alone. And she finally realized what a farce they'd been caught up in. Yet she'd clung to the misguided belief that she would be the one to save him, to bring him justice.

Stupid. Justice had nothing to do with it. After losing her mother and sister, she just wanted to be part of a family again. But that wasn't going to happen. Life was life in the federal system. Her dad would never be anything other than who he was: a killer, available only when he earned enough points to allow visitation.

She'd thought she'd toughened herself. That she could face life alone. Become the family hero. If she couldn't clear her father's name, at least she could help to restore the family legacy.

The idea came to her while researching the freedmen case that went before the Cherokee Supreme Court and through the federal district courts. At first it'd been a simple article for the law review, dissecting the historical foundation and current implications of the courts' decisions.

But when she'd discovered the Hale name included on the roster of Eastern Band freedmen families, it became more. A way to find family she'd never known she had. She needed that sense of connection, of legacy. Something she could pass on to her own children one day. Something to prove she wasn't really alone.

Her rocking slowed. So did her tears. As she quieted, she realized the thrumming noise pounding through her head wasn't her pulse, but rather the sound of fists banging against the outer wall. Frenetic at first, but now slower, softer. As if the chimps on the other side wanted to soothe her fears.

Maybe they'd also been drugged and stolen away. She wished she knew how long she'd been here—anything to orient herself. If the drugs had kept her unconscious longer than a few hours, she could be anywhere in the world.

She scooted back to the hole in the wall, trying to be quiet so she didn't create another frenzy among the chimps. Were they imprisoned together in a zoo? Held captive by some kind of deranged collector-slash-serial-killer?

Or had she been taken somewhere where chimps ran free?

Peering through the hole, she received few answers. It

was now dark outside, but there was enough moonlight that she could see movement as two—three—no, four chimps crossed the space in front of her peephole.

At least she knew it was night. She could start to keep track of the days.

The air was cold, smelled of Christmas trees, wood fires, and snow—just like in Evergreen where she'd been taken from that dive biker bar. Never should have gone there, but the man she was looking for worked there and she'd been anxious for answers. She shivered and hugged herself again, this time for warmth. At least she wasn't in some remote African warlord's compound.

Which left her still alone, still without any hope of rescue—no one would be looking for her—and still without any answers to the biggest question of all: Why had they taken her?

One last sob escaped her, this one born of terror that hollowed out her insides, leaving her collapsed on the floor. She stifled it with her hand, not because she was afraid of her captors hearing it, but rather because she knew if she heard it echoing through her tiny prison, she'd never find the strength to get back up again.

Please, God. She didn't dare to speak the words aloud for fear of what she'd do if He didn't answer. But she couldn't stop herself from thinking them. Prayer and faith had been constant companions all her life. They'd gotten her through Vonnie's and her mother's deaths, helped her through every bad thing she'd ever faced—even the anger she felt toward her father for abandoning them, wasting his life rotting in jail. For killing a man in cold blood.

Please, God. Help me. The words sounded pathetic and small inside her head, too weak to ever reach Him.

But then a miracle happened. As she lay on the floor,

facing up to Heaven, tears salty on her face, a small leathery hand reached through the wall and patted her cheek. Softly, gently, like she was a baby.

Lena sucked in her breath and froze. Suddenly she wasn't scared—despite the fact that here was a wild animal, carrying who knew what kind of diseases from who knew where, strong enough to rip through the hole in the wall it'd taken her hours to create, or to maul her, tear her arm off.

But the chimp didn't rip or tear anything. Instead it caressed, comforted. From beyond the wall it made a crooning noise, like a mother makes when singing her child to sleep.

God had answered her prayers. Again. Lena slowly raised her own hand to pat the chimp's. Then she carefully slid up to a sitting position. The hole in the wall was too small for her to see the chimp while the chimp had its arm inside. Why not ask the chimp for help in making it larger?

She held the chimp's hand as if they were shaking on a deal, stroked its fur with her other hand so it would know she meant it no harm, and guided it back through the wall to the outer layer of siding.

"If you guys can tear this off, I'll take care of the plaster," she said, molding the chimp's fingers around the outside edge of the hole and mimicking a ripping motion. "Then we can both deal with the wire." She hoped that once she enlarged the hole, she'd be able to find where the wire was fastened and tear it out. Maybe even figure out a way to use it as a weapon?

The chimp reached for her arm again. She redirected it to the wood siding. "If you want to help, this is the best way. Then we can figure out where we are and get out of here." It occurred to her that the chimps must have also been stolen. Who would keep chimps in the middle of the Smoky Mountains of North Carolina? "We can help each other."

The chimp—she decided to call it Smokey—made a cheerful noise and began pounding on the siding with wild abandon.

"No, no, this way," Lena said as she pushed her arm as far as it would reach through the hole and shoved against the corner of the siding. The wood was old and brittle enough that she was able to break off another chunk, earning her a splinter impaled in her palm.

Before she could pull her hand back inside, Smokey grabbed it. Held it gently. Lena tensed, hoping the chimp wouldn't mistake the blood for dinner. But the chimp made a soft keening noise as if she felt Lena's pain.

Lena slid her hand back inside. Smokey's fingers followed, curling around the edge of the piece of siding Lena had just splintered. Then the chimp tugged, the rest of the piece breaking away. She pressed her face against the larger hole, but seemed frustrated that she still couldn't get to Lena.

Lena removed the splinter and sucked the blood clean from her palm. "Do it again, girl," she urged the chimp. "Go on, pull another one."

Smokey made a whining noise, wrinkling her snout against the wire that separated them. But her fingers were curled around the edge of the next piece of siding.

"Just give it a yank. You can do it," Lena coached.

More out of frustration than following Lena's direction, the chimp snapped the piece of siding free. Good enough. At least Lena knew it was possible—as soon as she broke through the plaster and wire from the inside. And now that the chimp had enlarged the hole, there was no turning back. As soon as daylight came, her captors would see it.

Only one chance to get this right. Lena guzzled down an Ensure both for strength and to use the bottle as a tool, and went to work, hope fueling her efforts like a shot of adrenaline.

CHAPTER THIRTEEN

Caitlyn followed Route 19 through Evergreen to where the town's boundary met the southeastern border of the Indian reservation. It wasn't hard to find the VistaView Casino just across the town limits, on the reservation side of the border—in fact, it would have been difficult to miss given the sheer wattage of light surrounding the high-rise resort like a halo.

Bypassing the valet parking with its row of Town Cars and BMWs waiting, she pulled into a spot in the underground garage. Down here the Subaru looked more at home, parked between an F-250 with a sagging bumper and a Jeep Cherokee. Vehicles designed for the whipsnake curves of the lonely mountain roads.

As she carried Eli's papers back to the trunk to stow them, an armored truck pulled into the loading dock at the rear of the casino. Two casino guards emerged from the VistaView rolling handcarts loaded down with bags of coins. The guard from the armored car company stood by, more concerned about checking his watch than anything.

Figures. Who'd want to steal a couple hundred pounds of quarters?

She grabbed her go-bag and crossed to the elevator bank leading up to the casino. As soon as the elevator doors whispered shut, the air felt different. It tickled her nostrils, made her want to breathe deep, leaving her feeling a little giddy.

The elevator took her up two flights to the lobby level. Inside the resort the excited feeling intensified and she felt suddenly energized. The air left a faint metallic residue on the back of her tongue, tasted of ozone.

Extra oxygen pumped into the ventilation, she realized. Giving the casino players a jolt so they'd stay longer at the gaming tables and slots.

The elevators opened onto a large hall filled with rows of slot machines. The lighting was brighter near the elevators and dimmer at the far end so she could only focus on the twirling neon banners above the slots along with the players hunched over them. There was less noise than she expected, a thick burgundy carpet muffling much of it, allowing her to hear two jackpot bells coming from somewhere inside the labyrinth.

The cynic in her wondered if they had some way of timing the slot wins to coincide with guests arriving from the elevator. She'd never been inside a casino before, so she took her time to observe the players as she traversed the maze.

They were older than she'd imagined. Retiree age. Many were Native American—ironic since the casino was meant to supply them with revenue, not take it away again. Caitlyn could see none of the glamor Hollywood portrayed casinos with; these people were frowning, cranking slot handles, and jabbing buttons as if their lives depended on it.

Threading her way past the machines, she made it to the registration desk. Away from the distraction of the slots, she finally had time to take in the decor. It had a kitschy, 1980s feel to it, which made sense since the casino was built in 1990, the year after she and her mom had left Evergreen. Light ropes formed the illusion of chandeliers overhead. Mirrors reflected the light without amplifying it. Red-and-gold velvet wallpaper in the same shades as the carpet completed the decor.

She'd always imagined that the VistaView would showcase more of its Native American heritage, but instead it felt the opposite: all chrome and glass, no wood. Instead of local handicrafts, the glass display cases were filled with high-end designer clothing designed to entice shoppers to the stores in the atrium behind the lobby.

Vegas transplanted to the mountains of North Carolina. She could imagine Uncle Jimmy pitching the project. Why should Nevada have all the money and glamour?

"Can I help you, miss?" the registration clerk asked.

"Yes. There should be a reservation for me. Caitlyn Tierney."

The clerk, a twenty-something Cherokee wearing a black skirt and blazer with a crisp white blouse featuring the VistaView monogram on her collar, bent down to her computer. Caitlyn leaned against the desk, watching a man check in a few stations down. He was tall, muscled yet lean, wearing jeans, a black T-shirt, black leather jacket, and sunglasses. Some kind of movie star? With his long, blond hair and scraggly beard, he reminded her of Viggo Mortensen. Especially the way he looked up at her over the rims of his glasses, making eye contact with an alpha-male confidence that was designed to make her want to look away in self-preservation. Like he was too dangerous to look at safely, especially this up close and personal.

She kept staring. He gave her a small nod and a smile that began at the left-hand corner of his mouth before making it all the way across, revealing his teeth. As if he appreciated her daring to face the big bad wolf head-on.

Asshole, she thought, arching an eyebrow and purposely turning her back on him. Not that she still couldn't see him in the mirror behind the desk.

"Oh, Miss Tierney," the clerk said with sudden respect. "Your uncle said to call him as soon as you arrive. He's in with the security chief."

"Don't disturb him," Caitlyn said. All she wanted was a place to throw her stuff while she began to retrace Lena's footsteps. Then later, maybe a hot shower before she went through Eli's papers.

"He left orders." The clerk made it sound like she'd rather disobey a federal agent than Jimmy. Two bellhops appeared from nowhere, one reaching for her bag, the other standing guard.

"No. Thanks. I'm fine," she said. No way she was going to let any stranger carry her bag. It had her laptop and backup piece in it. "I can take that." She grabbed the small duffel and swung it over her shoulder. The bellhops stepped back, looked to the clerk for orders.

"But your uncle," the clerk protested. "Mr. McSwain said—"

"Just tell me where my room is. I'll deal with my uncle." Caitlyn held the bag to her chest when one of the bellhops edged closer. She stared him down and he backed off again. The Hollywood-wannabe watched the whole thing;

his smug smirk made her itch to show him her badge and Glock.

"There's my favorite Ginger, always causing trouble," a man's voice said from behind her.

She'd hoped he'd forgotten the nickname she hated, but that didn't stop her from turning around with a smile. "Uncle Jimmy."

It'd been almost fifteen years since she'd seen him last, but he looked exactly the way she remembered him. Just tall enough for a good bear hug, slight paunch struggling to escape from his belt, blond hair neatly trimmed. He, like her mom, dressed as if every day was Sunday, only now his suit hung perfectly from his knobby shoulders. Tailored.

He embraced her in a hug that lifted her off her feet for a moment. "How are ya, Ging? Still shooting first and asking questions later?"

He meant it as a joke, Uncle Jimmy meant everything as a joke, but after what happened last summer, it hit a little too close to heart. She released him and stepped back, holding her bag across her chest, a small barrier.

"You look great, Jimmy. The casino business must agree with you." When she was a kid her dad always looked upon Jimmy with a touch of scorn as Jimmy turned his attention to everything from day trading to patent applications to land development. Sean Tierney often scoffed—out of his wife's hearing, of course—about Jimmy's ability to make money at anything as long as it didn't involve a day's hard work.

Jimmy chuckled, his gaze moving across the lobby assessing the take from the gamblers in sight. "It's going to kill me in the end, Ging. Always something new to worry about, from cheaters to corporate theft to the gaming board. But, that's life." He waved away his concerns and planted both his palms on her shoulders. "C'mon, let me show you around."

"I'd love to, but I really need—" Before she knew what was happening, Jimmy had slid her bag from her shoulder, handed it off to a bellhop, retrieved a keycard for her from the desk clerk, and was escorting her behind the desk through a door marked PRIVATE.

She looked back, ready to retrieve her bag, but the bellhop was already traversing the path through the slots to the elevators. At least the Glock 27 wasn't loaded—it used the same ammo as her service weapon and she had two clips stashed in her coat pocket, more secured in her vehicle.

Besides, if you couldn't trust family, who could you trust? It was clear the employees held Jimmy in high esteem; they'd never risk his wrath.

As she turned to follow Jimmy, she caught the eye of the hunk in black. Mr. Hollywood was retrieving not one but three separate keycards. When he caught her staring at him, he fanned them like a royal flush and winked at her.

Rolling her eyes, she let the door close behind her and hoped her room wasn't anywhere near his.

Jimmy led her through hallways lined with administrative offices to a private elevator. "I checked on that girl you asked about. She never stayed here." As they rode up to the second floor, he said, "Your mom called. She's pretty upset. About you getting mixed up in all this. After all, Eli Hale is the reason your dad is dead."

That was Jimmy. Straight shooter—at least he pretended to be. She remembered more than once as a kid being fooled by his constant smile. There was always a catch with Jimmy, whether it was the old "pull my finger" routine or mesmerizing her and her cousin with three-card monte.

"Eli Hale is dead." The words came out flat, no hint of apology.

"So she said. Said you were caught up in some kind of prison riot."

"It wasn't a riot. I wasn't in any danger."

The elevator stopped. "Maybe you should try telling that to your mom. She worries, Caitlyn. When was the last time you visited her? I mean, I understand why you've never come home, here, too many memories, but a daughter should visit her mom every once in a while."

"I'm sorry I didn't make it to Aunt Lacey's funeral." Lacey had died of cancer while Caitlyn was at the FBI Academy.

His footsteps slowed. He stopped outside a paneled door leading to an executive suite. Suddenly he looked old, wrung out. Not the always-laughing Uncle Jimmy she remembered.

Then he brightened and laid a hand on the doorknob. "I have a surprise for you."

He opened the door before Caitlyn could protest that she was in no mood for surprises. His office had a wall of windows overlooking the casino floor, a large mahogany desk sitting on top of a luscious, thick Karastan rug. And her mother sitting in the leather Aeron chair behind the desk.

"If Muhammad won't go to the mountain," Jimmy chuckled, "then, you know." He stood watching, pleased by the shock on Caitlyn's face.

Not that she didn't enjoy seeing her mom. But she was

here to work and Mom was, well—*high-maintenance* was the best term to describe Jessalyn Tierney.

Jessalyn stood up, her posture regal, and glided across the room to greet Caitlyn with a hug and kiss on the cheek. She wore a designer suit with modest diamond earrings that along with her perfectly styled signature French twist added just the right touch of elegance.

"I knew I was right in coming up here. You sounded so distressed on the phone." She laced her arm through Caitlyn's as if they were best friends shopping for prom dresses. "Mama will cheer you up. I've already scheduled facials and massages and Jimmy reserved us front-row seats for the show tonight."

"Tyne Daly in *Gypsy,*" he gushed. "But first, let's catch up over a nice dinner. My treat."

He took Caitlyn's other arm and she suddenly felt like she was nine again, being towed into Sunday school against her will. But the smile on her mother's face was too bright to resist—especially when mixed with the guilt Jimmy's words had brought. She did avoid her mother; she could be a better daughter.

The search for Lena could wait another hour or so, she told herself. Somehow that did little to soothe the feeling of foreboding that made her rest her hand on the butt of her Glock, reassuring herself it was still there.

Goose would've spotted Caitlyn Tierney even without the clerk's heads-up or her bright red hair. The woman didn't walk. Instead, she strode like an old-time gunslinger, weight balanced against the extra two pounds of weaponry she carried on her right hip, gaze constantly in motion, assessing risk, absorbing details, ready for anything.

When she arrived at the registration desk, she swung her head as if she was used to having longer hair than the short cut that framed her face and made her look less like a cop and more like a fairy-tale elf.

An elf with scars. One along the side of her head, peeking out from beneath her hairline. Another skimming up along her breastbone. He liked her for not trying to hide it beneath a turtleneck or buttoned-up blouse.

She had a nice figure, obviously in good shape. Not too skinny or too fat, with narrow hips but a generous bust. No artificial enhancements. Not that she needed any, at least not to his taste. Goose was of the definite opinion that too much of a good thing didn't necessarily make it better.

Then she arched her neck as she swiveled her stare onto him. He gave it right back to her. No sense trying to hide, too late for that. Plus he wanted to see what she was made of. Poppy had said to find out everything he could about the fed. Goose might be better able to do that by getting in her face rather than by lurking in the shadows.

The smile he gave her as she rose to the challenge and didn't flinch from his gaze was genuine. Best job Poppy'd ever given him. Most fun, too. Maybe he'd misunderstood Poppy and Weasel. Caitlyn didn't seem like she could be a threat to the Reapers.

He watched her reunion with Jimmy McSwain, grinned as Jimmy called her Ging, then took the keycards the clerk Poppy had bribed gave him. One to Caitlyn's room, one to each room adjacent to Caitlyn's. He had bugging equipment ready to place, a keystroke recorder he'd plant on her laptop, as well as a GPS tracker for her car. Everything he needed to get the lowdown on why a federal agent was chasing after the same law student Poppy wanted to find.

Goose had no idea what the law student had stumbled across or why it was so vital to bury it and her; that was between Poppy and whoever was pulling Poppy's strings. But he figured it was in his best interests to find out as much as he could about both Lena Hale and Caitlyn Tierney. That way he could figure out how to protect both women from the Reapers while also keeping the Reapers happy. A win–win for everyone and no need for violence.

Caitlyn gave him one more glance before following her uncle into the private administration offices. Goose winked at her, enjoying the view from behind as much as he had from in front. Then he hustled to catch up with the bellboy carrying her bag. It bulged like there might be a laptop inside. If so, he was itching to see what was on it. More he knew, the better he could do his job.

Hopefully without anyone getting hurt.

CHAPTER FOURTEEN

The MC's clubhouse was crazy busy, gearing up for the big poker run tomorrow. Reapers were arriving from all over the Atlantic seaboard, including a crew from the home charter in Florida. Bernie was the low man on the totem pole, prospect-wise, despite it being his home turf.

As he ran beers to and fro, carried buckets of empties, restocked the bar, and dished out chicken wings and fries, Bernie couldn't stop thinking of Lena and the poor leopard. It'd been a day and a half since he'd been able to break free long enough to go check on them, and worry was churning his guts into acid.

All he'd wanted was to save some animals. And then he'd overheard Poppy talking to someone on the phone about a girl who was close to knowing too much—too much what, Bernie had no idea—and that she had to go. When Lena had stopped by the clubhouse and he'd seen her talking with Weasel, he knew she had to be the one, so he'd grabbed her before Weasel could.

He hadn't counted on her being so out of it for so long

after he'd tranked her. Just like he'd had no idea how hard it would be to get a stupid leopard to eat.

He'd read online that big cats didn't need to eat every day, that in fact it was bad for them. He'd also read about a host of diseases they were prone to if not fed properly while in captivity. Everything from all their teeth falling out to blindness to liver disease.

There was a break in the action as the guys moved outside to start in on the pig being roasted in an oil barrel. Bernie took advantage of the pig pickin' to call the guy in Pigeon Forge, the one they'd taken the animals from in the first place. He needed to know what the leopard liked to eat and if it maybe needed any medicine.

"Mr. Manson, please," he said when a woman answered the phone.

She sniffed hard as if she'd been crying or something. "Who's calling?"

"It's an old business friend," Bernie improvised, thinking hard about what to say. "I used to sell him—er—merchandise." He grimaced, knew it sounded lame, but he didn't know the exotic animal industry well enough to know what Manson would have actually bought from anyone. Dummy. Except animals, of course.

Didn't matter. The woman bought it. "You'll need to take your business elsewhere, mister. Manson died."

"Oh. I'm sorry to hear that." Bernie was about to hang up when he had a thought that grabbed at his throat, making it hard to swallow. Like Manson's ghost himself wanted him to ask. "My condolences, ma'am. Can I ask what happened? I just saw him last week and he seemed fine."

"He got jumped coming out of a bar. Beat up. They took him to the hospital but then"—she sniffed again, her voice choking out the rest—"he didn't make it."

"That's terrible." Bernie stumbled over the words, not sure what to say. His stomach began to flip-flop, churning out more acid. He reached for his Tums. "Do the police have any idea who did it?"

"No, sir. Not sure they care too much. 'Round these parts, as long as it doesn't involve anything that would drive tourists away, they don't too much mind what happens. Especially not to folks like Manson."

The police might not know who killed Manson, but Bernie sure had a good idea. "Sorry for your loss, ma'am," he said without thinking and hung up.

Goose. Who else would Poppy send to see if Manson had double-crossed them and stolen his animals back from the club? Who else would Poppy ask to take care of club business except the new enforcer?

No wonder Goose had come in so late last night. Looked so tired when Bernie saw him this morning.

His throat tightened again, but this time it wasn't a ghost clutching at him. It was his stomach ready to hurl at the thought that he'd almost confided in Goose. About the animals, about Lena, about everything.

He grabbed his jacket and keys, ran out the back door before anyone spotted him. There was no way he could stay and face the Reapers as they partied. No way he could continue to hide the truth. But if they knew he knew, he'd be the next one lying on a slab in the morgue.

Uncle Jimmy insisted on dinner in the dining room reserved for high rollers. As they entered, Jessalyn on his arm, he pointed out various celebrities, smiling and nodding and waving to them. Caitlyn didn't recognize any of their names, but names weren't her strong suit.

"How's Bernie?" she asked once they were seated. If

she was stuck in a family reunion, might as well get caught up. But apparently it was the wrong thing to ask.

Jimmy scowled down at his silverware and beckoned the waiter to replace a tarnished salad fork. "Bernie is Bernie," he said with a sigh. "The boy is hopeless."

Jimmy's tone was exactly the same one her mother used when talking about Caitlyn. Poor Bernie. Her cousin had always been a dreamer, one of those kids with their noses buried in a book or sitting hypnotized, too close to the TV. Caitlyn doubted she'd heard him utter more than a dozen words.

Her phone rang just as the salads arrived. "Sorry." She glanced at the screen. Didn't recognize the name. But not many people had her private cell number. "I should take this."

"Caitlyn, surely it can wait," her mother said. "We're having dinner."

"It's work."

"It's a family dinner. You haven't seen your uncle in fifteen years." For Jessalyn family always came first. The fact that Caitlyn's dad's job often made that an impossibility for him was a constant disappointment.

And Caitlyn was just one more disappointment to her mom. Long ago, Caitlyn had given up trying to meet her mom's high standards. But she could never give up a secret hope that maybe one day she'd do something to make her mother proud. Obviously that day wasn't today. She left the table and answered the call.

"Caitlyn?" The voice was female with a South Carolina accent. "Have you found Lena yet?"

Caitlyn riffled through her mental associations of names and faces. She knew she should recognize the voice but couldn't picture who it was. She answered the woman's question to buy more time and see where this was going. "No."

"I've been calling and calling her cell but it goes right to voicemail," the woman continued in a rush. "But then I thought of using our Find Me apps—"

Suddenly it clicked. The roommate. Caitlyn couldn't remember her name but it didn't matter. "Find Me apps?"

"You know. You load them on each other's phone before you go to a party with a friend. That way if you get separated you can find each other—unless you hook up and don't want to be found, then you just hang a DO NOT DISTURB sign on your cell and it goes to the friend's as well."

No. Caitlyn didn't know. Things sure had changed since she was in college. Suddenly she felt old. "So, did it work?"

"Kinda. I'm not sure. It says Lena's near Evergreen at a bar called the Pit Stop." The girl's voice upticked as if she was asking a question. "I Googled it and it looks like some kind of biker bar. Definitely not the kind of place Lena would go. So maybe someone stole her phone? Anyway, I thought it might help."

"Thanks. It does." Caitlyn had a vague memory of a log cabin above the river, motorcycles crowded out front. "Does it say when she went there?" Probably too much to ask, but worth a try.

"Oh sure. Let me look. It says she arrived there Wednesday at eight oh four PM. At least that's when she turned the app on. Oh. I guess that means she didn't have her phone stolen. Because why would a thief turn the Find Me app on?"

"I'll check it out. Is there any way I can access the history of where her phone's been through the app?"

"No. Sorry, it only reports when and where the app was turned on. Last time listed is a concert we both went to a few weeks ago."

"Thanks for trying."

"When y'all find her, tell Lena to call me, okay? I'm getting kinda worried."

"I will. Bye." Caitlyn hung up. She remembered the Pit Stop—it was a dive when she was a kid, what her mom called an eyesore. No reason to think it'd be any better twenty-six years later. The bar was Reaper territory, a motorcycle club that verged on outlaw status. Her dad had ended up in the ER a few times getting stitches after encounters with the Reapers, trying to shut down bar fights and all-night parties.

Why would Lena go there? Unless it had changed since Caitlyn was a kid.

She returned to the table. "Jimmy, is the Pit Stop still run by the Reapers?"

"They took it over, it's their private club now. Good thing, too. I keep them out of the resort for the most part, but sometimes they have big rides that attract plenty of law-abiding motorcycle enthusiasts, like the poker run this weekend, so I try not to judge. Why?"

She grabbed her coat. "Looks like I'm headed there."

Jessalyn jerked her chin. "What? No. You can't, we're in the middle of dinner."

Caitlyn gave her mom a peck on the cheek. "Sorry, gotta go."

"Caitlyn Matilda Tierney, you come back here this instant." Several diners looked around. Caitlyn was certain they expected to see a wayward toddler running away. She was out the door before her mother could repeat her summons.

There was going to be hell to pay when she got back, she knew. But a solid lead was a solid lead. Even if it did mean hanging out with a bunch of bikers.

Jimmy McSwain had given his niece a two-room suite on the Executive level. Nice digs if you could afford them, Goose thought as he surveyed the rooms to decide where best to place the bugs and pinhole cameras. Since he'd left Asheville, he slept in the trailer behind the clubhouse, a drafty single-wide with a plasma screen, all the porn you could watch, four bunk beds stuffed into two small bedrooms, and a dozen guys fighting over them on any weekend night. Weekdays it wasn't so bad, usually just him and Bernie crashing there.

After he'd lost his job and the Reapers invited him to go from being a hanger-on, partying with them on weekends and making the occasional ride down to Daytona, to a prospect, Goose had sold everything that wouldn't fit in the back of the cab of his pickup or in the saddlebags of his bike, loaded the bike onto the truck, and moved here to Evergreen.

He sat down on the king-sized bed, taking care not to wrinkle the fancy coverlet folded at the end. It was kind of a relief, not having to worry about anything like insurance or condo fees or bullshit like that. But after fifteen months of living out of a duffel, he wouldn't mind a night or two on a real bed like this.

Caitlyn also packed light; her bag was even smaller than his. Inside it he found her laptop, an unloaded Baby Glock in an ankle holster, a pair of black cargo pants, blue jeans, silk long johns, assorted panties and sports bras—nothing from Victoria's Secret, more's the pity—two fleece pullovers, and two off-white button-down blouses. Combined with the suit she was wearing, apparel that could be used anywhere from a boardroom to a SWAT raid.

Goose liked the way her mind worked. He'd Googled Caitlyn on his phone while waiting at registration for her to arrive and discovered she was something of a FBI celebrity, had made all the major news outlets six months back. Saved a town in upstate New York from a psychopath Russian mobster and had uncovered some government corruption while doing so. All while almost dying herself.

With her red hair and freckles and tale of death-defying action, no wonder she was such a media darling. He'd bet the FBI brass hated that. Wondered if they even knew she was here. Chasing down a missing law student wasn't exactly something the FBI would take on outside of the movies.

He checked out her laptop. She had an encrypted password, but that was okay; the keystroke recorder he loaded onto it via the battery pack would take care of that. Anything she typed, he'd see on his own machine.

After finishing with her laptop and zipping her bag shut again, he placed his bugs. Looked around the rooms once more: nothing out of place, nothing visibly disturbed. Not that she would know since she hadn't even been up here yet, but double-checking details was what made him good at his job. A single digit out of place could bring down everything, so yeah, even while playing I-spy for the Reapers, he sweated the small stuff.

He was just reaching for the door to leave when he heard the click of a keycard being swiped from the hall. Plastering himself to the wall behind the door, he hoped she'd walk far enough into the room that he could slip out without her noticing.

The door opened. He held his breath and sucked in his gut, fists at the ready in case it came to that—although he'd never actually hurt her. Poppy's orders were hands off; they didn't need the feds raining down on them like the wrath of Khan.

The room was in darkness and she'd have to pass the entrance to the bedroom in order to reach the lights. If he was quiet, he should just make it.

Caitlyn moved past him. He grabbed the edge of the door to keep it from shutting, ready to sidle around it once she was far enough away not to notice the movement.

Before he could make his move a man barreled through the door, blindsiding Caitlyn and knocking her into the bedroom. Goose left the safety of the shadows and was ready to intervene when he saw it was Weasel. Trying to help him, no doubt.

Caitlyn landed an elbow to Weasel's side, but she was fighting from a disadvantage, on her knees beside the bed, Weasel's heavier weight on top of her from behind. Before she could twist her way free, Weasel grabbed the coverlet from the bed, threw it over her head, wrapped it around her tight, and pushed her to the floor. He held her in a choke hold, his mouth next to her ear.

"Go home, fed. Forget about Lena Hale. You're messing in something ain't none of your business."

He shoved her headfirst half under the bed. Then he and Goose raced from the room, pulling the door shut.

"Hey, what's the deal?" Goose protested once they were safely behind the locked door of the room next door. "Poppy doesn't trust me? Sent you to spy?"

"I just saved your butt." Weasel waved him to silence as they both listened to Caitlyn's door slamming open, footsteps stomping down the hall, then back again to her room. Goose ran over to where his laptop was set up on the desk and activated the bugs he'd just placed.

"What's she doing?" Weasel asked, keeping his voice low.

Goose listened on the headphones so there was no chance of the sound carrying through the walls. "Calling her uncle. Asking if he can pull security tapes for this floor." He turned to Weasel. "Shit. We're screwed. All because you had to play the heavy. Poppy said to keep things quiet."

"Relax. These feds aren't as tough as they think."

"You sound like you have some experience there."

"You been with the club long as I have, you learn there's a public side of things and a private side of things." Weasel narrowed his eyes at Goose. "Let's just leave it at that."

Goose pulled up the video feeds. Caitlyn had changed into jeans and was loading her Baby Glock and strapping on an ankle holster. "What about the security cameras? She'll know we're here, see our faces."

"Don't worry. Poppy will take care of it. Let's roll."

"Don't you want me to stay here, monitor things?"

Caitlyn grabbed her leather car coat and left her room. Her footsteps echoed past their door and down the hall again.

"Only if you want to miss all the fun. I'm betting she's heading to the clubhouse right now."

CHAPTER FIFTEEN

Once Lena poked a few holes higher up, the section of plaster wall collapsed under its own weight, filling the small room with dust, choking her as she dodged the heavy slabs. The crash shook the room and left her ears buzzing.

If her captors were nearby there was no way they'd miss hearing that. Before the dust had a chance to settle, she climbed over the rubble and began clawing at the wire and wood lathing separating her from the outside wall. The lathing was thin, popped free of its nails easily when she leveraged her weight against it, but the wire wouldn't budge. Eyes tearing with dust, fingers bleeding, she searched for the end of the wire where it was anchored to the wood beams supporting the wall.

Adrenaline and anxiety sped her heartbeat through her veins with the force of a hammer driving nails. What she wouldn't do for a crowbar, she thought as she wiped blood from her hands onto her pants, mixing it with the plaster dust. All she needed was a few inches clear between the two-by-fours, just enough for her to shimmy through to freedom.

The chimps had done their part. Once Smokey began tearing at the siding, her three buddies had joined in on the fun. The outside siding was now riddled with gaping holes, including a sizable one directly across from Lena.

Lena shivered against the night air hitting her sweaty skin. She wanted to howl in frustration. Only the wire separated her from the outside world.

Clawing her fingers through the holes in the wire, she shook it, leaning her entire weight against it. She knew she couldn't tear it apart but hoped to bend it enough to loosen it from whatever anchored it to the wall. When that didn't work, she tried weaving one of the thin pieces of wooden lathing through it and leveraging it away. It gave slightly—at least she imagined that it did—but refused to pull free.

She tunneled through the plaster debris on the floor—the stuff was heavier than sin—and searched for the bottom edge of the wire sheet. It was anchored all right. Not just stapled in place. No, the sick, twisted bastards who'd built this place had nailed it to the outside of the two-by-six-footer with thick eight-penny nails bent over, the sharp edges of their heads driven into the wood. She might have been able to pull them out, given enough leverage, but she was on the wrong side of the footer and there was no way she could reach them through the wire.

Okay, Lena, okay. No need to panic, just because you've pretty much destroyed half the house and there's no way the bad guys won't notice it when they come back and that could be anytime now and they're going to be so very angry and who knows what they might do . . . Stop it! Work the problem.

An encouraging *chrumph-hurumph* sound came from outside. Lena looked up to see that Smokey had returned.

The chimp squatted beyond the hole in the siding, regarding Lena, tilting her head one way then the other as if examining Lena's predicament.

"Think you could help me again?" Lena asked. The chimp didn't move for a moment, then bounced up and down. "Here, can you pull here?" Lena wiggled her fingers through the bottom of the wire, pointing to its edge. "Be careful, it's sharp."

Smokey touched the wire, tapped a finger against the nails, making a gurgling noise in the back of her throat, like asking an uncomfortable question.

"I know, it's not going to be easy," Lena said, making eye contact with the chimp. "It's probably going to hurt." She pressed her palms against the wire, forcing it as far forward as she could. The chimp leaned into the hole in the wall, sniffing the blood on Lena's hands, the short hairs on her snout tickling.

She screeched and reared back, agitated.

"Wait, don't go!"

Too late, Smokey had disappeared into the night.

Lena wiped her face on her sleeve, ignoring the tears and mucus and plaster dust she smeared over her best wool coat. Her job-interview coat, the one she'd found at a thrift store, the price tag still on it. Anne Klein, only five bucks. It'd seemed like a sign from God that good things were coming her way, she remembered thinking at the time.

Idiot. She knew better than to put her faith in signs and portents. There was only one thing that could help her survive this: God. She just had to trust in Him.

A wave of tranquility swept over her, the night noises, the rasp of her breathing, the pounding of her heart all vanishing into a peace-filled silence. She closed her eyes, the better to see His vision for her. *Whatever you need, God. I'm trusting in you. Please just give me the strength and courage to walk the path you lay before me. Amen.*

A deep breath in filled her lungs with crisp, clean air. Another one out, expelling her doubts and fears. She opened her eyes, renewed energy tingling along her nerves.

Smokey had returned and sat watching Lena, arms wrapped around her chest. She looked very sad.

"It's okay," Lena reassured her, perching on the pile of debris and mimicking the chimp's posture. "We'll think of something." She tugged the belt on her coat tighter, trying to block the wicked winter wind. Then she looked at the belt buckle. Nickel. And the fabric was wool. Strong enough?

Thank you, she whispered to the heavens. She wove the belt through the wire immediately above the nails. The wood footer and heavy-duty nails were stronger than the wire—especially where it had been cut along the floor. All she needed was enough leverage to tug a few of the wrapped strands free.

Once she had the belt secured she braced her feet against her side of the wall and leaned all her weight back, stretching the belt taut. With loud grunts and screeches, Smokey cheered her on.

The wire fought, bent, and twisted. Smokey clapped as Lena strained, pushing with all her might. Finally, the bottom strands beneath the nails popped free. One inch, then two, then *pop-pop-pop,* the wire gave up the battle. Lena fell back, releasing a fresh wave of plaster dust while Smokey flew head over heels then somersaulted back to the wall, banging on it in victory.

"Thank you, Jesus!" Lena shouted, doing her own jig, floundering over the chunks of plaster.

She tossed bottles of Ensure through the opening, followed by her coat. Wrapping her scarf tight around her face to prevent being ripped by any stray splinters or nails, she sucked in her stomach and crawled through the wall to freedom.

The night sky was filled with stars, shimmering with halos as the mountain mist scudded across them, carried by a brisk westerly wind. Never had shivering felt so good.

Hope filling her heart, Lena slid back into her coat, filled the pockets with all the Ensure she could carry, and looked out into the darkness of a black vista of trees with no signs of civilization in sight. Smokey returned, cautiously, taking her time as she walked around Lena, assessing her. Lena stood still, holding her hands out, palm down.

"It's okay, it's just me," she cooed to the animal.

Smokey stopped, cocked her head again in consideration, then stepped forward and slid her hand into Lena's. An act of complete trust. Lena's tears broke past her willpower. Together they faced the wilderness surrounding them.

Which way, Lord? I will follow, wherever you lead.

CHAPTER SIXTEEN

Caitlyn winced and rubbed her left shoulder as she steered the Subaru down Route 19. Six months ago she'd broken that collarbone. It'd healed fine—until some Reaper goon decided to tackle her and throw her to the floor to land on it again.

She knew it was a Reaper because she'd torn a Reaper lapel pin from his collar while grappling with the asshole. At least she'd gotten in one or two good shots. Still, it rankled. Definitely not her finest moment.

How the hell did that guy get the drop on me? was the question foremost in her mind. He'd come from the direction opposite the elevators, from the guest rooms down the hall. Must've been in a room not too far from hers, because he wasn't in the hall when she unlocked her door.

Maybe a room across the hall? He could have been watching for her, familiar with the layout, aware that she'd be in the dark for a few steps, her back unguarded? She made a note to ask Jimmy to check which rooms were occupied and if any maids were missing keycards.

Unfortunately, since she had no idea what the guy looked like, until they got the security footage, it might not help much.

Jimmy wasn't even sure if the security cameras covered that far away from the elevators and ice machine area. Protested that they'd never had any problems—like it was somehow her fault, coming into town and stirring up trouble. He'd acted more concerned that none of his other guests heard the commotion than he had been about her safety.

Her breath steamed the windshield, and she cranked up the defroster. In a way, she guessed it was her fault. Trouble sure as hell seemed to find her no matter where she went: a secure federal penitentiary, a crowded resort. She passed Santa Land and drove through Cherokee headed south. This time she was taking trouble to them. The Reapers weren't going to assault a federal agent and get away with it.

It was amazing how much Cherokee had changed since she was a kid. Where there'd once been only a few ramshackle trading stands selling traditional Qualla crafts or housing bingo parlors, there were now strip malls and motels and a brand-new hospital. All thanks to the VistaView.

The Pit Stop, now the Reaper clubhouse, was just as Caitlyn remembered it. A long two-story log building with a few smaller outbuildings behind it. Tonight the parking lot was filled with Harleys, many sporting out-of-state licenses, as well as an assortment of pickup trucks, SUVs, and even two minivans. The lighted sign out front announced a charity poker run over the weekend. That explained the out-of-state plates, especially as the Reapers' home chapter was in Daytona Beach.

Caitlyn didn't even try to find a parking spot in the lot. Last thing she wanted was to get boxed in; she liked having an escape route handy. She pulled into the lot of the abandoned service station across the street, backing into the shadow of the unlit sign at the front edge of the lot. This way she could pull right out when she was ready to leave and had an unobstructed view of the clubhouse while she decided on her approach.

The crowd was going to make things both easier and more difficult. Easier to blend in as a stranger; more difficult to actually learn anything useful. Not like the Reapers were going to be talking club business in a bar filled with outsiders. She debated showing Lena's photo around, but it didn't feel right. More likely to bring her attention than answers. Best to wait until she had a better feel for the Reapers.

She slipped a knife into the front pocket of her jeans where it was just about unnoticeable, slid her ASP retractable baton into her coat pocket, but locked her service weapon in her trunk. The Glock 22 was too easy to spot and would mark her as law enforcement immediately. The smaller Glock 27 at her ankle would have to suffice.

Besides, if she did this right, her best weapon would be her smile. And the lapel pin she'd ripped off the Reaper who jumped her. She pinned it to the collar of her shirt, pulling the collar over her leather coat so it was easily visible.

Hanging offense for a non-Reaper. *Bring it on, boys.*

She strolled across the street and wove her way through the rows of bikes to the main entrance. The building was surrounded by a wide veranda that—despite the windows facing out from the front room—remained mostly in shadows. The heavy bass line of rock music made the wood floor dance beneath her boots as Buckcherry wailed about a crazy bitch.

"A chick walks into a biker bar alone," a man's voice greeted her as she crossed the porch. "Sounds like a a opening to a bad joke."

She was going to let it pass as a drunken come-on that backfired except he didn't sound drunk. Turning to face him, she saw the blond from the VistaView's check-in desk leaning against the outside wall of the bar, his black clothing blending into the shadows. He nodded to her, raising a bottle of Yuengling in greeting.

"You following me?" she asked.

"Looks to me the other way around," he said. "After all, I've been here long enough to have a beer, get tired of the smoke and noise, and step outside for air."

"You're a Reaper?" He wasn't wearing a cut—the leather vest with patches designating a member's status and home charter.

"I can be anything you want, darling. You looking for a Reaper? With the charity ride there are tons here tonight. Lots of folks who aren't Reapers, too. Motorcycle enthusiasts. Like me."

Didn't answer her question, but she wasn't going to push the issue. She almost went inside but the thought of leaving him behind her ruffled her instincts. He noticed her hesitation and smiled that sloe-gin smile again. The one that had irritated her so when she'd met him earlier.

"Would you like an escort?" he asked, pushing away from the wall. Then he noticed the silver Grim Reaper on her lapel. "Maybe you don't need one? Wouldn't want to tread on another man's territory."

"Look, mister—"

"Goose."

"Excuse me?"

"Goose. That's my name." He waited. "And you are?"

She hated pushy guys like him. Arrogant bastards. Controlling. But in a place like this, that was going to be all she found. Of the bunch this "Goose" was probably least objectionable. Certainly better looking than most. She softened her expression, managed a smile, and said, "Caitlyn. Nice to meet you, Goose."

He inclined his head as if he'd watched too many Gary Cooper movies. "Pleasure's mine, ma'am. I don't suppose you'd care to dance? Or maybe play pool," he hastened to add when she hesitated. "At least let me buy you a beer."

"No to the dancing, but yes to the beer and a game of pool." Hard to talk or overhear conversations while on the dance floor, but around a pool table she was much more likely to get some idea for the lay of the land. Maybe even hear a familiar voice, like that of the guy who'd blind-sided her earlier this evening. One could only hope.

"You sure you're supposed to be wearing that?" He nodded to her pin once more. "Didn't just pick it up in the parking lot or something, did you?"

"Trust me. I know what I'm doing."

"If you say so. Right this way, then." He opened the thick, rough-hewn log door, releasing a barrage of misogynistic lyrics from the Ying Yang Twins—the Reapers' musical tastes seemed more focused on degrading sexual acts than any particular genre—and followed her inside the clubhouse.

The tables and chairs had been pushed back to make more room for dancing. If you could call it dancing. More like dry-humping, the way the women were grinding on the men. Caitlyn was seriously overdressed compared with the other women who, no matter their size, all seemed to have bare midriffs, jeans that barely clung to their hips, and spaghetti-strap tops—the ones that had straps. And tons of colorful tattoos to draw attention to all that naked flesh hanging out.

The men were more conservatively attired in layers of denim, flannel, and leather. Most wearing black leather Reaper vests on top of everything. Like the women they ranged in age from barely legal to qualifying for Medicare.

Goose definitely drew attention as he ushered Caitlyn through the crowd to the pool tables in the far corner. Caitlyn scanned for exits. Between the two pool tables was a fire door propped open to let in air. Probably another down the hallway leading behind the bar where the restrooms were, but she didn't like that option: too many unmarked doors and places to get jumped. With the noise no one would ever hear her if she needed help. Best to stay in the open with her back to the wall and eyes on the crowd.

A tall brunette sidled up to Goose. "What can I get you, honey?"

He tilted his Yuengling back, finished it in a gulp, and handed it to her. "Another. And?"

"A Black and Tan and a shot of Bushmills," Caitlyn ordered.

"Only Irish we have is Jameson."

Caitlyn shrugged. She wasn't planning on drinking it anyway. A shot glass of whiskey could be an effective distraction or weapon. She might chance the Yuengling if it came with the bottle top still sealed. "Whatever."

"My tab," Goose said. The waitress pouted at that and wove her way back through the crowd toward the bar.

Both pool tables were in use, but the game in the far corner was winding down. Caitlyn made her way to the rear wall where she could watch the crowd and be close to the exit. Plus it was a little quieter here; she could actually hear what the men were saying.

Too bad they got real quiet real quick when they noticed her. Suspicious stares at her Reaper lapel pin followed by raised eyebrows aimed at Goose. He said nothing, but stood close enough to her to make it clear to all she was under his protection.

The thought rankled her, but it was a necessary evil in a place like this. By the time the waitress returned with their drinks, the pool players had lost interest in her and finished their game.

"Ladies first." Goose handed her a cue stick after racking the balls.

Caitlyn set her drinks down, took the cue, and purposefully made a bad break. She was more interested in having time to watch the room than focusing on the table. Plus, it would stroke Goose's ego, showing off for the little lady.

"Too bad. I'll take stripes." He bent over the table, aiming his shot, and his hair fell forward far enough for her to see the outline of a tattoo that began on his neck and traveled up onto his scalp. A Reaper trademark. Even their prospects got tatts there, forever sealing their fates alongside the full-fledged club members.

He made his shot and lined up his next. Just as he was pulling his elbow back, she asked, "Where's your cut?"

He didn't react but missed an easy shot. "Excuse me?"

"You're a Reaper. Shouldn't you be wearing your cut in here?"

He stood, holding the cue still, and stared at her. Like he couldn't believe how stupid she was, challenging him here of all places.

She flicked her lapel, the silver Grim Reaper glinting

in the overhead lights. "Maybe you're not wearing it because you lost this?"

"Girl's right." An older man with gray hair and dark, flat eyes stepped forward. "Mickey," he ordered someone without looking at them, "go fetch Goose his cut."

His own leather vest indicated that he was an original member of the Reapers and president of the Carolina Mountain Men. "I'm Poppy," he said genially but without offering his hand across the pool table. "Looks like I should know you, and yet I don't."

Other Reapers began to gather, although her exit route was still open except for one twenty-something she could deal with, need be. Caitlyn cleared herself more room by leaning over the table and lining up a shot, angling her stick to move twenty-something back farther.

"Name's Caitlyn," she said after making the shot. "Caitlyn Tierney."

"Nice to meet you, Caitlyn. Want to tell me what your business here is?"

Suddenly it was all about her and Poppy. Goose had stepped back away from the table, chalking his cue as if his life depended on it.

Caitlyn abandoned the next shot she'd set up and straightened, looking Poppy right in the eye. She leaned her cue stick against the table and reached into her pocket, enjoying the twenty-something Reaper's flinch as if he thought she was going for a gun. Not in this crowd, not unless she had to.

She flipped Lena's photo face up in front of Poppy. "Trying to find this girl. Heard she came by here a few nights ago."

Poppy didn't even bother to look at the photo before

flicking it back at her with a snap of his fingers. Caitlyn re-pocketed it.

"You're in the wrong place. In case you hadn't noticed, someone like her would've stood out around here. Just like this gentleman did."

The crowd behind him parted. Two men hauled a third one forward. One of them held a gun to his head.

Paul.

CHAPTER SEVENTEEN

Lena and Smokey ran into the darkness. She quickly regretted leaving the sleeping bag behind, but it'd been buried under the fallen plaster and there was no way she could take the time to dig it out. She had grabbed some of the old newspaper and shoved it into her socks as insulation. The wind off the mountaintop worked hard to blow her over, her coat no match for it. And she'd lost her gloves somewhere.

She leaned forward, wrapped her arms around her chest, trying to block the wind and save as much body heat as possible, and stumbled over the irregular ground. They came to another cabin. Single-story, cheap wood siding, it appeared identical to the one she'd been held inside. Unless she'd run full circle? No, the wind had been in her face the entire time and she hadn't come that far.

Smokey dropped her hand and circled the building, Lena following warily. There were no lights but she could hear strange sounds coming from inside. Scratches or gnawing. An image from an old campfire story popped into her head: a man with a hook sharpening it before going on a killing rampage.

Her stomach rumbled and she couldn't tell if it was fear-induced nausea or simple hunger. She hadn't been hungry inside the cabin, partly an aftereffect of the drugs, partly because she was too scared to think of eating, but out here, running in the cold air . . . Her teeth chattered and her body shook so badly she kept tripping over her own feet.

She looked back the way she'd come. At the edge of her vision, she could make out the lines of the cabin she'd fled from. Two cabins. Her brain seemed fogged as if making that simple observation strained it to the point of exhaustion.

The snow flurries changed to a steady fall, her coat collecting a white sheen. She looked at the cabin before her, at the trees whipping in the wind behind it. Shelter. She needed shelter.

The noise came again. Smokey returned to her side, screeching and doing a jig. The chimp didn't like this cabin, either. Together they skirted past it.

"Not the forest," Lena told Smokey, her lips so cold and numb she was surprised she could force the words out. "We need another house. Someplace warm."

The chimp bobbed her chin as if she understood and led Lena along the tree line downhill. In the distance another cabin, just like the first two, came into view, but Smokey didn't lead her there. Instead the chimp took her to a larger log cabin, a substantial building compared with the others—at least three times as large and two stories high.

Lena tugged Smokey's arm, wanting to examine the

log cabin, but Smokey kept trying to lead her past it. Lena's feet felt like deadwood, barely able to shuffle across the uneven ground. She stumbled and fell facedown, only catching her fall at the last minute. Her hands smacked against the cold ground, stray pine needles and twigs cushioning the blow.

She lay there, face pressed against the snow-covered ground, uncertain if she could get back up again. Why should she? She could just go to sleep right here, everything would be fine, just fine . . .

Vonnie's voice called to her from the darkness. "Hurry up, Lena. We're waiting."

"Five minutes," she murmured, eyes closed. "I'll be there in five minutes. I promise."

Vonnie was insistent. "C'mon. You know we can't be late. Daddy's waiting." The jangle of coins in a Baggie punctuated her words. "I'll let you be in charge of the quarters."

Lena opened her eyes. Their mom hovered in the background, wearing her best black hat, the one with the peacock feather. The one she let Lena wear for her make-believe tea parties if Lena promised to be extra-special careful.

Vonnie wore a red velvet dress that matched Lena's. Christmas. Oh how she remembered those—getting up extra early because the line for visitation would be extra long. Falling asleep in the car because it was still dark outside; falling asleep on Mom's lap while they waited to be processed; falling asleep sitting at the table waiting for Daddy.

It was years before she realized that most kids woke early on Christmas Day to presents under a tree and turkey dinner, not lines to get inside a crowded room filled with strangers and dinner bought with quarters from vending machines.

"Lena. Get up."

Anger surged through her and she waved her sister away. "Let him wait. Bastard's guilty. Did you or Mom ever stop to think that? No, you said keep the faith. You believed in him—*we* believed in him. Wasted our whole lives on the bastard. Well, no more. He can rot for all I care."

The heat of Vonnie's slap shook Lena. "Don't you say that. Don't you ever even think that. Now get up!"

Lena tried. If only to put her big sister in her place, let her know how wrong she was. But her eyelids were so heavy. Her entire body weighed too much to move.

So instead she curled up tighter. "Go 'way, Vonnie. Let me sleep."

It took all of Bernie's courage to sneak past the partying Reapers and leave the clubhouse early. But he had to make sure Lena and the animals were okay.

And the longer he hung out with the Reapers, imagining what they'd done to Manson, what they'd do to him if they suspected . . . he just couldn't take it.

As he drove his pickup through Cherokee, past the VistaView, and turned west up the corkscrew road that led up to the Teddy Roosevelt Lodge, he tried his best to untangle the complications his life had become ensnared in.

Had been so damn proud of himself, how slick and smooth he'd been, grabbing the animal tranquilizer and syringe the zoo guy had given them, guessing her weight, drawing up just the right dose, following her to the restroom and injecting her, bringing her up here before anyone at the clubhouse even realized they'd lost her.

He'd felt so brave, defying Weasel and Poppy. It wasn't until he got her up to the cabin that he realized he had no idea what the hell to do with her. And then when she didn't wake up for almost a full day, he about shit himself with panic that he'd overdosed her.

He told himself that as soon as she was awake and the effects of the drug wore off, he'd explain everything to her, help her do whatever it took to keep her safe and clear of Poppy and the Reapers. Even if it meant betraying the only family he cared about.

But he hadn't counted on the party last night keeping him away so long. Now he could barely swallow without fear that she or the leopard or those stupid chimps had come to harm.

If they did, it would be all his fault.

All because he had a dream. Of a home. Someone to take care of. Maybe even someone who would take care of him. Maybe.

Snow was falling steadily by the time he pulled the truck up in front of the cabin where Lena was. He wanted to make sure she was okay; then he'd see to the leopard.

When he'd checked on her last, yesterday morning, and given her back her necklace with the gold cross, she'd still been groggy and out of it, singing hymns and praying with words that made no sense. In no shape to talk to anyone but God.

Hopefully she was better now, because he sure as hell couldn't figure this out all on his own. Not when Poppy and Weasel were whispering something about the feds being involved, looking for Lena as well.

What the hell had such a sweet girl done to have so many people after her?

*　*　*

Vonnie left her dreams but Smokey wouldn't abandon Lena. The chimp kept nuzzling her face with scratchy whiskers, tugging at her arm like she was a rag doll.

"Leave me alone." Lena batted the chimp away. She rolled over. Snow filled her nostrils, choked her into alertness.

"What the—" She sat up. Dark. Black, black dark rushed her vision. She blinked back vertigo until she could see again. Snow. And cold, oh so cold. Hugging herself, she staggered to her feet. There was a building. Warm, she had to get warm.

Smokey chattered and cavorted, blocking Lena's path. Lena ignored the chimp, focused only on shelter and warmth. She could die out here. The thought drove her forward, one painful step after the next.

The snow wasn't deep but was wet enough that her makeshift booties had long ago soaked through. Her feet no longer hurt; instead they were numb, heavy, like moving two concrete blocks. *One, then the other, then the other, keep going.*

She counted her steps like words of a prayer. The most important prayer of her life. *Please God, don't let me die . . .*

The porch railing was salvation. Using it, she hauled herself up to the veranda. The door wasn't far now, not too far. A strange keening noise that barely cut through the sound of the wind made her stop, waver. Something was in there.

She almost gave up, almost sat down right there and embraced death. It was only the thought of how very disappointed Vonnie and her mom would be that kept her going. One step, two steps, three . . . She hit the door, fumbled with the heavy latch securing it. Old-fashioned. Lift and slide and pull.

The door opened. She fell inside. Closed her eyes again. Didn't even open them when she heard the soft thud of something large leaping to the floor in front of her.

CHAPTER EIGHTEEN

Surprise ricocheted through Caitlyn, leaving in its wake a heavy, sinking feeling of dread. Shit, no, no, no. This couldn't be happening. "Paul." She blurted out his name before she could stop herself. "What the hell?"

"Your mom was worried. Sent me to get you." He stood tall, looking directly at her, as if she was all that mattered. Didn't seem to even notice that he was the only black man here, much less the only man not carrying a weapon.

"Hear that, boys?" Poppy said. "It's true love. He's come to save her."

Paul shrugged off the two men restraining him, pointedly ignoring the one with the gun aimed at him. Despite her anger and fear, Caitlyn had to admit it was kind of sexy. If not for the fact that suddenly her half-assed plan had gone from getting the lay of the land to a critical hostage-taking incident.

"Look," Paul said in his most measured and reasonable physician voice. "I'm not sure what's going on here, but I'm sure it's all a simple misunderstanding—"

"Shut up, Paul," Caitlyn snapped, desperate to keep him from making the situation worse.

He glared at her and opened his mouth again when Poppy said, "Do what the lady says, Paul."

The Reaper with the gun jabbed it sharply into Paul's belly, just below his rib cage, hard enough to make Paul gasp. Caitlyn took note of the man: middle-aged, dark hair, short, mean-looking face that had seen its share of fistfights. Not as mean looking as when she finished with him, she promised herself. Not by a long shot. The name on his leather vest was WEASEL. It fit.

The crowd on the dance floor behind them kept gyrating and shaking their booties the way only white folks with no sense of rhythm could, as if what was happening here was happening behind an invisible force field. Not a part of their world. No help would be coming from that quarter. It was all up to her.

The Reaper whom Poppy had sent for Goose's cut returned, holding it in two hands and presenting it to Goose with respect. Once Goose donned it, she saw why. Asshole was the chapter's damn enforcer.

As soon as the leather vest was in place, Goose's demeanor changed. His gaze narrowed, assessing her, ignoring Paul, and taking good measure of the mood of the Reapers who now surrounded the pool table—including a few from the home chapter. Which upped the ante because the Carolina Mountain Men would need to save face in front of the bigwigs from Daytona.

Great. Just great.

Possibilities streamed through Caitlyn's mind, all examined and rejected until only one was left. The one option she hated, but it was the only way to prevent bloodshed. Surrender.

She pulled the silver Reaper from her collar and leaned over the table, bowing her head as she stretched her left hand to place it as close to Poppy as possible. Her movement and the table concealed her right hand sliding down to grab her Baby Glock. When she straightened, she held the Glock at her side, below the table, aimed where it would cause Poppy the most pain, and her left hand rested on her ASP, ready to deploy it.

Unfortunately three other Reapers, including Goose, now held pistols and at least four more had their hands where she couldn't see them, presumably on their own weapons.

"I made a mistake," she admitted, her pride about choking her. "Now let him go."

Poppy held her gaze for a long moment, spinning the silver pin between his fingers. "What do you say, Goose?"

"I say we've got a lot of people enjoying our hospitality tonight." Goose nodded to the dancers behind Poppy as he holstered his weapon at the small of his back. "I think a heartfelt apology should suffice."

Poppy jerked his chin to the men holding Paul. They immediately dropped their hands and stepped back.

"Get out of here, Paul," she said, not relaxing her guard one iota.

"Not without you." He stood his ground like he was Sir Galahad protecting her honor. Couldn't he see how delicately the balance of power teetered between her and Poppy?

"The lady is free to go as soon as she apologizes," Poppy said.

Paul jerked; obviously he thought it would be the Reapers apologizing to him.

Before he could say anything that would send the

situation spiraling into violence, the noise of sirens sounded through the open door behind her. The gyrations on the dance floor had morphed into a full-fledged brawl. Nice timing.

Amazing how fast weapons disappeared and the Reapers vanished into the crowd at the sound of cops approaching. All except Goose, Poppy, and the short man who'd held the gun on Paul. Weasel. Whom she now noticed was missing one of his lapel pins.

Caitlyn took advantage of the disruption to step around the table and grab Paul, yank him to the door. "Go, now. I'll meet you back at the hotel."

He pivoted out of her grasp. "No. I'm not going anywhere without you."

"This is my job, Paul. You need to let me do it." Adrenaline rushed her words as she positioned herself to cover both sides of the doorway.

Paul didn't move. "Do you have any idea how hard it was for me to come here? I knew what kind of crowd I'd be walking into. But I promised your mother I'd keep you safe."

Caitlyn felt a rush of shame that he'd ventured into danger because of her. She had to get him out of here before things escalated. "The best way to keep me safe is to let me do my job. And I can't do that while I'm watching over you." He stared down at her. Caitlyn sacrificed a precious moment of her attention to meet his gaze. "Please."

Finally he nodded. "Okay. I'll wait in the car."

"No. My mom will be worried. You go ahead and I'll meet you back at the VistaView." The sirens were louder now, almost here. A beer bottle flew past, coming from the direction of the dance floor.

Reluctantly he wove his way between the vehicles

crowding the parking lot. She covered his back until he was safely in his Volvo. He pulled onto the road just as the first sheriff's car pulled in from the opposite direction, followed quickly by two more squads and an SUV.

Caitlyn was about to make her own escape when she heard a voice behind her. "If you're still here tomorrow, we'll be by to collect that apology, Special Agent Tierney."

Weasel. The same voice as the man who'd tackled her earlier in the evening, confirming her suspicions. *Nice to meet ya. Again.*

Caitlyn turned and flipped him the bird. Just in time for a sheriff's deputy to spot the gun in her other hand.

"Hold it! Show me your hands!"

"Sheriff Markle wants to talk to you." The deputy escorted Caitlyn from the back of his car but didn't say a word as he walked her over to a white Tahoe emblazoned with the Balsam County Sheriff's Department insignia.

Markle was in his early sixties, trim except for the slightest hint of a double chin, upright posture, salt-and-pepper hair trimmed in a buzz cut. Former military, Caitlyn guessed. Local boy, returned home, settled in. And, she thought as she caught the changes in his expression when he spotted the civilians gathered in the parking lot, a born politician.

"Do you respond to all the Friday-night drunk-and-disorderly calls, Sheriff?" she asked, getting a jump on the conversation. A frown creased his eyes but his smile never wavered. Superglued in place.

"Only when they involve a federal agent, Ms. Tierney. Can I ask what your business here is?" Translation: Why the hell are the feds messing in my sandbox?

"Looking for a missing person."

"Looking? As in the FBI is looking or you are? Because it's customary to notify local law enforcement when you're working a case in their territory."

"I'm looking. Daughter of a friend." Not the total truth, but close enough. She handed him Lena's photo. "Sorry, Sheriff. I planned to stop by in the morning. Had no idea tonight would be so . . . eventful."

"Uh-huh." He nodded as if he wanted to be helpful but his eyes slit in disapproval when he glanced at the picture. "The Hale girl? Sure, I know her. Been a pain in my butt the past few years—always sending requests for information, coming down on the weekends and school breaks to pester folks who remember her dad's case. Not that many are left—or care. Haven't seen her for a while, though."

Not what the deputy who'd been keeping her company while they waited for the sheriff to arrive had said. "Your deputy mentioned that he'd seen her at the station a few days ago."

His shrug was larger than it needed to be. "Don't know. We've got nothing to hide. You can ask my men all you want, As long as it's not while they're on duty." He leaned his weight against the Tahoe's fender. "Now, about this mess here tonight. I'm assuming you don't want me calling your supervisors and letting them know you were involved in an assault?"

A not-so-subtle threat. She waved it away like a stray snowflake. "I'm sorry, Sheriff, someone seems to have misinformed you. If you look at the witness statements, you'll see that I didn't assault anyone. I was the one who was assaulted while trying to protect a civilian. And that man"—she pointed to Goose, forcing herself not to roll her eyes at the biker's nickname—"and several of his fellow Reapers pulled guns on me and an unarmed civilian."

Unfortunately Weasel was nowhere to be seen or she would have gladly fingered him as well. Markle didn't look at Goose, instead kept his stare on her as if waiting for her to buckle.

"I understand the recreational bikers bring a lot of tourism dollars to the county," she continued. "I'm sure you don't want a loose cannon among the Reapers running around threatening civilians. Not to mention the good citizens who elected you."

Across the parking lot, the older biker called Poppy, the one with the dead eyes, gestured to Markle as if he were the boss of Markle. Probably was. The sheriff pushed away from the Tahoe. "Thank you, Ms. Tierney. I'll take care of everything."

Then he swung back to Caitlyn. This time his smile was genuine but no less menacing. "Tierney? Any relation to Sean Tierney? We were deputies together."

"I'm his daughter."

"Really? Well, how about that. Your dad was a good man, good cop." He gave her another look of disapproval. "You'd think his daughter would have more common sense about poking a hornet's nest. Especially with civilians around."

Caitlyn was silent. Already beating herself up enough, thank you very much. Not to mention looking forward to hearing it from Paul and her mother and probably Uncle Jimmy as well. But what was she supposed to do, let the Reapers get away with anything they damn well pleased?

"Funny you looking for Lena Hale." The sheriff stopped, waited. Forcing her to break the silence and ask.

"Because of what her father did?"

"No. Because her last request for information was the case file on your daddy's suicide." He continued past her, waving a hand over his shoulder in dismissal without turning his face to look at her. "You have a good night now. Caitlyn."

He said her name like she was a nine-year-old. Probably how he remembered her. And about the age she'd acted tonight, letting the Reapers get under her skin.

Caitlyn wandered over to the Subaru and sat on its hood, thinking. Why would Lena be researching Caitlyn's father's death? Eli Hale had said Sean Tierney's death had something to do with the same mysterious "they" he thought were threatening Lena, but she'd written that off as the paranoid delusions of a man incarcerated for a quarter century.

Still, Lena was definitely missing. And the people of Evergreen were lying about her—at least some of them were. The trick would be in separating the truth from the lies.

If Eli was right and Lena was in danger, then she'd better move fast.

A deputy escorted Goose to his squad car and placed the Reaper into the rear seat. One obstacle out of the way, Caitlyn thought. Now to deal with the next: Paul.

She sighed and got into the Impreza, heading toward the VistaView. She still had to sort through Eli's papers, placate Paul, and come up with a game plan to find Lena. It was going to be a long night.

But all that wasn't what kept her hunched over the steering wheel as the Subaru rounded the twisted curves leading up the mountain to Evergreen. It was the thought of her father, lying in his own blood, his service weapon at his hand.

Why would Lena be investigating a twenty-six-year-old suicide?

CHAPTER NINETEEN

Lena's cabin was silent and Bernie wondered if she was sleeping. He tiptoed through the front room to the walk-in closet where he'd left her. Didn't want to disturb her. The air in the cabin was a little chilly. There was no central heat, but he'd banked the woodstove before he left yesterday. It must have gone out.

A floorboard creaked beneath his weight. He listened. No sound from Lena, not even that crazy-mixed-up praying-hymn-singing she'd been doing yesterday. She had such a beautiful voice. Listening to her was like nothing he'd ever experienced. Fear shuddered through him— what if she'd had a reaction to the drugs? What if something was wrong?

He fumbled for the key to the padlocked door, finally found it, twisted it in the lock, snapped the padlock off, and pulled the door open. Dust filled the air, making him sneeze. He turned on the light.

A mountain of plaster filled the center of the closet. And the outside wall had a giant hole gouged through it.

Lena was gone.

Bernie stood, his breathing so hard and fast it about pulled him out of his boots. "Lena!"

His shout swirled through the plaster dust. He turned and ran outside, circling the cabin to the hole on the side wall. Just enough snow to reveal her footsteps, thank God.

He raced to the pickup, grabbed a flashlight, and ran back to her trail. Large, bare feet stomped over and across Lena's trail. The chimps. If they hurt her, he'd shoot them, kill them all, he swore.

Bernie always carried his granddaddy's bear-hunting pistol with him when he visited the leopard. The gun was an old Smith & Wesson .44 magnum revolver, big thing, heavy, too. Although Bernie had shot plenty of game with long guns, he'd never actually aimed Granddad's revolver at any living thing.

The two times he'd come across black bears in close proximity he'd had a shot but just couldn't bring himself to take it. Seemed a shame to destroy such beautiful creatures. Not without good reason, anyway. So he'd kept the revolver holstered while he and the bears had themselves a quiet conversation. Both times things ended with the bears sauntering off into the woods, ignoring Bernie like he wasn't even there.

Now he pulled the .44 free of its holster. Held it in one hand and the flashlight in the other as he bent low, straining to make out the tracks in the windblown snow. They led in a semicircle bounded by the tree line. Thank God, she was too smart to go into the woods. She'd be lost for sure in there, a city girl like her.

"Lena." He called her name again but the wind swept it away.

An indention in the snow in the shape of a woman's

body grabbed his attention. She'd lain down. In the snow. Why? Was she hurt?

He found no blood, just more chimpanzee tracks. A handprint—a woman's. She'd pushed herself up, staggered onward. He followed once more then raised his head.

The tracks led to the log cabin where the leopard was. He raised his light and saw that the door was open.

Before he could move a woman screamed.

"Lena!"

Questions spun in Caitlyn's brain. But that was okay: Finding answers was what she was good at. Sometimes because she could see patterns and possibilities others were blind to. Sometimes because she was lucky. Mostly it was simple, pure, unadulterated stubbornness.

Like tonight. Clearly the Reapers were involved with Lena's disappearance. Lena must still be alive or they wouldn't have warned Caitlyn to stop looking for her. Did they have Lena and want Caitlyn off their trail? Or were they looking for her themselves and wanted the competition gone?

If the Reapers were involved with Lena, odds were they were also behind Eli's death. Which meant they might have had something to do with what put Eli in prison in the first place.

Could everything she'd believed for the past twenty-six years be a lie? What if Eli was innocent?

A chill shook her despite the Subaru's heater. What if her dad didn't kill himself?

The thought was a familiar demon, one she'd tangled with all her life. Trying to excuse Sean Tierney, to find ways to love him without being so furious that he'd abandoned them—abandoned her. Didn't he love her enough to stay with her and Mom, face whatever he was frightened of?

She'd learned over the years not to follow that path. It only led to heartbreak.

But still the insidious whisper that had haunted her all her life came: *Maybe he didn't love me. Maybe I don't deserve to be loved.*

No. She blinked hard, turned the windshield wipers up higher to fight the snow whipping through the dark outside.

Lena didn't have time for Caitlyn to be distracted by would've, could've, should've wishes from the past. As it was, the present held too many what-ifs, not enough leads.

She pulled over into the empty parking lot of a strip mall that featured Mexican, Chinese, BBQ, and McDonald's alongside a Korean nail joint and a Dollar Store. Something for everyone.

Grabbed her phone and dialed. "Boone, it's Tierney."

"You any idea what time it is?"

"Shit. No. Sorry, did I wake you?"

"No." He sighed and she realized he wasn't being sarcastic. "Don't sleep much anymore. What's up?"

"You guys have any sets affiliated with an OMG called the Reapers?"

"Thanks to the ATF we've got just about every outlaw motorcycle gang in the country represented here. Bureau of Prisons tries to spread them around, avoid trouble while they're inside." Like shipping the Surenos from California to do their time. "So yeah, I'm sure we got a few Reapers. They hooked up with the Aryan Nation boys as well? We got tons of those guys."

"I don't know. Not exactly my area of expertise."

"What do the Reapers have to do with my little slice of heaven?"

"There's a chapter in Evergreen, Eli Hale's hometown. I think they might be involved in the hit on him."

"Care to explain why? Hale never had any problems with any of the OMG guys—or the AN, for that matter. Why target him now?"

Good question. "I'm working on it. Just see if you can find anything, would ya?"

"Sure, because I'm Santa and it's Christmas every day around here."

He hung up, leaving her in the dark with more questions than ever.

Okay, back to tonight. It was no accident the Reapers ambushed her in her room at the VistaView. Obviously Goose had overheard her room number. Or they'd bribed the desk clerk. If they had her room number, how hard would it be to get a key?

Maybe Weasel had tackled her from behind the door to her room? Had been inside lying in wait?

She reran the few seconds in her mind. Didn't feel right. He'd had enough momentum to propel her the whole way into the bedroom. Plus, it was a pretty stupid thing to do after going to the trouble of getting her room number. Assaulting a federal agent? It was sure to get her pissed off. No way they could actually believe that stunt would make her turn tail and run.

So why had he ambushed her? Must have been to distract her. Or get her out of the room for a while.

Which meant someone working for the Reapers had probably been in her room while she was at the clubhouse. Going through her stuff. Who knew what else? Bastards.

At least they hadn't gotten to Eli's papers. Those were safely locked in the trunk of the Subaru. And she wasn't about to let them have a chance at them. As soon as she got back, she'd grab her stuff and leave the VistaView. No, better. There was nothing in the room she needed tonight. She'd check into one of the cheap motels along 19. Go through Eli's stuff there, keep it safe where no one could find it.

One problem with that plan: Paul.

She dialed his number. "Hey, what's taking you so long?" he answered.

"Where are you?"

"In our room, of course."

"Which room? The one my uncle gave me?"

"Yes." He paused. "Why? Did you not want me here? What's going on, Caitlyn?"

Not the place or time to hash this out. But he definitely sounded in no mood to meet her at a second-rate roadside motel, either. "Nothing. I just didn't really care for that room." Or for the folks who might have a key to it. "I'm almost back to the VistaView. Would you mind grabbing my bag and checking us into another room?" He was going to think she was paranoid, start asking even more questions. Then inspiration hit. "On another floor. Away from my mother?"

She had no idea where Jessalyn's room was, but he didn't know that.

"Right. Your mom." Relief and a touch of humor colored his voice. "Okay, sure. I can do that."

"Don't worry about checking out. And use your name, not mine. Text me the room number and I'll meet you there."

"Will do." She almost hung up, but he continued, "Caitlyn, we need to have a long talk about tonight. You can't keep me in the dark like this. It isn't right and I deserve better."

No denying that. Didn't mean she was looking forward to it.

"I'll see you soon." She hung up before he could say anything more.

Smokey's scream jolted through Lena. She sat upright, the dim light coming through the open door barely enough for her to make out the chimp's shadow. But more than enough to reveal the feline outline that had agitated Smokey.

A very, very large cat. Mountain lion? Who cared, it was big and huffing like it was mad, and it stood between Lena and Smokey and the door.

The cat lunged toward Lena. Smokey shrieked again, jumping to protect Lena. The cat swatted a paw at Smokey, but slowly, as if it was testing the chimp. Smokey dodged it easily. Lena stood, keeping the chimp between herself and the cat. Cowardly, she knew, but what choice did she have?

She touched Smokey's arm. The chimp trembled with fear and shook her off without turning her attention away from the cat. Smokey's fur stood on end, as if a few extra inches of bristling hair would be enough to convince the cat that the chimp was a threat. The cat yawned, unimpressed, its mouth a gaping abyss of large white teeth. Very sharp teeth.

Lena backed away. The stench of urine and rotting meat gagged her. "C'mon, Smokey. Let's not bother the pretty kitty. Good kitty, now, shoo." Her tongue was thick with cold and her words sounded slurred. Crazy trying to talk a mountain lion into leaving its dinner behind anyway.

The light from the door hit the cat as it paced, its head cocked as if it considered Lena's words. There were markings across its coat. Not a mountain lion. A leopard? What the hell was a leopard doing here?

Question for later. After the leopard was on the other side of the door and she and Smokey were safely locked behind it.

Thankfully, the leopard seemed to be thinking the same thing. It swung its head from Lena and Smokey to the open door, nose high, scenting the air. But then it focused on the prey in front of it once more.

Suddenly a shadow blocked the doorway. A man. A light shot out, blinding Lena as it pierced the darkness. She shielded her eyes, stumbling backward. Her foot slipped on something wet. Losing her balance, she flailed her arms but fell to the floor, the collision stunning her.

The leopard sprang. Not at Lena. At the man aiming the light at it. The cat made a low *hrumph*ing noise, the kind of noise that could be the very last sound its prey heard. It sideswiped the man with its paw, shoved him aside, and bolted for freedom.

Smokey screeched, jumped up and down, swinging her arms to protect Lena from the new threat. The man sagged against the door, dropped the light. It spun across the floor, like a disco ball, illuminating what appeared to be an old hotel registration desk. Lena didn't know whether to get up or play dead until the man cleared the doorway and gave her room to escape.

He pushed himself to his feet, fumbled something into his coat pocket, and approached with his hands held palms up to his side, trying to convince her he wasn't a threat. She wasn't sure she bought it, but her feet were still too numb to try to run past him—hell, last time she'd tried to use them, she'd fallen, so she'd have to come up with a Plan B. Maybe Smokey could create a diversion, buy her time?

"Shh, now, I'm trying to help. Let me just check her, make sure she's okay." The man crooned softly to the chimp as he took one step then another toward where Lena lay. Smokey calmed, her posture relaxing.

So much for Plan B. Lena's mind felt like it was struggling through an avalanche, almost as numb and cold as her body. It was so hard to think clearly, much less convince her freezing body to cooperate.

"You remember me, don't you, girl?" The man stretched out a hand. Smokey sniffed, then took it, patting her palm up and down his arm and chest as if re-familiarizing herself with him. He stood in place, waiting for her to finish her exploration. Only once she'd accepted him did he dare to crouch beside Lena.

Smokey mimicked the man's posture, her paws gently nudging Lena. She made a worried keening sound and turned to the man. As if she trusted him to take care of Lena.

Lena didn't move. Couldn't move. Because even in the dim light she could make out the stranger's eyes.

Pale blue with silver flecks. The same eyes as the man who'd kept her prisoner.

CHAPTER TWENTY

Paul had gotten them a regular room on the floor above the atrium. It had a king-sized bed, a small table with two uncomfortable-looking chairs in front of an interior window beside the door. She didn't like the window, it was a security risk, but Caitlyn felt better for having moved. Not that she'd be letting her guard down, but for tonight this worked.

She'd hauled Eli's box up from the car. Wasn't about to let it out of her sight until she had a chance to go through it.

"What the hell was that all about?" Paul asked as soon as she walked in the door and dropped the box onto the table in front of the window. She'd been hoping he'd be asleep. No such luck. "Back at the bar?"

"That was me doing my job. Until you showed up."

He didn't look convinced. "Were those bikers really going to shoot us over a stupid little pin?"

"It's a matter of honor. That pin represents the entire MC."

"Honor my ass." Wow, he really was pissed. She'd never

seen him like this before. "Bunch of racist hoodlums. And what were you thinking? You could have gotten yourself killed. Going up against a gang like that on your own. Are you crazy?"

"I know what I'm doing."

"Your mom told me this is about some girl you haven't even seen for twenty-five years. It's not your job. Even if it was, shouldn't you have backup or a team or a plan or something? You don't just go charging in—"

"Sometimes you do. Shake things loose. I had it covered until you blundered in."

"Didn't look that way from where I stood." He blew out his breath. Had that resigned look he got when he had to play the adult in the relationship. She hated that look. "I admire your loyalty. To your job. Even to friends you haven't seen in years. But when are you going to start being loyal to yourself? To your family and the folks who love you?" He laid his palms on her shoulders and looked down at her. "Caitlyn, I don't know what I'd do if anything happened to you."

Adrenaline fled, leaving her bones ready to melt. She surrendered to exhaustion and let Paul hold her even though she knew she'd regret her cowardice in the morning. He was so strong, it was tempting to forget everything else and just let him take care of her.

"I hate it when we fight," he said, his words ruffling her hair. "Hate it even more when I feel like I'm the only one fighting. For us."

His words brought more guilt with them. She should love this man—what woman in her right mind wouldn't? He was sweet and thoughtful and honest and handsome and tonight had proved his courage. She was attracted to him, enjoyed being with him . . . maybe that was love?

Maybe she'd been waiting to feel something that didn't even exist? How the hell was she supposed to know?

The silence lengthened but he relented, not pushing her for a commitment. Add kind and patient to his good qualities. She hoped he never tried to make a similar list about her. It'd be damn short.

"This case," he said, his face still buried in her hair. "It's not official business, right?"

She pulled away, looked at him suspiciously. If he was going to ask her to give up—

"So, that means you can tell me about it and maybe I can help," he finished. He sat down on the edge of the bed. "Start at the beginning."

She wasn't about to let a civilian get involved— especially not Paul. He'd almost gotten himself and her killed tonight trying to help. But talking this tangle out might clear her head, give her a direction to go in. She sank down onto the chair, pulled her knees up to sit cross-legged, and propped one elbow on the table, resting her chin in her palm.

"The beginning? I'm not even sure where that is. I thought it was with the murder Lena's father committed twenty-six years ago, but now I'm not sure."

"Her dad killed someone?"

"A Cherokee tribal elder named Tommy Shadwick. Beat the guy to death with a hammer then torched the body and his house to cover it up."

Paul's eyes went wide. So typical of a civilian. Give them blood and gore and suddenly they got interested. "Really? Why?"

"I was just a kid at the time. But when I read about it later the only motive mentioned was that Tommy opposed Hale's efforts to have his family placed on the tribal rolls.

There was a big case started in Oklahoma about former African slaves of the Cherokees being given full tribal status. I guess with the new Indian gaming law passed back then, Hale thought his family should get a piece of the action."

"The casino was the reason he killed a man? Just to get a share of the profits?" Paul seemed dismayed; he'd been expecting something more dramatic, less ordinary than greed.

"The casino wasn't built then—I don't think it was even approved until after Tommy's death. Uncle Jimmy's company didn't get the contract to develop it until after my dad died and we'd moved."

"This guy beat a man to death and burned down his house just *in case* the casino got built and his family might make some money off it?" Paul's frown mirrored her own. "Eli Hale must have been pretty nuts to do that. Was he violent with his family? Did he ever hurt you? Is that why your mom is so against you helping his daughter?"

Caitlyn pushed her chair back and stood. Wished the room had more space to move in. "He was never violent. He was best friends with my dad. The best dad I knew—second to mine, of course. He worked hard but he laughed hard, always put his family first. He was—fun."

"But he bludgeoned a man to death? You were just a kid. Maybe there was more going on you didn't know about. He was bipolar or something."

"No. Lena would have used something like that for an appeal." It took her six steps to pass the bed and reach the bathroom. Another six back. "He confessed. Never changed his story. All the evidence pointed to him. Except my father couldn't believe Eli was guilty."

"Did your father have proof?"

She shook her head, straining to piece together the fragments of memory, newspaper articles she'd read once she was old enough to find them on her own, and the transcript of Eli's sentencing. "No. He was with Eli that night but there was still a window of opportunity so it didn't hold up as an alibi." Another six steps. And six steps back. She stopped in front of Paul. "But there should be a better motive. A crime like that is personal, intimate."

"Is that what Lena was here to research? Her dad's case?"

"No. Lena researched her dad's case already. Found no evidence of his innocence and nothing to base an appeal on. Plus, he maintained his guilt right up until he died— they had a huge fight at Butner a few weeks ago and she told him she finally realized he was guilty and she wasn't going to keep wasting her life on him. That was about the time she started researching Eastern Band Cherokee tribal archives from the eighteen hundreds."

"Wait. You lost me. Eli Hale is guilty—he says it and everyone believes him, including his own daughter. So what do Indian archives from over a century ago have to do with anything?"

"I'm not sure. Her roommate said it was research for a law review article. Tied in to a Supreme Court ruling about the freedmen in Oklahoma."

"The same case everyone thinks got the tribal elder killed back in 1988?"

"It finally made its way through the court system." She had no clue what a case about an Indian tribe in another state had to do with Lena's disappearance. And no good ideas about where to start looking. "Maybe you could help me with that? Do some online research about what Lena was researching and see who she might be visiting here?"

"Maybe. But what are you going to be doing in the meantime?"

"You know how hard it is for me to read on the computer." God, she was a slug, using her traumatic brain injury and the resultant migraines to get him to do her work. But if that work kept him safe and sound huddled over a computer, it was worth it. "It would be a huge help."

"Okay. I'll do it. In the morning. After we get some sleep." He stood and pulled down the duvet. "But on one condition."

Conditions. She hated conditions. "What?"

"You don't go anywhere near those bikers again. And you keep me in the loop."

That was two conditions. Didn't matter. There was no way in hell she'd be able to honor either. A civilian was not going to dictate her investigation. She didn't answer, instead pretended to be busy searching for her toothbrush, trying to decide whether to lie to Paul or not.

No matter what she told Paul, she was going to find Lena. She owed Eli Hale that much.

Especially since she was beginning to think her dad might have been right all along. There was damn little evidence except Eli's confession to tie him to Tommy Shadwick's murder. And even less motive.

What if Eli Hale was innocent?

CHAPTER TWENTY-ONE

Goose lay back on the steel bench outside the holding cells, his handcuffs rattling against the railing they were attached to. Not exactly the comfortable bed he'd hoped for tonight. At least he wasn't inside one of the two small cells, crowded with drunks, at least one of whom had already tossed their cookies.

Once they'd spied his top rocker labeling him a Reaper officer, the deputies had allowed him to stay outside the holding cells. The only other casualty of tonight's ruckus that they'd shown equal deference to was one of the guys from the home chapter.

It wasn't out of respect, that much was clear. It was because the sheriff knew how to best keep peace around here. With the population of Reapers in his territory increased tenfold for the weekend, he wasn't going to risk igniting a war. Not when a little common courtesy could keep things quiet.

Smart man, the sheriff. Almost as smart as the fed, Caitlyn. She'd really gotten under Poppy's skin. Goose smiled at the memory of her flicking that photo of Lena

Hale onto the pool table like she was turning up the ace in a royal flush. And waltzing into the clubhouse wearing that Reaper pin? Most men wouldn't have the balls to do something like that.

Her poor boyfriend was gonna get a new one ripped, wrecking her power play like he had. What kind of idiot was he, crowding in on her plan like that?

He considered that. Then again, maybe she wasn't so smart, hanging out with a guy that clueless. Maybe she should be hanging out with someone who knew how to play the game, someone like Goose.

The thought made him smile. As soon as he was out of here, he planned on finding out everything he could about the pretty fed. Best way to save her ass now that she'd given the Reapers a reason to target her for real.

"Get up." The deputy nudged him before Goose's fantasy could take him any farther. "You've made bail."

The deputy uncuffed him. Goose stretched, taking his time, luxuriating in the freedom. He followed the deputy out to the front office where Poppy waited, collected his personal belongings—knife, cell phone, Browning Hi Power 9mm plus magazine, wallet, and keys—then followed Poppy out to the Reapers' van. Weasel sat behind the wheel, but otherwise the van was empty. They must have already run the guy from Daytona back.

"The fed's at the VistaView," Poppy said as he climbed into the front passenger seat, leaving the backseat to Goose. "We need to know what she's doing."

"She had a box of shit with her," Weasel put in. "Papers. You should grab those."

"Do you care how?" Goose asked.

Poppy considered it. Goose knew he didn't want to make waves, not with the national president, Caruso, coming in for the poker run tomorrow. "Under the radar would be best. Keep her off balance."

"You know she's not down here on official business." Goose leaned back, waiting for their response.

"How would you know?" Weasel whipped his head around to aim a glare at Goose.

"Easy. No FBI agent on a real case would bring their boyfriend with her. And when I saw her and her uncle together at the casino, it looked like a family reunion. He said something about her mother as well—I mean, come on, who's gonna risk their mom working a job?"

"He's got a point," Poppy said.

"Besides, feds don't work alone, right? So where was her backup when she needed them?"

"What makes you such an expert on how feds work?" Weasel snapped.

"When's the last time you saw anyone in law enforcement walk into our clubhouse without backup?"

"Yeah. Okay. But then why's she looking for the girl?"

Ah. It was the girl they really wanted. So much for Weasel's story about giving her directions and sending her on her way. "Who cares why? We let Tierney lead us right to her."

Poppy was silent a moment, then nodded his blessing. "Okay. But no one touches Tierney without my say-so. She's still a fed, and we don't need that kind of hassle."

Weasel looked surprised at that, giving Poppy a look Goose couldn't interpret. Goose had thought once he was a club officer he'd learn more about how the MC actually got the money to keep its members—mostly unemployed drifters like Goose—fed, housed, and supplied with all the booze, dope, and women they could ask for. A few of the guys had even had the MC buy out the notes on their houses so they wouldn't lose them to the bank. Taking care of their own—one of the reasons why the Reapers would remain loyal "till Death us do part," as their initiation oath required.

"What about the guys from Daytona?" Weasel said. "Caruso's gonna be asking questions."

"You let me handle Caruso. All we need is for him to keep his boys focused on the poker run. While we're taking care of business."

Goose leaned back, hiding his face in shadows, waiting for them to say more. But they pulled up to the clubhouse and parked, leaving him without answers. Were they going to ask him to TCB, take care of business?

He climbed out of the back of the van, weighed his options, and decided to keep silent and wait to see what they wanted of him. Weasel already had a TCB patch on his cut—the only Mountain Man besides Poppy who had earned the right to wear it.

The snow had coated the bikes and trucks in the lot with a frosty layer of white, made them look like something out of a fairy tale. Or a nightmare.

Goose wanted to get out of there, get far away as fast as his '05 Softail Springer would take him. Before Poppy and Weasel asked him to do something he just couldn't do. He wasn't naive; he knew "taking care of business" meant more than breaking the law.

He'd had a lot of fun with the Reapers; after a year of living with them, considered them more than friends. But there was a line he wouldn't cross.

Only question was: How could he stop them from killing the fed or the girl, Lena, without the Reapers turning on him? The only thing the Reapers hated more than feds interfering with their business was a traitor.

And the penalty for betraying the Reaper Code? Death.

* * *

It took everything Bernie had to stay on his feet long enough to calm the chimp and check on Lena. Was she dead? Had he been too late?

His left arm burned with pain and hung uselessly at his side. Trickles of what he feared was blood gathered at the crook of his elbow, caught by the folds of his sweatshirt. All he could taste was acid and bile and fear. Tears pricked at his eyes, but he didn't give in to them. Long practice at the hands of his father.

Lena's eyes blinked open. She was alive! He helped her up with his good arm. "Are you okay? Can you walk?"

She said nothing, staring at him, white showing all around her eyes. "It's okay," he tried to reassure her. "I'm here to help."

Still she remained silent. But she allowed him to haul her up. The effort made his head swim and stomach lurch, but he took a few deep breaths and his vision cleared. "It's not far to my cabin." He needed a deep breath to stay on his feet. Had to stay strong—for Lena. "We'll go out the back."

He'd dreamed of showing her how nice he'd fixed up the guest cabin he'd originally put her in. He'd washed an old crazy quilt that was mainly shades of pink and purple calico, put new sheets just bought from the Kmart in Sevierville on her bed for her, had even left a vase with dried sunflowers on the dresser.

Last thing he'd wanted was for her to see his place. The small cabin was mostly taken up with the 1992 Super Glide FXR he was in the process of rebuilding. Parts strewn about, soaking in pans of degreaser or lined up on newspaper, waiting for him to clean them. His clothes were piled on the bed—he usually slept in the old recliner anyway. There was a radio that played cassette tapes but got no reception other than an AM Bible-thumping station, no cable TV or Internet, and nothing to eat except cans of soup and tuna fish. Maybe some peanut butter, although he'd run out of bread and jam, hadn't had time to pick more up.

Not exactly an auspicious first impression. But it was the closest cabin and with the leopard out there on the prowl and him leaking blood and her so very weak with the cold, he couldn't risk their being exposed for long.

The chimp didn't help matters, circling around them as he and Lena stumbled through the empty lodge, avoiding leopard scat and rotten venison, to the rear door. He had to let go of her while he fumbled it open. For a second he thought she might run, but she just leaned against the door, staring at him like he was the hunter who'd shot Bambi's mom.

"It'll be okay," he tried to reassure her. "You'll be safe. I promise."

The night wind blew a bushel of snow at them as they crossed outside. He wished he'd been able to hang on to the light. Not that it would have helped against the leopard—the .44 in his coat pocket was the only thing with any hope of doing that—but the snow had brought a fog that clung to them like ghosts fresh sprung from the grave.

He shuddered. The chimp must have also been spooked, because it bounded into the mist. Bernie believed in ghosts—his gram had the Sight, and he knew better than to poke his nose into the business of the dead. He pulled Lena tighter against him, she was shivering so hard she nearly knocked him off his feet, and together they crossed the empty stretch of grass between the rear of the lodge and his cabin. He tripped on the steps but she kept him upright. The door didn't have a lock—Bernie had nothing worth stealing—and it slammed open with a twist of the knob and the help of a gust of wind.

He flicked the lights on, threw his weight against the door and the wind to shut it, and turned to Lena.

"Sorry about the mess" was the best he could come up with.

She stood, trembling, hugging herself, lips pressed so tight she wouldn't be able to talk if she did have anything to say.

Way to go, Romeo, he thought. He ignored the pain lancing through his arm to grab a fleece blanket from the recliner and offer it to her. She hesitated then took it. "Tea?" Shit, no. He didn't have any tea. "Or coffee? It's instant, but—" He almost tripped over a saucepan filled with machine screws from the Super Glide. Had to catch himself on the bureau, red spots dancing before his eyes. Still, Lena was silent. Idiot, of course she was silent—he hadn't even told her his name. "Um. I'm Bernie. Bernie McSwain."

That got a reaction. She jerked up, her expression confused. "Bernard McSwain?"

"Yep. That's me." He reached for the coffee, forgot and used his hurt left arm, releasing an explosion of pain. Not to mention the oh-gee-that's-really-bright-red blood seeping from beneath his cuff.

"But you—you're the one I came to find. Why—how—"

Her words tumbled through Bernie's mind like raindrops bouncing off the river as he stared at the blood on his hand. Right before everything went black.

CHAPTER TWENTY-TWO

Caitlyn woke a few hours later. Paul was turned away from her, the space between them a DMZ without the razor wire. He'd been upset when she wouldn't agree to his conditions. Had used that to start a conversation about their relationship. Her response had been to duck into the bathroom for a shower. No wonder he'd moved apart from her in his sleep. He wanted to talk; all she wanted to do was run. Classic Caitlyn.

But this time she had a good reason. She wasn't running away from Paul, she was running out of time to save a girl. Surely that counted for something?

She slipped out of bed, grabbed a fleece top and the coverlet to keep her warm, curled up in one of the chairs, and began going through Eli's box. At least the window was good for something: It allowed her to crack the drapes enough that she didn't have to turn the room light on to see.

She hoped to find something mentioning her father or some clue as to why "they" were after Lena—or even what Lena was after herself. But there was nothing except pages and pages of drawings. No written words except in the address book and a few legal briefs. Not only that, all of the drawings were famous architectural wonders except for the sketches in a pocket-sized spiral notebook: images of every corner of the house Eli Hale had built for his family, sketches of his family, a few of Caitlyn playing with Vonnie—she wasn't quite sure how she felt about that, a killer sketching her as she appeared twenty-six years ago, back when she'd been an innocent kid and neither of them had blood on their hands—and one line drawing of her dad fishing, caught in the process of casting, his head high, body stretched long as if the rod were an extension of him.

God, he looked so alive. Like nothing could ever stop him. Her vision blurred and she had to look away. She missed him so damn much. As much today as she had when she was a nine-year-old girl, lost without her hero, her daddy.

Her mom had tried hard to fill that void, but with her father's death something had broken inside Caitlyn, something had been lost. How could she ever trust, fully give herself or her heart to anyone—even her mom—after her dad betrayed her the way he had?

Why had Sean Tierney thrown it all away? Just because he thought Eli Hale had betrayed him? That was worth leaving her and her mom, ending it all?

Anger knotted her shoulders, and she was tempted to tear the sketch to pieces. Hated that Eli Hale of all people had been able to capture her father's essence. No. Hated that Eli Hale had lived and her father was dead.

The fact that Eli had died before her eyes couldn't erase decades of rage.

She closed her eyes against tears, tears that even after

all these years she refused to acknowledge. Tears of sorrow over her father's death, tears of anger over the life she could have lived, tears for her mother's sacrifices . . . she had no idea. All she knew was they needed to stay hidden, buried inside her. Otherwise . . . She choked them down, opened her eyes again.

To hell with otherwise. She had a job to do. Find Lena.

She thought about what Sheriff Markle had said. That Lena was asking about Sean Tierney's death. Again the temptation to forget about Lena and focus on her father. But that way lay madness—besides, Lena hadn't even gotten the records on her dad yet, had only requested them. Dead end.

She finished with the papers, returning them all to the box except for the small notebook she shoved into her coat pocket. If Eli Hale's cryptic message to the chaplain was right and all the answers she needed to help Lena were in his papers, then it had to be in there. She was just too tired to see it right now.

This could still all be a wild-goose chase orchestrated by a paranoid delusional convict. Which she'd be all too willing to believe if it weren't for the fact that she'd almost started a gun battle simply by showing Lena's photo to the Reapers.

The Reapers. If they were so interested in Lena, could they have had something to do with Tommy Shadwick's murder twenty-six years ago? What would an outlaw motorcycle gang have to do with a Cherokee elder and the man who'd confessed to killing him?

She opened her laptop, pulled up archived accounts of Tommy's death. The level of violence certainly fit with an OMG. But where was the motive?

The Reapers. Originally begun in Daytona, they'd

spread throughout the Southeast and up the Atlantic seaboard as far as Maryland. The Carolina Mountain Men chapter had been established in 1987 by Peter Oren Parker, aka Oren Parker, aka Poppy. She was surprised to learn that Parker was only sixty-one; he'd appeared older. Years of hard living.

According to the NCIC he had several arrests, all "dismissed for interest of justice," which meant no convictions. Pretty slick—Poppy either had a damn good lawyer on retainer or a judge in his pocket. Maybe both.

She had no legal names for Weasel or Goose, but guessed their sheets would look about the same. She tried to find any connection between Poppy and Eli Hale or Tommy Shadwick but failed. Other than living in the same area at the same time, there was no indication they knew each other.

As a deputy Dad would have covered the entire county outside the Indian reservation. If there had been a connection, he would have known. Maybe his old partner, Sheriff Markle, could help.

The words on the screen fuzzed as she tried and failed to blink away her exhaustion. She wanted to go through Eli's papers one last time, promised herself she would in a minute. But for now she just needed to rest her eyes . . .

When the man collapsed, Lena bolted for the door. He didn't move to stop her, just lay there making an unnerving sighing noise like a tire losing all its air. She glanced back as she yanked the door open. Blood seeped from under his left arm onto the dingy linoleum of the kitchenette.

Leopard must have clawed him. Served him right. She ran onto the porch, the night darker than ever, snow twisting across the floorboards in mini tornadoes. The cold pricked at her almost as much as her conscience. The man had been hurt trying to protect her. Shouldn't she help him? Wasn't that what a good Christian girl would do?

Her mother had had very strict ideas about what good Christian girls did and didn't do. She would have been heartbroken to see Lena's last argument with her dad, when she told Eli she wasn't coming back anymore. And to leave an injured person without helping him . . .

Lena shook off her guilt and raced down the creaky steps. She'd send help for the man as soon as she reached a phone. Her feet burned with pain when she hit the snow-covered grass. There was only an inch or two, but that didn't make it any less cold.

Where was she going to go? The only light came from the cabin behind her; the moon was now totally obscured by clouds. The closest building was the lodge where the leopard had been—who knew what horrors lay behind the doors of the other cabins?

Movement caught her attention. Not coming from the cabin she'd fled from, but from the nearest one to her right. The clouds parted long enough for a stray moonbeam to silhouette the leopard as it paced along the porch roof. It froze, its eyes glinting in the moonlight—at least Lena imagined she could see them—fixing on her.

No way she could outrun it, especially not with two half-frozen feet. No way she could fight it. And nowhere to go—except back inside the cabin she'd just escaped from.

The leopard took flight, soaring through the night with such grace Lena's heart froze as she watched. Every primal instinct told her to run, but she fought them, instead retracing her steps backward, her gaze never leaving the leopard on the grass twenty feet away. Her hip struck the porch railing, and she reached behind her to grab it as a guide.

Instead she found a man's hand. He pulled her up the stairs, putting himself between her and the leopard for the second time tonight, although he leaned heavily against the railing. She spotted the large pistol in his hand and realized if he meant her harm he could have killed her at any time.

"Get inside," he said, steadying his aim with both hands. The leopard crouched down, ready to pounce.

"You come, too," she said, yanking at his leather vest. It had silver patches sewed onto it; one was of a Grim Reaper, the other said PROSPECT.

He hesitated, and she knew he didn't want to kill the beautiful animal. "I wish I had a tranquilizer gun," he muttered as he drew in a breath and took aim.

The leopard seemed to read his mind because instead of rushing them, it scurried away in the opposite direction, disappearing into the woods.

"Come inside before it comes back," Lena said.

He followed her inside but didn't shut the door. In fact, he moved so that he didn't block her escape.

"I know you must be scared," he said. He stretched his arm toward her, handing her the pistol, grip first. "I'm just trying to help. Really."

She took the gun. It was heavy. Deadly at close range. You didn't have to know anything about guns to know that. She weighed it in her palm for a long moment, looked at him swaying, barely staying on his feet, blood dripping from his arm, then slid the gun into her coat pocket, her decision made. God had a plan for her, all she had to do was follow it.

"You're not going to be much help if you pass out again," she told him. "How about if you sit down and let me take a look at that arm?"

Her mother would have approved.

Despite the snow—or maybe because of it—Goose decided to take his Harley instead of his truck. He needed to clear his head. Navigating treacherous curves with the wind blowing in his face was the fastest way.

He drove into Cherokee but instead of heading through it to the edge of the reservation where the VistaView was located, he stopped at a small family-run motel, parked his bike out of sight, and went to a room in the back.

A woman answered the door. She wore a black leather vest, jeans, and tattoos. One of them said: PROPERTY OF WILSON. "You're late."

Goose didn't reply, merely walked past her to where Wilson sat at a small table holding a cold can of beer against a black eye that was swelling fast. Wilson looked suspiciously like a young Jimmy Buffett. Except instead of a Hawaiian shirt and flip-flops he wore a Harley Davidson T-shirt and steel-toed boots heavy enough to crack ribs.

"Nice timing on starting the fight." Goose took the beer Karlee handed him, touched cans with Wilson in a salute, and popped the tab.

"Hope it was worth it. Did it buy you enough time to search the vans?"

"Got to the support van from Georgia and the one from Daytona. The cash isn't there."

"There's no way in hell they're hiding three million in a bunch of saddlebags." Wilson gave up on the eye and cracked his own beer open.

"You sure you heard right?" Karlee asked, leaning against the wall behind Wilson. Her tone implied that not only didn't she trust Goose, but she seriously questioned his competence as well.

Goose didn't bother wasting a glare on her. Instead he focused on Wilson. "Poppy said over three million was coming in this weekend and that the poker run was the perfect cover."

Ordinary citizens had no idea the Reapers operated a huge money-laundering business, servicing most of the drug, gunrunning, and prostitution operations in the Southeast. Not only was it how the Reapers stayed in business, it posed a lot less risk than actively participating in dealing drugs or guns themselves—crimes that often attracted unwanted federal attention, not to mention biker-on-biker violence.

It had taken Goose over a year to get the inside scoop on the Reapers' cash operation. All he needed was for everything to go right this weekend and he'd be home free by Monday morning.

"Maybe Caruso's bringing the cash himself?" Wilson asked.

The national president would be traveling with his own entourage, including a support vehicle. "Maybe. Seems risky, though."

"Risky, but smart. Only people near it would be hand-picked by him."

"When is he getting here?" Karlee asked.

"He's due in this morning. Supposed to lead Church tomorrow night after the run, followed by a big party."

Karlee pushed off the wall, bouncing with anticipation. "So, problem solved. You find the cash and we go in for the score."

Goose finished his beer and stood to leave. They made it all sound so easy. Conveniently forgot it was his ass on the line if the Reapers ever suspected he was betraying them.

"Is Caitlyn Tierney going to be a problem?" Wilson asked. "If so, we can do something about her."

Goose hesitated. Remembered the way Caitlyn had strode into the clubhouse, fearless. Reckless. Last thing he needed was to be worrying about her sweet ass in addition to his own. "Yeah, that might be a good idea."

CHAPTER TWENTY-THREE

Lena watched Bernie sleep. She'd stopped the bleeding and cleaned the gashes as best she could. He'd fainted again—not from blood loss, just from the sight of it. Made her wonder if she was mistaken and he wasn't the man who took her. After all, twice already he'd stood between her and danger, saved her life.

He fell asleep in the kitchen chair, obviously exhausted. Fine with her, it gave her a chance to search the cabin, see if he was who he said he was. Her mom and roommate always said she was too trusting; this seemed a good time to be a bit skeptical.

She found nothing to make her suspicious of him. Besides pieces of the stripped motorcycle, Bernie's decor reminded her of her own room in Durham: books, books, and more books. His were all classic pulp science fiction and mystery, dog-eared dime store copies. And comics. Boxes and boxes of *Avengers* and *X-Men* and others she'd never heard of. He had a TV/VCR but it got no reception, which explained the stacks of videos that looked like they'd been collected from garage sales, most missing their cases. Classic movies and TV shows, none newer than the last century.

He snuffled in his sleep, a raspy noise that made her wonder if he was coming down with something. Poor guy didn't seem like much slumped in the chair asleep. The only threatening thing about him was the Grim Reaper tattoo across the back of his neck and scalp. She bet that hurt, getting a tattoo there.

A thud came from the roof followed by the sound of heavy footsteps. The leopard back again, letting them know it was watching, waiting. Lena shuddered. She didn't like being at the bottom of the food chain.

There'd been no sign of the chimps but there also wasn't anything she could do to help them if the leopard was stalking them. Just like there was nothing left she could do to help Bernie. Funny. Things weren't really much better, but she wasn't scared anymore. As if last night and almost dying had burned it out of her. Or maybe it was something about Bernie. Maybe God had sent him to her in answer to her prayers—or maybe He'd sent Lena to Bernie to save him? Who knew? She ate peanut butter smeared on a banana, drank some of his milk, sat by the window, and waited for the sun to rise.

Whatever it was that God had in store for her, at least now she had someone to share the burden with. A man brave enough to stand between her and danger.

She didn't understand the danger, had no idea what she'd stumbled into. But for the first time in days—no, years, since her mom and Vonnie died—Lena felt like she wasn't fighting alone.

* * *

Running, she was running through the trees, blood on her hands. So much blood. She stopped. Stared at her hands. Started to scream.

"Caitlyn. Caitlyn, wake up." A man's voice silenced her screams.

She blinked away the blood. Saw Paul leaning over her. "You're having one of your dreams." He crouched down beside her chair, pulled her close to him, his warmth easing her shakes. "I thought I should wake you before—"

Before she began screaming in real life. Like she had so many times before.

She pushed him away, sucked in a breath to steady herself. Paul knew too many of her vulnerabilities. She'd taken that—him—for granted. Started to depend on his strength rather than her own. Fine when she was recovering from brain surgery and almost being killed by a psychopath. After all, who could resist Paul's easy smile and the way he offered comfort so readily? She'd thought she wanted dependable, reliable—that was Paul. Now she realized it was a mistake. Big mistake.

She needed to depend on herself, not someone else. Not even someone as nice as Paul.

"I'm fine." The tremble in her voice said otherwise. "What time is it?"

"It's around six." He slid onto the other chair, his gaze never leaving her face. She turned away from his scrutiny. "Don't you think it's time you told me about your father?"

She breathed in and out again. The air in the room felt heavy—or maybe that was her heart. Weighed down by memory. And the thought of leaving Paul. She felt like she owed him this, the final answer, the reason why she could never be with him. Be with anyone. "I never told you how he died, did I?"

"No. Just that you were the one who—that you found him."

She nodded even though she still faced away from him. "I was nine. My dad worked long hours. Four days or nights a week for the sheriff, then days off he'd work for my best friend's father, Eli Hale, help him build houses."

"Hale. And now you're searching for his daughter."

"Lena. Eli's youngest. Just a baby when I saw her last. Anyway, it was a beautiful spring day and my father wasn't working so I skipped school and stayed home, hid beneath the porch—my favorite hiding place, warm in the winter, cool in the summer. Dry most of the year. I thought my father would be fishing, such a beautiful day, and I wanted to go with him."

She remembered the sun slanting through the latticework, casting shadows on the packed earth at her feet. So warm. Dad would be angry with her about missing school but he'd also laugh at her boldness. He always told her never to be afraid to be brave or bold if she knew it was the right thing. And with so much going wrong in Evergreen recently, she knew taking her father fishing, making him laugh and forget his worries if only for a day, was the right thing to do.

"The grown-ups were all so worried and frightened," she continued. "Tommy Shadwick had been killed on the reservation a few weeks before. Beaten to death with a hammer and his house burned down. Folks whispered and locked their doors for the first time ever. But us kids, to us it was all an adventure—something exciting had finally happened in our tiny, dreary town."

He scooted his chair closer to hers, wrapped his arms around her from behind. Sheer reflex had her leaning into his embrace. She just couldn't help herself. At least that was her excuse. "Your dad, he was investigating this man's death?"

"No. Tribal police were. And the FBI. The sheriff was working with them, of course. But Tommy Shadwick's death was more than a case to Dad. He wasn't sleeping, was always arguing with Mom and Mr. Hale. Mr. Hale was getting ready to do something Dad didn't want him to do, something Dad thought was wrong. We didn't understand it at the time—all we knew was every time we walked in a room with the grown-ups, they'd shush and send us away. Then came the day Mr. Hale came and told my dad to arrest him. Said he'd killed Tommy Shadwick. They found the hammer in his truck, blood still on it. My dad came home that night, didn't know I was awake, waiting for him. First time I ever saw him cry."

Paul stiffened and she realized he'd already figured out the ending of her sorry story. "So that day you skipped school—"

"I fell asleep under the porch. The sound of the shots woke me up. I ran upstairs. And there he was. Blood. Gun at his hand. Dead. All because of Eli Hale. I learned later Dad had initially provided an alibi for Eli. Even after Eli confessed, Dad maintained his innocence, said he couldn't have done it. But obviously he was wrong. Eli killed that man. Just like he killed my dad—or good as."

"So that's why you're always running. You need to abandon everyone before they have a chance to abandon you." His hands tightened around her, and he lay his head on her shoulder. "You can stop your running now. I'm here for the long haul, Caitlyn."

Yes, but was she? She rubbed at the scar on her temple,

drew in her breath, searched for the courage to tell him the truth: she was broken, damaged beyond even his ability to heal. But she couldn't find the words. Knowing herself a coward, she pulled free of his embrace. "What are you, a radiologist or a shrink?"

His smile was forced but he didn't push the issue. "I'm whatever you need me to be."

"Well, right now I sure could use a fresh pair of eyes and someone who knows their way around a search engine." She showed him the materials she'd listed from Lena's research and law review project. "Think you can help me fill in the blanks?"

"Sure, no problem. Are you going to get some sleep?"

She wished. "No. I need to visit an old friend. It won't take long."

"Your mom and uncle invited us to brunch at eleven. I think it'd be nice if we both were there. On time." Paul was ten minutes early for everything, just like her mom. Drove her crazy that to them being on time—give or take a minute or two—was the same as being late.

"Don't worry, I'll be there."

Goose about shit himself when he got back to the VistaView and Tierney wasn't in her room. No way he was about to tell Poppy he screwed up.

He still had no idea where the law student fit into anything, but if Wilson did his job, Tierney wouldn't be a problem after today. Then all they'd need would be to find the cash.

He found Tierney's car in the garage and placed a GPS tracker on it. Then he went to bed, his cell phone and laptop set to alert him of any activity. Surprisingly it was the laptop that buzzed him awake at around six in the morning, the keystroke recorder faithfully creating a copy of everything Tierney did.

Nice. Now that he had her password, once she logged off, he could gain access to her computer. From the WiFi code, she had moved to room 313. He couldn't see the result of her Internet searches but he could see what she was searching for. What the hell was she working? Some kind of antique fraud involving Indian artifacts? She was looking at stuff from the eighteen hundreds but also checking out the Reapers and Poppy and some Indian guy who got killed a quarter century ago.

Maybe she was sleep surfing. Because he sure as hell couldn't fit it all together.

One thing for sure. This was about a lot more than some missing law student.

His curiosity nagged at him and he set about re-creating her searches on his machine. No links that he could find between the tribal elder's death and the Reapers, but he did figure out what she was looking for in the Eastern Band's history. The elder dude was opposing some law that would allow the descendants of the Cherokee's black slaves to become tribe members. And his argument was based on something called the Freedmen Pact that the tribe had negotiated way back after the Civil War. Mirroring Caitlyn, he searched for a copy of the pact but came up empty.

That's when his phone alarmed. Tierney was on the move. But how could she be? She was still typing on her computer.

Shit. It was the boyfriend doing all the searches on the Indians. Probably the only thing Tierney had checked out was the Reapers. Made sense, the guy looked like an academic, had no clue how to handle himself in the real world. What did a woman like Tierney see in a guy like that anyway?

He grabbed his laptop, shoved it into his bag, and ran down to his bike. He could just leave her to Wilson and Karlee, but something about Tierney pulled at him. That pixie haircut, the scars she didn't hide, the way she faced the world head-on . . . he had no idea but he couldn't deny the temptation.

Wherever Tierney was going, he was going with her.

CHAPTER TWENTY-FOUR

It never hurt to play nice with the locals—in fact, compared with her colleagues at the Bureau, Caitlyn was usually pretty darn good at it. Blame it on her dad, but she had a soft spot for small-town law enforcement, understood the pressures they were under and the uphill battle they fought with limited resources.

Despite it being a Saturday morning, Sheriff Markle was in his office, sipping coffee with one hand and hunting and pecking on a keyboard with the other. No sign of a secretary, probably couldn't afford the overtime, so Caitlyn knocked on his open door to announce herself.

"I should've made an appointment," she said. "You look busy."

"It's this damn poker run. Got all my men working traffic." He looked up, nodded to the chair in front of his desk. Leaned back in his own, both hands wrapped around his mug of coffee. Didn't offer Caitlyn any—not that she wanted any, from the looks of the brown stains on the coffeemaker sitting on the credenza behind him. "So, what can I do for the FBI?"

She tried a conciliatory smile. "Not the FBI. Just me."

"Just you." He took a sip of coffee and considered that. "Daughter of an old friend, former colleague, guess I can spare you a few minutes. What can I do for you, Caitlyn Tierney?"

"I'm still looking for Lena Hale."

"Right." He tapped his computer screen. "Durham PD issued an ATL, so my guys are all looking for her or her vehicle."

The attempt to locate would help—if any law enforcement officer spotted Lena's Honda and ran the plates through NCIC, it would show up.

"I was hoping you could tell me more about the research she was doing here," Caitlyn said. "Her roommate told me she was researching Cherokee tribal laws from the eighteen hundreds, but you said she was asking about my dad's death. I don't get how the two could possibly be related."

"You know anything about the man Eli Hale killed?"

She decided to play dumb. Better to hear it firsthand from someone involved in the investigation than old newspaper articles. "Just that he was an Eastern Band tribal elder. That's what bought Hale the federal time. And that my dad thought Hale was innocent."

"Elder's name was Tommy Shadwick. Good guy but liked the limelight—always had to take the opposing view on anything, just so he could have his say. Know the type?"

"I've worked with a few."

"Pain in the butt. The council would approve something, say, new street signs so emergency crews could get where they needed to be faster. Then at the last minute, Tommy'd insist they be printed in both English and

Cherokee. You got any idea how expensive and time consuming it is to hand-letter a few hundred street signs? In reflective paint, no less? But that was Tommy. Said he just wanted to keep the tribe connected to their roots."

"Isn't that out of your jurisdiction?"

"Sure. But around here there's a lot of miles to patrol and not so many lawmen to do it. So me and the tribal police chief, we keep in touch. Try to have lunch together every week or so. Sometimes the Bryson City chief or the chief ranger from the park stops in as well. Kind of a mutual-aid, intelligence-sharing thing."

"So this Tommy Shadwick was a bit of a rabble-rouser. What was Hale's beef with him?"

"Now, that's where the ancient history comes in. You've heard of the freedmen?"

"Yes."

"Hale wanted his family reinstated on the tribal rolls, and Shadwick was blocking it."

Didn't seem like much of a motive for murder. "And that's why Hale bludgeoned Shadwick with a hammer and burned his house down to try to cover it up?"

"Yep. That's what Eli Hale confessed to. It was his hammer. Because of the damage to the body done by the fire, the time of death was only approximate, so your dad's alibi for Hale wasn't enough to clear him. Plus the fire destroyed any other evidence. And did I mention the man confessed?" He shook his head. "Never did understand why your dad stood by him. Refused to let it go. Stubborn." He raised his mug in a salute. "Guess you inherited that from him."

Caitlyn couldn't deny it. Her stubbornness had gotten her into—and out of—more trouble than she cared to admit. "Still, sounds like a pretty circumstantial case. Why didn't Hale just shut his mouth? Any decent lawyer could've gotten him off."

"Guess the guilt got to him. Once he confessed he never wavered on any of the details. Man was like a broken record. He drove to Tommy's house, they argued, he got his hammer from his truck and went back, killed Tommy, doused the body in gasoline, lit a match, and left. The end." A phone rang in the outer office. The sheriff looked past her for a moment, but otherwise ignored it. "Twenty-six years no one ever questioned Hale's guilt or tried to prove him innocent. Except your father and Hale's girl."

"Do you think he was guilty?"

He shrugged. "Not my case, not my call. But why would a guy confess and serve life for something he didn't do?"

Good point. "And my dad's death? Why was Lena asking about him?"

Funny how she shied away from the term *suicide* now. In the past she'd always forced herself to face it head-on—bolstering her armor by refusing to deny it. But now . . . now it didn't feel quite right.

"I'm not sure. There was never any question who killed Sean—you know that better than anyone. It was just you and him at the house, you found him minutes after the shot was fired. Nothing to question."

She sighed. "Yeah. I guess."

The phone rang again. Caitlyn pushed herself to her feet. "Thanks, Sheriff. I appreciate your time."

"You need anything, just holler. Do me a favor, though. Stay away from the Reapers. We got enough on our plates right now with so many of them being around for the poker run."

"I'll try."

His glare said she'd best do better than try.

"What can you tell me about the Reaper you arrested last night? Goose, they called him."

"Goose? You mean Jacob Clay. Never caused me any problems until last night. Some kind of computer software guy from Asheville until his job got downsized. Moved here full-time a little over a year ago."

"He still in lockup? I'd like to have a little chat with him."

"Sorry. Nothing to hold him on—he had a carry permit for the gun. He probably made it home before you did last night."

Great. "And the other one, Weasel?"

"Lionel Underwood. Nothing to hold him on, either. But he's a mean one. A few arrests for assault, extortion, one for kidnapping."

"So why isn't he locked up?"

"Never made it to trial on any of them. Witnesses all either recanted or vanished." He shrugged again but this time it was less resigned, more defensive. "Not much I can do about it. I just pick 'em up. Up to the DA to see they stay behind bars."

Caitlyn made it to the door but then turned back. "Look, you knew my father, right?"

"Sure. Small department. We all knew each other pretty well." His eyes narrowed. Then he opened his hands and spread them wide. "What do you want to know?"

"Well, I guess—" She swallowed, shifted her weight from one foot to the other, suddenly feeling like a little girl. "What was he like? Was he good at his job? I mean, why—I just don't understand—how could—"

She hung her head, blinked fast, trying to force back the emotions that suddenly overwhelmed her. Some professional. She raised her head, ready to let Markle off the hook and beat a hasty retreat with at least some of her dignity intact.

Markle surprised her. He stood, left his desk, and closed the door, shutting out the sounds from the outer office. He gestured to the chairs but Caitlyn shook her head; she didn't trust herself to move without crumbling into a giant jellyfish of grief. Markle leaned against his desk, facing her, but staring past her, giving her some privacy.

"Was Sean Tierney a good deputy? Yes. One of the best. Stubborn, but with a good head on his shoulders— always seemed to understand the truth behind the truth, if you get my drift. Good people skills. Had a way of sizing up a situation, or a person, real fast, then surprising them by coming at things from a whole other direction from what they'd expect."

"But then, why—" She couldn't finish, the image of her father's bloody corpse choking her into silence.

"Why did he do what he did?" She appreciated his tact. So many cops would have used shorthand—*ate his gun* or the like. "I'm not sure. Sean was, well, *intense* is the best word for it. He'd get an idea in his head and you couldn't knock it loose with a two-by-four. And loyal— guess that was his downfall. Too damn loyal. He just couldn't accept it that Eli Hale, his best friend, would go and do something like what he did to Tommy Shadwick." He grimaced. "I guess, in a way, what Eli did broke Sean's heart. You ask me, I think he did it because after being betrayed like that, after realizing how wrong he'd been about a man he trusted, he just couldn't face thinking about what else he could have gotten wrong."

Markle pushed off his desk and reached past her to

open the door once again. "I hope that helps in some small way, Agent Tierney."

Her smile was bitter. "Yes. Thank you. I guess it does." Then she remembered why she'd come here in the first place. "Did Eli Hale have any connection with the Reapers?"

He looked surprised by the question. "No. Hale always stayed clear of any of that. Hardworking family man, surprised us all when he killed Shadwick. Guess it just shows how little you know about anyone."

"What about my dad?"

"Involved with the Reapers? You mean other than arresting them?"

"Yes."

"Guess maybe through your mom. But I doubt it."

"My mom?" Now it was her turn to be surprised.

"Well, her brother. Jimmy McSwain used to ride with the Reapers. Was about ready to join them for real, until your dad set him straight." They reached the outer door, and he opened it for her. "You take care now."

She walked through the door and was halfway to the Impreza before she realized it. Uncle Jimmy had almost joined the Reapers? She couldn't picture him without a suit, much less hanging out with a bunch of bikers. The thought of Uncle Jimmy in biker leathers made her smile. A little piece of family history best left buried.

She got into the Subaru and debated. Where to next? It was only nine forty, plenty of time before brunch and the archives wouldn't be open yet.

Nothing she'd learned here explained why the Reapers were so damn interested in finding Lena. God help Lena if they found her before Caitlyn did.

CHAPTER TWENTY-FIVE

A bright light stabbed at Bernie's eyes. He squinted them tighter, squirmed in his chair. His arm throbbed with pain and a metallic taste filled his mouth. Lena. The leopard. It was going after . . . "Lena, look out!"

He opened his eyes and she was right there. Sitting beside him at the table. "It's okay," she said. "You had a bad dream."

Maybe he was still dreaming. To have her here, in his house, taking care of him. Best dream ever. "What happened?"

"The leopard clawed you. I stopped the bleeding but I think you should see a doctor. I'm worried about infection."

His arm felt heavy; even turning his head to look down at it hurt. But he couldn't leave her. Not with the Reapers after her. "You, you said you came looking for me. Last night. You knew my name."

She got up, poured him a glass of water, and handed it to him. "I was looking for the owner of this land."

"You want to buy the Teddy Roosevelt?"

"No. I'm interested in the freedmen's land. I found an old copy of the pact that said it was in this corner of the reservation. Your land and the national park share boundaries with it. I was going to ask permission to cross your land, see if there was any evidence of my family ever living there."

He frowned. The water wasn't helping to clear his head. Of course, it was hard to think with her big doe eyes staring into his like he had the answers to everything. "Freedmen land? What's that?"

"Land the Eastern Band granted their emancipated slaves. Including my family."

"And you think your family lived up there?" He shook his head, regretted the movement as pain shot down his arm. "No one has ever lived up there. Hunted, yes. But lived, built homes? No. It's too steep, rock ledges, crevasses, waterfalls—about the worst land you could imagine to build on."

She sat back, disappointment clouding her face. Bernie was sorry he was the one to put it there. "No houses? Not even back over a hundred years ago? Maybe there's just no evidence of them left anymore."

He couldn't bear to tell her no. "Maybe. But we have more important things to worry about. You know people are looking for you, right?"

She pushed her chair back, got up to stand behind it, as if she needed protection from Bernie. "Are you the one who drugged me? Why? What do you want? Is it about my father?"

Bernie couldn't face her. He stared down into the empty glass, trying to make sense of how tangled everything had gotten. He'd only been trying to do the right thing. How had it all gone so wrong? "I was trying to save you. That night when you came to the clubhouse—"

"I was looking for you."

"Something you said upset Poppy—he's the leader of the Reapers. Anyway, he sent Weasel—you don't want to meet Weasel, believe me—after you. They were going to hurt you. So I, I—" He fumbled for words to make what he'd done seem less awful. There weren't any. "I needed to get you out of there fast and quiet, so I gave you the drugs I had for the animals. And I brought you here."

She backed away from him, as far back as she could go, until the wall stopped her. "What do you want?"

"Not me. I only wanted to help. I had no idea the drugs would make you so out of it for so long—you were singing and talking gibberish. That's why I locked you up when I had to go back to work. If I didn't show up, they'd know and come looking for you here. So I had to leave. But I was worried you'd hurt yourself or wander off and get lost or something. I'm sorry. I didn't mean to leave you that long."

"How long? What day is it?"

"It's Saturday."

"Two days. You left me two days in that room?"

"A day and a half." Her eyes widened with anger, and he held up his good hand. "I'm sorry, Lena. But they were going to hurt you and I couldn't let that happen. I was trying to protect you, save you." He hung his head. "Guess I didn't do such a good job of it."

So typical, his father's voice echoed through his brain. *My son, the loser.* Dad was right. He was a loser. Only now it was Lena who might pay the price.

She was silent for a long moment, thinking. "Why? What do they want from me?"

"I was hoping you could tell me so we'd know what to

do next." His stomach churned, acid biting the back of his throat. He fumbled in his pocket for his Tums. "Because I have no idea."

Caitlyn decided that despite the sheriff's request, her only option was to talk with Oren Parker, aka Poppy. Given what she'd seen last night, they were probably still at the clubhouse partying. She might even run into Jacob Clay, aka Goose, again—or better yet Weasel, aka Lionel Underwood.

Too bad she didn't have enough proof to arrest the men; wouldn't that be a great way to start the day? But they didn't know that. She might have enough leverage to get a few answers and a direction to follow.

Unless Paul turned up something in his research, learning why Lena had been at the Reapers' clubhouse was the only clue Caitlyn had left.

Both the clubhouse parking lot and the old service station across the street were filled with motorcyclists registering for the poker run, tinkering with their bikes, vendors selling official, licensed Reaper paraphernalia, and food stands. There were even several TV news crews covering the festivities. A Reaper directing traffic stopped her.

"Spectators can park down near the river," he told her, gesturing to a narrow lane on the other side of the clubhouse. "There's free public parking down there, plus a picnic area."

The temperature hovered slightly above freezing, but apparently to the Reapers this was picnic weather.

"I'm here to see Oren," she said, hoping Poppy's real name would get her in.

He frowned and tapped his Bluetooth, passed on her request. "Name?"

"FBI Supervisory Special Agent Caitlyn Tierney." Technically she wasn't here on FBI business, so she didn't show him her credentials, but it wouldn't hurt reminding Poppy that she had a bit more clout than the locals.

The frown turned into a scowl. Then he gave her a grudging nod as he hung up. "You're clear. Go down the drive, past the trailer, to the large white house."

Past the trailer translated into a mile along a gravel drive that climbed up a bluff overlooking the river. The topography and crowded evergreens shielded her from view of the clubhouse, the road—well, just about everything and everyone.

She called Paul, to let him know where she was. No answer. Great. She left a voicemail, hoping he hadn't forgotten his phone in the room. Constantly hounded while at work, he tended to disconnect from communications devices when off duty.

A large white house sat in a clearing that hugged the side of the mountain on one side and had a sheer drop down to the river below on the other. It could have come out of a Norman Rockwell painting. True-blue Americana.

Except for the thirty-odd assorted Harleys parked in the grass and along the drive. Each accompanied by a Reaper.

The drive was circular, which gave her some comfort as she pulled past the glowering bikers. The lane behind her was too narrow to turn around. She decided to forget about confronting the Reapers' leader, simply follow the drive until she was headed back the way she came, and get the hell out of there. Talking to Poppy one-on-one or even half-a-dozen-on-one she was comfortable with. Three dozen to one? No bet.

She almost made it. But just as she passed the house

the men up ahead mounted their bikes and blocked the road. The ones behind her closed off any chance she had of backing up. Seemed like Poppy was as anxious to talk with her as she was with him.

Too bad. She shifted down to second and steered the Impreza across the lawn. He could bill her for the landscaping later. Despite the ground being a bit soft from the melted snow and frost, the Subaru responded nicely, barely a shimmy when she splashed through a large puddle.

Unfortunately, the Reapers had her outnumbered and outflanked. Before she could reach the road again, they had her surrounded, circling their bikes in ever-tighter circles until she had to choose between stopping the car and running one or more of them down.

Mood she was in, she actually considered the later. But they hadn't shown any weapons, hadn't threatened her, were merely trying to intimidate her, so she stopped the car. Besides, if she had run them down, the paperwork would have taken the rest of the weekend—and who would look for Lena?

If she wanted answers she had to play by their rules. They stopped, their bikes circled bumper-to-bumper, revving their engines until the noise was enough to shake the ground. Bullies.

Play by their rules? They had no rules, other than their code: till Death do us part.

Smart money and the FBI's bible would have her remain in the relative shelter of her vehicle. Just sit there and ignore their rude gestures as they laughed at her and suggested couplings that weren't anatomically possible.

She thought back to the agent in training she'd made cry two days ago. The bad guys are just as blinded by adrenaline—and in this case, testosterone—as the good guys, she'd told her. Think beyond that, search the possibilities.

Great advice. So what possibilities did she have here? The Reapers didn't want her dead—that would bring a reign of terror down on them, unwanted scrutiny from every domestic law enforcement agency, local, state, and federal. They did want to send her a message, that much was as obvious as a gorilla beating its chest warning off the competition.

What were they competing for? Lena?

Why?

The rank and file wouldn't know. Poppy might. Which meant getting out of the car.

Only question left was whether to play it like a wolf in sheep's clothing or a sheep in wolf's clothing. They were used to treating women like property. Should she go all meek and docile? It had saved her and Paul last night.

Or give in to her anger and face them head-on?

Then it struck her. They played by their rules—and they'd be assuming she'd be playing by the feds' rules. Which would basically prevent her from striking first or doing anything other than defending herself.

She glanced at all the mirrors in turn as she pulled her ASP from her pocket and made sure her Glock was clear of her coat. She'd be most vulnerable when she climbed out of the driver's seat. Only one chance to get this right.

A few of the Reapers got off their bikes, including one guy the size of the Jolly Green Giant who climbed off a lovingly restored classic Harley with a custom paint job complete with a naked blonde named DEEDEE.

Time for Caitlyn to unleash her inner bitch.

CHAPTER TWENTY-SIX

The sheriff's station made sense, Goose thought as he followed Tierney's Subaru. But Poppy's home? On the morning of a run when the national president had just arrived?

Woman was either a fool or had a death wish.

He sped down the drive to Poppy's house, hoping he was in time to see which. Not that he cared, of course. He had to stay focused on the money. Three million cash. Nothing to sneeze at. Virtually untraceable, given that it came from illegal drug, weapons, and prostitution transactions.

Despite the Reapers' focus on racing and partying, Poppy and Caruso had built a finely tuned criminal enterprise. Almost seemed a shame to throw a wrench in the works. But three million was too much to let the opportunity pass.

When Goose arrived at Poppy's house he saw Tierney had also thrown a wrench in the day's program. The Daytona Reapers, freshly arrived after tearing up the highways in an all-night party/predawn run, had her little Subaru Impreza WRX surrounded. He held back to see how she'd get herself out of this one.

One thing about the fed. She was damn entertaining to watch in action.

One of the Daytona guys, nicknamed Tiny because he was built like a brick wall, got off his bike and lumbered toward Caitlyn's door. Tierney didn't wait for the Reaper. Instead, she threw the door open and popped out of the car in one fast movement. Tiny stopped, shooing the rest of the crowd of Reapers back. Not because he was scared of the gun in Caitlyn's hand—he wanted room to maneuver.

Caitlyn stared him down. Tiny just smiled and shook his head like a buffalo getting ready to charge. The air was so cold his breath steamed, heightening the illusion. But Caitlyn didn't back away or retreat to the relative safety of her car.

Instead she flipped her left wrist, snapping open a weighted extendable baton. Now she had the longer reach, despite Tiny's towering almost a foot above her. His smile turned into a grin, enhanced by the fact that he was missing a few teeth. Beauty and the Beast.

Tiny shuffled like a boxer, moving to his right. Caitlyn did the same, moving to her right. She was also smiling. Why was she smiling? Goose wondered. It was a real smile, showed her dimple, so she wasn't faking it in a show of bravado.

She twisted her wrist, making the ASP crack through the air like a whip, took one more step to her right—and he had his answer.

"Move another step and DeeDee gets her head gasket blown off." She placed the muzzle of her Glock against the naked woman painted on Tiny's Road King Classic.

The Reapers didn't gasp but the air clouded as they all exhaled simultaneously and bared their teeth. You could mess with a man, but mess with his ride? A hanging offense.

No Reaper would risk Tiny's bike. Without shedding a drop of blood, Caitlyn Tierney had taken the entire crowd hostage.

Caitlyn used the ASP like a lance, touching a Daytona prospect on the shoulder. "You. Run inside and tell Poppy I'd like a word."

No one moved while the prospect jogged to the house, up the porch steps, and vanished inside. Well, no one moved unless you counted various grunts and growls and hissed promises as movements. Caitlyn decided it was best to ignore them.

Thankfully the prospect returned before the fire in the not-so-Jolly-Green-Giant's glare could spontaneously combust. "Poppy says come on inside."

Right. Like she was an idiot. "Out here will be just fine, thank you."

The prospect turned toward the house with an elaborate shrug. Moments later Poppy appeared, accompanied by a second man. If Poppy was a cross between Willie Nelson and Jerry Garcia with Charlie Manson's dead eyes, the second man was more of a John Travolta minus the *Pulp Fiction* suit. He wore jeans, biker boots, and a black tee under his black leather cut, but no tatts were visible; he was clean-shaven with a haircut that spoke of an hour in a stylist's chair and a twenty-dollar tip.

She would have pegged him for a hanger-on, some banker biker wannabe, if not for his eyes. Same I-always-get-what-I-want stare as Poppy. Like the men around them were objects, not humans. Then he drew close enough for her to read the patches on his cut. National president. This was Caruso himself honoring her with his presence.

The other Reapers parted, clearing a path for Caruso and Poppy, their expressions filled with respect and macho deference. A few cut their eyes her way, eyebrows raised in anticipation, as if they expected Caruso to call down lightning to strike her dead for her blasphemy.

No wonder they called their club meetings Church.

Caitlyn took the initiative. "Good morning," she called out in a chipper tone. "Beautiful day, isn't it?"

Poppy's glare darkened. Caruso chuckled. "Yes, yes it is. A great day for a ride." Guy even sounded like a bank manager.

They reached the circle of bikes surrounding her and her vehicle. Poppy gave a curt nod to the others and they quickly sped away, leaving just the two of them, Caitlyn holding her gun on the painted nude, and the Giant shuffling from one foot to the other, torn between protecting his bike and obeying his leaders.

Again, Caitlyn took action before they could request or demand anything. Keeping the upper hand was imperative in these kinds of confrontation, but she also didn't want to do anything to push their anger to the point where they'd be forced to act to protect their status.

With a flourish she bent on one knee to slam the ASP against the Subaru's front tire, collapsing the baton. Then she nodded to the Giant and holstered her weapon. He rushed to his bike, rubbed his palm over the nude, checking for the most minute scratches in the paint.

"Go," Poppy said. The Giant gave Caitlyn a death stare that said she'd better never meet him in any dark alleys then revved his bike and pulled away to join the other Reapers gathered in front of the house.

Now it was just the three of them. Oh, and there was Goose, her hunky shadow. All this party needed was Weasel. The hairs on the back of her neck rose at the image of him out there wrecking havoc—and she thought of Paul. She'd left him parked in a front booth at the casino's café, in full sight of anyone on the gaming floor or helping themselves to the buffet. Hopefully he had the good sense to stay there out of harm's way. Knowing him, he was so lost in his research he probably had no clue where he was or what was going on around him. Just like when he stared at videos of angiograms, following the trail of dye through arteries, veins, and capillaries one frame at a time.

"Do you know who I am?" Caitlyn asked.

"The bitch who won't keep her nose out of our business?" Poppy said.

Goose closed the distance between them, staying within earshot in case he was needed. She kept her hands on her weapons, her weapons at her side, and favored him with a quick glance of acknowledgment. He nodded, keeping his hands where she could see them. Showing a little respect. About time.

"Besides that," she said.

Poppy blew out an exasperated breath. Gestured to Caruso then Caitlyn. "Meet FBI Special Agent Tierney."

"Supervisory Special Agent," she corrected. "Sorry to interrupt." She kept her voice contrite, realizing Poppy needed to save face in front of the national president. "I just have a question or two for Mr. Parker."

Caruso stared at her long and hard before nodding. "Make it quick, we've our own business to attend to."

He turned on his heel and walked back into the house. Caitlyn arched an eyebrow at Goose, but instead of leaving he sidled closer to Poppy and crossed his arms over his chest, settling his weight like he was the Rock of freaking Gibraltar. Fine. Whatever.

Poppy rocked on his heels, appraising her. "You're the spitting image of your old man. He was a pest, too."

Caitlyn decided to take that as a compliment. "Thanks. How about if you tell me about Lena Hale? Make life easier for us both."

"I wish I knew anything. I really do." He sounded almost sincere. Except for the flat gaze that never wavered. Usually Caitlyn's habit of staring made others look away, but this time she was the one fighting the urge to break eye contact. "If you find her, let me know. I have my guys searching—figure last thing we need is blame for some missing law student lost in the mountains."

"Seems funny the last place she was seen was your clubhouse."

"Told you. She asked for directions and left." They stared at each other in silence for a few seconds. This time Poppy was the one to break. "You calling me a liar?"

She was silent, assessing any potential chinks in his armor. Caruso appeared on the porch steps, beckoning to Poppy.

"Let me know if you find that girl. It'd surely ease my worries." He walked away, Goose falling in step behind him.

Frustrated, Caitlyn hopped into the Impreza and drove off before any of the Reapers—especially DeeDee's owner—got the bright idea of stopping her. If she hurried, she'd make it to the VistaView in time for brunch.

Lena sank to the floor, hugging her knees to her chest. She almost wished she was back in her tiny closet. Things were so much easier there. Just her and God working a plan. Who knew escape would lead to more danger and confusion than ever before?

"You thought some bikers wanted to kill me and that's why you kidnapped me?" She was glad she had the gun. Maybe Bernie wasn't the nice guy he appeared to be. But, despite doing all the wrong things—oh, so very wrong—he genuinely seemed to be doing them for the right reasons.

"Yes. I couldn't let them hurt you." His voice was pleading for her to understand and trust him. Could she?

"But you don't know why they wanted to kill me?"

He frowned, his eyebrows coming together in one scraggy ridge that shadowed his eyes. "Poppy told Weasel they couldn't take any more chances that you wouldn't find out. That's all I heard." His face cleared and he met her gaze. "Does it help?"

"Wouldn't find out what?"

He shrugged, winced with pain. His face was flushed, and she wondered if he was getting a fever. Who knew what kind of germs leopards carried?

"Why do you have leopards and chimps here in the middle of the mountains?"

"I saved them." His grin made him look like a little boy on Christmas morning. "The Reapers were going to let them loose, have hunters pay to shoot them. So I took them. Just like I took you. Gave them a new home." His smile faded. "Only the leopard worries me. Won't eat. And the chimps got away the first night—they've been running around, teasing me ever since."

His concern for the helpless animals—well, not as helpless as Bernie thought, obviously—made her want to like him. And stealing them from a biker gang? He'd risked a lot to save them. Just as he'd risked everything to save her. "Aren't you worried about the leopard being loose? What if it goes after someone else?"

"No one else up this far on the mountain. It'd have to go through the woods around to the other side to reach the trout farm and below that the Tierney house and of course your dad's old place." He stirred in his chair. "I read that they're nocturnal, so I'm hoping it goes back for the meat I left in the lodge. I left the front door open. Maybe I can trap it again before it gets hurt."

"Leopards don't eat chimpanzees, do they?" she asked, worried she hadn't seen Smokey since last night. She pushed to her feet and ran to the window. Nothing moved outside except for wind pushing snow across the lawn in swirls of white.

Bernie struggled to stand and joined her. "No. I don't think so."

He didn't sound very certain. She looked at him once more. He seemed different from the guys she usually hung out with. Not dumb. Just . . . simple. Innocent. Childlike.

Then she noticed the sweat rolling off his forehead. She touched his cheek with the back of her hand. Hot. Too hot. He turned his face away, his blush deepening—or was it the fever?

"I'm sorry I ever got you mixed up in this," he mumbled, sagging into her arms. She barely made it to the bed, gently laid him across it. "Should have known I'd screw up." His eyes fluttered shut.

"Bernie. Wake up. Bernie!"

No response. It was up to her. No idea what was going on, where to find help—or who she could trust.

CHAPTER TWENTY-SEVEN

When Caitlyn got back to the VistaView, Paul was right where she'd left him, undisturbed, nose deep into her laptop at the restaurant on the main floor. "Turns out this freedmen thing is a big deal," he said when she slid into the booth beside him. "We're talking a lot of money if they become full tribal members, especially if you added it up retroactively."

"Worth killing for?"

"I guess so."

"But what would the Reapers have to gain by getting rid of Lena? The Reapers have no claim with the tribe."

"Maybe someone with the tribe is paying them to protect their interests?"

She frowned. Sounded desperate. Especially as the court rulings on the Oklahoma case were mostly in favor of the Cherokee Nation. Why go to such extremes? "No. There has to be more going on."

"Well, Lena's research was correct. Her family and twenty-one others were included on the tribal rolls of 1883. The other families have all moved away, generations ago.

Even the Hales haven't lived on the reservation since the only surviving Hale son returned home from World War One." He shook his head. "All that history, lost."

"Not entirely. There must be something left that Lena found. Enough to get her father killed." *And maybe Lena as well,* she didn't add.

Paul shut the laptop and stood. "We're late."

"Aren't we meeting down here?"

"No. Your uncle is having brunch served up in his penthouse." He grinned. "I can't wait to see the view from up there. He gave me the code to his private elevator. C'mon."

She groaned but stood and followed him out. "So no leads for me to follow up on?"

"I found a name. A librarian at the tribal archives." He wove his way through the crowds around the slots like an old pro and led her to a secluded elevator.

"Good. Who is it?"

He shook his head and punched in the code. The doors opened immediately. "Oh no. I give you the name and you'll rush off to ruin some poor librarian's weekend and leave me holding the bag with your mother and uncle. Not going to happen."

"Paul—" Her ears popped as the elevator whisked them to the penthouse suite on the eleventh floor. Altitude or the effort of swallowing her frustration with him, she wasn't sure. "Just give me the name."

"I'll text it to you. After we eat." The doors opened onto a panoramic view of the Smoky Mountains. "Better yet. I'm coming with you."

Before she could protest, Uncle Jimmy and her mother rushed into the foyer to greet them.

"Caitlyn," her mom said, taking her arm. Today Jessalyn wore a simple navy sheath dress with a gold-and-navy brocade jacket. "You're late. What have you been doing?" She brushed her fingers over Caitlyn's coat. "There's mud all over you."

Being surrounded by bikes in a field could do that to you. "I took a drive, sorry if we're late."

"No matter. We're all here now. Isn't this lovely?" Jessalyn gestured at the skyline and the sumptuous feast waiting on a chrome-and-glass table covered in linen and silver-gilded china. Caitlyn looked down at her muddy jeans and boots. Brunch. Wasn't that supposed to be scrambled eggs and waffles? Maybe throw in a fruit plate?

This looked like the final supper on the *Titanic*. Platters of salmon and roast beef, eggs Benedict, broiled tomatoes and ham, shrimp bigger than her thumb arranged in a circle around a martini glass filled with cocktail sauce . . . and those were only the dishes she could identify. Two waiters flanked the doors to the kitchen, ready to spring into action. If Jimmy was trying to impress, he'd succeeded.

Jessalyn appeared to be right at home, walking directly to her seat at the far end of the table to Jimmy's right, waiting for Jimmy to pull her chair out for her. Paul hurried to do the same for Caitlyn, but too late, she'd already taken care of it herself. Jessalyn threw a disapproving glance her way. Caitlyn ignored it, realizing her stomach was ready to rebel if she didn't give it something to digest.

She reached for the eggs. Jessalyn shook her head. Jimmy cleared his throat and raised a champagne glass filled with a pomegranate mimosa. "It's not often that I get the chance to entertain such lovely company." He nodded to Paul and Caitlyn. "I'd like to propose a toast. To family."

Paul and Jessalyn chimed glasses as Caitlyn grabbed hers and did the same. "To family."

She took a sip, the bubbles tickling her nose, then set the glass down and reached for the real food once more. That's when her phone rang.

"Sorry," she said, glancing at the number and seeing it was a Quantico extension. "I really need to take this." She looked longingly at the spread, grabbed a strawberry, and, ignoring her family's irritated expressions, headed out to the foyer. "Tierney."

"You picked the worst day ever to skip work. I hope you're lying in a hospital bed somewhere with a doctor's excuse."

"Gee, nice to talk to you, too, LaSovage. What's the problem?"

"The assistant director came to observe the evaluations yesterday. That's the problem."

By taking a leave day, she'd left him a man short. "I'm sure you found someone to fill in as a bad guy."

"You don't get it, Caitlyn. It's not *my* problem. It wasn't me he wanted to observe."

A waiter walked past, asked if she needed anything. She shook her head and mouthed, "I'm fine." Then LaSovage's words penetrated. "Yates was there to see me?"

"Bingo. He heard about what happened Thursday."

"Thursday?" So much had happened since then she had to rack her brain to remember what he was talking about. "You mean with those new agents in training?" One of whom she'd made cry.

"Guess someone told him. Welcome to the new FBI, guaranteed no more tears."

"But I didn't do anything wrong—"

"Caitlyn, Caitlyn." He sighed. "You don't get it, do

you? They want you out. You don't have to do anything wrong, you just have to not do everything right."

"Nothing I can do about it now."

"Actually, there is. That's why I'm calling. Yates left a message that he wants you back here. Today."

"Is he coming to supervise the training—wait, it's Saturday, there is no training scheduled."

"There wasn't any. But I'm putting together a little extracurricular project." His voice brightened. "I think you'd have fun with it, actually. We're expanding off your impromptu scenario from the other day."

Jessalyn appeared, looking angry. Uh-oh. "That's nice, but I'm tied up with my mom and uncle. I can't make it back today."

"What should I tell Yates if he asks?"

Caitlyn hesitated, torn. Family or job? Choosing either would mean abandoning Lena. And Caitlyn was the closest thing to family Lena had left.

"Tell him family comes first." She hung up even as Jessalyn reached out a hand, ready to snatch the phone from her like she was a nine-year-old again.

"Come here, we need to talk," her mother said with that she-who-must-be-obeyed tone Caitlyn loved to rebel against.

"But Jimmy and Paul—"

"Can wait." Jessalyn led Caitlyn into a large study with a wall of windows, velvet curtains, chrome-and-glass tables surrounding two large black leather couches. She whirled on Caitlyn. "You need to quit this foolishness. Right now."

"You mean looking for Lena?"

"I mean the FBI." Jessalyn blew out her breath, her lips pursing to reveal wrinkles Caitlyn had never noticed before. "All I've ever wanted is what's best for our family. What's best for you. I've sacrificed everything for that."

"How is my quitting my job what's best for me or the family?"

Jessalyn's gaze focused on the scar running up Caitlyn's sternum toward her throat. Her souvenir from a psychopath. "The FBI has almost gotten you killed twice now. Sweetheart, do you have any idea what that does to a mother? Especially after your father—"

She looked away, blinking hard. Jessalyn never could talk about how Sean Tierney died; in twenty-six years this was the closest she'd ever come. At least with Caitlyn.

"Mom, it's okay." Caitlyn's anger drifted out of reach as she comforted her mother with a hug. Arguments with Jessalyn always ended this way. "Nothing's going to happen to me."

"You don't know that." Tears brimmed in Jessalyn's eyes, threatening to spill over. "You can't know that. After everything I've been through I don't think it's too much to ask. If you like detective work, Jimmy can put you on at the casino. Sneaking around undercover, catching card cheats. At least it wouldn't be dangerous. And I could finally sleep at night without worrying that I'm going to get another call—"

She broke down, collapsing onto the couch without even smoothing her dress to prevent it from wrinkling. That's when Caitlyn realized this wasn't one of their usual melodramatic arguments about trivial matters blown out of proportion. Jessalyn was truly worried, scared even.

Caitlyn heaved out a breath as she sat beside her mother, one arm around Jessalyn's shoulders. Her mom never showed this much emotion—drama, yes, but never true tears. She never let her guard down far enough to expose her heart. It was something she and Caitlyn had in common.

"Mom, I can't quit. It's my job, my life. I've fought so hard to get where I am—"

"Your life? You mean your death. Caitlyn, if you don't quit, that job is going to kill you." The tears splashed from her eyelashes down onto her cheeks, streaking her impeccable makeup. "Please. I've never asked anything from you, but I'm asking you now. Caitlyn, you need to quit. I'm begging you."

Her mother was right: Jessalyn had never asked her for anything. Although she'd made it perfectly clear that she'd given up everything when she left Evergreen to give Caitlyn a better life. Away from all the turmoil surrounding her father's death. All her mother had ever expected in return was for Caitlyn to love her and be a good daughter. Caitlyn was the first to admit that maybe she'd done the first but failed at the second. Could she refuse her mother's one request now?

Paul had basically asked her to leave her job as well. And her bosses at the FBI would love it if she made life easy for them and quit before they had to find a place for her. They were just biding their time until they could find cause to dismiss her without embarrassing the Bureau. Did Caitlyn really want to work in that kind of atmosphere?

She slid her arm away from Jessalyn, touched her fingers to the scar at her temple. Maybe Mom and Paul were right. She couldn't believe she was even thinking it, but maybe they were all right. She should quit while she was ahead.

Standing, she turned to the window and drew back the

curtain. The mountain vista was comforting, welcoming her home. To her real home.

A life without the Bureau. She couldn't even imagine it. Her entire life she'd dreamed of being a FBI agent. It wasn't just her dream, it was her dad's, the one thing she could do for him, know he would be proud of her even if he wasn't here to see it.

What would Dad do? She pressed her palm against the cold glass rattling in the winter wind cutting across the mountain range. Would he want her to quit, take the easy way out?

Anger spiked through the memory of his face, his blood. Just because he took the easy way out . . .

Jessalyn sensed her ambivalence, rose and stood behind her. "You don't have to decide now. Take some time off. Go to the beach with Paul. You deserve a break."

"I can't. Lena—"

"Lena isn't family. You don't even know the girl. She's none of your concern. Besides, you said yourself the local authorities could do a better job in finding her. It's not your case. You need to take time, focus on what really matters, what you want for your future." She lay her hand on Caitlyn's shoulder, rubbing her arm in slow, soothing motions, just as she had when Caitlyn was a little girl.

Seemed like Caitlyn had spent most of her life learning how to calm down, swallow her anger and outrage. Jessalyn had taught her well. Maybe that's really why she needed her job. Not just for the prestige of working for the FBI, of living her father's dream. She needed it because it let her channel the emotions she kept buried into something productive, something bigger than her.

A chance to change the world. Stop the bad guys. Maybe save lives.

Even save herself.

The Bureau frowned on the idea of its agents being heroes. Indoctrinated them into understanding that they were simply well-trained cogs in a paramilitary machine, following orders, protecting their country and its citizens. They were anything but "special," replaceable by the next agent waiting in line to serve and protect.

And Caitlyn refused to serve. At least not blindly. She'd risen fast—promoted to supervisory special agent years before most—because of her inability to keep her head down and obey orders. She always had to push things, which is how she'd broken the cases she'd broken. The Bureau loved the good press she brought them, hated the truths about their own inadequacies she exposed with her maverick methods, and wanted her either gone or safely encased in a bubble-wrapped office tied down in red tape where she could do them no harm.

She'd hit the ceiling at the FBI. Hit it hard, at meteoric velocity.

But quit?

Shrugging her mother's hand away, she turned around. "I can't, Mom."

Jessalyn's posture went rigid, pulling back from Caitlyn. "You mean you won't. Stubborn, stubborn child. That's what you are. Can't look past yourself to see the way you're hurting the people who love you most."

Sharp words. With an added edge since Jessalyn spoke the truth. Caitlyn blinked back her pain. "I'm sorry. I'm not quitting."

Her mother stepped away, her face twisted with rage and regret. "I'm sorry, too, Caitlyn. Believe me, I'm sorry, too."

She walked out, not even bothering to slam the door on her daughter.

* * *

While the regular club members headed off on the run to Gatlinburg, Poppy and Caruso sat smoking cigars by the fire in the huge stone fireplace that filled one wall of the farmhouse's living room. Goose and the national club enforcer, a guy named Hopper who said nothing, stood guard at the door.

It was meant to be an honor, standing there in the presence of Reaper greatness, but Goose had too many things on his mind to stay still and the conversation between the two presidents was boring. Stuff about enrollment and what to do about members not paying their dues because they were out of work. Caruso talked the way he looked: like he was some kind of CEO of a Fortune 500 company instead of running a bunch of outlaw bikers. It was funny watching Poppy try to mimic the national president's cultured manners, but Goose was itching with a need to get out of there and back to work.

"So you don't want me to keep following Tierney?" he asked during a break while Poppy and Caruso refilled their bourbon glasses. They were drinking the good stuff: Maker's 46.

"Not for now." Poppy and Caruso exchanged glances. "If Weasel isn't back soon, we might have another job for you. Can you handle it?"

"Sure. Whatever you need." It was the only right answer with the chapter president and national president staring you down. "Where is Weasel?"

Goose hoped the club VP was doing something with the cash the Daytona crew brought up with them. Wilson was tailing Weasel in the hope that he'd lead them to the money. They had to find it before the Reapers transferred it to the casino, where it'd be lost forever.

"None of your business," Poppy snapped. Goose returned to leaning against the wall, keeping in the shadows. Waited for Poppy and Caruso to decide what the hell they wanted him to do. Hopper slanted a glare at him with an eye roll that said, *Amateur.*

It'd be great if they put him back on Tierney. Following her gave him the freedom to search for the money. They didn't realize that he could keep perfect tabs on her from his phone and laptop. Of course, watching her in person was more fun, but business before pleasure. He smiled at the memory of how she'd handled the situation earlier, almost reducing Tiny to tears. All without a drop of blood shed.

"He has a point," Caruso said, his words emerging slow as if he'd thought long and hard about the topic. "What are we going to do about your Agent Tierney?"

Poppy jerked, covered the movement by reaching for his glass. "Nothing. There's nothing to worry about."

"You should have told me a fed was snooping around." Caruso's tone was undercut with disapproval.

"You don't need to worry about her. I have leverage if we need to turn her." That made Goose perk up. What kind of leverage could Poppy have over an FBI agent? "And it might be good for business to have a fed in our pocket."

Caruso snorted. "That one isn't about to sit in anyone's pocket. The girl's a firecracker waiting to be lit."

Silence. Poppy fiddled with his cigar, relighting it, then took another swallow of bourbon. Caruso lounged in his chair, feet stretched out, crossed at the ankle, and watched the older man.

Finally Poppy spoke. He didn't look at Caruso, instead

stared into the bottom of his glass. "What do you want me to do?"

"Get rid of her. Now. Before we move the money."

Goose tried to act casual, hide his excitement. They hadn't moved the money to the casino yet. There was still time for him to find it.

Poppy nodded, set his empty glass aside. "Let me make a few calls. She won't be a problem."

"No. I don't mean send her away." Caruso glared at Poppy as if suspecting Poppy of treason. It was clear Poppy had deliberately misunderstood the national president's order. "I mean take care of business. Today."

Shit. Was Caruso nuts? He'd just ordered a hit on a federal agent.

Poppy's face blanked. He nodded. "Of course."

The front door burst open and Weasel stomped inside. "Son-of-a-bitch. I told you that kid was a liability." He stopped short when he noticed Caruso. "Oh, sorry."

Sorry? Hell, even Weasel was intimidated by Caruso. So far the national president hadn't impressed Goose as anything other than a politician with his fake smiles and handshakes, but there must be something he was missing given the way the other Reapers deferred to the man. Caruso didn't even have a TCB patch on his cut, although it was obvious he had no trouble giving the order to have someone killed. Typical manager. Didn't get his hands dirty.

"Excuse me a moment," Poppy said, rising.

"Anything I need to know about?" Caruso's tone was relaxed but not his gaze. Goose had a feeling the national president knew everything going on with the Mountain Men and wasn't too happy with Poppy's leadership.

"No. Just one of our prospects slacking off."

"Can't have that. You should make an example out of him." Caruso puffed on his cigar.

Poppy's shoulders went rigid. "You're right. We will." Poppy joined Goose and Weasel, motioned them across the hall to the dining room. "What'd you find?" he asked Weasel.

"Bernie was a no-show so I went by his place. Didn't make it but two steps into the lodge when I found part of a dead deer—"

"*Inside* the lodge?"

"Yeah. Parked there like it was a freaking all-you-can-eat buffet. It gets better. There was a leopard chewing on it. The kid stole our freaking leopard!"

Poppy waved that aside. "What about the girl? Any sign of her?"

"I ran out of there and was heading around to see what was in the other cabins, if he had our other animals, when I found her car. He has her. But you know that place. The way it's spread out. They see us coming, they'd be off into the woods or they could get the drop on us."

"Drop on us?" Goose said. "That doesn't sound like Bernie." Kid was so gentle-hearted that when he cleaned the clubhouse, he routinely scooped up spiders and ants and took them outside rather than killing them.

"I'm telling you, he's got the girl up there with those animals. Kid's gone off his rocker."

"What do you want to do?" Poppy asked.

"I slashed the tires on the girl's car and Bernie's truck, so they're not going anywhere anytime soon. Let me get a few of the boys together and we'll go on our own hunting trip. We'll nail them both and problem solved."

They were talking about killing Bernie—one of their own—and the girl. For no good reason. At least none that made sense to Goose. But he knew better than to argue; it'd only make things worse. Maybe he could get away and call Wilson, have him go find Bernie and the girl, get them away. Warn Caitlyn as well. Wilson would be pissed, the money was his priority, but still—this was murder. Of two innocent kids and a fed. Goose couldn't let that happen.

"Not quite all our problems," Poppy said, glancing over his shoulder into the living room where Caruso waited. "Bernie and the girl can wait. The fed paid us another visit. Embarrassed us in front of Caruso."

Weasel touched the knife on his belt. "Bitch. I'll deal with her."

Poppy shook his head. "Goose says she's been searching the Cherokee archives online."

Goose didn't correct Poppy, tell him he suspected it was Tierney's boyfriend doing the Internet searches. No reason to add one more innocent to the club's hit list.

"Think Lena talked to her?"

"Or maybe Eli Hale somehow got a message to her. Either way, she needs to be dealt with, before she puts the pieces together."

They were serious. No way. He hadn't signed up for this.

They both stared at Goose, assessing him. "What do you say, Goose? Up to taking care of business?"

Despite the chill pouring through his veins, Goose forced his best poker face and nodded. "Whatever the club needs. How do you want it done?"

Poppy clapped him on the shoulder. "Knew you had it

in you. Make it look like an accident. Last thing we need is the feds looking our way."

"I'm on it."

"I'm trusting you and Weasel to finish this. Today."

CHAPTER TWENTY-EIGHT

Caitlyn stared after her mother. Jessalyn always had to have the last word. On everything. But this was different. This felt . . . permanent.

Her mom had worked all her life to make sure Caitlyn was strong enough to face anything. Why couldn't she trust her daughter now?

Caitlyn stood, not noticing the sun playing off the scudding clouds, reshaping the mountains before her eyes. Family first. Jessalyn's creed. How was Caitlyn betraying that by staying loyal to a job she loved?

Confusion warred with resentment. She just wanted to do her job, damn it. But no one, not Jessalyn, not Paul, not the freaking FBI seemed to understand that.

Hell with them. She was going to find Lena Hale. Then she'd figure out the rest.

She left to find Paul waiting for her in the foyer in front of the elevators. "Figured you might be hungry." He handed her a bagel turned into a sandwich, ham and a fried egg shoved between the two halves.

"Thanks." She devoured the starchy concoction without

really tasting it before something else could happen to keep her from eating. They took the elevator downstairs.

"Where to?" he asked.

She was grateful he didn't mention Jessalyn or the fiasco known as family brunch. Appreciated that he didn't ask questions. But hell if she was about to adopt him as a partner in this investigation. "You keep working on the research. I'll go talk to the librarian at the archives. What was his name?"

He smiled. One thing about Paul, when he wanted to, he could charm a snake out of its skin. Even without resorting to his Barry White impression. "You mean the name of the guy waiting to talk to *me*? C'mon. I'll drive."

"I'm driving." That way she could ditch him there among the dusty papers and books. Safest place for him and he'd love it. She'd figure out some special assignment to make him feel important, something esoteric that would take him all day to ferret out, even with the help of the librarian. While she'd hit the streets. Best way to let her do her job and keep him safe. Although Paul probably wouldn't agree if she stopped to discuss it with him.

The archives were one of a row of tribal offices in a modern single-story whitewashed cement-block building with a metal roof. Other than Caitlyn's Subaru the lot was empty.

Turned out the librarian wasn't a librarian at all. He was an archivist. Name of Judas Bearmeat.

"You'll find Bearmeats on the rolls as far back as you can go," he said proudly as he escorted them past an empty reception area and behind a counter. "Including my namesake on the Hester Roll of 1884."

They passed shelves filled with stacks of microfiche, well-tended ledgers, stacks of newspapers, and library card catalog files. In the rear of the building sat a small conference table stacked with books. The corner behind it had been turned into an office without a door or walls. A metal desk sat diagonally across the corner with horizontal file cabinets on either side, one with a tea set and coffeemaker on top, and two metal chairs in front of it, although Caitlyn doubted Bearmeat entertained company very often. He was late fifties, early sixties, with the rapid-fire speech of someone who spent way too much time alone and couldn't shut up when he finally had the opportunity to talk with another human.

"What did Lena ask you to help her with?" Caitlyn cut to the chase while Bearmeat fiddled with coffee for Paul and tea for himself after she declined.

He took his time in answering. It was obvious he would have rathered it was Paul doing the talking—they spoke the same language. Academics. Fine with her. It would keep Paul entertained after she left.

"As I told Dr. Franklin"—Bearmeat nodded to Paul and handed him a cup of coffee in a porcelain cup with the Eastern Band crest on it—"Ms. Hale and I had any number of discussions. She was a delightful lady with a spirited mind. Would have made a fine researcher."

"She's not dead. Only missing," she reminded him. Six minutes in his company and she was already irritated by his pedantic speech. "The last time you spoke with her. What was the topic?"

"As you may know, Ms. Hale was researching Eastern Band rolls and trying to locate other freedmen families in addition to her own. She was curious about how recent court rulings on Oklahoma Cherokee freedmen tribal membership might impact our own freedmen descendants."

"Right, I know. Law review, Supreme Court. But

something got her interested in my father's death. What does restoring her family and the other freedmen to Cherokee rolls have to do with my father?"

Bearmeat sat down with his tea and crossed his legs. He placed a napkin over one knee of his chinos before resting his cup and saucer on it. "And who might your father be?"

"Sean Tierney. He was a Balsam County deputy. Died twenty-six years ago." Bearmeat didn't need to know Sean had killed himself. Or why.

"Tierney. Oh yes, I remember. Lena wasn't so much interested in his death as she was in the Freedmen Pact."

"What's a Freedmen Pact?" Caitlyn asked, about ready to turn Bearmeat into his namesake.

Paul answered. "You know about the Trail of Tears, right? In 1839, when most of the Cherokees were forced off their land and moved to Oklahoma. But a number stayed behind, and many returned to North Carolina. They couldn't own land, but a white man adopted by the tribe, Will Thomas, began buying the land in the Qualla Boundary with his own money for his fellow tribe members. Then came the Civil War. Thomas gathered a company of Cherokees from this area to fight for the Confederacy."

Caitlyn shook her head; dates and history had never been her strong suit. "So they fought on the losing side."

"That's not the point," Bearmeat said. "Owning slaves was abolished by act of the Cherokee National Council in 1863. Then, a year after the Civil War ended, the former slaves, the freedmen, became citizens of the Cherokee Nation in accordance with a treaty negotiated between the Oklahoma Cherokees with the federal government."

"So the freedmen are Cherokees."

"That's the controversy. What Lena was researching."

"You see," Paul said, "the cases have been going through both tribal courts and federal ones since the 1980s. But those cases didn't apply here to the Eastern Band of Cherokees."

Bearmeat took over. The two men were in sync, even though Bearmeat had spent a lifetime studying this and Paul had only had a few hours. If she was less confident and less impatient, Caitlyn might have been intimidated by their intellectual superiority. As it was, she was struggling not to interrupt and ask them to cut to the chase.

"After the Civil War, the Eastern Band made a pact with their freedmen," Bearmeat said. "They couldn't negate the treaty with the federal government, not without risking losing the tenuous status they had gained after siding with the Confederacy, but they realized that their strength, indeed the only way to ensure their continued existence as Cherokees, was to maintain their racial purity. So they formed the pact."

"Still no idea what the pact is." Neither man noticed her tone. If they had, they would have hurried up.

"It was an agreement with the freedmen," Paul explained. "The Eastern Band couldn't just kick them off the reservation, not without repercussions from the government. So they offered the freedmen land for their own use. They could live on the reservation as members of the Cherokee Nation as recognized by the federal government but they would give up their rights as tribal members."

"After the Civil War, most around here couldn't afford to own land. Here inside the Qualla Boundary, the freedmen were given land for free, theirs to use in perpetuity. If they agreed not to seek full tribal membership."

"Why would Lena think my dad had anything to do with a treaty signed over a hundred years ago?"

Bearmeat didn't answer. Instead he rose, carefully placed his teacup and napkin beside the coffeemaker, then pulled open one of the thin flat drawers of the steel filing case it sat on. At first Caitlyn had thought the drawers held maps since they were extra wide and deep but thin. Instead of a map, though, Bearmeat withdrew a large sheet of paper: a facsimile of an old parchment or sheepskin.

He walked past her and laid it out on the empty conference table outside his door. She and Paul followed.

"This is just a modern photocopy," he said, despite the fact that he treated the piece of paper like it was King Tut's tiara. Caitlyn crowded in between Paul and Bearmeat to take a look. There was a flourish of handwritten English on the top and beautifully drawn characters below, followed by a row of signatures. One of the signatures belonged to an Elijah Hale, one of the Hale family ancestors.

"So that's Cherokee writing on the bottom?"

"Correct." He sighed. "We lost the original. Back in 1988."

"That's when my dad died."

Bearmeat shrugged. "No idea about that. Last time I spoke with Lena she was taking a copy of the pact to a Cherokee translator."

Caitlyn's shoulders drooped in disappointment. For a moment there she'd thought the archivist might know what connected her father's death to Lena's disappearance. Maybe even give her a lead, either to Lena or the truth about her dad.

Then Bearmeat looked up from the text of the old document. "Unless—I don't suppose your father had anything to do with Tommy Shadwick's murder? Because he was the last person who checked out the original pact from the archives. Same night he was killed, in fact."

* * *

Bernie was burning up. Moaning in his sleep. His eyes were turning yellow—that couldn't be good. Lena checked his arm where the leopard had scratched him. The wounds weren't bleeding anymore and although they were a little bruised and swollen, there wasn't any redness or signs of infection. Plus, it'd come on so fast. Maybe he'd been sick before the leopard clawed him?

Didn't matter. He needed help. Now.

She searched his cabin. Found parts from motorcycles, dirty laundry, canned goods and frozen dinners, economy-sized bags of dog food, and stacks and stacks of comic books and old paperbacks. Portrait of a lonely man.

But she didn't find what she'd been looking for: a phone or computer. Some way to call for help. She searched Bernie's pockets. Found a handful of bullets. Checked the gun he'd given her, figured out how to open the wheel that held the bullets and found it empty.

He didn't trust her with a loaded gun. Was that because he was trying to fool her or because he wasn't stupid enough to give a loaded gun to a scared girl who'd never held one before?

There was no safety she could find, so she decided it was probably the latter. The leopard still paced the tin roof overhead. The sun was up; shouldn't the animal be in bed?

She gingerly slid four bullets into the little slots on the gun. Then she closed the wheel, snapped it into place so that there were two empty holes lined up for the next shots. That meant she'd have to squeeze the trigger three times before shooting anything. It was the safest way she could think to carry the weapon. And no way she was going outside without it. Not with the leopard still on the prowl.

She arranged a chair between the window and Bernie's bed, alternating between trying to get him to drink some Gatorade and watching for the leopard. Finally it leapt to the ground and vanished into the trees. If she was going to go for help, this was her chance.

"I'll be back," she told Bernie.

He groaned and gripped her hand. Sweat had soaked through his shirt and the sheet. "Don't go. Not safe."

"You need help. I'll be back." She wiped his face with a damp cloth. "Is there a car?"

He nodded. "Beside your cabin. Take my truck. It's cold."

Chills made his teeth chatter and she wasn't sure if he was talking about the weather or his fever.

"Lena." He said her name like it was something special. "Be careful." He slumped back on the pillow, the few words draining him.

She grabbed her coat and glanced once more out the window. No sign of the leopard. Now or never.

The sun was bright enough to have burned away the thick fog that had surrounded the cabin most of the morning. The snow was already melted as well, although clouds building over the mountains to the west promised more to come. She buttoned her coat tight against the wind. The gun felt cold and heavy in her naked hand.

In the light of day, she understood why she'd gotten so disoriented last night. A clearing had been carved out of the forest for the lodge and the surrounding cabins. It was large enough that each cabin had privacy, maybe fifty to sixty feet separating it from its neighbors. Looking toward the center where the lodge stood, its log walls darkened by age, you had the feeling of wide-open spaces. But along the perimeter trees towered over the single-story cabins, swaying in the wind like they were playing Red Rover and daring anyone to leave the cleared space with its illusion of civilization and come over to the wild side.

Past the trees to the south and east was empty sky, only the faintest hint of mountains beyond the valley below. To the north and west, craggy peaks covered in ice and fog, their shadows crowding out the sunlight.

Long way from the Hayti neighborhood Lena had grown up in in Durham. She was totally out of her element.

She bent her head to the wind but tried to keep an eye out for any movement as she hurried across the clearing to the cabin where her little Honda sat beside a big, black pickup truck. As she approached the cars she heard a chattering noise behind her.

"Smokey! You're okay." She pocketed the gun and held her arms open, surprised by how relieved she was to see the chimp. Smokey rushed her, pulling back at the last minute so she didn't bowl Lena over, not hugging her but pressing her nose against Lena's chest, face, neck as she patted Lena's body as if checking for injuries.

"I'm fine. Where are your friends?" Lena looked around. No sign of the other chimps. Hopefully the leopard hadn't gotten them. No. If it had, it wouldn't have been hanging around Bernie's cabin all morning, it would have been feasting.

She took Smokey's hand, feeling better for having the chimp with her. How crazy was that? But in less than a week her entire world had been toppled, everything she believed cast into doubt. All she had left was her faith in God, and even that had been strained. But look what He'd done to deliver her. Sent her Smokey and her family, sent her Bernie just in time to save Lena's life, sent her comfort and solace in the midst of her despair.

As she and Smokey crossed the brown grass made mushy by last night's snow, she sent a quick prayer of thanksgiving aimed at the highest mountaintop above them. A large bird appeared, spiraling upward toward the sun, and she smiled. God was still listening. What more could a flawed human like herself ask?

The answer came faster than she would have liked. Just as they reached the Honda, Lena saw that it had sunk into the mud up to its hubcaps. Tires flat. All of them. The truck's as well.

Someone had been here, done this. Bernie? No, he wouldn't prevent his own escape. All he had to do was hide the keys.

Glancing over her shoulder, she walked around the two vehicles. Bernie's truck keys were in the ignition. So, definitely not Bernie who'd slashed the tires. And not a leopard or bunch of chimps.

She stopped at the passenger side of the Honda on the opposite side from Bernie's truck and the cabin where she'd been imprisoned. Hairs on her neck prickled and she whirled around, expecting to see a man wielding a knife. Nothing. Just wind blowing dead leaves across the lawn.

The feeling of being watched didn't go away. She turned back to the cabin, about to go inside to search for her belongings, when Smokey began making a low, throaty noise and tug at her arm.

Lena looked up. The leopard was on the cabin roof, back legs bent as it prepared to pounce.

CHAPTER TWENTY-NINE

Caitlyn whirled on Bearmeat. "You think Tommy Shadwick was killed because of a piece of paper?"

Bearmeat shrugged. "Do you know almost no one talks about Tommy anymore? Much less the reasons why he died. He was the only council member who opposed the VistaView, thought the casino would corrupt our people. No one remembers that or how he fought to protect our language and culture. Without him we wouldn't be teaching Cherokee in our schools, much less preserving our oral traditions."

All fine and well but it didn't get her closer to understanding why Shadwick was killed or what that had to do with Lena or her dad.

Paul chimed in, "Eli Hale said he killed Tommy because Tommy opposed giving the freedmen tribal membership. Maybe Eli thought destroying the pact as well as eliminating Tommy's opposition would help the freedmen?"

"Destroying the original pact wouldn't help," Bearmeat said. "There are copies here and in Raleigh. In fact, the only reason the original was here was because the tribal council had organized a display of important Eastern Band land grants and deeds for the general meeting where the vote on the casino development would take place. Its value lay in the fact that it was a historical document, not that it was irreplaceable."

More jibber-jabber, still nothing concrete for Caitlyn to follow up. "You said Lena took a copy to an interpreter?"

"Yes, Sharleen LittleJohn. My own Cherokee is rudimentary at best," Bearmeat confessed. "I was raised in Bryson City, didn't return here until after I graduated with my Ph.D." He drew Caitlyn a map on a piece of paper and added directions in careful block print.

"Paul, could you keep working with Mr. Bearmeat?" Caitlyn asked. "I think we're on to something here, I'm just not sure what."

"Sure, okay." He was distracted by a bound selection of old maps lying on the conference table. "Meet back here?"

"Call me if you find anything." She thanked Bearmeat and ducked out before either of the men noticed.

She'd just reached the Impreza when her phone rang. "Is this the fed looking for that black girl?" a woman's voice asked.

"Who is this?"

"Never you mind. You want to find that girl before it's too late, you'd better hurry. She's at her dad's place on McSwain Mountain."

The woman hung up before Caitlyn could ask anything else. Number blocked. Of course.

She sat in the driver's seat waiting for the car to warm up. Using a woman to make the call was smart—they'd think she'd be less wary. Too bad they didn't know Caitlyn's motto—*Trust no one, assume nothing*—had been drilled into her at a young age.

Abandonment issues the bureau shrinks would have diagnosed if she ever gave them a chance. Idiots. A nine-year-old girl finding her father's body, realizing her hero had betrayed her, left her? And then growing up with a mother who treated her more like a roommate than a daughter? No shit she had issues.

But it was those issues, trust, abandonment, whatever you called them, that had kept her alive this far. She wasn't about to change now.

The question wasn't if the phone call was a trap, it was how to use it to her advantage.

The plan was for Weasel to wait for Tierney at the old Hale house. One of his girls back at the clubhouse would call Tierney and send her there while Goose trailed behind to make sure she came alone and to block her escape.

That was the plan. Goose had no intention of carrying it out. As he idled on his Softail on Route 19, waiting for Caitlyn to leave Cherokee, he called Wilson. "How's it going?"

"Weasel isn't going anywhere anytime soon," Wilson said. "I filled his gas tank with water." Better than sugar and less obvious. "He won't know what's going on. I'm headed back to cover Caruso now."

"Did Karlee call the cops?"

"She tried. Talked to a dispatcher, told her about the girl and Bernie. Wasn't sure if they believed her or not."

"They're safe enough with Weasel out of the way," Goose decided. "I'll talk to Tierney, send her after them."

"You sure about this? It could backfire big-time."

"Don't worry, we'll get the money. Without getting blood on our hands."

"It's not the money I'm worried about," Wilson snapped. "It's what the Reapers will do to you if they ever find out."

"It's all cool. Just find that money, I'll take care of the rest." Caitlyn's blue Impreza turned onto 19 from Acquoni Road. "Gotta go. Showtime."

"Be careful."

"Yes, Mother." Goose hung up and put the bike into gear, falling in behind Caitlyn.

Once they were past the VistaView there was little traffic on the road. The bikers on the poker run would be halfway to Gatlinburg or on their way back, and they'd left the tourists behind in Cherokee or at the casino. The road curved up the side of the mountain. He made his move, speeding up to come even with her. She spotted him in her driver's-side mirror and pulled ahead.

Damn it. They were almost to McSwain Mountain Road. He had to stop her before she turned onto it, otherwise Weasel would know he was involved and everything would be ruined. A car coming the other way kept him behind her, riding her bumper, but once it passed, he shot forward once more, motioning to her to pull over.

She surprised him, the Subaru showing some nice giddup-and-go as she swept past him and tore around a sharp curve, out of sight.

He leaned over and geared down even as he sped up and took the curve almost horizontally. Couldn't risk losing her now. There was one last road between here and McSwain Mountain, a dirt road that corkscrewed over the mountain and headed back onto the res, ending up near the trail at Mingo Falls.

He had to get her to either stop and listen to him or

take that road. He came out of the curve and spotted her Impreza, a bright blue dot against the brown of the trees and black pavement. He shot ahead, passing her, then spun to a stop, leaving rubber on the asphalt, blocking both lanes. No room to pass on the right without going off the side of the mountain; the only place to maneuver was onto the Mingo Falls road. Unless she ran him over. Which, given that she'd be coming out of a curve and might not see him right away, all depended on her reaction time and the Impreza's braking power.

His bike vibrated beneath him, tempting him to abandon his plan and take off, when she came around the corner heading right for him.

Stupid, stupid idea, he thought. But he stood his ground.

CHAPTER THIRTY

Caitlyn had no idea what games Goose was playing, trying to run her off the road, but she was about ready to pull her service weapon and take him into custody herself. She'd tried calling the sheriff's office for backup but this stretch of road between Evergreen and Maggie Valley had spotty cell reception and she couldn't get through. Leaving just her and the Reapers' enforcer playing chicken with a sheer drop-off on one side and the mountain on the other.

Thank goodness the Impreza WRX was up to the challenge. It didn't look fancy, but in addition to the all-wheel drive, it had an engine similar to a Porsche. Goose's Harley roared past her as he sped ahead and vanished around a hairpin curve, the last switchback before the turnoff to McSwain Mountain Road. Maybe he was setting up an ambush on the single-lane road up to Hale's house?

She steered out of the curve. There stood Goose, his bike blocking both lanes. Adrenaline fired her synapses as she stomped on the brakes and clutch while throwing the gearshift from fourth to second. He hadn't waited for the turnoff to stop her—but did the idiot have a death wish?

She pulled on the emergency brake, the stink of burning rubber filling her nostrils. Both hands fought the steering wheel as the car skidded out of control. Instead of trying to keep it straight, she steered into the curve, angling toward the mountainside and a small gap between the trees: a dirt road.

Yanking the wheel viciously, she turned the skid into a J-turn, coming so close to Goose and his bike that he filled the side window as the Subaru twisted across the wrong side of the road, finally facing the opposite direction, half on the pavement, half on the dirt.

Although she managed not to hit anything—including the idiot biker—the car stopped so violently that Caitlyn flew forward, hitting her head on the steering wheel. Not enough to black out, just enough to make her lose a second or two to the sudden pain. She kept her wits, enough to draw her weapon and hold it at her side.

Goose ran over and yanked her door open. "Are you okay? I just needed you to pull over. I wasn't expecting Steve McQueen."

She moaned and raised her head. Blood smeared the tan leather of the steering wheel. She undid her seat belt, keeping the Glock hidden from his sight. "De Niro. *Ronin* definitely had a better car chase than *Bullitt*."

"Okay, we'll compromise. Hackman." He cupped her chin in his hand and peered at the cut on her forehead. "No pain anywhere else? Like your neck?"

"No. I'm fine. Hackman. *French Connection*. Sounds good to me."

He leaned into the car, wiping her forehead with his bandanna. "I don't think you'll need stitches. Nasty bump, though."

That's when she jammed the pistol into his chest.

Pushed him back as she climbed out of the car. Then she sidled beyond his reach, holding the Glock steady despite the trickle of blood seeping down her forehead and dripping into her eye.

"Turn around, hands up over your head, and look up at the sky."

He obeyed, moving slowly, showing her he was no threat. "It's not what you think. I'm trying to help and we don't have much time."

"Trying to kill me is more like it. Did you really think I'd fall for that fake phone call?"

"Wasn't all fake. Lena Hale *is* in danger. But she's not at her dad's old house. If you want to save her, I know where she is. All I'm asking is that you listen to me."

She considered that. Something about Goose had bothered her since she first met him. It'd be good to get the truth out. "Okay. Talk."

"Not here." He twisted his head to look over his shoulder at her. "Someplace private. I can't been seen talking with you."

"What'd you have in mind?"

"Up there." He jerked his chin at the dirt road. It led up to Mingo Falls—her dad used to take her up there all the time when she was a kid. The Reapers could have set a trap up there, but this seemed an awfully complicated way to get her there. Everything about Goose's posture said he spoke the truth.

Caitlyn decided to listen to her instincts instead of playing this by the rules. She lowered her weapon and nodded to his bike. "You first, no more than five feet in front of me." No way she was going to let him ride with her, and if they left the bike behind and any Reapers saw it, they might follow.

Goose said nothing but the tension drained from his shoulders. He gave her a smile—not the smirk she was used to seeing from him, but a real smile that made it to his eyes. "Thanks."

The dirt-and-gravel road was empty—tourists hardly ever came to the falls in the winter, and when they did, they took the paved road from the reservation side of the mountain. It didn't take long to reach the parking lot, a secluded patch of cleared land at the trailhead.

Goose dismounted and waited for her, hands open and at his sides. No threat.

She got out of the Subaru, her weapon in her hand but not raised. Not yet. She remained far enough away that he couldn't make a move on her but close enough that he'd regret it if he tried. Her head throbbed and her stomach felt queasy with the pain and aftershock of adrenaline. Not that she'd ever let him see any of that.

"What the hell's going on here?" she demanded. He sighed, ran his fingers through his hair, and she had the sudden impression he wasn't used to wearing it so long.

"My name's not Jacob Clay," he started. "It's Jake Carver."

Only one reason for someone to have an alias that stood up to the sheriff running it through NCIC when he was arrested. Well, hell. She knew there was something off with him.

"You're investigating the Reapers. ATF? DEA?" Those were the usual suspects when it came to outlaw motorcycle gangs.

"All the swap meets and gun shows around here, the Reapers can buy any guns they need legitimately. And the only drugs I've seen them with are strictly personal recreational use."

"So what's their deal?"

"Money laundering."

"Shit." She eyed him. "You're with the Bureau. Financial crimes?" Most of the guys she knew working white-collar crime were the suit-and-tie type. Anything but the muscled, tattooed, leather-and-jeans specimen Goose presented himself as.

"Worse. IRS."

She couldn't stop her snort of laughter.

He sighed and slumped against his bike, but smiled at her, eyes crinkling, telling her he was used to the jokes.

"You're an IRS agent?"

"Originally. Reassigned to the FBI the past few years."

"So that makes you a"—she gave a shudder of mock terror—"CPA?"

"And a CFA. Certified forensic accountant."

Good God, what were they thinking? Sending an accountant undercover as a biker? "How long you been under?"

"Fifteen months, six days. Not that I'm counting."

"Where's your cover team?"

"Tricky keeping them close given that everyone knows everyone around here, so they usually rotate in and out as gamblers or tourists, fishermen. Two of them were on the dance floor the other night, started the fight that so conveniently got you and your boyfriend out of trouble."

"Where are they now?"

He shrugged. "Nice thing about new technology, they don't have to stay in line of sight to hear everything."

The Bureau routinely outfitted cell phones with omni-directional microphones and recorders. But, although those could record anywhere, they wouldn't get a signal to his cover team when there was no cell reception. Which meant he'd spent the better part of fifteen months basically on his own. "Yeah, but that also means they can't back you up if there's trouble. At least not quickly."

"As opposed to you coming in, stirring things up all by your lonesome. At least I have backup." He turned to her, his expression serious once more, a glint of the bad-boy Reaper Goose reemerging. "Point is, we're almost ready to nail these bastards. Not just the Reapers but the men behind them."

"And I'm in your way."

"You have no idea. I'm here now because Poppy wants you dead. He sent me to kill you."

CHAPTER THIRTY-ONE

The big cat leapt, landing in Bernie's truck bed. Lena yanked the Honda's rear door open and tried to shove Smokey inside. The chimp balked. The leopard stretched, its front paws balanced on the wall of the truck bed. Lena met its gaze, fear holding her hostage.

Smokey saved her. The chimp finally scampered into the rear of the Honda, giving Lena room to jump in and pull the door shut just as the Honda rocked violently.

The leopard was on the roof.

Lena leaned forward to the driver's seat and clicked the locks shut. Then laughed as she realized the futility. Like a leopard was going to use a door handle. She laughed so hard tears squeezed from her eyes. Smokey made a cooing noise and patted her head, combing Lena's hair with her long, leathery fingers.

The chimp's maternal instincts made Lena want to curl up onto her lap and give in to the tears. Instead she wiped them away.

The leopard scraped at the metal above them with its claws. She drew the pistol from her pocket. Smokey recognized it, tried to slap it out of Lena's hand, her teeth bared. Lena yanked it back as the chimp curled into the farthest corner of the backseat. Then she realized she couldn't shoot the gun, not inside a car—what if the bullet ricocheted and hit her or Smokey?

She returned the gun to her pocket. Nothing to do except wait out the cat.

Smokey calmed down, inched back across the seat toward her, draping her arms around Lena's shoulders. There was a strange squeaking noise. The leopard slid backward down the windshield to the hood. It sprawled across the hood, its front paws against the glass, nose pressed to the windshield, and peered in at them, looking confused to see them so close yet unable to reach them.

Lena was tempted to blow the horn but wasn't sure if that would scare it off or just make it angry. She decided to pretend to ignore it, hope it would go off after easier prey. Her messenger bag was on the front passenger seat where she'd left it two—no, three—nights ago. She stretched a hand and hauled it back to the rear seat.

Smokey sniffed at the canvas bag, trying the buckles and yanking on the straps. She jerked back at the sound of the zipper. Lena rummaged inside the side pocket and found her cell phone. Dead. It'd been on four days straight. And her charger was with her suitcase back at the VistaView.

The only other items in the bag were a few energy bars—which she tucked into her coat pocket before Smokey could tear into them—her notebook, and a few books she'd checked out of the tribal archives: a bound edition of the Joseph G. Hester 1883 Eastern Band of Cherokee tribal census and Dr. Bearmeat's own doctoral dissertation from 1987, a history of the Eastern Band that discussed the Freedmen Pact at length.

Dr. Bearmeat had been so excited by her interest in the pact and the prospect of seeing his work used for the *Duke Law Review* that he'd told her she could keep the books longer than the usual seven-day lending period. After all, he'd said, no one else had checked them out in decades.

They'd had several lively discussions on the legal ramifications of the pact, especially given the recent rulings in the Oklahoma Cherokee freedmen case. He'd used the special large-format printer to make her a copy of the pact, which she'd dropped off with a woman he'd recommended as a translator.

The most fascinating thing—and Dr. Bearmeat agreed—was how no one seemed to remember or even care about the pact. No Freedmen had lived on the land granted to them for generations; in fact, the Hale family was the last freedmen family who'd lived anywhere near the Qualla Boundary, and they'd moved away after Eli was sent to Butner.

"It's like someone wants to bury our history," she'd said as he fixed them tea. The several times she'd visited the archives no one else had come in. She had the feeling Dr. Bearmeat was a very lonely man, anxious to share the knowledge he had before he died and it was lost in the masses of documents he so painstakingly tended.

"Computers," he said, stirring milk into his Earl Grey with more vigor than he needed. "I blame the computers. If they can't find something in two nanoseconds on Google, people assume it never existed. They aren't patient enough to trace the original sources, not like you." He beamed at her like she was a star pupil.

"You said the original pact was lost?"

He squirmed and focused on his tea. "Yes. When Tommy Shadwick's house was burned."

"By my father." Over the past few weeks since Eli had ordered her to stop appealing his conviction, she'd come to terms with the fact that her life had built upon a lie: her mother and sister's belief in his innocence. As she accepted Eli's guilt, she felt a guilt of her own, a strange impulse to seek out her family roots and find some way to restore the Hale name. Learning of the pact signed by her ancestor seemed like a Heaven-sent opportunity.

Dr. Bearmeat nodded. "Yes. When Tommy died and his house burned, we lost an irreplaceable historic document. Of course, no one other than myself saw it that way. As long as there were copies, they couldn't care less. Back then these archives were merely stacks of boxes dumped in my dad's garage. The Bearmeats have long been the history keepers for the tribe, so folks got used to collecting any papers or old books they found and giving them to us like hauling out the trash."

His voice filled with scorn. "That was the 1980s. Everything had to be rebuilt, shiny and new and chrome. Modern. They all wanted modern. Forgot about their heritage."

"Not everyone, Dr. Bearmeat." She patted his arm. "If it wasn't for you, all this would be lost."

He smiled at that. "And you'll carry on the tradition. Let the world know about the pact."

More than that. Now that her time wasn't filled with conjuring legal arguments to appeal Eli's conviction, Lena wanted to settle down. She liked it here in Cherokee. The mountains, as stern and forbidding as they looked down from the heavens, felt like home. She began to fantasize about using the pact to restore her family name on the Eastern Band rolls, getting a job helping Dr. Bearmeat, maybe even setting up a small practice here. Combining history and the law to help people. It felt right.

Until she'd taken a good look at the books she'd checked out. Dr. Bearmeat was right: no one had taken the books on the pact from the archives in decades. Twenty-six years to be precise.

When Sean Tierney had checked them out. The week after Tommy Shadwick was killed. A few days before her father was arrested and Sean died. Dates all indelibly etched into her memory.

If Eli killed Tommy because the elder refused to give freedmen tribal status under the terms of the pact, then maybe Sean Tierney was simply curious about Eli's motive. Wanted to understand what had driven his best friend to kill a man.

Made sense. Except for a sliver of paper she'd found tucked between the pages of Dr. Bearmeat's dissertation. A handwritten scrawl with a question: *Casino?*

The casino was the Hale family's current source of income. Before his conviction, Eli had invested heavily in it through Jimmy McSwain's development company. Tommy Shadwick had also opposed the casino development— which only added to Eli's motive, although no one had ever mentioned it during Eli's short trial.

But given that Sean Tierney's note was shoved between the pages containing the maps of the Qualla Boundary and the area allotted to the freedmen under the pact, she couldn't help but wonder if Sean had stumbled onto something more.

Something that maybe had gotten him killed. By her father, his best friend.

CHAPTER THIRTY-TWO

Goose seemed to expect some kind of reaction with his pronouncement, but Caitlyn was more interested in answers.

"Who are these people behind the Reapers?"

He narrowed his eyes. "We don't know yet. Even if I did, I couldn't tell you. But I can give you one thing."

"What?"

"I really do know where Lena Hale is. And she doesn't have much time. Poppy put out a hit on her and Bernie, one of the Reaper prospects, who's been helping her."

"Bernie—Bernard McSwain?"

"Yeah. He's your cousin, right?"

"I haven't seen him in years."

"I suggest you get going now before you miss the chance at a family reunion. Permanently."

"You just want me out of your hair."

He shrugged. "Two birds. But Lena and Bernie really are in danger. And I can't help. Weasel isn't going to be tied up for long. I can't risk my cover. Not to mention an operation that's taken a year and a half out of my life."

He was right. She knew exactly where he was coming from—years ago she'd worked undercover in Boston. Nothing was more important than preserving your cover and finishing the op.

But if she went after Lena and Bernie, she might miss her chance to get the answers she needed from the Cherokee interpreter. Although Lena might already have all the answers. Then another thought occurred to her. "If Poppy's coming after me, he'll be after Paul as well."

Shit, shit, shit. And here she was, standing around talking. She holstered her weapon and yanked the Subaru's driver's door open.

"Pick him up after you get Bernie and Lena. They're at the old Teddy Roosevelt Lodge."

"The lodge?" She glanced at his Harley. "That thing any good on rough roads?"

"Yeah, why?"

"The lodge is only a few minutes away if you cut across the old logging road just down the mountain. You watch over Lena and Bernie while I get Paul. I'll meet you at the lodge, pick up the kids, and you'll be in the clear to wrap up your operation."

He frowned. "I can't take too much time. We still need to find the cash. Tie it to the principals."

"Is it tagged?"

"Yeah, some of our guys in Florida managed to slip marked bills into a stash used for an arms deal with the Nomads. They gave it to Caruso to launder. Now we need to document Caruso taking it to the bank."

"You mean the casino." Millions of cash flowing in and out every week, the VistaView made for a perfect money-laundering center. "How are they doing it?"

"Not sure. The casino is off limits to the Reapers. My

team's been in there monitoring operations during times when we know the money is being exchanged, but came up empty every time. At first we thought it was a few of the dealers at the tables or one of the cashiers, but we haven't been able to get any concrete evidence."

"Have you talked to my uncle Jimmy or his security chief? I'm sure they'd cooperate. It hurts the casino as much as anyone if it's being used by the Reapers."

He was silent. And the penny dropped. "You suspect my uncle."

"Not just him. We suspect anyone connected with the VistaView. That much cash walking in and out every day, there's a dozen ways from Sunday they could be making the exchange."

"Why are the Reapers so interested in Lena? She doesn't have anything to do with the money laundering, does she?"

"Nope. I have no idea what they want her for. Poppy acted like it was maybe personal. You know about her father, right? Killed some tribal elder a while ago."

He obviously didn't know much about the local history—or her own family history. "Yeah, I know. He's dead. Killed at Butner."

"Really? When?"

"Yesterday. About two minutes before I was about to question him."

"Well, hell. Anything to do with my case?"

"I don't see how. The VistaView wasn't even built last time Eli Hale was in Evergreen."

"I don't like coincidences."

"Me neither. But until we have more answers, we'd better get the civilians off the playing field."

"Okay." He blew out his breath and swung his leg over

the Harley. "I'll secure Lena and Bernie. Just until you get there. Where's this logging road?"

As she drove back over the mountain to Cherokee, Caitlyn couldn't stop thinking that she'd missed something. Some key that tied Lena's research into ancient history to the Reapers. But no matter how she twisted the little she knew, she couldn't make anything fit.

The one fact that stood out was Lena's interest in the pact. But there were copies readily available, so why would that make the law student a target?

The only thing Caitlyn could think of was that most of the world, even many living on the reservation, didn't speak or read Cherokee. Could the translation of the native language trigger a reinterpretation that would set up a new legal battle for the freedmen?

But why would that be worth killing for? The Oklahoma freedmen's court case had been going since 1985. Not exactly the Reapers' kind of quick and easy payday.

Still. If Lena's interest in the pact had triggered the Reapers' interest in her, then the interpreter might be the key.

She turned onto Acquoni. The parking lot in front of the archives office was still empty, the lights on against the early-January twilight. The interpreter didn't live far, maybe three minutes out of her way. Poppy would never think to look for Paul at the archives; he'd be safe a few minutes longer while Goose protected Lena and Bernie.

She passed the archives office and kept driving. Maybe it was just curiosity that wouldn't allow her to give up her search for the answers; maybe it was instinct. She had no idea, and she hoped she wasn't making a huge mistake, putting lives at risk. But she couldn't pass up a chance at solving the mystery.

* * *

Logging road, his ass, Goose thought as he bounced the
Harley over the hard-packed trail gouged out with tire
treads. At one point something flew off the bike, but it
didn't seem to affect the engine or steering, so he ignored
it. Thankfully the bike's suspension was good enough
that he didn't risk permanent damage to his internal or-
gans. Not that that was much protection as his spleen
slammed against his rib cage every time the bike cata-
pulted over a rut or off a rock.

Tierney had been right—the trip only took a few minutes, rough as they were. He emerged from the trees between two cabins. A large two-story log building stood in
the center of the plateau. He idled for a moment, remembering what Weasel had said. Something about the leopard being inside the lodge. Okay, leave that as the last place
to search.

The sun had already vanished behind the mountain
peaks to the west, leaving the area shrouded in shadows.
The wind had picked up and brought with it a few snow-
flakes. There were no lights in any of the cabins or smoke
coming from any chimneys. Had Bernie and Lena left on
foot? Or were they hiding?

He decided to search the buildings in a counterclock-
wise pattern. Parked his bike but left it idling in case he
needed a quick escape, and opened the door to the first
cabin. He had a small Maglite with high-intensity LED
bulbs, tiny but very bright. A strange musty smell greeted
him from the darkness within the cabin. He swept the light
around, revealing a dead tree, leaves hanging from its
branches, lying across the center of the floor. Then the
light reflected from two large eyes that blinked slowly,
winking out of sight.

He moved the light and saw the three-toed sloth's large claws clinging to the tree. "Lena? Bernie? I'm here to help."

No answer except for the rustle of another creature out of sight in the shadows. Good enough. He slammed the door shut and rode the Harley to the next cabin.

This time when he opened the door he was greeted by a lion's roar. He slammed it shut before even getting a look at the creature. *Damn it, Bernie, what the hell were you thinking?*

He slowed down in front of the third cabin but didn't stop as the Harley's headlight found Bernie's truck parked beside the cabin two doors down. Alongside it was Lena's Honda.

And sprawled across the Honda's hood was the leopard.

The leopard leapt up at the sight of the headlight. It didn't run; rather, it turned to face Goose, its head swinging in time with the bike's motion, tracking it. It stood on all fours, its chest pushed out as if protecting the car.

Then he saw what it was really guarding. One of the rear doors of the car cracked open and a girl shouted, "Help us! Please!"

The leopard whipped his head around at the motion of the car door and she pulled it shut again.

"It's okay, Lena," he called back, although he had no idea if it really was okay. How the heck could it be okay when there was a freaking leopard between him and her? Not to mention the Reapers who might be on their way here anytime now. Plus Wilson was going to kill him if he ended up blowing the operation.

First things first. He drew his pistol, a Browning 9mm. It looked very small next to the leopard on the car. A wounded cat would be more dangerous, and he doubted he could kill it easily. But he didn't have to kill the damn thing, just spook it enough that it ran and gave him time to reach the car and Lena. How the hell had she gotten herself trapped in there?

"Get down," he shouted to Lena. From the shadows in the back of the car, looked like she wasn't alone in there. Bernie had a gun; why hadn't he taken care of the leopard himself? Probably couldn't bring himself to hurt the animal—kid was simply not cut out to be a killer.

Not that Goose was too happy about it, either. He raised the Browning, took careful aim, and shot. The bullet hit the hood a few inches away from the cat. The cat jumped. First to the roof of the car; then, when Goose fired another near miss, it leapt across the truck and to the roof of the cabin. Then Goose lost it in the darkness.

He didn't give it any time to return, speeding the bike to the Honda. As he approached Lena jumped out, pulling a chimpanzee by the arm.

Holy hell, could this day get any more messed up?

CHAPTER THIRTY-THREE

Sharleen LittleJohn lived in a single-story frame house with a small porch whose roof sagged to one side. Caitlyn walked slowly up the front path, giving Sharleen time to know she was coming—common country courtesy that she seldom had the chance to use. Her usual approach to a residence was to park several houses away, check through the windows first, then finally knock with one hand on her weapon.

Mrs. LittleJohn answered the door before Caitlyn reached the top of the steps. "You're late. Judas Bearmeat called ages ago, said you were coming."

She wasn't the wizened elderly woman Caitlyn had pictured. Sure, she had plenty of wrinkles and crow's-feet, but she wore a purple velour tracksuit complete with New Balance cross trainers, also in purple. She gestured Caitlyn inside, bobbing her head impatiently as Caitlyn explained why she was there.

The frame section of the house was a modern addition to an older log cabin in the rear. The decor was eclectic: framed family photos, grandkids of all ages prominently displayed, hunting trophies, and gourds painted in the traditional Qualla fashion.

Mrs. LittleJohn took the initiative. "Don't know nothing about that girl. I took her money but I didn't do anything wrong."

"I'm not saying you did. What exactly did Lena ask you to do?"

"Had copies of some old papers. Wanted them translated from Cherokee to English. Never came back for them."

"Did she explain what she was interested in?"

"She had an English translation right there with them, I told her that, but she said she wanted to compare it to mine. At first I thought she was trying some kind of bullshit university experiment or something, testing to see if my Cherokee was any good, but then I realized what she was after."

"What was that?"

"There was a difference between the two documents. Subtle, you'd never notice if you weren't looking, but it was there." She motioned for Caitlyn to follow her and led her to a dining room. There were no chairs around the table or anywhere in sight, maybe because the table itself, a massive slab cut from a tree, polished to reveal every ring marking the tree's ancient history, took up most of the room.

"Been in my family for generations." Sharleen gestured to the table. "Not that anyone cares. Can't get the grandkids to even visit here anymore. When they come all they want to do is hole up at the casino, play video games, and slide on the waterslide."

A stack of folders sat on one side of the table. Mrs. LittleJohn opened the top one and spread its contents faceup in front of Caitlyn.

"What are these documents, anyway?" Caitlyn asked.

"These papers are the original land grant to the freedmen that accompanied the pact."

Caitlyn turned to the final page of the English document. Signing as representative of the twenty-two freedmen families was Elijah Hale. Lena's ancestor. "Was Lena tracing her family tree?"

"Nothing to do with family trees," Mrs. LittleJohn said with a sly smile. "Everything to do with the land. Here's the original Cherokee." She pointed to a photocopy of beautifully formed characters that danced across the page. "See this here? It's the word for 'south.' But here in the English it's been changed to 'north.'"

Caitlyn squinted. The English version was hard to read, also handwritten in old-fashioned script. But when Mrs. LittleJohn pointed out the text she was talking about, Caitlyn could see she was right.

Mrs. LittleJohn crossed the room and returned with a large framed map. An antique, hand drawn and labeled in Cherokee.

"The English version says northeast corner of the Qualla Boundary." She pointed on the map. "That's here."

"Nothing there today except forest bordering the national park and the Teddy Roosevelt Lodge." Which meant no roads, no possibility for development. Worthless. Although it did explain why Lena had gone to the lodge. To explore the land across from it. "But you said the actual land deeded to the freedmen is south."

"Right. Back then that land would have had little value to my people. Most of the timber was already cleared, it was too far down the mountain to be any good for hunting, and it's not close to the river."

"Where's the real land tract located? The southern area that really belongs to the freedmen."

Mrs. LittleJohn's smile grew wider and she traced her finger down, coming to a stop at a point on the outer edge of the reservation. Right where the casino was built.

"Holy shit." Caitlyn breathed as she realized the enormity of what Lena had stumbled across.

"Exactly."

As Caitlyn took photos of the documents with her cell phone, she thought hard, trying to fit all the pieces into their correct places. "If the original pact was correct, then the English translation wouldn't have been altered until at least 1988 when the Indian Gaming Act was passed and the casino was planned."

"Right. Unless the original translation was wrong to start with. Who's to know?"

"Too big of a coincidence. Had to happen in 1988." She remembered Bearmeat lamenting the disarray of tribal archives. Even with the technology back then it wouldn't be too difficult to make a small alteration. And who would bother digging up the original to check? No freedmen were left in the Qualla Boundary—the Hales were the last who lived close by. Which meant no one to protest or know the difference.

"It had to be 1988," Caitlyn decided. Right around the time of a tribal elder's murder, Hale's arrest, and her father's death. Which meant whoever was behind all of this had not wanted the casino development project moved—or delayed. "Who else besides Mr. Bearmeat knows Lena brought these to you?" The old woman might be a target.

"I live alone at the end of a dead-end road no one else

lives on. Hell, can't even get my own kids to visit. So who would know?"

"Still. I'm not sure you're safe here. If I found you, others might as well."

At first she thought Mrs. LittleJohn would put up a fight, insist on staying, and Caitlyn would need to find some way to protect her. But the older woman nodded. "I had a feeling you might say that. That's why I told you all this. Now I'm not the only one who knows."

She walked past Caitlyn to a door at the end of the hall and emerged rolling a purple suitcase in front of her. The wheels spun along the irregular boards of the wood floor. "I'm seventy-three years old. About time I see some of the world, don't you think, Agent Tierney?"

Lena wouldn't leave the chimp and they didn't have time to argue, so Goose ended up ferrying them both to another cabin, the girl hugging the chimp tight to her chest with one hand and holding on to Goose's jacket collar with the other. No sign of the leopard, Weasel, or any other wild animals, thank God.

"You have to help Bernie. He's sick, needs a doctor," Lena shouted into his ear over the roar of the bike. They stopped in front of the cabin, and she and the chimp hopped off. The chimp held her hand but stopped to turn and shriek at Goose, baring her teeth. Goose figured he was getting off lucky, damn thing could've taken a bite out of him anytime during the ride.

"Hey, I got you here in one piece," he told the chimp. "What more do you want?"

Neither the chimp nor the girl answered as they bolted up the steps to the cabin. "Bernie?" Lena called, turning on the lights. Goose arrived just in time to see her fall to her knees beside Bernie's still form on the bed. "Oh God, he's dead!"

Had to admit the kid looked bad. Skin was pale and sallow, with a strange yellow tint, eyes sunken, lips parched. But corpses didn't sweat. Goose raised Bernie's wrist. "No. He's got a pulse. It's pretty darn fast."

"Call for an ambulance."

Goose grabbed his phone. No bars. He tried anyway but couldn't get through. But Caitlyn should be there soon. "Don't worry. Help's on the way."

Maybe this was for the best—not only would he be able to keep his cover, but Caitlyn would be safely out of the way if she was with Bernie in the hospital. He'd just have to make up some story for why she never showed up at Hale's house. As long as Weasel didn't shoot first and ask questions later, he was safe.

Caitlyn called ahead and Paul was waiting outside the archives when she arrived. He waved good-bye to Bearmeat and hopped in the car.

"Where have you been?" he asked as she pulled away, speeding down Acquoni back to Route 19.

She waved him to silence. Thankfully it was too dark in the car for him to see the cut on her head—otherwise she'd never get him to shut up. She called her mother. Goose might be suspicious of Jimmy and everyone else at the VistaView, but there was no way her mother could be involved. Plus, Jessalyn was staying in one of the apartments behind the casino, away from the crowds. Where better to stash Paul, Lena, and Bernie?

"It's me, I need a favor," she said when Jessalyn answered the phone.

"First you run out on your family and now you call for a favor? You really are like your father."

Harsh. But maybe deserved. Caitlyn didn't have time to parse their mother–daughter dysfunction right now. "Can Paul and a few friends stay at your place? Just for a little while?"

"Why not get them a room at the resort? I'm sure Jimmy—"

"See, that's the thing. I need for no one to know they're there. Not even Jimmy."

A long pause. Which felt even more surreal since she was passing the VistaView as she spoke. Was tempted to drop Paul off but she'd already kept Goose away from his job too long and she needed to get Lena and Bernie to safety.

"What's this about, Caitlyn?"

"Just a few people who need a safe place to stay. Only for an hour or so." Or until she was sure Goose didn't need her help. "Then I'll get them out of your hair." It would be so much easier if they could trust local law enforcement or if there was a FBI office closer than Asheville, but given Goose's situation, she couldn't risk blowing his cover and getting him killed.

Jessalyn's sigh coincided with a gust of wind that shook the Subaru. "Okay."

"Thanks. We'll be there soon." She hung up just as they reached the turnoff to the Teddy Roosevelt.

"Where are we going?" Paul asked as she sped up the narrow, twisting road. "What was that all about? I'm not staying with your mother. And who are these other people?"

"One of them is Lena Hale." A fact she'd conveniently forgotten to tell her mother. Whoops.

"You found her? Caitlyn, that's great."

"Maybe. There are some not-so-nice folks after her. I need you to watch her while I take care of business."

"Not alone. You're going to call the cops, right?"

Depended if she could figure out a way to involve the sheriff without exposing Goose. Trust no one, assume nothing—that's what kept undercover operatives alive. There was a damn good reason Goose had waited so long before telling her the truth.

"Yeah, sure," she told Paul. "Just as soon as I get you guys to safety."

The lie kept him quiet long enough for them to reach the lodge. Only one building had its lights on, so it was easy to find the others. As she pulled up, Goose appeared, holding his 9mm at the ready. He didn't relax until he saw her emerge from the Subaru.

"Change of plans," he told her. "We've got trouble."

CHAPTER THIRTY-FOUR

"What's going on?" Caitlyn asked Goose as she hustled Paul inside the small cabin.

"Bernie's sick. Real sick. He needs a doctor."

"Paul, take a look, will you?" He stared at Goose but then looked past the biker to Bernie. Caitlyn followed his gaze; the kid really did look sick. Like next-to-dead sick.

"What were his symptoms?" Paul asked, dropping to one knee beside Bernie's bed and taking his pulse.

Lena came out of the back room, a chimpanzee holding her hand. Caitlyn recognized the girl from her photo—the chimp was a stranger. "What the hell?"

"Things are more complicated than we thought," Goose said in a wry tone.

"No shit." No time for reunions with long-lost best friend's baby sisters. She beckoned Goose outside to the porch. "Tell me everything."

"The Reapers took a bunch of exotic animals as payment for a bad debt, were gonna use them for target practice. Kid couldn't bear to see them killed, so he stole them from the Reapers, brought them here. There's three more chimps and a leopard running loose, a lion over there in that cabin, a sloth and some other monkey-things in the one beside it—"

"Wait. Did you say there's a leopard running loose?"

He shrugged one shoulder. "Told you it was complicated. But it gets worse."

"What?"

He held up his phone. "GPS tracker on Poppy's SUV. He's headed this way. Probably not alone."

"Your cover team?"

"Haven't been able to reach them, but they've got my GPS signal."

"But they won't come unless they know you're in trouble, right?"

He nodded. "Plus, they're following Caruso and his men, hoping they'll lead them to the money. Might not even be looking to see where I am. Last they knew I was supposed to be sitting around with Weasel, waiting for you to walk into our trap."

"How much time do we have?"

He consulted his phone. "Poppy just turned off 19. Maybe twelve, fifteen minutes tops."

That wouldn't give her time to tell Lena about her dad. Keeping the living alive had to take priority.

"Ideas?"

"Only vehicles we have are your car and my bike. How about if you take the others over the logging road in the Subaru and I'll play decoy?"

She gave him half an eye roll. "Don't be stupid. You'll blow your cover and they'll probably kill you on sight."

"I could say I was waiting for them—" He interrupted himself before she could do it for him. "No, that won't work. Weasel and Poppy will wonder why I wasn't at

Hale's house like we planned. Okay, what do you suggest?"

"My dad taught me to hunt here in these woods. I think with a few minutes' head start I can set up some diversions to slow them down. While you take the others down the mountain in my car."

He frowned, clearly not liking her plan. Hey, she wasn't so keen on it, either. But there was no better way, not with three civilian lives at stake. "A lot of the Reapers hunt around here, too."

She shrugged. "That'll keep it interesting. Let me see what supplies I can rustle up."

"I'll hide my bike."

"Good idea. Why don't you park it with the lion?"

He laughed and leapt off the porch. She opened the Subaru's trunk and removed her weapons and spare ammo. Wished she had brought her Remington. Next time for sure. She grabbed a roll of duct tape, stomped on it to flatten it to fit in her coat pocket, then added a small roll of twine left over from when she'd hauled her Christmas tree home. Knife, ASP, two 40-caliber Glocks, almost a full box of ammo, a little night-vision help from her surveillance monocular, good to go.

Goose returned. "Might want to do something about your hair and face—you practically glow in this moonlight."

She grinned. "You've the heart of a poet."

"And the paycheck to match." They moved inside. Bernie was sitting up, sipping at a plastic glass Lena held for him. The chimp had climbed up onto the nightstand and squatted, combing his hair with her fingers. If Caitlyn had more time, she'd have snapped a photo because no one was ever going to believe this.

"How's Bernie?" Goose asked.

"I gave him ibuprofen for his fever and that's his second glass of Gatorade," Paul said, turning from where he was washing his hands at the sink. "But he's icteric and I can't do anything more for him here. We need to get him to a hospital."

"Working on it," Caitlyn said as she opened and closed each door, familiarizing herself with the cabin layout and searching for more weapons. No locks on anything, not even the exterior doors. Kid sure had a lot of books—including an entire walk-in closet filled with paperbacks and comic books. She took a black ski mask from a coat hook. "Bernie, do you have any guns?"

"Just the one." His voice was hoarse, as if it took all his energy just to answer her.

Lena left Bernie and handed Caitlyn a Smith & Wesson .44 magnum. She wouldn't look Caitlyn in the eye, as if Caitlyn scared her.

Caitlyn wished they had more time. She could tell Lena stories about when she was a baby, hear all about Vonnie's life, tell her that her dad had died.

Paul scowled at her, seeing her face for the first time in the light. "What happened to your head?"

"I'm fine," she protested as she checked the revolver. Four bullets.

"No. You're not. Let me check you out."

"Leave me alone. I said I was fine," she snapped, her patience frayed. She had no time for distractions.

Thankfully Goose intervened, wrapping one hand around Paul's upper arm and almost lifting him off his feet as he hauled him away from Caitlyn. "Let the lady do her job."

"Idiot." Paul's tone was scathing. "Her judgment is obviously impaired."

"She seems fine to me. I vote for letting her save our sorry asses."

"She had brain surgery a few months ago. And now she might have a concussion. I need to check her out."

"He's exaggerating," Caitlyn said, scanning the darkness from the window. No sign of the Reapers. Yet. She dared to look over her shoulder at the two men. Paul stood in the center of the room, face twisted in frustration, while Goose leaned against the far wall, angled so he could keep one eye out the other window and one eye on Paul.

"You almost died," Paul said.

"Before the aneurysm repair. I'm fine now." Why the hell were they having this argument and wasting time? "Goose, you need to get them out of here before the Reapers find us."

"Why him?" Paul argued.

"Because I need to create a diversion."

"You come with us. Let him stick his neck out. He's nothing but trouble anyway."

Silence. She couldn't break Goose's cover, not even for Paul.

"We could make that work," Goose said, offering her an out.

Didn't they just have this discussion? Impossible. If the Reapers caught him, they'd know he was a traitor and kill him.

"No. We can't. You have friends out there"—she emphasized the word *friends,* hoping he caught her drift, "who can back you up. Once you're in cell phone range, they can get Paul, Lena, and Bernie to safety. Then you can come back for me."

He frowned but nodded. "Let's go, Doc."

"No—" Paul protested. For a moment she thought Goose was going to slug him and haul him out on his ass.

"The lady has a good plan. Let's not mess with it." Goose glanced at his cell phone then handed it to her. "They've stopped about two-thirds of the way up."

She gave him hers in exchange. "That's the last switchback before they'll be in sight of the lodge. If I were Poppy, I'd send an advance guard on foot. That means I'll have the chance to set up an ambush at the choke point, take them one at a time."

"If Poppy thinks like you. Either way, we're out of time."

Paul stood, frowning at Goose then at Caitlyn as he followed their conversation. "But as soon as we get out of here, we send help back, right?"

"Right." Caitlyn smiled and nodded without actually looking at Paul. And Santa Claus really had reindeer that flew.

Goose glanced at Caitlyn before mirroring her smile and nod. "I'll come back for her myself."

"No," Paul said. "I mean real help. The police."

"Oh, of course." Goose's expression never changed. Caitlyn could see why he'd be good at undercover work. They both knew the odds of her eluding Poppy and the other Reapers weren't good. Most likely any help would be too little too late.

But it was the price she'd pay for their safety. She gave Paul a hug, kissed him hard. "I'm sorry about this weekend," she whispered.

"That's okay," he said but she could tell he didn't really mean it. "You'll make it up to me."

Such a nice man. "Someday you're going to make some lucky lady a great husband."

He stared at her long and hard. Blinked slowly. And

she knew that he finally understood what she'd been trying to tell him for days. "But not you."

She shook her head sorrowfully. "Not me."

He thought she was breaking up, had no idea she was
saying good-bye. Forever.

Probably best that way. She turned to Goose. "You keep
them safe or I'll chase you to hell and back."

He smiled that sloe-gin smile that had first caught her
attention. "Yes, ma'am. I will."

She zipped her coat tight, pulled Bernie's knit cap over
her head, grabbed her weapons and Goose's cell phone,
and was out the door before she could change her mind.
Just had to stay alive long enough for them to get down
off the mountain. How hard could that be?

A low growl echoed through the darkness from the
trees before her. Harder than she dreamed.

CHAPTER THIRTY-FIVE

"What did you mean back there when you said her judgment was impaired?" Goose asked once they had Bernie and Lena—and the chimp—loaded and were headed across the compound to the logging road. He had Paul drive with the lights off, leaving his hands free in case he needed to shoot. "She's carrying a weapon. The FBI wouldn't let her do that unless they cleared her."

Paul hunched over the steering wheel, peering into the moonlight as the sullen silence grew. "They did clear her. But she's smart. She knows how to fool the tests and their doctors."

"But not you?"

"She still has problems. Associating names and faces. Remembering dates. Recognizing people she doesn't know well. She hides it, has a ton of ways to cope, but she'd be better off without this job."

"Better off sticking with you, you mean." It was so obvious the man was in love with Caitlyn, and just as obvious that he was not the right man for a woman like her.

He'd smother her, douse the fire and passion that made her good at her job, made her who she was.

Goose fiddled with the defroster, trying to get a handle on his own feelings. He knew nothing about Caitlyn, so why did he feel so upset by Paul's interest in her?

"Better off with me than dealing with lowlifes like you, yes," Paul said defiantly. "I don't understand why she fights so hard to keep her job. The FBI doesn't appreciate her, she has to deal with all their bureaucratic crap just so she can risk her life—it's not worth it."

"You want her to quit." No way a woman like Caitlyn would ever quit. Goose couldn't see her giving up on anything—she'd see it as a challenge. Just like recovering from her brain surgery.

"We were supposed to go away this weekend. To the beach. I had it all planned." Paul turned away from Goose, face aimed at the darkness flitting past the window. "I was going to ask her to marry me."

"Sorry about ruining your plans," Goose said, only half meaning it. "Let's start with saving your ass so you can try again some other time."

"Not sure if there will ever be another time."

They reached the logging road. "I can't do this without lights," Paul said.

Goose nodded. Under the cover of the trees, it was as safe as it was going to get. Paul clicked the lights on and bounced the car onto the primitive dirt road. From the backseat Bernie moaned and the chimp made an anxious chattering noise.

"Hang on, guys," Goose told them.

"What do we do if they find us?" Lena asked.

Good question. They weren't going to like the answer.

"If it looks like we're going to get caught, then you're all going to have to trust me."

"And why should we do that?" Paul asked. Goose couldn't see his sneer, but it came through loud and clear. To Paul, Goose was just another lowlife biker helping Bernie, his fellow Reaper.

"You can trust him," Bernie's voice came from the back, weak but earnest. "What's the plan, Goose?"

"If they stop us, I bail and run for help."

"Like hell—saving your own sweet ass," Paul said. "What about us? They'll kill us."

"Not if they need you alive." Goose was totally improvising, but he had no choice since he had no clue what Poppy's endgame was. "Lena, they want something from you. Any ideas?"

The girl hesitated and looked at Bernie, who nodded. "I think it might have to do with the original Freedmen Pact. But I'm not sure. I was in the middle of my research when—"

"That's okay. Just act like you have something they want. All you need to do is keep them talking until either Caitlyn or I can bring back help."

"Okay." Her voice quavered. "I guess I can do that."

"Hopefully it won't come to that. We'll get off this mountain and everything will be fine." Except for the fact that in the past ten minutes they'd barely gone a hundred yards. Paul's driving would make a slug seem like a speed demon.

Then Paul stopped the car.

"What's the problem?" Goose asked.

"Over there. Down the mountain. See them?"

Lights. Moving. Toward them. Goose rolled down his

window. The night was shredded by the sounds of a dozen motorcycles straining their engines as they tore up the logging road. Coming right at them.

Caitlyn stopped at the edge of the road beyond the switch-back's curve. She was above the Reapers, out of sight of them, although she could hear the rumble of their bikes' idling. She decided to start with a simple surprise if they did ride their bikes up. She strung the twine across the road, tied to two trees at neck level, double thickness. Probably not enough to do serious harm, but it was invisible in the shadows and if it threw one rider on the narrow road, it would slow them down.

Next she planned her escape route. She'd stay in the trees; head up the mountain to the Mingo Falls trail then take it across and down to Route 19. In case any Reapers tried to follow her, she set a few quick traps: hemlock boughs covering a narrow crevasse where the stream had carved the granite into a sheer drop, bent sap-lings anchored with duct tape and rocks she could kick away as she passed, and more twine, this time tied at an-kle level across the path at strategic points.

Ten minutes later she was in position behind an out-cropping of rocks looking down on the Reapers through her night-vision monocle. No sign of Poppy but Weasel was there, riding in a big SUV, pump-action shotgun in his hands, along with six Reapers on their bikes and two more pickups at the rear. Nice. She didn't even have to wait for them to make the first move; she could keep them pinned down from here with minimal risk.

She started with Bernie's .44. It would be the loudest and have the greatest impact at this range. Took aim at the engine block of Weasel's SUV and fired two rounds at it, quickly followed by two more at the nearest pickup.

A shout went up and the men scattered. A barrage of gunfire aimed her way filled the night sky but they were at a disadvantage: shooting uphill and blind. None of the bullets even came close.

She changed to her Glock and got off several more shots before Weasel had his men organized enough to kill their headlights. She watched through the night-vision monocular; she hadn't managed to hit anyone with the Glock, no surprise given the distance and the moving targets. Several Reapers began to climb the mountain toward her while the rest gave them cover fire. Good strategy if she couldn't see them coming. As it was, all she had to do was follow her retreat path, cross the road, and reposition herself a little farther up the mountain. It meant giving them a bit of extra ground, but gained her what she really needed: time.

From her new position she shot at the men on foot. The men quickly scrambled down to take cover behind a fallen tree trunk. Now three others were trying to get past her on their bikes, hoping to outflank her.

She moved to a better angle to take aim at the road, waiting until they hit her twine trap. As she suspected, the first rider didn't see it until it was too late. Startled, he spun out on his bike and ended up with one leg pinned beneath it. She needed his comrades to follow her into the woods, not continue up the road to the lodge, so she purposely broke cover, letting them spot her before she returned to the shadows and pulled Bernie's ski mask over her face and neck.

A few shots rang out in her direction. She fired back,

barely aiming, mainly just wanting the noise as she moved farther down her escape route paralleling the road so she could cover it in case they didn't come after her. Then there was silence.

Puzzled, she scrambled up a nearby hemlock and hid in its branches as she observed them through the monocular. Weasel was talking into a satellite phone, waving his men back down to him. What the heck?

There could only be one reason why he'd be giving up so easily. She crawled around to the other side of the tree, the side facing the lodge, and used her monocular. She didn't need her night vision setting to see the Subaru's twin headlights flanked by several motorcycles as it was escorted back to Bernie's cabin.

She'd thought she was the diversion but it turned out Weasel and his men were just playing with her, wasting her time.

Poppy. It had to be. And Weasel was on his way to join them. What they'd do to Goose—she didn't even want to begin to imagine. And Paul and Lena? God, poor Bernie. An icy chill shivered down her spine. She told herself it was the wind sneaking beneath her collar, but knew better.

After what happened six months ago, she knew fear. On a very intimate level. The chill landed in her stomach and spread out across her body, leaving her frozen in place.

CHAPTER THIRTY-SIX

Goose felt awful. Not just the blisters tearing his feet apart as he bushwhacked down the side of the mountain in boots made more for stomping heads than stomping dirt. More than the knowledge that the people he left behind faced an uncertain fate. Or that they thought he was betraying them, saving himself. All except Bernie.

More than even the fear that he might let them down. The feelings churning his gut, tangling with adrenaline, leaving him breathless, had to do with Caitlyn Tierney. The look in her eyes as she said good-bye—she didn't expect to return.

It was Caitlyn he couldn't bear to disappoint. A stray branch slapped him in the face and he almost lost his balance, slid headlong into the embrace of another tree. He pushed off and kept going. Down, always down. To the road, to civilization, to a goddamn phone.

Bernie wasn't sure if he was dreaming or not. So much rushed together in a whirling kaleidoscope of color and sounds. He was hot yet freezing at the same time, couldn't stop his teeth chattering, not even as Lena and the stranger hauled him back out of the car.

Car? Where were they going? Nice to go places with Lena, just like he'd dreamed.

"Can we get more ice cream?" he asked. "Sprinkles on top?"

"Of course, Bernie. Just lie down and rest," she whispered.

Then she was gone and rough hands ran over his body. "Hey, leave him alone. Can't you see he's sick?"

Bernie was falling, falling . . . the bed caught him but oh, it didn't feel so soft. Every bone in his body ached. Then Lena was back, her hands soothing the pain.

"Lena?"

"I'm here, Bernie."

"You're so much better than ice cream." His eyes fluttered, her image blurring like an old movie exposed too long. Then everything went dark.

Caitlyn barely made it back to the cover of the trees near Bernie's cabin before Weasel and his men came roaring up the road, coming to a stop alongside her Subaru and the other Reapers gathered in front of the cabin. Most of the idiots sounded like they were drunk—a few were even drinking now, as if this was their idea of a party.

Using her monocular, she could see through the windows of the cabin. Bernie lying on his bed and Paul and Lena sitting on kitchen chairs beside him, their backs to the wall. A Reaper held a gun on them but she saw no signs of restraint—and no signs that they'd been hurt. But Goose, where was Goose? Had they killed him?

No. She hadn't heard any gunfire from this direction.

So not dead—gone for help? It was just a hope, a vague long shot of a hope, but she held on to it.

Poppy emerged from the cabin to greet Weasel. She inched closer, straining to hear their conversation over the sounds of the other bikers. It had been a long time since she'd hunted in the woods, even longer since she'd hunted in these woods, but her body remembered how to move silently in the dark.

What scared her was that she wasn't alone. Something moved nearby and it wasn't a Reaper. Something sleek and deadly and silent except for a faint chuffing noise that made her toes curl with the urge to run. The leopard.

She swallowed her fear and crept closer to the cabin. Poppy and Weasel were talking in the relative privacy at the back of the SUV.

"There's only one way out for her," Weasel said as he pulled a hunting rifle from the back of the SUV and slung it over his shoulder. "She has to be heading up to Mingo Falls, then she'll take the trail across and down the mountain."

"You think you can catch her?"

Weasel pulled a pair of night-vision goggles from a small case and adjusted them onto his forehead. He looked more like his namesake than ever: mean and nasty, ready to do some damage. "Oh yeah. That bitch is good as dead."

"Don't let me down, Weasel."

Weasel nodded curtly and took off across the clearing, heading back toward where he'd seen her disappear into the woods. Hopefully the escape route she'd created before setting up her ambush would keep him busy for a while as a false trail. If he fell into one of the traps she'd left, so much the better. Now if she could just isolate Poppy . . .

Poppy stayed behind the SUV for a moment, talking into his phone. A satellite phone like Weasel's. That's how they'd coordinated all this despite there being no cell service out here.

She smiled. That phone was how she was going to get everyone off this mountain safe and sound. Poppy pocketed the phone and headed back inside the cabin. All she needed was a little distraction for the bikers out front.

The leopard moved, heading farther into the woods. Fine with her, because Caitlyn was planning to move in the opposite direction, around the perimeter of the clearing. All the way to the cabin where Goose said there was a lion.

Bunch of half-assed, half-drunk Reapers wouldn't know what hit them.

CHAPTER THIRTY-SEVEN

Caitlyn could smell the lion before she got anywhere near the cabin's door. A strange acrid combination of urine, rotten meat, and sweat socks. Hopefully the stench meant the animal would leap at the opportunity for a little fresh air and some nice hunting.

She pressed her back against the far side of the cabin door and opened it, using the door as a shield between her body and the lion. Nothing happened. Good grief, was she supposed to call, *Here, kitty, kitty*?

Then she heard a snuffling sound followed by a wheezy cough. Poor thing had a cold. She was about to give up and take her chances sneaking into Bernie's cabin without a diversion when she heard tentative paw steps. Good enough. She slid back around to the tree line behind the cabins and skirted the shadows to Bernie's place.

He had no locks on any of his doors, so getting in wouldn't be a problem. The problem would be what greeted her on the other side of the door.

Then came the sound she was hoping for: a loud roar followed by men yelling. Even a few gunshots—which made her feel guilty, poor lion, but given the shooting skills of the Reapers and the alcohol they'd been imbibing, she doubted she or the lion had much to worry about.

She inched the door open, peered through it. Poppy and the other Reaper had their backs to her as they watched the confusion out front.

The lion gave another roar, covering the tiny squeak as Caitlyn stepped through the rear door of the cabin. Poppy stood directly in front of her, yelling directions to his men through the open front door. The second Reaper held a gun loosely aimed at Paul and Lena, but his gaze kept flicking to the window.

The lion must have leapt onto the porch because the second Reaper jumped while Poppy slammed the front door shut. Caitlyn rushed in before either man could respond, jamming her service weapon into Poppy's ear and spinning him to use as cover between herself and the other Reaper.

"Drop it," she ordered. The Reaper raised his hands then remembered he had the gun and looked at it uncertainly. "Put your gun on the floor and back out the front door. Unless you want to see his brains splattered all over those pretty boots of yours, do it now!"

Poppy nodded to the Reaper. "Do what she says."

His voice was calm, too calm for her taste, but that was okay. There was enough adrenaline rushing through her system for both of them. She jerked Poppy back away from the door, giving the Reaper room to go through it.

"Paul, get his gun. Lena, secure the doors, front and back."

Paul picked up the gun, holding it like he'd seen in the movies.

"Finger off the trigger, please," she coaxed him. "Just hand it to me. Good. Now search Poppy for weapons."

"This is a mistake," Poppy said.

Caitlyn ignored him. "Take his phone as well," she told Paul. Lena was having trouble with the doors. "Shove a chair under the knob. And close those curtains. Be careful, stay low, below them." It was like having kindergartners as partners. She wished Goose were here.

Paul finished searching Poppy. Caitlyn would do a more thorough job as soon as she had the man restrained. She handed Paul the duct tape and moved to the side while Paul taped Poppy's wrists. "Tighter. That's it. Take the tape the whole way up to his elbows."

Where to put the man? She wanted him out of the way so she could concentrate on the rest of the plan—which she hadn't quite come up with yet. She remembered the large, windowless closet where Bernie had his stash of comic books. "Lena, clear as much out of that closet as you can—take the clothes bar out as well."

A few minutes later she had Poppy on the floor of the closet, his ankles bound, and all his weapons or anything he could use as a weapon removed. She squatted before him, still holding the Glock as she perused his satellite phone. "I'm betting I'll find a whole bunch of calls to my uncle Jimmy on here."

He smiled—the kind of smile that would make a rattlesnake turn tail and run. "Of course you will, he's a friend. We chat all the time."

His answer only confirmed her suspicions. Sorrow and disappointment at Jimmy's involvement tried to crowd out the adrenaline surging through her. She shoved the emotions aside to concentrate on getting them out of here alive.

"Yeah, I'll bet. So much to talk about. Like killing a tribal elder to quash any opposition to the casino, framing an innocent man and sending him to jail, arranging for his execution twenty-six years later when he was about to talk, chatting about the best place to kill his own niece. Tons to catch up on. Oh, and don't forget the whole reason behind all this: the money laundering."

He rolled his eyes and chuckled. "I have no idea what you're talking about."

"Sure you do. Only thing I don't get is the part about Lena and the pact. The whole thing makes no sense. You already controlled Hale—why upset things now by having him killed?"

He shrugged at her. "Caitlyn, you're delusional. Paranoid. Let me go now and we'll get you the help you so desperately need. An FBI agent, recently recovered from major brain surgery, suffering from PTSD after killing a man, now taking hostages? This isn't going to look good."

Ahh . . . and the final piece of her plan crystallized. "You're right. Thanks, Poppy."

She slammed the door on him and returned to the main room. Lena was helping Bernie to sit up and drink another glass of Gatorade. God, she looked so much like her big sister, Vonnie. And Caitlyn was going to have to tell her her dad was dead. Shit, sometimes life sucked.

Bernie's color looked better, but that wasn't saying much. The chimp had reappeared as well. "Where did it come from?"

"That man, he made me lock her in the bathroom," Lena said, patting the chimp with her free hand. "Poor Smokey. Yes, you're such a good girl." She looked up proudly. "She bit two of them before they got us in here. You should have seen her."

"Maybe I should put her in there with Poppy to stand guard."

The chimp bared her teeth in a smile that made Caitlyn think that wasn't such a good idea—not if she wanted to keep Poppy alive. And she needed him, for now.

Paul paced in front of the window, stopping to look through the crack in the curtains, then resuming his death march. "What are we going to do? They're never going to let us out alive. Not after this."

He didn't sound so appreciative of Caitlyn's rescue efforts.

"Relax. They're not going to risk Poppy."

"How can you be so sure? They're a bunch of maniacs. They have no respect for the law or one another."

"You're wrong. They respect Poppy. He's not just their leader, he's like their father."

He shook his head at her, eyes narrowed in disbelief.

"Just trust me."

"Yeah, that's what your friend the biker said. Right before he took off running, leaving us to save his own skin."

So Goose was okay. Relief rushed over her. "He went for help."

"It's been a while," Lena put in. "And Bernie needs a hospital. His fever's back."

"Help him out, Paul."

Paul didn't back down. "That's not going to do him any good if we can't make it past those guns." He gestured to the Reapers outside. Had already dehumanized them. Primal instincts: us versus them. "Caitlyn, we need a plan."

She understood. He was a doctor and a man. Every instinct, hormone, strand of DNA was urging him to take charge of the situation. She lay her palm flat against his arm, felt the stress tightening his muscles. "I have a plan."

Kinda. Sorta. The beginnings of one. A plan that would hopefully get them all out of here alive: reapers and civilians alike. "Trust me, Paul. This is what I do. Tactical situations. Hell, this is what the Bureau pays me to teach."

He frowned, his eyebrows pulling together at first in disbelief then surprise. She kept herself from rolling her eyes. Even after all this time, Paul was like so many civilians, thought her job was like in the movies: running around in high heels, waving a gun, catching bad guys before the commercial break, and returning to lounge in a cushy office filled with expensive gadgets.

"You have a plan." His tone was uncertain.

"I do. And you have a patient who needs you." He still hesitated. "Keep him alive a little while longer, and I'll get you all out of here alive. I promise."

Paul knew she never made a promise she couldn't keep. Part of those control and abandonment and whatever-else-was-screwed-up-inside-her-psyche issues.

He nodded. Surprised her by pulling her close and kissing the top of her head. "Okay. I trust you. I believe in you."

The simple words stole her breath. She couldn't remember anyone ever saying them before. Not to her.

Paul grabbed a bottle of ibuprofen from the kitchenette and moved to help Bernie. Caitlyn raised Poppy's phone as she took a look out the window. No sign of the lion. No blood that she could see, either. Lion 1, Reapers 0.

The Reapers had arranged themselves in a semicircle, weapons pointed at the cabin, but they were arguing about something. Without Poppy or Weasel to lead them, they were confused about how to best save Poppy.

A few of them were even leaving. Good.

But that still left way too many guns in a way too volatile situation. She needed more good guys here to contain things. And fast.

She used Poppy's sat phone and started with the sheriff's department. Then called the state police. And finally the FBI office in Asheville, just to let them know what was going on. Between the three jurisdictions and the mutual aid Sheriff Markle was calling in from Bryson City and the tribal police, she figured she'd have plenty of good guys here. Only problem was, it was going to take at least forty minutes before the first SWAT team could be mobilized and make a safe approach up the mountain—they couldn't risk flying in directly, too easy for a Reaper to take down a helicopter.

Who could get here faster? Without the Reapers shooting at them? That had been the question she'd been wrestling with. Until Poppy provided the solution.

Caitlyn raised the phone once more. "This is FBI Supervisory Special Agent Caitlyn Tierney. I need to reach the film crew on location for the Reapers' charity poker run. No, I can hold. You might want to tell them it's an exclusive on a hostage situation. Am I a hostage? No, ma'am. I'm the hostage taker."

CHAPTER THIRTY-EIGHT

Lena curled up beside Bernie, trying her best to look brave for him, to stay calm. Smokey knew the truth, that Lena was anything but calm, that she was terrified, and lay her head against Lena's thigh, patting and rubbing Lena's back.

Men with guns, men who wanted to kill them—kill her—Bernie so very sick, car chases and motorcycles and, and, and . . . it was all too much. She wanted to be home. With her books. Or in the library. Or talking history with Dr. Bearmeat. Or watching one of those old TV shows with Bernie. Anywhere but here where she was scared and confused and lost and alone.

So very, very, alone.

Her mother's voice filled her head. *Hush, hush. You're not alone, child. You're never alone. I'm here and Vonnie and your Father. Trust in your Father.*

Lena knew she was just imaging her mother's gentle words, but they helped to focus her. God had saved her. Over and over. He had protected her. Mom was right: Lena had to trust Him now. Keep the faith. It was the only thing that would save her.

Caitlyn sent the other man, the doctor, to the back of the house. Something about standing guard. Then she turned and sat on the edge of the bed, looking at Lena with sorrow in her eyes.

"I remember you when you were still in diapers."

"You knew my sister."

"Vonnie was my best friend. Best friend I ever had. I was sorry to hear about her and your mother."

Lena looked away, blinked hard. She felt ready to crack like a glass plunged too fast into hot water. She closed her eyes, steeling herself. Caitlyn was trying to tell her something, something bad.

Her fears were confirmed when Caitlyn reached past Bernie's feet and Smokey's body to take Lena's hand. "I saw your father yesterday."

Lena opened her eyes but couldn't look at Caitlyn.

"I'm sorry, Lena. He's dead."

It took all her energy to absorb the words. Bernie pushed himself up and held her as she fought to twist Caitlyn's words into something else, some lie she could hold on to. Like maybe he was hurt or he was ill, not . . . but there was no denying what Caitlyn had really said. Eli was dead.

"How?"

"Stabbed. They caught the men who did it."

Lena just kept nodding. She couldn't stop herself. If she tried, she knew she'd fall apart, never pull herself back together again. She hugged herself, hard, one hand reaching for Bernie's. Then Caitlyn pressed something into her other hand. A small pocket-sized sketchbook. "He wanted you to have this."

Lena's fingers tightened so hard around the notebook that she folded it in two. She sniffed and rubbed her eyes with her free hand, then wiped the tears from her hand onto her slacks. Bernie pressed his body against hers from behind, Smokey from the side. Their warmth was comforting. She stared at the notebook. Something of her dad. She'd never had that before. Never had anything except memories that she'd finally realized were lies. Lies within lies. What was inside here, the truth at last?

Finally she opened the book, began to flip through the pictures. Her house, their house, the house her father had built with his own hands. She barely remembered how it looked when she was a child, but she had visited it every time she returned to Evergreen, examining every joint and crevice, seeking the man her father was.

She knew every inch of that house as well as she knew the lines that crossed her own palm. She traced her fingers along the cornice Eli had built in the dining room, the lines of the octagonal window he'd hung above the front door, the curve of the banister.

Then she stopped. Puzzled.

"This isn't from our house." She looked up at Caitlyn, holding the book open to the unfamiliar drawings. "Why would my father spend so much time drawing these, leave them here?"

Caitlyn stared at Lena. "Let me see."

She sat down beside the girl and took the book from her hand. The pages were in the last third of the book, mixed in with detail sketches of a stair railing and kitchen cabinets. She'd missed them when she went through the book last night—she'd been looking for written clues, not visual ones.

"Look." Lena pointed. "This one of the fireplace mantel. And here where he does a detail. And this one looks like it's zooming in on some kind of carved medallion. None of this is in our house."

Caitlyn remembered the Hales' fireplace: brick from ceiling to floor with a nice thick plank of heart of pine for the mantel, matching the floors. Nothing like the drawings here.

"What was he drawing?" Lena asked. "And why?"

It was Caitlyn's turn to tremble. She held the book so tight her fingerprints smeared the edge of the page. "I know where this is."

"Where?"

Caitlyn didn't answer. Because Lena's second question was more important. She handed the book back to Lena and stood to move about the room, checking the windows. Her plan had to work. They had to get out of here.

Because now she knew why Eli Hale and her father had really died.

CHAPTER THIRTY-NINE

Caitlyn returned to Lena. If things went wrong, it was best that they both knew as many of the facts—and suspicions—as possible.

"We were all looking at whether your dad was guilty or innocent. None of us could understand why he'd confess and go to prison for a crime he didn't commit." She took Lena's hand in hers. "You, Lena. He did it to protect you and Vonnie and your mom. He did it to save you."

"How do you know that?" Lena looked up at her, confused.

"It's the truth, Lena. I'm certain of it."

"My father did what he did to save his family?" Lena was crying, slow, silent tears that she didn't even seem to be aware of. "I wish he could have told me. I was so angry at him for so many years. The last time I saw him—" She buried her face in her hands.

Caitlyn stared, unsure if she should tell Lena the whole truth or if it would upset her more. How could she comfort the girl? Bernie came to her rescue, holding Lena tight against his chest while she wept. A few minutes later

Lena sniffed hard, swallowing her tears, and looked up. "If my father didn't kill that man, then who did?"

"Good question, but not the right one. The who doesn't matter as much as the why." Caitlyn paused as she spotted movement at the edge of the yard. She stared into the darkness but couldn't make out anything solid. But they were out there. They'd be coming. Soon. She had to give Lena the info she needed and get her and Bernie to safety.

"Then why was Tommy Shadwick killed?" Lena asked.

"Everyone thought it was because he opposed your father's request that the Hale family be reinstated to the tribal rolls as freedmen. Then I thought it was really because Tommy opposed the casino and your dad was just a fall guy. But I think he died for the same reason your father was kept alive all those years."

"Kept alive?" Lena sounded angry. Good, she'd need that strength to get through this. "My father was kept in a cage with men who were animals for the past twenty-five years for a crime he didn't commit. You're talking like it was all some game he was there."

"Think about it, Lena. Once Eli was convicted, why not have him killed as soon as he got to prison? Why risk him saying the wrong thing to the wrong person all those years?"

"But you said he went to save us. They had what they wanted, a fall guy for their crime. Why not just leave him alone?"

"No. He was a risk. They gave him what he wanted: his family's safety. But he had some kind of leverage on them. And it all had to do with Tommy Shadwick."

"He had proof that he was innocent?"

"No. He had proof about why Tommy had to die. He

had the Freedmen Pact. The original. And he hid it for you to find after he died."

"Wait. The pact burned with Tommy's house."

"No. That's why they torched Tommy's house. They couldn't find it—but a few slips of paper, it'd take days to properly search a house. They knew Tommy was the last person who had it, so they took a chance and burned the house down thinking they'd destroyed the pact along with any evidence they were there. Except of course your dad's hammer. They planted that in his truck since everyone knew he and Tommy'd had been arguing earlier that evening. Your dad was the perfect patsy."

"But why is the pact so important? All it would prove is that my family signed away their right to ever be full tribal members. It has nothing in it that anyone would kill for."

"The version you have has nothing in it that anyone would kill for. It says that the freedmen's land is in the northeast edge of the reservation."

"Yeah. Right across from here," Bernie put in. "My dad said that's why the Teddy Roosevelt never got off the ground—no place to expand to with the res boundary and the park boundary sandwiching it in."

"That's what everyone thought. And who would tell them otherwise? No freedmen have actually lived on that land since after the Civil War when they moved down into town to make a living at the lumber mills or moved out of the area altogether. It was a new era; they could live where they wanted. Why stay on a ragged piece of mountain, right?"

They both nodded, still confused.

"Wrong. The real freedmen land deeded to them in perpetuity by the pact was in the southeast corner of the reservation. Not the northeast. Best I can tell the change was made in the existing copies of the pact—the ones you got from Raleigh and from Mr. Bearmeat, Lena—in the mid- to late 1980s."

Bernie still looked puzzled, but Lena's eyes grew wide as she realized the implications. "The casino. That's where the VistaView is. And the Indian Gaming Act was passed in—"

"Nineteen eighty-eight."

Lena left Bernie on the bed and sprang to her feet with fresh energy. "They knew the act was going to pass, and they knew the tribal council wanted the casino as far from Cherokee as possible. Putting it on the eastern boundary put it closer to the interstate and tourists and . . ." She swung her head to stare at Caitlyn.

"And Evergreen. Where my uncle Jimmy happened to own all that worthless real estate, just sitting there, waiting for something to come along and make it worth developing. Something like a huge resort and casino. I'm sorry, Lena. I think Jimmy might be involved."

"He killed Tommy?"

Bernie fell back against the pillows, looking paler. He met Caitlyn's gaze, and she gave him a sorrowful nod. The two fathers in his life—Jimmy and Poppy—were killers. Lena didn't realize it yet, the role Bernie's family played in all this. He turned his face away, buried it in the pillow.

"I think Jimmy and Poppy were in it together. Poppy provided the muscle, Jimmy provided the land and relationship with the council. All they needed was to get rid of the one opposing voice on the council and it was smooth sailing. After all, who else would the council appoint as their managing director but the man who put the deal together for them and who was getting them all that money?"

"But why bring my dad into it? Why him?"

Caitlyn continued. The best thing for everyone was to get the truth out. "Tommy opposed the reinstating the freedmen into the tribe, but he was a reasonable man, he did due diligence and researched your father's claim. While he was searching the archives for the old tribal rolls to see if the Hale family was listed, he must have come across an original copy of the Freedmen Pact."

"One that wasn't altered."

"Right. Since Tommy could read the original Cherokee, he realized that although it supported his contention that the freedmen not be allowed full tribal membership, it also meant that the land the casino was going to be built on actually belonged to your family and the descendants of the other freedmen families. It's still reservation land, but the freedmen descendants would control whether or not the casino was built there—and at what price. He must have told Eli and given him the pact for safekeeping."

"So where is it?"

Caitlyn pointed to the book. "Eli gave us everything we needed to find it. In his drawings. That fireplace with the carved medallion? It's not in your house. It's in mine."

CHAPTER FORTY

Goose had never met a woman trucker before. But the one who'd almost run him over then stopped and helped him, letting him use her WiFi to Skype Wilson, reminded him of his aunt Tilley. All blushes and flirts but really she was a tough cookie who liked living on her own and wasn't about to take up with any man for long.

With her help, he'd made it back to the cabin before any of the cops. Not just the trucker's help—good old-fashioned fear had pushed him up the trail and through the woods back to Bernie's. Fear of what he'd find . . . and fear of what he wouldn't find.

The curtains were all drawn in Bernie's cabin but the lights were on. That meant at least someone had to be left alive. Especially as the Reapers still congregated out front, although there were twice as many as before. What the hell were they waiting for?

A rumbling sound punctuated by a spotlight came from the sky and he had his answer. Couldn't be SWAT; they'd never risk a helicopter, not with the firepower in the hands of the Reapers. A few of the Reapers did raise rifles and pistols at the helicopter, then quickly lowered them as the door to the cabin opened and Caitlyn appeared, holding a gun to Poppy's head. Poppy's mouth was duct-taped, his wrists bound behind his back, and he looked angry enough to spark a fire with just a look.

The Reapers swiveled their attention from Poppy to the helicopter and back. Then the helicopter landed and a man with a camera on his shoulder hopped out, followed by a petite blonde in a skirt and a velvet coat that fluttered in the rotor wash.

"Smile, boys, you're all on candid camera," Caitlyn yelled.

Caitlyn let the camera crew catch a few shots of her as well as all the faces in the crowd. Amazing how fast the guns vanished with a camera in the midst. She almost regretted calling the staties for assistance—a pretty blonde with a microphone might be all she needed to clear the Reapers off the mountain.

Paul beckoned to her from inside the room. Shit. No time to celebrate. "Is Bernie worse?" she asked.

"I need to talk to you," he said. "In private."

She closed the door and hauled Poppy back to the closet, shut him inside.

"What is it?"

"He's back," Paul whispered, jerking his head toward the bathroom in the rear of the cabin. "Your loser friend."

Goose? Her heart gave a kick of joy. "Watch the doors," she told Paul and Lena. "Don't let anyone in."

"You're not going in there alone," Paul protested.

"I don't have time to explain everything. Just do as I say." She hated the wounded expression that crossed his face, but it was the truth. She didn't have time. And she couldn't expose Goose's cover. "Please, Paul."

He stomped off to the front door. She ran to the bathroom, gave a knock, and burst inside.

Goose grinned up at her from the toilet seat. "Hey there, Red. Will you still talk to me now that you're a TV star?"

"Best way I could see to keep the Reapers from rushing the cabin." She shrugged. "Not exactly SOP, but when you're outgunned and outmanned, you've got to make do."

"You up for one more acting job?"

She narrowed her eyes at him. "What do you have in mind?"

"I need you to take me hostage," he whispered earnestly. "Throw me in with Poppy."

"Why? To protect your cover?" The hungry gleam in his eye gave her her answer. "That's why you came back? You really believe there's a chance in hell Caruso is going through with it? If the man has any brains, he'll bury the money and come back for it next century."

"I've met the man—hubris is his middle name. Hell, he probably thinks he has less chance of getting caught now with this all going down, drawing attention away from him. He can blame it all on Poppy and the Mountain Men going rogue. He knows there's no way Poppy can talk, not without earning the same fate as Eli Hale once he's behind bars. All I need is for you to throw me in there with Poppy. The cops have nothing on me, they'll have to let me go. Caruso will think I was trying to protect Poppy as club enforcer, and it will buy me time to get to the money."

"You're insane. You really think Poppy and Caruso will buy it?"

"Why not?" He stood and stared down at her. "Tell me you'd do anything less if it was your op."

She sighed and sank onto the edge of the tub, rolling her shoulders. "Maybe Paul was right, I should quit."

"Why? Because you didn't recognize that Poppy was a step ahead of us? Hell, neither did I and I've practically lived with the man for the past year."

She shook her head. He didn't get it—how could he? "People have died because of me. Good people."

He sat beside her, his hand over hers, and waited.

"Six months ago. I was following a lead. No official case, but I knew there was something. I was right. Found a psychopath getting ready to slaughter an entire town."

"Good instincts. Told ya."

"The local officer working with me got killed." She blinked hard, talking to the floor because it was just too damn hard to find the energy to raise her head and face him. "He died saving my life."

"Was it your fault he died?"

"No."

"And how many lives did you go on to save?"

She shrugged. That was beside the point. "I couldn't save him."

"Are you God? Do you think you can save everyone?" His voice had an edge even as his fingers gripped hers. "Because if you do, tell me now. That's not the kind of partner I want to have watching my back."

"You'd rather have a screwup?"

"I'd rather have someone who knows we all screw up and who will do their damnedest to prevent it from happening. I'd rather have someone who thinks with their head instead of their gun and who sees the possibilities, isn't afraid to make the tough choices. Someone like you." He stood, pulling her back to her feet. "Face it, Caitlyn. We're both screwups in our own way. But you gotta admit, we make a helluva team."

She didn't try to stop her smile. "What can I say, Carver. When you're right, you're right." She dropped his hand, took a step toward the door. He surprised her by not following. "You ready to do this or what?"

"Just so you know, the money isn't the only reason I came back." He grabbed her by the elbows, pulling her tight to his chest, and kissed her so deeply her vision went wobbly before she remembered to breathe again. Then he released her. "Okay. Now I'm ready."

CHAPTER FORTY-ONE

Caitlyn yanked open the door to the closet. Poppy scowled up at her, a death wish in his eyes, making her thankful for the duct tape over his mouth.

"I have a present for you." She reached behind her and yanked Goose off his feet, hurling him into the room so hard he bounced off one wall before landing on the floor. Like Poppy, his arms were bound behind him and his mouth duct-taped. "You didn't really think I'm stupid enough to let this doofus get the drop on me, did you, Poppy?"

She slammed the door shut again, leaving them in the dark. The less said, the more Goose would have to play with later. If there was a later.

The satellite phone chimed. She grabbed it. "We're in position," the state police SWAT leader told her. "Just need a diversion out front to focus their attention away from the perimeter."

"Give me two minutes." She turned to Paul and Lena. "Get ready to move. Lena, it will be safer for Smokey if she's back in the bathroom." Last thing they needed was a chimp going nuts in a crowd of Reapers who were itching for a fight.

She called the news crew, made sure they were in position and out of harm's way. Paul and Lena helped Bernie to his feet. His eyes rolled back for a moment, but then he steadied himself. Together they shuffled toward the front door.

"You guys ready?"

They nodded. Caitlyn shoved the phone into her pocket, keeping an open line to the SWAT leader, grabbed her gun, and went to get Poppy.

He didn't fight her as she hauled him to the front door. She gave Paul a nod and he opened it, keeping himself, Lena, and Bernie behind it, waiting for her signal. The Reapers out front were getting agitated again, like a bunch of sheep who couldn't remember where home was.

"You want me to shoot him now?" she yelled. That got their attention real fast. She pushed Poppy in front of her onto the porch, holding her gun to his head. "No? Well, here's how it's going to work."

Most of them had holstered their weapons, but a few still carried long guns. "First," she told them, "everyone put their weapons on the ground. Then you're going to let the civilians walk over to that news crew. Then you get Poppy."

They hesitated, staring up at Poppy for his approval. She shoved the Glock into his ear, hard. "Tell them to do it."

He cut a glare her way but nodded his head. The Reapers scowled at her, letting her know exactly how this was going to play out once they had Poppy clear and safe, but they lowered their weapons and cleared a path to the helicopter.

"Good. Everyone, don't move." She marched Poppy to

the side of the porch, giving Paul and Lena room to come out, Bernie between them, his arms over their shoulders as they helped him down the steps. They'd just taken two steps into the crowd when a figure appeared between the Reapers and the helicopter. He raised his pistol, aiming at Bernie.

Weasel. Caitlyn raised her own weapon. Poppy used the movement to plow into her, knocking her gun to the floor. She scrambled away from him just as a shot rang out. Lena threw herself in front of Bernie, who was down.

The crowd went wild, Reapers reaching for their weapons, two of them jumping onto the porch to get to Poppy just as Goose barreled out of the door, knocking Poppy back down again, covering his leader with his body.

Nice touch, Caitlyn thought as she pulled her ASP from her pocket and with a couple of well-placed swings made her way to Lena and Bernie. She couldn't see Paul. Lena stood her ground, despite the fact that Weasel was advancing on her, along with several Reapers who had lined up on either side of him.

Help came from an unexpected direction. A blur of motion caught Caitlyn's eye as the leopard flew over the heads of the Reapers and landed beside Bernie. The cat stood over Bernie, in between Caitlyn and Lena, as if protecting him. A few of the Reapers ran, straight into the arms of the SWAT team advancing from behind them, but Weasel and his men rushed forward, screaming obscenities.

Caitlyn swung her ASP, trying to buy the few seconds it would take for the SWAT guys to get in and clear the crowd. With the wind, they wouldn't be using tear gas, but given that Weasel was the only one who seemed interested in using a gun, they probably wouldn't have to. The rest of the Reapers were in a blood frenzy, using their bare fists to take on the leopard.

The leopard did more than hold its own; of course it had more than fists to fight with. The Reapers quickly fell back, leaving Weasel holding his pistol, aiming right at Lena. Before Caitlyn could push the girl out of his way, the leopard leapt through the air.

Weasel fired. The leopard pulled back its paw and batted his head so hard Weasel dropped to the ground. The leopard pounced, striking him one more time. Then there was a tiny pouf of noise. A dart whizzed through the air and into the leopard's flank.

The leopard looked over its shoulder as if disappointed in the humans who interfered with its dinner, then dropped.

Caitlyn turned her attention to the civilians first. "Are you okay?" she asked Lena, checking her for wounds.

"I'm fine. He didn't hit me." Lena flung herself beside Bernie. "Bernie, Bernie?"

"We need a medic over here," Caitlyn called to the SWAT team. One of them separated himself from where they had the Reapers lying prone on the ground, searching and restraining them, and joined them.

"No sign of a gunshot wound," he said. "But he's burning up. In shock."

Paul appeared, his face covered with dirt and grass. "I'm a doctor. He needs a hospital. Can we use that helicopter?"

"We've got our own on the way now that the scene is secure."

While they made arrangements to transport Bernie, Caitlyn watched as Poppy was led away by sheriff's deputies dressed in camouflage tactical gear, differentiating them from the state police SWAT unit dressed in black.

Another deputy escorted Goose. She made eye contact and gave him a wink, but he had to stay in character and merely scowled at her, although his shoulders rocked with laughter.

The two SWAT leaders approached her. "Thanks for giving us the heads-up on the wild animals," the state police leader told her. "We have an animal control team on the way to deal with the others."

"You were amazing," the news cameraman gushed as he ran over to film them. "The way you and the leopard fought together, like you were totally in sync. This is going to win me an Emmy, big-time."

One of the deputies ushered him away. The two SWAT leaders turned back to her. "Seriously, good work," the sheriff's department leader said. "No way we could have handled that many Reapers without casualties."

"No one was hurt?"

"Only Lionel Underwood. Looks like the leopard broke his neck."

Weasel was dead. Somehow she just couldn't feel too bad about that. Except to hope it didn't get the leopard in trouble.

"Using the news crew to stall for time and pacify them was brilliant, even if it wasn't exactly SOP," the statie added. "I liked how you stayed one step ahead of them. You knew that without a clear leader they might get out of control, so you took charge, manipulated them every step of the way." He shook his head. "Twenty-three armed men, and you took them down with no civilian losses."

"Couldn't have done it without you guys," Caitlyn told them, trying to sound like she'd planned any of this instead of making it up as she went along. "I think the news crew is waiting to talk with you."

"Don't you want to tell your side of things?" the deputy asked, obviously surprised the FBI wouldn't be taking all the credit for the night's success.

"No, thanks. I'll just catch a ride with one of your guys and give my statement."

"Pleasure working with you, ma'am."

She shook their hands, her own starting to tremble with fatigue and the ebb tide of adrenaline leaving her system. "Thanks."

Was there anything more humiliating than having your mother pick you up from the police station where you'd been questioned most of the night? Caitlyn couldn't think of anything—especially as Jessalyn acted exactly like she had when Caitlyn was fifteen and got caught joyriding.

"What am I going to do with you?" she announced to the world. "You could have been killed. Again."

Caitlyn ignored the smiles of the law enforcement officers crowded into the tiny sheriff's station. All men and all enjoying her discomfort. Where were the colleagues who five minutes ago had been treating her like a hero and congratulating her on taking care of business without getting anyone—especially any law enforcement officers—shot?

"I'm fine, Mom. Drop me off at the lodge and I'll pick up my car."

"You'll do no such thing. You're coming home with me."

The station doors closed behind them and Caitlyn took advantage of the relative privacy to face Jessalyn. "No. Either take me to the lodge or take me home. To McSwain Mountain."

Jessalyn turned pale. "To our old house? Why do you want to go there?"

"There's something I need to get. Something Dad left for me."

Jessalyn thrust the keys to her Jaguar into Caitlyn's hand. "Fine. Go where you want. Are you leaving me here or can a mother accompany her own daughter after her daughter almost got herself killed?"

Caitlyn sighed. She hadn't slept in two days and was in no mood to deal with Jessalyn. "Get in."

"Let me just call Jimmy, let him know you're okay." While Caitlyn got into the driver's seat and adjusted the mirrors, Jessalyn stood outside on her phone. Jimmy was probably home in bed, warm and unworried. Why should he worry? Right now she had nothing to tie him to Eli or Tommy's murders except speculation. If there was any trail, it would only lead to Poppy, she was certain.

Sooner or later she'd have to figure out what to do about Jimmy. She couldn't start an investigation into him, but maybe Sheriff Markle could. Or even Goose if there was any evidence Jimmy knew about the money laundering. As it was, she wasn't even sure if they could get him for fraud on the original casino land deal. After all, he hadn't bought or sold the land under false pretenses—he'd only arranged for its development. It would be up to the tribe to compensate the freedmen, pay any damages.

Hell, the way the legal system got so tangled, Jimmy might not have even broken any laws. The thought made her feel beyond exhausted.

Jessalyn hopped into the car and they headed over the mountain. Home.

When they arrived, Caitlyn was surprised to see lights on in the house and a black SUV in the drive. She had to shake off a feeling that her dad was waiting for her, the house looked so warm and welcoming, exactly the way she remembered it.

"Jimmy's kept it up," Jessalyn said. "Just in case."

They got out of the car. Caitlyn stared at the old farmhouse, at the porch where she'd spent so many happy hours, at the stairs she and Vonnie used to race each other up and down. Wind from the mountain made the hemlocks lining the drive weave back and forth as if beckoning her. If she tried hard she swore she could hear her dad's laughter escaping the shadows.

Her phone rang. Boone. "Go on," she told Jessalyn. "I'll be right there." She was afraid to move since she miraculously had a wavering half bar of cell reception. "Tierney here. You're up early."

"Who says I ever went to bed?" Boone answered in his usual endearing way. "Got that call you wanted. Final call from Eli Hale went to a cell number registered to a casino."

"Let me guess, the VistaView?"

"Yep. The voice is a man's but we won't be able to trace ownership."

"Can you play it for me?"

"Sure. Hang on a sec."

Caitlyn huddled against the rapidly cooling car, praying that the gods of cell reception kept favoring her. Although a small part of her hoped the call vanished into the night—that way she wouldn't need to be the one to arrest her uncle.

"Here you go," Boone said. Then a woman's voice came over the line. "This is the operator at Butner Federal Correctional Institute. An inmate named"—there was a pause while Eli supplied his name—"would like to place a collect call to this number. Will you accept the call and the charges?"

A man's voice answered. "Yes. I'll accept."

It was Jimmy. Shit.

She squeezed her eyes shut as Eli Hale spoke from beyond the grave. "It's me. Just wanted to let you know my girl knows nothing. She's just tracing her roots. Wants to find her family, that's all. Do you understand?"

"Of course. No problem. We'll make sure she's well taken care of."

Then the click of a receiver hanging up.

Boone came back on the line. "Get what you need?"

"Yeah. Yeah, I did."

Caitlyn hung up and climbed the stairs slowly, feet dragging as if she were eighty-five instead of thirty-five. When she crossed the threshold into the front room, Jessalyn was nowhere to be seen, but Jimmy sat in her father's favorite recliner, legs sprawled out in front of him, sucking on a fat cigar.

"Stand up, you're under arrest." Her tone was as low as her mood. But somehow there was no surprise. It was as if, all her life, she'd been waiting for this moment. The final betrayal.

"Under arrest?" Jimmy looked surprised. "For what?"

"For arranging the murder of Eli Hale. Since he was in federal custody, it's federal jurisdiction. Get up, hands where I can see them."

"Goddamn it girl, you are just as stubborn as your father." Jimmy took a drag on his cigar before looking at Caitlyn again. "Don't tell me I'm going to have to kill you, too."

Caitlyn's hand went to her weapon. Not drawing it, but ready. "I'm going to call for backup, we'll go down to the sheriff's station, and then you're going to tell me every-thing."

He laughed. The sound was anything but funny as it echoed through the empty room. Nothing like the laugh-ter she remembered in this house.

"I'll tell you everything. And you're going to leave like a good little girl and keep that big mouth of yours shut. Forever." Then he smiled. "Maybe this isn't a bad thing. Having a fed on board might come in handy. I'll ask Poppy, see what he says. But I warn you, girl. He doesn't like you much. Not after you got him arrested last night. Might prefer a dead fed."

"He's out?"

"Of course. He'll never go to trial, not in this county. After all, it's all he-says, she-says evidence. No one was hurt and no one can say anyone broke any law except Weasel and he's not talking, now is he?"

She was so tired of this bullshit. Dealing with FBI politics was so much easier. "Put the cigar down and keep your hands where I can see them." Inside she shook like a leaf caught in a blizzard, but she managed to keep her voice steady.

He took one more drag on his cigar then complied with a dramatic flourish. "Jessalyn," he shouted. "You want to get the hell in here, talk some sense into your girl?"

Caitlyn stepped back so she could cover both the hall-way and Jimmy, hand still resting on her weapon. She would draw if she had to—but she prayed it didn't come to that. Her mother entered the room, gliding across the oak floors like a beauty queen, not a hitch in her step, hands in her coat pockets, holding it open as if it were an opera cape.

"Caitlyn, I told you not to get involved in this."

"He as good as admitted to killing Dad." Damn, there was a quiver in her voice at the end there. She sucked in her breath, focused on Jimmy. "Mom, I need you to call the sheriff. Tell them a federal agent needs backup."

"She'll do no such thing," Jimmy said.

"Mom—"

Jessalyn ignored her, instead waltzed past Jimmy, for one heart-stopping second crossing Caitlyn's line of fire. Caitlyn braced herself, drawing her weapon against the possibility that Jimmy would take his sister hostage. If he did, what would she do?

But he didn't. He simply lounged in his chair like he owned the world while Jessalyn stepped to the wall and yanked out the phone cord. Surprise flooded over Caitlyn in a wave of ice that made her skin crawl.

"You knew," she gasped. "You knew he shot Dad."

"I didn't shoot your father," Jimmy said.

Caitlyn whirled on him, weapon aimed. He was un-armed, a civilian, but at that moment she didn't care. Heat burned through her and for a moment all she could see was her father lying in his own blood, just a few feet away from where Jimmy sat now. "Shut up! You killed him. You killed my daddy."

The muzzle of the gun shook. She drew in a breath and steadied her aim. "Tell me everything. Now."

He didn't bother to hide his amusement or disdain. "Sure thing, Ging. But you're not going to like it."

"Just tell her, Jimmy," her mother urged. He glanced at her and she nodded, the slightest bob of her chin, a queen granting a royal boon. "It's time she decided for herself. Family or not."

What the hell was she talking about? The Glock felt heavier than it ever had.

"Your father had a choice," Jimmy began. "He could have chosen family. Instead he chose to place us all in danger. He could have chosen to protect you and your mom, to ensure your future. Instead he chose—well, I never really understood what he was choosing. That's why I was there that day, arguing with him."

"You killed my father." Words so bitter cold they made her heart skip a beat then race to catch up.

"No." Her mom. Defending her brother. "Your father made his choice. He abandoned us, Caitlyn. He'd rather see us dead than compromise his so-called honor."

"You think Poppy's a mean SOB now," Jimmy added. "You should have known him back then. I lost track of all the people gone missing around him. And the only thing they had in common was that they'd gotten on the wrong side of Poppy and his club."

"You mean *your* club. You run the Reapers as Poppy's silent partner. Hell, you gave them your only son as collateral. Poor Bernie has no idea he's not a prospect, he's a freaking hostage."

Jimmy didn't waste time denying the facts. "At least I know how to keep my family safe. Not to mention prosperous."

Money. It always came down to money with Jimmy. His idea of protecting his family was really protecting himself and his financial interests. That's why he had Tommy Shadwick killed. He didn't want the tribe to find the original Freedmen Pact and move the casino away from the land Jimmy owned in Evergreen and made a fortune developing after the VistaView was built. Greed. The bane of the McSwain family.

She glanced at Jessalyn. Looked hard at her mother. Jessalyn stood straight, no trace of guilt or remorse.

"Dad didn't betray us," Caitlyn said slowly, the words tasting metallic and bitter. "He was doing the right thing, doing his job, keeping an innocent man from going to jail."

"He betrayed me. Betrayed you. Would have taken your mother from you. Didn't even have to think twice about it."

"You knew? About what Jimmy was doing?"

"I kept his books. Who do you think came up with the money-laundering scheme in the first place?" Jessalyn sidled closer. "If Sean had arrested us, there's no way the Reapers would have trusted us not to talk. They would have killed us all—you as well. Sean, too. By doing his job he was condemning us all."

"No," Caitlyn protested, the barrage of hidden truths exploding around her like land mines. "No. Dad would have protected us. He would have saved us."

Jessalyn raised a hand. For a split second as their eyes locked Caitlyn thought her mother was going to slap her. "Your father betrayed us. He didn't care if the Reapers killed us all."

Caitlyn stepped back. Wished her mother had hit her; it would have hurt less. Because now she saw the final truth, the truth that sliced so deep she could barely breathe. "You. You killed him."

Jimmy's laughter pealed through the room once more. "Oh, this is priceless. Jess, you do realize that you've just given your daughter the same dilemma her father faced? Honor, duty, or family? Which will you betray, Ginger?"

Caitlyn swiveled her attention from Jessalyn back to Jimmy. Jimmy wasn't just laughing, he'd pulled a gun, a small 9mm semiautomatic. Aimed at her.

"There's only one right answer here, Ging," he said. "What's it going to be? Your family or your life?"

Before Caitlyn could react, before she could even re-member how to move her mouth to form words, much less raise her own weapon, Jessalyn pulled a gun from her pocket and shot Jimmy twice in the chest. His eyes went wide, hands started to rise as if to protect himself from the bullets, then he slumped in his chair, his pistol tum-bling to the floor.

Caitlyn whirled on her mother, her own weapon raised. "Drop it," she shouted, amazed her voice and body seemed to be reacting without her brain being engaged. It was a surreal, out-of-body moment as she stared down the barrel of her gun at her mother.

"You're not going to shoot me," Jessalyn said, her voice certain. But she did set her gun down on the floor, rising to face Caitlyn. "And you're not going to arrest me. That pistol belongs to Poppy. His fingerprints are all over it and the bullets inside." Caitlyn noticed Jessalyn still wore her leather driving gloves. "We were never here. Do you understand me, Caitlyn? We were never here. To-gether we're going to leave and everything is going to be just fine. I promise."

She walked past Caitlyn, heading to the door. Caitlyn stared after her, dumbfounded. Ran to Jimmy, no pulse. No surprise—the pistol Jessalyn used was a chrome-plated Desert Eagle .357 magnum.

"Caitlyn, let's go."

Caitlyn turned to her mother, still holding her Glock, but more out of comfort, not aiming it anywhere. She just needed something solid to ground her in reality. She reached into her pocket and grabbed her cell phone as well. "Why? I don't—"

Jessalyn frowned as if Caitlyn were particularly slow on the uptake. "What do you mean why? Family, Caitlyn. Blood always comes first. You're my blood, my daughter. I couldn't let Jimmy and Poppy bring us down—and you know they would. They'd cut a deal to save themselves, and we'd be the ones to suffer. So I came prepared to save us. You and me, Caitlyn. Just like always."

Caitlyn blinked at Jessalyn's twisted attempt to pull Caitlyn into her warped scheme. Suddenly her mother seemed very tall and Caitlyn felt very small. Like she was nine years old again. Her voice emerged in a hushed whisper. "You, you killed Dad."

"Of course. I told you, I had to save you. Jimmy didn't have the guts to do what had to be done. Men, they're all so weak. I'm sorry you're the one who found him—we had no idea you were there that day. We must have left out the back while you came in the front."

"And now you killed Jimmy. Your own brother." Caitlyn understood the words; she just couldn't force her mind to accept them as fact.

"Yes, dear. Now hurry up. Mama will drive, you seem to be in shock."

Shock. That was an understatement. Caitlyn stared at her mother, stared at her uncle, then stared at the spot on the floor where her father had died. Full circle. Didn't make anything right, didn't ease the pain, but . . . somehow it felt like this was the only way things could ever have ended.

She straightened. "I don't think so. You're not going anywhere except to prison. Let's go."

"Everything I did, I did for you. How can you be so ungrateful? Why do you always have to take your father's side? I love you. I sacrificed everything for you. Don't you dare talk to me that way!" By the time she finished Jessalyn was screaming just like any other felon Caitlyn had ever arrested. Gone was the facade of superiority.

All her life she'd been waiting for her mother to accept her, to be proud of her. Never going to happen. But as she ushered Jessalyn outside and shut her in the backseat of the car where she wouldn't have to listen to her, Caitlyn realized she'd earned something more precious. She'd gotten her father back.

The cost was incomprehensibly high—and she'd be paying the rest of her life, she was certain. But the thought helped to calm the turmoil rushing through her brain so she could stay focused on her job.

She found the cell phone sweet spot and put in a call to Markle. As she waited for his men to arrive, Caitlyn stared up at her home.

Her own mother. A killer. And Caitlyn had just arrested her.

She knew the words should have disturbed her, but standing there, the chill wind cutting across the mountain, she was too numb to care.

The sun rose across the valley, golden beams giving the house a glow. Home sweet home.

Then mist from the mountain crowded out the sunbeams, shrouding the house in snow flurries. Making the house look cold and lonely, just as it had every day since her father died.

Not a home, Caitlyn thought. Not anymore. Just another crime scene.

CHAPTER FORTY-TWO

Back to the sheriff's station. Back to answering questions. Back to dissecting her actions, forcing herself to stay unemotional and professional while inside she felt like her feelings were ready to boil over in a confused mess she couldn't even begin to label or analyze.

Finally a deputy drove her to her Subaru. She was tempted to just head home—didn't have the courage or strength to face Paul if he was still at the VistaView—but needed her laptop. And she wanted to pack up Eli's papers, arrange that Lena got them along with the original pact.

Paul, in his usual thorough thoughtfulness, had taken care of everything. When she got to the room, he was gone, her bags packed, and a note left for her along with a sandwich from room service. She sank into the chair, forced herself to eat even though every bite stung with regret.

A man like Paul. A man who'd take care of her, comfort her. She very much wanted to love a man like that. But she didn't. Maybe she couldn't. She was too exhausted to do more than blink away tears as she chewed her turkey club and read his note.

Caitlyn,

First, you need to know I love you. But I think we both need a little time and space to think about what happened here. To think about what we both want.

No, that's not true. I know what I want. But I need you to be certain.

I love you and I think you love me as well. Trust your heart, Caitlyn. It won't lead you wrong.

I'll be waiting. Love always,
Paul

Trust her heart? Laughter bubbled out of her. High-pitched, insane; if she didn't laugh she'd be on the floor sobbing. Love? Her mom loved her dad, look where that got them. Her mom loved her brother—whoops, that hadn't worked out very good, either, had it?

Her mom said she'd done everything because she loved Caitlyn.

Her laughter died. She shoved the sandwich away along with her emotions, tucked Paul's note into her pocket, grabbed her stuff and left. Paul was right about one thing: she did need time. To think. To feel. To understand.

But not now. Later.

Now she just wanted to go home.

As Caitlyn pulled out of the casino parking garage she met another vehicle coming in. An armored truck. With Florida plates.

This is silly, she thought even as she turned the Subaru around and parked where she could watch the truck. Made perfect sense that a casino would need spare cash on a Sunday, especially with all the tourists in town for the poker run.

Except. It just didn't feel right.

She grabbed her monocular from the glove compartment. The logo on the truck had a different style of lettering from the one she'd seen on Friday. Meant nothing. Companies changed logos, didn't take the time and money to update every truck. But there was also no agent operator license or US DOT number listed.

The truck she'd seen on Friday was picking up coins. This time the armored car guards were unloading shrink-wrapped bundles of bills from the truck under the direction of a man with a clipboard and another man who wore a VistaView security uniform. A large man dressed as a guard pushed a handcart loaded with bills out of the truck. Tiny, her favorite Jolly Giant. Bingo.

Wanting backup, she called Goose. "Where are you?"

"Sitting on Caruso. With the poker run canceled, looks like he's sleeping late."

"Forget Caruso. There's nothing in his saddlebags except dirty underwear."

"What the hell you talking about? Our guys—"

"If you want your marked money it's being unloaded from the back of an armored truck into the VistaView as we speak."

"And you know this how?"

She shook her head, too exhausted to even try to explain. "Truck's marked GUARDIAN SECURITY with Florida plates. Four men, at least three of them armed. I'd hurry if I was you."

She hung up before he could say anything. Goose wasn't her problem anymore. Neither were Lena, Paul, or her mom. Only thing Caitlyn had to worry about was what she was going to do with the rest of her life.

But still, she wasn't about to let Caruso get away with

it. The man with the clipboard turned around, and he looked familiar as well. He'd been at Poppy's house with the other Daytona Reapers.

The exchange was moving along nicely. The loading dock was equipped with an industrial scale. The guards would drive their handcart loaded with bills over the scale; the man would record the weight, then transfer the cart to the second man dressed in the VistaView uniform, who would hand him a check. Turning illegitimate money into legally obtained and documented casino winnings. It was elegant in its simplicity.

The exchange was obviously a familiar routine for these guys. Familiar and all too fast. There was no sign of Goose by the time they had the last handcart from the truck on the scale being weighed.

She was so damn tired, she actually thought about letting them get away. But Goose had worked so hard, sacrificed so much for this bust. He deserved it.

Caitlyn snuck out of her Subaru and crept between the other cars until she was at the front of the truck. A blind spot for the men at the rear, but by twisting one of the side-view mirrors she could see them easily. She held her Glock at the ready. The man with the clipboard was unarmed as far as she could see, both hands occupied. The two guards from the VistaView were loading bundles already exchanged onto a second handcart. Tiny was in the back of the armored car, making the final exchange.

Which meant they all had their hands full. And were close enough together that she could cover them all. Best timing she'd get.

She waited for Tiny to emerge from the cover of the truck, pushing the cart. Then she stepped forward, Glock aimed at them. "Freeze and keep your hands where I can see them."

Tiny stared at her, dropped the handcart, and raised his arms. Not in surrender but as if he planned to leap off the loading dock and tackle her.

"You," he growled. It should have scared her but after the wild animals of last night, it had no effect. "I'm gonna kill you, bitch."

The man with the clipboard laughed. The other two just watched—obviously not paid for their brains.

Caitlyn sighed, sighting on Tiny's no-miss target of a chest. Was she really going to have to kill someone again?

"Tiny, please. I'm in no mood to kill you. And that's what's going to happen if you try anything. First, I kill you. And then"—inspiration struck—"I go after DeeDee. Ever seen what happens to a bike sitting unprotected in a for-feiture lot for a year or two? Pushed around, scraped up, sitting in the rain, maybe even broken down and sold for parts? You want that for DeeDee?"

It was a long shot. Trying to connect with a sociopathic biker's soul.

At first Tiny's face grew red, but then it drained of color faster than sour milk going down a drain. "DeeDee—you wouldn't, you couldn't . . ." His voice was hardly a whisper, it was so choked with emotion, as he crumbled to sit on the concrete, hands on his head.

The man with the clipboard made a move for his jacket and Caitlyn shifted her aim to him. "Hold it."

There was a split second when everything seemed to move in slow motion. The clipboard falling to the ground, the man's hand reaching for a semiautomatic in a shoul-der holster beneath his blazer, Caitlyn's finger slipping from the trigger guard to the trigger.

"Do what the lady says." Goose came up behind the man on the other side of the truck, his gun aimed at the back of his head. Another man and a woman appeared from the casino entrance, holding weapons on the guards.

Caitlyn blew her breath out, took her finger off the trigger. So close, so close. "Nice timing," she called to Goose.

"Just returning the favor. Technically, I guess this collar belongs to you."

She shook her head and holstered her weapon. "Not me. I was never even here."

Caitlyn drove east until she reached Raleigh, where she should have headed north on I-85. Then she saw a sign for Route 64. The way to the Outer Banks. *What the hell,* she thought, as she steered the Subaru off the interstate. Because of the holiday tomorrow, no one was expecting her at work until Tuesday. Hell, they might not even notice if she didn't show up then—or at least not care.

It was almost nine by the time she reached Duck, North Carolina. Seemed like the Outer Banks pretty much closed down during the off season; she was lucky to find a tiny Mexican restaurant in a small strip mall north of Duck with its lights still on. The waitress and cook, obviously mother and daughter, recognized a weary traveler when they saw one and took pity on her, feeding her the best seviche and fish tacos she'd ever had.

"Where are you staying?" asked the daughter, who had a better command of English.

"Tonight? I don't know. Are there any hotels near here?" All she'd seen on the windy road up the barrier island were condos and large mansions.

The waitress spoke in Spanish to her mother, who

nodded and disappeared into the kitchen. A few minutes later she emerged with a slip of paper and a key.

"Our cousin is a Realtor, rents out condos, houses," the daughter explained. "We clean them between guests. He says you can stay as long as you like—family discount rate."

Caitlyn shook her head. Seemed like every family had an Uncle Jimmy. "Thanks. I'll just need it for two nights. I think," she added, wondering what it would be like to live on the beach. "I don't have much cash, can I put it on my credit card?"

"*Sí, sí*. There are fresh linens already there. You can't buy groceries tonight, but the Food Lion opens again at nine in the morning."

"You be okay?" the mother asked, worry crinkling her eyes. "Alone?"

"I'll be fine." She paid, leaving a generous tip, and stood to leave.

"You come back again," the mother called, waving her apron. "Tomorrow lunch. I fix you special."

"Thank you. I will."

The condo was a gorgeous two-bedroom, one half of a duplex that was on the second row from the beach. She couldn't see the ocean from her balcony in the dark, but she could hear it. The air was crisp, more tang to it than the mountain air, still chilly but promising sunshine rather than clouds and snow. She found cushions for the divan on the balcony, brought a comforter out from the bedroom, snuggled in to listen to the waves and think.

A man calling her name carried over the sound of the ocean. She struggled, trying to orient herself. Dad?

She shook herself awake. The moon was directly over-head, and she could see its reflection off the sand beyond the backyard. The tide had come in. There was the ocean; wave after wave of white frothy moonglow.

"Caitlyn!"

She looked down into the backyard. A familiar figure stood on the other side of the locked privacy fence. "Goose?"

"Can I come in?"

She ran down the stairs and let him in. "What are you doing here? How did you find me?"

"GPS tracker on your car. I never had a chance to take it off." He rocked on his heels, hands in the back pockets of his jeans. "You mad at me for coming?"

She thought about it. Somehow it didn't bother her that he was here, sharing a moment that she'd thought was reserved for her and her dad. That aching hole Dad's memory used to leave didn't feel so empty.

The head shrinkers at Quantico would probably have a field day with that, but she didn't care. She took his hand and led him back out the gate, following the boardwalk over the dunes to the ocean. "No. I don't mind. But why did you come?"

"You were right about the truck. We got them all. They're sending me to DC. Grand jury, debriefing, all that jazz. Trying to figure out what to do with me while I'm waiting to testify. Anyway, I figured I might not have the chance to see you again and, well"—he suddenly focused on his boots as if the shifting sands had left him off balance—"we never had a chance to say good-bye."

The high tide made the sand soft so that their boots sank into it as they walked. Caitlyn gave up and sank down onto the sand. Goose hesitated for a brief moment, then sat down beside her, stretching his legs out to where the incoming waves brushed against the soles of his boots.

"What do I call you?" she asked. "I can't stop thinking of you as Goose, but—"

"Goose is just fine. If you like it. Carver's fine as well. Or Jake." He shrugged. Obviously it'd been so long since anyone used his real name, he wasn't sure what to call himself.

"Why Goose?"

"When you become a prospect for the Reapers they shave your head. Then tattoo it." He ran his fingers through the back of his hair. "Guess my head looks a bit funny when it's shaved. Like a big, old—"

"Goose egg." She laughed. It felt good, not as painful as she thought it might. "My dad was going to bring us here when I was a kid," Caitlyn continued, smoothing her hands over the wet sand, feeling its grit and heft before it slipped between her fingers and was gone. "But then he died and I never made it until now."

"Really?" He leaned back on his elbows, gaze fixed on her—or the moon beyond her. "We used to come here all the time. Stayed a bit farther up the road, another five miles or so. Not so crowded there."

She looked up and down the dark beach. No lights visible except for the one she'd left on behind them at the condo. "Crowded?"

"We came during the summer when school was out."

"Sounds nice."

He sighed. "It was. Haven't been back in, wow, ten, eleven years."

"I hadn't been back home to Evergreen for twenty-six years. Guess maybe I should've stayed away longer."

"You still think of it as home? Despite everything?"

"I don't know. Not sure where my home is." The only

constant in her life as she'd moved from assignment to assignment was the old gun safe her father built. The one piece of him her mother hadn't gotten rid of. Now she wondered why. Maybe Jessalyn had a conscience after all, had been punishing herself all these years every time she looked at that beat-up old gun safe—or looked at the daughter who was the spitting image of the man she'd killed.

"You going back to Quantico?"

She'd thought she'd need a few days to think, but suddenly the decision was clear. "It's funny. Friday night when I got to Evergreen my mom and I argued about my job. She wanted me to quit. So did Paul. Everyone wants me out."

"What do you want?"

"I want to do my job. I'm good at it—damn good. Even if I have a hard time playing by the Bureau's rulebook. So"—she heaved in a breath—"yes. I'm going back to Quantico. I'm not quitting. If they want me out, they'll have to find a reason why. Hell, this time I didn't even shoot anyone."

He nodded as if her answer was exactly what he'd expected. Then he sat up, leaned in to face her. "Too bad. Because my understanding is that fraternization is against FBI rules."

A grin danced across his lips. Too enticing to ignore. She cupped his face between her palms, smearing sand through his beard and hair, and kissed him hard.

"You know me. I love breaking the rules," she said when they parted for air. Before he could answer, she pressed her weight against him, leaning him on his back in the sand, and kissed him again.

* * *

They spent the day walking on the beach. The water was freezing but Caitlyn couldn't resist taking off her shoes and playing in the surf.

Paul texted. Again. Goose watched as she stopped and read it. Again.

Heard about your mom. So sorry. Words fail. Call me. Love you.

Saltwater spray made her eyes water. She pocketed her phone, ignoring the text. Again.

"You're not going to talk to him?" Goose asked after the fourth time.

"He wants closure, doesn't realize he already has it. Better this way. A little pain now . . . Besides, he's a doctor. Has his work, his patients. He'll be fine." She wished, she hoped. Paul deserved better than she could give him.

"The man really does love you, you know."

"That's what *she* keeps saying, too." Jessalyn. Who did everything for love of family. Love for her daughter. Who wanted or needed that kind of love in their life?

She dug her toe into the sand, enjoying the cold sensation as the tide buried her foot. It hurt, a little, sharp needles freezing her skin. But she'd get over it. So would Paul.

"I think some people know how to give love but not how to receive it," she finally said. "Some can do both, some can't do either. After all, giving and receiving are different skill sets, you're not necessarily born knowing how to do both, right?"

"And which group are you?" His tone said he thought her theory a load of crap but was willing to humor her to keep her talking.

She didn't answer right away. "I'm still figuring that out."

* * *

Bernie woke to bright lights and a throbbing headache. He blinked, and the lights were blocked by a beautiful face smiling down on him.

"Lena," he gasped. "Where am I? Are you really here?"

She pushed a button, and his hospital bed raised up. "Of course I am, silly. Where else would I be?" Before he could answer, she raised a glass with a straw to his lips. "The doctor says to drink plenty of fluids. You got an infection from one of the animals. Leptospirosis. They're giving you medicine, you should be fine, but he said it was a close call. Your liver was inflamed and your kidneys almost shut down. But everything's fine now, you're okay."

He pushed the glass away, saw an IV poking out the back of his hand. "Never mind me. Are you okay? What about the animals? What happened? All I remember is—" Panic flooded over him. "Weasel. He had a gun. Did he shoot you?"

"Nope. It was a miracle straight from Heaven. He shot that gun four times but didn't hit anyone. Not even Lucky."

"Who's Lucky?"

"That's the leopard's name. She and the others are over in Asheville, at the zoo."

"They're okay?"

"Thanks to you, they are." She smiled and kissed him on the cheek. "Thanks to you, so am I."

"But did you find what you were looking for?"

She sat back, the light overhead giving her a halo. Like an angel. His angel. Smiling at him and only him. "I sure did."

The way she squeezed his hand he hoped she meant him. But . . . "The land grant you and Caitlyn were talking about. My dad, the casino—"

"I have the original pact. The tribe and the freedmen descendants will work something out so that everyone benefits. I'll see to it. Starting with the tribe taking responsibility for running the casino themselves now that your dad's gone."

"He's going to jail, isn't he?" Bernie sighed. He knew this day would come, but it was still hard.

Lena moved from the chair to sit beside him on the bed. God, she was even more beautiful than the first time he'd seen her.

"Bernie," she said in a low voice, taking his hand in both of hers, "I have some bad news. About your dad . . ."

Caitlyn lingered in Goose's arms as long as she could before leaving to drive back to Quantico. Who cared if she didn't shower or wear clean clothes when they were just going to fire her anyway?

The traffic gods smiled on her and it was only nine oh five when she arrived at the corridor outside her office. LaSovage waited, pacing the hallway, her office door shut behind him.

"This is it?" she said.

He seemed more upset than she was. "Assistant Director Yates is in there. Waiting for you."

So. The powers-that-be made the trip from their cushy offices in DC instead of summoning her to come to them. This did not bode well. Still, she just couldn't get too upset about it. She'd told Goose that she wanted to do her job—and she did—but one thing she'd realized lying awake last night was that there were always possibilities. She didn't have to work for the FBI to do the job she wanted to do. The FBI had been her father's dream, and she'd made it come true. But if it was time to move on, she could accept that.

She reached for the door but LaSovage stopped her. He handed her a DVD wrapped in a clumsily tied red ribbon. "No matter what happens, this is for you."

"What is it?"

He shuffled, nervous—totally out of character for the *über*-confident HRT guy. "Just a few clips of what you missed around here this weekend."

"Mike, what did you do?"

"Not me." Yates could be heard stirring on the other side of the office door. "Good luck."

He was gone, leaving her alone to face Yates. She opened the door, surprised to see the assistant director sitting in the spare chair in front of her desk, watching something on the TV.

"I see you received one as well," he said by way of greeting. He held up a DVD case labeled: FIRST ANNUAL ADVANCED TACTICS COMPETITION.

"Just now. What's going on?"

"You tell me, Agent Tierney." At least she was still "agent." For now, at least. He paused the DVD. "Seems your unorthodox teaching methods inspired some of the agents in training. Two of them held an impromptu review session in the commons Friday night, where they shared your tactical advice with the other agents in training. This in turn inspired Special Agent LaSovage to set up a voluntary tactical competition between the new class and the class due to graduate next month. He said he wanted to combat any skill deterioration the long holiday weekend may induce by creating a little collegial rivalry."

Didn't sound at all like LaSovage, but maybe bullshitting

was part of his skill set in addition to being a crack marks-man.

"I don't understand what that has to do with me or why you're here, sir." She added the last belatedly, but Yates didn't seem to notice.

"LaSovage used real-world scenarios not found in our training materials, judged by members of the HRT and some National Academy instructors who volunteered."

He hit PLAY on the DVD. LaSovage stood in front of a crowd of NATs sitting in the grass in front of the 9/11 Memorial. "And the first annual Golden Donut Award"—he held up a donut spray-painted traffic-stop orange—"plus this box of Krispy Kremes." He opened the lid, revealing a half-empty box of donuts. "Excuse me, what's left of this box of Krispy Kremes, goes to our newest class of agents in training."

A roar of applause drowned him out as a woman bounded up to accept the award. It was the female NAT Caitlyn made cry last week. What was her name? The image of a nun flit through her mind. Maria? No, Mary Ag-nes. Garman like the GPS.

Mary Agnes took the bright orange donut and held it aloft. "We couldn't have done this without the guidance of Supervisory Special Agent Caitlyn Tierney. Thanks for keeping us safe and smart, Agent Tierney!"

More applause. Yates paused the DVD again. "The new class beat the pants off the outgoing class." He left his chair and moved to sit behind Caitlyn's desk in her chair.

She had to stand, twist the chair he abandoned around—it was the only spare one in the tiny office—in order to sit facing him. Once she had, he arched an eye-brow at her and she wondered if he'd meant her to stay standing at attention.

Oh well, he could only fire her once. And at least the NATs had learned something from her. Pride flushed her cheeks, and she didn't care if Yates saw it. She blinked back a tear. Damn, she was going to owe LaSovage a beer after this.

"Every member of the New Agents in Training class added their personal endorsement to the end of the DVD," he said in a dour tone. "In case you ever want to start a fan club." He shuffled a few printed pages. "Which brings me to these." He flipped his reading glasses on. "Endorsements from a Butner SSI named Boone, a North Carolina State Police captain in charge of their SWAT team, and a Sheriff Markle from Balsam County."

Caitlyn sat there, stunned. Not sure how to respond. "Sir, I hope you don't think that I requested or coerced any of those—"

"That's the problem, Agent Tierney. I know you didn't. Which creates a bit of a conundrum for me. That footage of you taking down an outlaw motorcycle gang—with the help of a leopard?" He tilted his chin to gaze over his glasses as if in disbelief. "That's gone viral. You have a flare for closing cases in a way that makes the FBI look good to the public. Unfortunately those cases seem to rarely fall into our official purview, especially now that the Bureau is moving away from criminal investigations and focusing on counterterrorism and homeland security instead."

He lowered the papers, eyeing her over the top of his glasses. "But the public and local law enforcement still see us as primarily investigators. Blame TV and the movies, but we're stuck with the image. And in these days of local budget cutbacks, requests from law enforcement for our assistance in cases have quadrupled. You see my problem?"

"You want to maintain the image of the FBI, avoid any public backlash from our being unable to assist local law enforcement, while not actually using the Bureau's resources." Typical government gobbledygook. Didn't the idiots who decided where the FBI's focus should be realize that protecting the country and its citizens started locally? Most of their major counterterrorism busts had begun with tips from local law enforcement—there was no reason to treat smaller jurisdictions like they were idiot second cousins.

Yates nodded in approval. "Maybe there's hope for you yet. My understanding is that you want to remain in the Bureau, correct? Because if you want to resign, now's the time."

She stood and came to attention. "No, sir. I want to stay."

"Very well. Then I'm ready to give you your new assignment." He glanced up at her, his gaze softening. Maybe. A little. "You may not know it, but I began my law enforcement career as a sheriff's deputy in a small county in Nebraska. We were understaffed, overworked, undertrained, and always short on money. But we served our constituents well. I'm just as proud of the work I did there as I am of the work I do now for the Bureau. So"—he inclined his chin to the right—"let's just say that I understand the challenges facing local law enforcement. As it seems you do as well. Which is why I've decided that you're to remain here, based at Quantico, part of the Critical Incident Response Group. But you'll be operating independently with an official title as local law enforcement liaison."

Sounded great. She stifled her grin before he could see it. There had to be a catch. "Exactly what would my duties entail?"

"You'll have a minimal budget, no staff, and you'll be on call twenty-four seven. You'll be expected to triage requests from jurisdictions across the nation. The vast majority you'll be forced to decline—and do it in a way that doesn't cause any public relations backlash. The cases you decide to accept will be approved by me. I'll assign you any resources I deem necessary to aid in your investigations. You'll report directly to me and the executive assistant director."

Tight leash, tons of administrative bullshit—not to mention the whole diplomatic aspect of saying no to locals asking for help—but she got to choose her own cases, cases anywhere in the country?

"Count me in, sir."

"I wouldn't rush in so fast, Agent Tierney. Most of these cases will be unsolvable or political quagmires that local law enforcement can't afford to get caught up in. You're not going to be making many friends out there."

"But I get to do my job, my way? Take a case as far as I can, right?" She couldn't hide the excitement in her voice.

"As far as your resources allow you, yes. As long as there's no negative backlash on the Bureau."

He didn't say anything about obeying rules or regulations. Maybe Yates was smarter than she gave him credit for.

She stood and extended a hand. "Thank you, Assistant Director Yates. I accept."

But where did the nightmare begin
for Caitlyn Tierney?

Turn the page for an extract from C.J. Lyons'
first book in the Caitlyn series:

BLIND
FAITH

The huge *New York Times* bestseller:
a thriller to keep you up all night.

Available in paperback and ebook now.

June 6, 2007:

WALLS PRISON UNIT, HUNTSVILLE, TEXAS

CHAPTER ONE

Sarah Durandt flinched as faded blue-checked gingham curtains rattled open to reveal the prisoner strapped to a gurney.

One of the women behind her gasped. Sarah leaned forward, one hand flattened against the glass that separated them from a monster. She breathed through her mouth. It was the only way to choke down the heavy air trapped inside the tiny cement-walled room.

She and the other witnesses were gathered behind glass so thick halos circled the objects in the white-tiled execution chamber on the other side. Bulletproof glass. Who did they think would be doing the shooting? The condemned man already woozy from sedatives or those who came to watch him die?

Sarah curled her hands one into the other and held them still on her lap, shivering as the air-conditioning blew a frosty stream down on her. Eleven others were crowded into the room with her, families representing the other victims. She barely noticed them. They were here for closure. She needed answers.

Her gaze narrowed to a laser-sharp focus aimed at the prisoner beyond the glass. His arms were extended, needles inserted into veins on both sides of his body. Seven leather straps crossed his body and limbs, holding him in a position eerily reminiscent of a crucifixion. But this man was no Messiah.

This man was the devil incarnate.

Damian Wright was medium sized, someone who would not stand out in a crowd with his bland face, blander features.

Sarah knew better. She knew his cunning. Hidden behind his façade of normalcy smoldered a sick desire to torture and maim. Even here, on his deathbed, he persisted in tormenting her. Denying her the slightest measure of comfort or peace.

She wasn't sure why, of all the victims, Damian had focused his sick power plays on her. She wasn't anyone special, just a schoolteacher from upstate New York who lived in a village of less than five hundred souls. Her brown hair was usually pulled back into a ponytail and forgotten about, leaving it free to fall around her shoulders on special occasions like today—the execution of a serial killer.

Damian's sweat-beaded skin glistened as he lay beneath a large, round surgical light. His eyes were squeezed shut against its unflinching illumination. The warden nodded to a black-suited man with a small silver cross on his lapel. The man stretched out his hand, his wedding ring shimmering as it passed through the beam of light, and pulled a black microphone down. Sarah rubbed her own ring finger, tracing the plain band Sam placed there six years ago.

Uncoiling like a cobra, the microphone bobbed hypnotically above Damian's lips. A click, like a muffled gunshot, echoed through the witness room as the warden switched on the intercom. The scratchy sound of Damian's breathing filled the room.

Sarah found herself inhaling in time with Damian, could almost smell the antiseptic and surgical tape and the stench of sweat and nerves emanating from beyond the window. Alan Easton, who sat beside her, gave her hand a comforting squeeze.

"You okay?" he asked, his tone that of a friend rather than her lawyer. She was the only family here to bear witness for Sam and Josh. The only family Sam had left. And Josh, how could she not be here for her son?

She nodded, her attention focused on the events in front of her. The execution chamber held only three men: the warden in his navy suit, bleached white shirt, and narrow tie; the black-suited minister; and Damian Wright, the man who had destroyed her life.

If Sarah were to describe the Death House to her sixth-grade students back home, she would have said the theme of the room, of the entire building set far apart from normal prison housing, was containment.

Nothing was meant to ever escape this tiny building with its cement walls painted an institutional green. The utilitarian execution chamber beyond the viewing window made no efforts to soften or hide its purpose. A flat surgical table, arms splayed wide, bolted to the floor was its only piece of furniture.

"Any last words?" the warden asked the condemned man.

Sarah came to attention. A fly trespassed into the profane proceedings and beat its wings against the cage shielding two flickering fluorescent lightbulbs, its buzzing deafening. Damian Wright, convicted murderer and child rapist, opened his rheumy eyes and stared directly at her. She pulled her hand free from Alan's, fisted it tight.

Tell me. Say something. Give me a clue.

Her prayers went unheard. Damian remained silent, muscles slack, not fighting his restraints. Only his chest moved, rising and falling as he counted down to his last breath. Sarah's lungs squeezed tight, ready to burst from pressure. Damian stared at her, a smile creasing his eyes.

She blinked first, not ashamed to surrender; she'd do anything if it helped her to find Sam and Josh.

Damian's smile widened. But he remained silent.

Fury knotted her gut. Did he torment her, refuse her the closure she so desperately yearned for, because she'd been away at that damn mandatory in-service on the day he took Josh? Or was it because of all the boys he'd killed, only Josh had a father willing to fight, to die for him?

Alan said it was probably because Sam interrupted his ritual with Josh. Forced him to deviate from his sick, twisted fantasy to kill Sam before he could return to Josh.

The minister intoned from his Bible, his eyes never rising from the written word to gaze upon the lost soul he prayed over.

The words of the Psalm, words that twenty-two months ago would have brought Sarah comfort and solace, were now reduced to meaningless noise with less significance than the buzzing of the fly. She pressed her palm flat against the cold glass, more intent on gleaning the answers she needed from Damian than listening to the word of God.

She'd spent her entire life listening. Where was God when she'd needed him most? Where was he when her husband and son needed him?

"I'm sorry we couldn't stay the execution," Alan whispered. "I know how much you hoped—"

She shrugged his words away, her entire universe consisting of the gaze of a killer. The man who had confessed to killing Sam and Josh—but who refused to tell her where they were buried.

For a year and a half she had fought. Fought Damian Wright's silence, his refusal to see her. Fought the new Texas law that allowed executions to be "fast-tracked" with an unprecedented efficiency. Fought her own desire to see Damian die. A desire superseded only by her need to find her husband and son.

The warden strode forward, reading from a document in a monotone that floated just beyond the periphery of Sarah's awareness.

Where are they, you sonofabitch? Sarah tried to broadcast all her loathing and hatred into her glare, hoping to loosen Damian's tongue in these, his last seconds on this Earth. Her fist pounded against the thick glass, creating only the smallest of muffled thuds.

The killer didn't flinch or look away from her. Nor did he speak. Instead his expression turned to one approaching pity. As if she were the one condemned, not him.

The warden finished and removed his glasses, aiming a small nod in the direction of the executioner's booth. Sarah had researched the procedure. Behind the one-way mirrored glass, an unseen man flipped a switch. Medication flowed into Damian's veins. First more sedatives, then a paralytic, finally the potassium chloride to stop his heart.

Time stopped. Sarah didn't blink. Damian didn't blink.

Three minutes later, the minister stood aside as a man clad in a white coat stepped forward and listened with a stethoscope. He straightened, reached a hand out to Damian's face, and closed the killer's eyes.

The blinds snapped shut.

A collective sigh swirled through the room as the other

witnesses shifted in their seats. Through the haze filling Sarah's vision she heard several women and a man sobbing, felt the rustle of their movements as the room emptied. She remained frozen, not blinking, eyes burning.

Alan touched her elbow, pulled her fist away from the glass, and drew her up onto unsteady feet. "We have to go now," he murmured.

She kept her face craned toward the darkened window until the last possible moment. Finally, Alan led her out into bright sunshine, Texas heat and humidity bearing down on her with the intensity of a ten-ton truck.

For a moment she was the one suffocating under the weight of paralyzed lungs. Her chest tightened. For an instant it was her heart that stopped.

She blinked and pain returned. An ice-pick stabbing behind her eyes, her constant companion for twenty-two months, unmitigated by any sedatives or hope of release. Unlike Damian Wright's pain.

And she knew she was alive. At least her body was. Her mind was. Her soul—that was buried in some unmarked grave back home, up on Snakehead Mountain.

Alongside Sam and Josh.

It's over, it's over, it's over . . . The words threaded themselves through Sarah's mind, spinning a cocoon that blocked out all feeling, providing a soft, safe place to hide. A place where there was no need to think, to do, to react. To be. *It's over, it's over, it's over* . . .

Sarah hugged herself tighter and leaned against the car window, her back to Alan as he drove them away from the prison. She'd promised herself no matter what, she wouldn't break down, at least not in front of anyone.

But Alan wasn't anyone. Alan understood—he'd been through it himself. His wife had been killed by a drug addict who stormed their house looking for cash. That was why he'd left his corporate law practice to focus on victims' rights, to help people like Sarah.

How could she have survived the past two years without Alan?

The tires spinning against the highway carried her away from Damian Wright, away from her last chance to find Sam and Josh. *It's over, it's over, it's over . . .*

Her body sagged against the door frame, her right hand automatically reaching for the single ring on her left. She had no engagement ring. Instead, Sam had given her his most valuable possession, a guitar pick used by the legendary Stevie Ray Vaughan, and promised that when he sold his first song he'd replace it with a diamond. Seven years later, the pick still sat in its black velvet jewelry case on her dresser.

Her hand felt cold, but her wedding band radiated warmth, as if she touched Sam. She spun the ring in time with the words weaving their way into her soul, inviting her to surrender. *It's over, it's over, it's over . . .*

No! It can't be. Not like this.

Tears pressed against her closed eyelids, burned as they fought to escape. Sarah's grip on the plain gold band tightened. Her last link to Sam and, through him, Josh. She was tired, so very tired. She should give up. What more could she do?

After all, she had a life to live. Sam would want her to be happy. Someday. A ragged breath tore through her and she felt Alan stir beside her. Alan—could she imagine a future with a man like him? A man who'd devoted almost two years of his life to guiding her through this morass of pain and grief, who'd brought her back into the light, had given her this one last chance.

Last chance, last hope, last rites.

It's over, it's over, it's over.

Sarah straightened, opened her eyes, and blinked against the harsh Texas sun. She uncurled her legs, smoothed out the soft cotton of her navy blue dress. She refused to wear black, not until Josh and Sam were laid to rest. The dark highway stretched hypnotically into the future.

"You all right?" Alan's gaze left the road to stare at her for a long moment.

A sad smile curled Sarah's lips. "Yes. I'm fine."

It's over, it's over, it's over . . . the words sang through her mind, pounding insistently like a toddler throwing a tantrum, banging his head against the floor when he didn't get what he wanted. Josh had thrown a few of those in his day. Until he learned that when he did, he never got what he wanted.

It's over, it's over, it's over!

Sarah gave a small shake of her head—the only warning Josh needed now. She'd shake her head, smile, and he'd leave his whining behind, take her hand, and snuggle against her. *Sorry, Mommy. I forgot.*

But I haven't.

It's over, it's over, it's over . . . *No. It's not.*

It's just begun.

Wednesday, June 20

CHAPTER TWO

Supervisory Special Agent Caitlyn Tierney didn't look up at the tentative knock on her open door. Instead she raised a hand in the universal palm forward gesture of "wait" and kept reading the report on her computer screen. Her latest group of New Agents in Training was in their final week of training before graduating from Quantico. Nerves were frayed as they waited to learn their field assignments, so this hadn't been the first interruption of Caitlyn's morning.

She finished reading her NAT's scores on their critical incident projects and nodded with satisfaction. They'd done as well as she'd hoped. Even Santos, the diffident, intense twenty-six-year-old with a background in particle physics, had managed to integrate himself as part of the team. Caitlyn shut the lid to her laptop and looked up at her visitor, half-expecting to see Santos himself.

Instead, it was one of the lab geeks. Ah, man, she knew his name; he worked in DNA. Not Rogers, no, something close. She smiled, keeping her face blandly genial as she forced her brain along its circuitous route to match the face of the man before her with his name.

Finally, it clicked. But it took at least twice as long as it would have two years ago, before her accident. Something she'd never admit to anyone.

"Hi, Clemens," she said heartily, gesturing the tech to one of the two wooden chairs beside her overflowing bookcase. "What brings you over here to Jefferson? Teaching a class?"

He shook his head. "Thought it would be easier than asking you to make the trip to the lab building." He was right; the forensic analysis center had more security than Fort Knox. Even FBI staff like Caitlyn needed a special invite and authorization for a pass to enter. Clemens glanced at the open door and shifted his weight in his chair.

She might not be as good with names as she used to be, but Caitlyn was still a pro when it came to nonverbal communication. She rose to her feet, folded her reading glasses, and nonchalantly closed the door as she crossed over to sit beside him.

"What's up?" she asked, leaning forward and engaging him in direct eye contact.

He fumbled a file folder from his briefcase. It wasn't marked "top secret" or even "sensitive," so she wondered what all the cloak-and-dagger was about. Then she saw the name on the file. Damian Wright.

Her first assignment two years ago after she'd returned to work. She'd hated everything about that case: the crimes, the travel, the blinding migraines that blurred her thoughts and almost crippled her with their unrelenting pain and nausea, and most of all she'd hated her fatuous asshole of a boss, Assistant Special Agent in Charge Jack Logan. Logan had swooped in and taken over the case without any warnings or explanations, something unheard of. ASACs led from behind their desks via memos and directives; they never ventured into the field.

"You know Damian Wright's dead?" she asked the lab tech. "Executed in Texas." She glanced at the calendar. "Two weeks ago."

"I know." Clemens' voice was mournful. "I'm sorry."

Caitlyn's spine went rigid. Bright flashes of light sparked at the periphery of her vision. "Sorry? You can't be saying you found anything exculpatory?"

Caitlyn agreed with most law enforcement officers that death was too good for a lot of these sickos—but it was the best punishment they had. That didn't mean that she, like other LEOs, didn't also live in fear of putting an innocent man on death row.

Which was why she'd reviewed the Texas evidence against Wright herself, even though by the time Texas took over she was off the case. Their case had been rock solid. Not only had he been caught with the still-warm body of his last victim, butchering the boy, but Wright confessed to everything, refused to allow any appeals on his behalf, and became the first person under Texas' new law to be fast-tracked to execution. Twenty-one months from arrest to death, a new record.

Clemens shook his head. "No, Wright killed those boys in Texas, Vermont, Tennessee, and Oklahoma." He paused. Caitlyn took a deep breath, forcing the flashing lights to fade into the distance. "It's the ones in New York I'm not too sure about."

"Hopewell, New York. Josh Durandt and his father. Right before Katrina hit." Caitlyn remembered. No bodies recovered in that one. The crime scene had been halfway up a mountain; she'd been wearing a skirt after being whisked away from a memorial service for the second

Vermont boy. Logan had laughed, giving her no time to change into more appropriate attire and cutting her no slack when her migraine made her sick during the drive down. After she puked her guts out on the side of the road, he'd joked, asked if she was pregnant, adding that was the problem with "today's FBI." He never had to worry about any of the guys letting him down because they went "hormonal" on him.

"See, I was clearing the backlog and I found these samples in the pile to be disposed of," Clemens said, his tone hesitant as he shifted in his seat, obviously having second thoughts. "You know the new director's protocols. All evidence reviewed prior to disposal, even in closed cases. Turns out the results from Hopewell were never recorded. Not anywhere. Case like that, they should have been top priority. Instead they were almost trashed. If it wasn't for the new rules—"

"What do you have?" she asked, sliding the folder from his hand and spreading it open on her lap. The familiar dark lines of a DNA analysis filled the first page.

"The DNA from the Hopewell crime scene—it wasn't Wright's."

"There were two blood samples found, right? The dad's and one other. We assumed it was Wright's since the field kit said it was his blood type and we had his prints on the memory card found there."

"Yeah, it was his print and the card came from his camera. Wright's reflection can be seen in some of the photos. He definitely took them."

"Who was at the crime scene with him? Are you saying he had an accomplice? There was no evidence of that at any of the other scenes." She ran her hand through her shoulder-length hair, absently rubbing at the puckered skin above her right ear. Her hair hadn't even grown out when she was in Hopewell. Back then it had been so short it barely covered the surgical scar.

Clemens blew his breath out. "That's where it gets a bit weird."

Caitlyn straightened. It never boded well when a lab geek called evidence weird. "How weird?"

"Conspiracy theory, cover-up, Area Fifty-One, political and career suicide kind of weird." He grimaced. "I've gone over everything a dozen times. The data is correct. It's the facts surrounding it that are wrong."

"You mean *my* facts, *my* investigation?"

He looked down at his scuffed Adidas and nodded. "Yeah." He looked up again, pushed his hair back when it fell across his forehead. "Well, yours and Assistant Special Agent in Charge Logan's. He was the agent of record. His name was on all the paperwork. But since he's retired, I thought I better come to you." He gave her a hesitant smile. "Maybe you could tell me what to do with it."

Caitlyn stared past him, through her small window that looked out over the expanse of forest home to the Yellow Brick Road, the academy's famed obstacle course. Sunlight streamed in, reawakening her headache. She'd always suspected Logan of hiding something. He'd hustled her off the Wright case as fast as he could, claiming she was needed to help with the Katrina cleanup efforts. She'd spent weeks working with the National Center for Missing & Exploited Children, identifying over forty-eight hundred kids and reuniting them with their families. An area more suited to a woman's talents, in Logan's words. Since they'd had Wright cold on the other murders, she'd let it go.

She turned to Clemens. "Tell me everything."